Initial Words

The 2005 Marguerite Press, Best Reviewer Award Winner Said

Big Tymers is an exhilarating, suspenseful, and provocative action packed novel that will steal your attention and hold it hostage until the very end. **Crystal without a doubt is the new diva in urban fiction** and **she's taking this genre to the next level.** In other words, she's creating a new genre that has yet to be named.
Monique Bruner, Reviewer Looseleaves.org
OKC, Okla

Asia,
Daddy's Girl

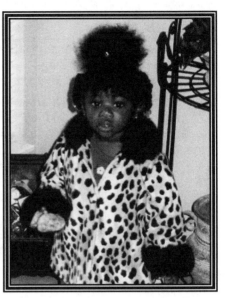

"Hey! What's this
Hood Rich stuff all about
anyway?"

"Wrong story, baby girl. This is
Big Tymers!!!
AND
Asia Prince is all grown up."

WHAT PEOPLE ARE SAYING about...
Big Tymers

"Big Tymers is a raw and captivating novel. *I put my pen down to ya Crys. You did the damn thing."*
Meisha Holmes, Author Brooklyn Jewelry Exchange

"Big Tymers is a sure fiya **summer hit!!!** *Crystal's changing the game with this classic.* **Bravo girl, all** *your novels provide the key points avid readers look for in a great book; adventure, stimulation, suspense, and a quality written tale!* **Get ready, `cuz you're on your way."**
Amaleka McCall Author of A Twisted Tale of Karma
Washington DC

"People gon' read BIG TYMERS and say two words, **GAME OVER!** Authors are going back to the drawing board after this. **You did that** Ma. And **your literary skillz are stoopid."**
Kerry E. Wagner, Author of She Did That
Houston, TX

"Big Tymers is a well written masterpiece, a raw adventure that will take you on an enjoyable ride. Big Tymers is guaranteed to leave you with your mouth wide open. READ REFLECT and REALIZE that Asia Prince's story is a roller coaster ride of a lifetime."
Tureko Virgo Straughter, San Francisco, CA
Coast 2 Coast Readers

"BIG TYMERS, WOW!!! I anxiously awaited this sequel. Hood Rich was my favorite novel of all times. BUT.....**this sequel is everything I expected it to be and more.** I don't know, it's giving the prequel a run for its money."
Anita Kilpatrick, OKC, OK
5th St. Baptist Church Book Club

"BIG TYMERS is the kind of read you never want to end. Once again Crystal takes urban fiction, puts it on her back, and carries it to the next level. It's reality based fiction at it's best. This novel is action packed and full of so much suspense and drama that you literally **Can't Get Enuff."**
Delonya Conyers, C2C Readers
South Bronx, NY

"From Alpha to Omega, this joint takes you beyond your climax. **Crystal has bonded the ultimate marriage of suspense and deception to birth a seductive masterpiece.** This novel is sexy, classy, and arousing to ones psyche. **Simply speaking, Big Tymers is "THE TRUTH."**
Terryonto #02469-087 Detroit's Finest
Beaumont USP

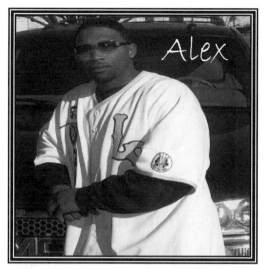

"Real **Big Tymers** don't die, we multiply. Oh yeah, we believe in gettin' that money by any means necessary, and if a nigga invades our territory, we takin' prisoners. Step to a true hustler illin' and it's yo ass. But hey ... that's how it goes in the jungle of bling, dope, and fast scrilla. Understand that if you play in a Big Tymers world, you better be ready for the shit that goes with the game. Feds, Lock Down, Drama, you name it, we've been there....and done that."

"When you've flourished from nothing, real *Big Tymers* respect what they've become. Most importantly, when they take a moment to ponder on where they could have been, they value themselves even more and the journey they had to endure to make it to the top."

Edited   1/2006
First print   4/2006

BOOKSTORE DISTRIBUTION
Contact:

CRYSTELL PUBLICATIONS
P.O. BOX 8044
EDMOND, OK. 73083-8044
(405) 414-3991

Place orders via our website
www.Crystalstell.com

ISBN: 0-9740705-8-0
Library of Congress Control Number: 2006902655

Cover Credits
Model: Teretta ....Teretta.net
Photographer: Erik Sivad
Cover Design: Kevin.........Info@ocjgraphix.com

Printed in the United States of America

Big Tymers
Can't get enuff

A Novel by: Crystal Perkins-Stell
Essence Bestselling Author

*A **Big Tymer** is a nigga with looong bread who can take care of himself, and most importantly, ME..... Can you say rent, shopping sprees, car payments, and trips around the world?*
If yes, Great.... Now ask yourself can you finance them, and if you can, look a diva up.

*"Sis, a real **Big Tymer** ain't talkin' bout no, "How much!"*
Oh, and he also lives up to my motto:
"Broke niggas, don't break no bread, Rich niggas, gettin' broke off head."
If you gettin' em how you live, and you living LARGE....
It's a wrap, you're a Big Tymer."

Acknowledgements

I asked God to bless me with a gift I could share with the world, and he gave me the talent to write as well as the spirit to love others. Makya, mommy is so honored to call you my baby. Your book, *Jazzy Little Five-Year-Old* is more than just a children's story, it's truly what you are in my eyes. Know that you mean the world to me. No book or anyone could ever take your place in my heart. Always remember that Mommy is trying to soar like an eagle and you inspire my altitude.

To the first family…Mom, Pooh, Marcus, Kim, my loving nephew Three, and my pretty l'il niece Kaylee, you all are simply the best. I thank God we're a part of each others lives. Damon, and all my family and friends who support me, you know who you are, I appreciate all you do to aid in my literary career. Big thanks to my peeps, Jackie Pagan, Del, Wanda, and T-Bell. Moe-Luv wa'sup, I wish you could have shared in my childhood, but thanks for being in my life now. Miles Sr., thanks for stepping up and being a father to me and a grandfather to my daughter. The Horton's and Perkins' family, Dawn, Shirley, Sharonda, Musa, Tyrell, Monty & Scooter, Love you… Mean it. Mike May, thanks for being my big brother, my very best friend in the world, and my ear when I'm whining. There are simply no words for you. I am speechless. Just thanks for believing in me. You have been such a great friend and a beaming star in my life for the past twenty years. May I never forget the blessing you've been 4 me. WUUD w/2HoLLoTyp$ thanks for the help on my Audio book. Casonya Lucas, you're wonderful. Auntie Bonnie, gurl you and your book club are 2nd to none. Thanks for embracing me. Invite me back for wings.

Annie Guess, (God Ma) thanks for all the long talks. Richard and Roberlyn, with Urban Knowledge, Marc Flemon, Monique and Nych in Jersey, Monique in OKC, and my DST'sorors, y'all are simply the bomb. Debbie Lynn, you always come through for me. Thanks for helping to restore my sanity. To all the wonderful college students in my life from LU and OU, you guys give me hope and keep me young. I couldn't even write this kind of grit, if I wasn't so inspired by you all.

D. Brown, Teretta, and Jermaine, *Hood Rich* made the Essence Bestsellers list thanks to your help. I must also extend a super special thanks to my Big Tymers models. My baby girl Kya, for givin' us a little Aisa to love in Hood Rich, Teretta, for repin' Big Asia. CoCo and Ashley, for bringing Kell and Nikk to life, Rondell, for being Alex, Kwame, you could be Kerby fa'real. Mook, Ant is so you, and Silk can't nobody B U but U. Y'all are simply the best. Smooches and much love to each of you for believing in me and helping a sista bring my mental vision to life. Kevin BIG TYMERS is SICK, Naw man.. as one of my great author homies would say…. **IT'S STOOPID!** Mrs. Higgins, thanks girl 4 everything you do 4 me.

Kevon Thomas, you are one of the hardest working book sellers I've ever met in this purple world. I love your professionalism and your spirit. One day you're character is going to take you far in life and when it does, remember me. I need to be sporting a royal crown with ya. Jamaica, Queens, I'd be slacking if I didn't rep the first street vendor that ever gave me a chance to rock the block. Massamba, you're simply fabulous. Your hospitality is top-notch. Thank you so much for allowing me to come to 164 and Jamaica Ave. to learn about the book hustle.

Now with all the snakes in the garden of Hood Lit, I'm so glad God put a few beautiful butterflies amongst me. Toschia, and the author's of the Divine Literary Tour, I can't wait to hit these 53 cities in 06. O'Shea, get that novel out this year. Kelvin King, you showed a sista mad love at your university, thanks. Kerry, you're so giving and so wonderful..Game Over! Lisa, hey boo. Amaleka, thanks for unselfishly telling DC about me. Now I gots ta' spread some luv the Brooklyn Way, Meisha, gurl you're a dynamic friend, thanks for grinding my books on the block.

Hey, I couldn't give shout outs without sending mad love to my favorite bookstore in the city of Detroit. Nefertiti, Diane, and all *The Truth Bookstore* affiliates, *thank you so much for everything*. When I was looking for an opportunity to shine in my own city, you embraced me first, and last. Thanks for giving me a chance and a venue to showcase my craft. Most of all, thanks *for making Hood Rich #5 on Essence Magazine's Bestseller's list. God Bless You.*

To all the bookstores, book clubs, and dedicated readers who have purchased my books and supported me in my efforts to accomplish my dream, I say thank you. I'll never forget how you embraced me as a new author. Radiah of Urban Reviews, thanks for your support and for picking me as one of the Top Five Underdog Authors for 2005. Rawsista's, Pastor Brian and Sherry Coleman, the Fifth Street Reading Ministry, and O.O.S.A., thanks for your support. Coast2Coastreaders.com, *Thanks for making Hood Rich C2C's Book of the year for 2005.* Hot, Glam, Virgo, Scorpio, MzCrys, Shyste, Greeneyerican, Mskiki, Kathyj, Rayamon, from the gate, y'all helped make me a hit in the land of C2C. I'm so glad I followed my dreams. Thanks for helping my novel blow up and become game and conversation worthy. Blackmeninamerica.com, thanks for the 6 out of 5 stars and a Literary Hall of Fame prediction on *Hood Rich*. Looseleaves, thanks for giving me my first book club review ever. Nardsbaby, girl you ain't no joke. You tell it like it is and I promise I'll be anxiously awaiting your analysis on Big Tymers. (wink)

Finally, I'd like to say thanks to my Reps on the inside and out. To my number one salesman from the D. Terryonto, I appreciate the letter regarding how *Hood Rich* touched your life. You will never know how seeing someone take actual notes on my book blessed me as an author, not my ego, but my heart. I gots mad luv 4 ya playa. You're a true example of why I wrote Hood Rich, so thanks for letting me know that my lit inspired you to believe that *your life has real purpose*. Tyrone, and Ma Shirley, y'all are the greatest. Melvin A, Latif L., Rico B. thanks. Leonard, thanks a thousand times over for bringing Tink-Tink to life. May *Jazzy Little Five-Year-Old* be to children's lit, what Oprah is to Television. "A real money maker." K. Young and Mrs. Barnett, thanks for always reading my work. Cassandra and Neisha, you two motor city divas are not only the best, but my peeps. It's amazing how a great book can bring dynamic people together. Charles B. and Lexy, much love 2 you. Ant (A.K.), Quan, Cliff, Me, Chawntese, Manirah, thanks for using your hard earned coins to go with me to NY. The next one's on me. Luv u..Smooches.

And1 last BIG UPS. Thank to Steve B. for the assistance with understanding the NBA and other organized basketball leagues. 2 guard/guard 2, whatever, I got it right in the book. I typed that part right after you explained it. Thanks for the blur. To all I neglected to name, charge it to my head, not my heart. Luv u 2, just forgot.

Get out and get your copy today

Number 5
Essence Magazine Bestseller

The Prequel

Opening Scene
Big Tymers

Why Simps always want to try a Big Tymer…. is beyond me. The game of Ballin' is like the game of life, every moment is precious and nothing's promised. Silk always said that most niggas focus on the lifestyle cause money, fame, and hoes are the key ingredients that make up this thing we call "Grindin." Thug-lyfe and thug living ain't shit. Oh yeah I said it, but that's because so many young bucks are loyal to the word, without truly understanding the commitment that comes along with the territory. Stuntin' Dope Boys hit the dust everyday, but the Savvy Big Tymers, huh, those are the ones that thrive and make it in the end.

What's a Big Tymer? Hum, it's funny you would ask. I've questioned myself on those very words. I guess it could be a number of things. It could be a top flight heavy hitter, a star athlete, a rap group, a song, a massive drug deal gone right for the Feds, or a legit ass nigga like myself. No matter how it's broken down, it all comes back to this, *"Someone or something of major status."*

Major status. Ump! Speaking of that, once you make a name for yourself, it's something how it gets lonely at the top. I wonder do all Big Tymers feel the same as me? I wonder if after all the money is counted, the dope distributed, and the women are gone, do other Ballas feel the same kind of void I feel? I wonder if they honestly find true satisfaction in being ruthless killers? I used to, but after loosing a child, a few homies, and a brother along the way, my mind is in turmoil. My heart, damn, it's bitter. And my gangsta, though at one time it was on point, it doesn't seem to hold the same value it once did.

Somewhere along the way, I got soft. Somehow with the passing of each new day, I started to care about myself and those I was putting in harms way. When I was fresh on the come up, my boys always teased me, talking 'bout, "Oh hell naw, you ain't no real Thugizzo." And, I guess to some extent they were right. I say that because I believe what really happened was somehow, I discovered that my life had real purpose, but ballin' wasn't it. DAMN! I wish I would have realized that long before all my losses. Then maybe I'd feel better about my current position and my life choices. My grandma, GG always told me the decisions I made while growing up could and would affect me and all those connected to me, for the rest of my life. To bad I didn't clearly understand what she meant then. It's a damn shame that life came to this for me, before I truly decided to change my ways. More than anything, I wonder why a nigga got ta be stripped of everything to realize his worth. I know you're clueless as to what I'm talking about or even who I am for that matter, but I hope you read ***Hood Rich*** that way you'll be up on the playas in this tale. If not, I'm gon' turn this over to Asia. She'll take it from here, and when she's done, you'll understand where I'm coming from.

Chapter 1
Recapping Hood Rich

I'm sure you're wondering who in the hell was talking in the opening. Well give me a few seconds to take you where my family's been, then allow me to bring you to the present. Once that's done, then everything will make sense.

My daddy, DeMarques Prince always told me that being ***Hood Rich*** was far more than driving around in a fancy car or sporting some iced-out jewelry. He vowed that it was more than a certain state of mind or even having the finer things in life. Well, that could have been some serious food for thought, but the value of Dad's wisdom was diluted to me, considering that he'd come up with such a definition after serving fifteen years in Michigan's penal system. At the time, he was trying to spit knowledge, I was only sixteen, so for that reason alone, Dad knew I was on some grown shit like most teenagers my age. You know, can't nobody tell us a thing about life when we got our minds set on doing what we wanna do. So to make a long story short, his facts fell on deaf ears, and I got my ass kicked by Hard Knocks 101.

I don't know why Daddy thought he could save me from going through my own series of life lessons, but I guess that's something every parent does. When he was going through his trials along with my Uncles, Ant and Silk, I'm sure my grandma Bean did the same thing for him. Nonetheless, the consequences of Dad's actions were grim. After a life sentence from DOC and all the dirty family secrets that surfaced, my dad's a real trooper to still have some damn sanity. I know a lot of what came out after Grandma Bean died still bothers him to this day. He never said much about the secrets or how they really affected him, but one thing for sure, Dad was gon' try to take 'em to his grave. I believe in his effort to keep the family's secrets secure, Dad decided before coming home from prison that he would rather be burdened with the stress of confidentiality than dog out his mother after she died.

To ensure that I started a new Prince legacy, without placing my focus on the Balla's fascination, Dad made sure he stayed in my ass about niggas that loved to make fast money. Considering his temper as well as the fact that both sides of my family had history in the game, I decided that I was gon' do me, and I didn't have to take Dad's advice. But, I sure wasn't stupid enough to let him know that.

"Asia, regardless of all the negativity thrown my way, a real Big Tymer like me allowed hard times and bold environments to transcend me into a prosperous achiever. After getting out the joint, I based my new dreams on the knowledge I gained from prison and the hood. You know there are too many sista's looking for love in all the wrong places. In the end, they come up with knuckleheads that don't give a shit about 'em. I don't want that for you. Once you understand that there's more to life than material things, you'll select men that treat you like a lady and love you unconditionally. I'm tellin' you now, I ain't gon' tolerate you bringin' home no bum ass nigga, so you better make good choices or else I'm goin' back to the joint for breakin' one of these young punks off."

Daddy always had something to say, and so for that reason alone, he spent just as much time as my mom did trying to inspire me to search for brothas of quality. Yeah Daddy tried his best to keep his baby girl from falling for a gangsta, but I was a Prince and just like him, I was gon' do what I do. *Shit, gangsta blood is in my genes. Plus, my pussy is already more valuable than black gold. Well, at least that's what Alex says when he's dropping scrilla on dem gifts. I don't know who Daddy's tryin' to punk. Hell, he already know... if I got to sneak to get mine, den I'm gon' do just dat. No matter what he says, things gon' go my way and niggas gon' love me just because.*

4

Chapter 2
My Thoughts

Once I became older, those father-daughter discussions between Daddy and I became very dear to me. As I matured, they changed the way I viewed men, my desire to be loved, the things I valued in life, and my future. You see, though I went on to college and later became a professional woman, I must admit that in my younger days, there were three things wrong with me. First, I was the daughter of DeMarques Prince. I was spoiled as hell and used to getting things my way. I also came from a family of flamboyant nigga's, so I liked nice shit. In my teenage years when my daddy wouldn't do what I wanted him to, I needed a man with deep pockets, who could and would deliver my hearts desire. Since I thought I knew what I wanted in a man, I always keyed in on the kind that could bring it in an instant.

Secondly, I was a cutie that grew up on the block. I knew I was a fine muthafucka and men that crossed my path in general let it be known on a daily basis. Now my downfall was that I was attracted to nothing but paid ass dope men. I mean, I admired everything about them. The way they walked, the way they checked hypes, and the manner in which they held their dicks while kicking it with their dawgs. I liked their stylish dress codes, from their jean hook-ups, to their custom suits with matching gators, which they rocked to some of the most elite events the city would ever see. I loved the flashy cars they drove, and that hard core mannerism they flaunted to let a nigga know they weren't to be fucked with.

Finally, I was that teenager that knew everything. Nobody could ever tell me shit, and if my parents or anyone else objected to my behavior, "So damn what," I was gon' do it anyway. I was that chick that was down for my man in spite of the drama it caused in my home.

My biggest problem was that I wasn't one to be on no lames with small pockets. Broke brothas couldn't afford me, my time, or the poonachie, so I made it a point to stop the legit nine to fivers from trying to holla at me straight out the gate. This cat named Kenny was a perfect example. Poor Kenny, I remember dissing him just because he was a nice guy.

"Asia, when you gonna hook up with a brotha?"

"I'm not interested playa, don't you work at Burger King on Grand River and Prevost."

"Yeah, and?"

"And nigga you can't afford me."

"What?"

"You heard me."

"See Asia, pretty bitches like you make honest, hard working brotha's like me fuckin' sick."

"Naw, pretty sista's like me, makes lame ass nigga's like you recognize off the top that you reachin' way out of yo league."

"Fuck you, trick."

"I wasn't a trick just a minute ago."

"That's when I thought you had some class, but I see you a dirty money rat."

Dirty Money Rat...I was not, so I didn't even trip cuz that's how nigga's I dissed usually played me. It's a shame a brotha can't take rejection without getting all pissed off. Anyway back to the story....

When I first started pullin' street nigga's, I didn't have no home girls in my life to teach me all there was to know about the role of being a dope man's woman. But from observing, I thought I knew enough. Shit, I didn't need no seasoned hoe's up in my business trying to school me anyway. Hell, I adopted what I wanted from a few of the sista's I checked for and did my own damn thang.

I'll admit a hard head gets a sore behind, so a few lessons I most certainly had to learn the hard way. I don't know why, but somehow I got hooked up with this ill bastard named Alex who was tickish as hell, and taught me how to take some serious dick. I added that fact because this brotha put in some long heavy stroking I wasn't used to. Sad part about that was that no matter how much I grunted when it hurt, before it was all said and done, he had me lovin that dick.

Is my self-esteem that low? I wondered, once I started trying to shake Alex. You know what, when I think about it, I believe it was, considering all I tolerated from him. I say that because no matter how bad he treated me, I convinced myself that that's the way a man treated his woman to prove his love. For some women, getting ourselves involved in domestic violence is a whole lot easier than getting ourselves out. And when the abusive relationship thing found its way into my life, like anyone else, I struggled to leave as well.

…♦♦♦…

Right after Daddy was released from prison, I met Alex while I was in Detroit visiting my father for the summer. Our first few months together, Dad was like a guard dog. I mean, he was tripping hard about everything, especially boys. Actually, because he was so adamant about me not being out there, he didn't leave me any room to breathe. I had to sneak around to do just about everything. Dad rode me about the way I dressed, the kind of young men I found myself attracted to, and my strong sassy attitude. *Oh here we go,* I would always think seconds before simply tuning him out. "And Asia, while you're out there trying to be so damn grown, you better remember what I told you. And if I find out you sak chasin', I'm splittin' a nigga's head to the white meat, then I'm comin' for you." *Be serious, Daddy, people don't even say sak chasin' no more. Plus, I'm sixteen, touch me and it's gon' be on,* I thought without saying, cuz I knew Dad wasn't the one.

It was always one kind of threat after another, so when I met Alex, I never told Dad. Since neither of them wanted me to date, he and GG would have had a fit. Besides, I didn't want to hear no lectures.

I think my GG was the one that got on my nerves about boys the most. She used to always get onto me about being to grown. *"Asia, you need to put some dang clothes on and stop walking around here looking like you're lookin'. That's what's wrong with you youngins today; you always want to expose yourself. You ain't leavin' a thang to be imagined, so a boy gon' know all of what you got before he should."*

"GG, this is the style."

"Style my ass. If God wanted you to have all yo butt crack showin', clothes wouldn't exist. Wha'cha gotta have that low cut stuff on for anyway. It's got you lookin' like a tramp."

"I'ma…"

"You ain't gonna do nuthin' but get raped. Men are horney these days, they'll take yo little stuff and not think twice about it."

My attempt to hip GG was hopeless. *"See, Grandma Bean would have loved these jeans. That's why I miss her so much. She let me be myself."*

"Don't throw Bean or nobody else up in my face."

"GG, these clothes are just an expression of my personality."

"I got an expression for your personality," GG fussed, making an ugly face at my attire. *"Yo Grandma Bean would have liked those pieces of scraps because she was hot just like you at your age. Hell, that's why she*

had kids so young," GG paused with the most serious look on her face, then asked, *"You are on the pill, Right?"*

I was not finna talk about my sex life with my great-grandmother. I could just see myself telling GG about my favorite positions, or my freaky tales. *Forget this,* I thought before getting up to go to the basement to watch rap videos.

Week two, Dad immediately forced me off on a cruise, talking about some bonding time. I'd already met Alex by the time we left for our trip, so in all reality, Dad didn't stop nothing more than a week of chit chatting. I won't lie, we did have a ball. Not to mention that it was a much needed trip for us both. By the time we made it home, I was ready because I'd thought about Alex my entire trip.

When we got back, Alex talked about how much he missed me, but I thought he was just shooting game, so when he started trying to come see me and asking to take me out, I went crazy trying to come up with excuses as to why neither could happen.

To be honest, when I think back on it all, I don't even know why I got so caught up with Alex anyway. I could see that we were different from jump, so I knew he was a nigga to beware. All the signs were there, but I ignored them. He was charming, said all the right things, and to win me over, he bought me lavish shit that no other dude I'd ever dated could afford. Besides, I really didn't know how much of a fool he really was until after the verbal abuse became a regular occurrence. To this day, I wonder did I tolerate him for as long as I did because I thought I was lacking something in my life. Who knows? I guess I'll just get on with the story and let you be the judge.

…♥♥♥…

Chapter 3
Introducing Alex

In June 2001, I ran into Alex at T-Bell's corner store and things took off from there. Alex was purchasing some *Swisher Sweets* while I was at the counter paying for a Papaya juice and some Jay's Flaming Hot chips. Suddenly, he was making small talk.

"Yo, what's up with you sexy?" He asked, giving me this bright smile with his pretty white teeth.

"Excuse me?"

"Where's yo' man?"

"I ain't got no man. Where's yo woman?"

"I'm talkin' to her," he said, immediately winning me over.

"Oh, is that a fact?"

"It can be, if you feelin' a playa like he's feelin' you."

This nigga got hella game, I laughed. "You're cute, but I ain't one to be jockin' no dope boy," I lied to avoid being viewed as a gold digger.

"Good, cause I ain't one to be on no bitch."

"Bitch! Who you callin' a bitch?"

"I ain't callin' nobody a bitch, Mami. I said, I don't be jockin' no bitches."

"Oh, I thought so. Clean it up, cuz I was 'bout to say."

"You was 'bout to say what?" he smiled.

"I was about…"

"Yo' l'il fine ass wasn't bout to say shit," he interrupted.

"You don't know what I was gon' say."

"It wasn't gon' be much."

"And why you so sure about that?"

"You smilin' too hard, which means you're feelin' a nigga and his conversation. If you was gon' tell me anything, it was gon' be your name and 'dem digits."

I snickered, cuz he was right. Alex was tall like Lebron, thugged out like Shug, sexy lips like LL, tatted up like Pac, smooth pretty skin like Li'l chocolate like Whizzey, and well groomed like Usher. Shoot, before I could get out of the store good, *I had it bad.*

"Maybe we should start over." I suggested, extending my hand to shake his. "Hi, my name is Asia."

"Alex," he replied, pulling out a phat knot. "Let me get dat?"

"Oh, I got it, but thanks anyway."

"Thanks anyway, I'ma need a l'il mo' than just a thanks."

"A little more like what?"

"Like some digits."

"My number? Oh you must be 'bout to spend more than three dollars then."

"It ain't like I can't."

"Well since you put it like that, it's 414-5555," I stated, watching him program it into his celly.

"Cool, I'll call you later."

"Okay."

When I walked out that store, I switched a little more than usual cuz I knew he was looking. And since he was starin' so hard, I wanted him to peep all the hips and ass I was draggin. *Yea, I think I'm the shiz..nit.* I nodded, continuing on with my thoughts. *Oh I'm bout to hook him, and he's paid, too. Shit a sista could use some bling and a new pair of Coach Boots with a phat bag to match for the fall. Huh, don't these niggas know, they can't expose new millennium hoes to their scrilla on day one. Shit, diamonds are a girl's best friend, right after money that is, and I'm 'bout to get paid, I say I'm 'bout to get paid.*

....◆◆◆◆....

Alex was fresh on nineteen and had just started to come up in the game. He was a runner for this "Big Tymer" named Calvin Shaw. Al was loyal as hell when it came to having his back, too. He didn't talk much about Cal's business, which made me a little curious about how big time he really was. But from what he shared, he expressed that Calvin and his boy Melvin put him on when he was only thirteen. I think most of Alex's drive to be as loyal as he was to Cal came from seeing first hand what dope money could do for one's lifestyle. During that time, Calvin owned this lavish club called *Big Fellas*. Now that place was the hottest spot during the early Y2K era, and Al always spoke highly of it. Every now and then, Calvin let him hang in V.I.P., which was known to most as BBO, "Big Ballas Only." Al said everybody that was somebody in the D reserved tables in BBO weekly and packed *Big Fellas* out way beyond capacity on holidays. One time he told me about this Mauri cat that had long money. Mauri owned a few clothing stores, a limo service, and was an older player who did business on the DL with Calvin from time to time.

People like Mauri were interesting to me. All I know was hearing Alex's stories made me crave my own adventures. I wanted to experience *Big Fellas* and that fast lifestyle for myself. You know, gather my own memories and have my own wild dirty money tales to share. After Alex got me hooked on his BBO saga, I knew it was only a matter of time before I'd be up in the house drinking *Chris* and mingling with some of the greatest ballas in Detroit's history.

Actually, the longer Al and I dated, the prouder I was to be the woman of a legit gangsta in the making. I say legit because Alex wasn't just treated like a gofer, he got mad respect from Calvin, which aided in his anxiousness to one day be the man himself. Most often, all I could ever think about was how I was gon' come up. My being so young and naive at the time, I thought being a ballas main bitch was a glamorous lifestyle to live. I was so caught up on the hype that it was rare that I even considered the risk that came along with the dope game. However, drama quickly opened my eyes to it, and I wasn't ready.

I remember how ampted Alex was after Calvin promised him the world for his loyalty, but before Al could really prove himself, Melvin ended up missing and Calvin came up dead. Whatever went down with those two was seriously brutal, and due to Alex's association with both of them, Calvin's murder had me on spook. That incident should have been my sign to flee, but foolish me, I was gon' ride or die for my nigga, cause "I loved him like that."

Yeah, that's right, dumb ass me, I stuck it out for the longest because Alex was my first love. I wasn't going nowhere, and with the seriousness of Calvin's murder, all I could do was hope that no one was looking for Al too. I don't know why, but I worshiped the ground Alex walked on. I mean, I loved his dirty draws, and because he wasn't no punk, I believed if something went down, he could and would protect me.

I did get a chance to meet Calvin Shaw the summer before he got killed. I was getting ready to return to Chicago, so Alex took me out to dinner. On our way back to my friend Nikki's house, he stopped by Calvin's club to do a pick up.

"Big Fellas," I said, reading the sign. "Why are we here?"

"I got bi'ness. Hold tight... I'll be right back."

"Ut'un, you ain't 'bout to leave me out here. Anything could happen."

11

"Come on then, scary ass," he teased, grabbing my hand. "I want you to meet Cal anyway."

"You been tellin' him about me?" I asked, thinking maybe he was really feeling me. Anyway, we walked into the club and rode a glass elevator up to Calvin's office. *"Damn this is nice," I replied, stepping out onto the floor known as BBO.*

"Yeah it is the shit. One day all this gon' be me. Cal said when he gets tired of running thangs, I'm the next in charge."

"And you gon' need a dime on yo' arm like me to keep the prowlers away."

"Baby, I 'ont want nobody but you."

"Yeah, that's what you say now. Wait 'til you got a big butt and a smile up in yo face then tell me that same shit," I teased, walking into Calvin's office.

As soon as I entered, Calvin looked at me as if he'd seen a ghost. After frowning at this horrific picture he had framed on his wall, I kind of stared back at him, trying give off the affect that I too was a down ass individual. He nudged his head at me, as a form of a greeting, and I returned the gester.

"Yo, Cal, what's up my man?" Alex said.

"Chillin'... Who dis?"

"Oh, this is that little fem, Asia I told you about."

"Sup... Asia, that's a fittin' name for a little cutie like you."

"Thanks," I responded, kinda uncomfortable.

"Al's been talking about you. You're the first to have his nose wide open like this."

"Is that right? Well, what can I say?"

"I know you better not break my boy's heart."

"I won't," I smiled, giving him dimples galore.

"Al, you better be good to this one. She's a keeper."

"Fa, sho, man. I told you she was a hottie."

"Asia.... Hum...I like that," he said, staring once again.

At that point, I had no more words for Calvin. To igonore him, I locked in on that ugly damn painting once again and thought, *You'd think a balla of his status would have better taste for fine art. That damn painting looks like shit.* Suddenly, I was distracted and became a little uneasy with the way Calvin was staring, so I inconspicuously tapped Alex to inform him that I was ready to go. *This nigga Calvin is checking me out. He must want me for himself or something..... Nah, that's crazy.* I quickly dismissed that foolishness, considering that Al was like a son to him.

Calvin was somewhat handsome, but had this dry gaze that was kind of creepy. Actually, for a Kingpin, I found him to be a rather nice guy. Nonetheless, I don't exactly know what he did to end up pushing up daises, but I will say that for whatever reason he got hit, someone took him out with a real vengeance. Whenever I asked questions about Calvin, Alex never said much to me about what happened, but I did overhear him telling his boy Terrell that "Cal cashed out on the **wrong nigga**." He never said who the "Wrong nigga" was, but I assume the guy was someone just as prominent, because when Calvin got tagged, someone cut off his lips and toes, stuffed them in his mouth, and duck taped his face.

I knew from just listening to my daddy and Uncle E that brutality like that meant Calvin stepped to a heavy hitter, and in some way his loose lips obviously sank his ship. When they found him, his hands and legs were bound, and then he was obviously pitched into the lake like a squirming worm. I heard he was alive when they tossed him, too. I say that because when his body was recovered, I remember reading News-on-detroit.com while in Chicago. The article said the victim drowned, and I guess Melvin's body was weighed down so well that he became fish food. After hearing about all that went down with Calvin, I really knew I was a fool for staying with Alex. Actually when I considered the distance between us, I really didn't think Alex and I would work out anyway. And because I lived in Chicago and was only in Detroit for holidays and summer breaks, I wasn't worried about us getting serious.

We tipped that entire summer without getting busted, but once I returned home, as far as I was concerned my fling with Alex was just that. Much to my surprise, after about two months, Alex started driving to Chicago. Every twenty to thirty days, he'd do a drug run for Calvin. He'd call as soon as he hit the city limits. Hell, since he was frequently in the Chi on business, he had a legit excuse to drop in to see a diva. After his business was completed, he'd scoop me up, we'd go get a room, and then fuck like rabbits. For some reason, when it came to him, my sex drive was out of control. He had turned me into a real freak while I was in Detroit. That's why he knew if he wanted to keep me honest, some serious lovemaking was required every time he hit my city.

...♦♦♦...

We did that long distant thang for almost a year straight and a few months short of my high school graduation, Alex started talking to me about moving to Detroit.

13

"Alex, I can't move there. My parents have money put up for me to go to college. If I don't go to school, they'll have a fit."

"I didn't ask you not to go to college, I said move to Detroit. I want you closer to me, so I can see you on my terms and treat you like the fly muthafucka you are."

"But what about going to college?" I asked, smiling about his response.

"Michigan has schools. Get on the internet and start lookin' now? That way by the time you get ready to leave, you'll at least know where you want to go. And Baby money ain't gon' be no problem, cuz one thing Calvin told me was, '*Al she's a doll. Man, if you gon' keep her, you better treat her like she's the daughter of a Prince.*"

"He did?"

"Yeah Boo. Cal thinks you're good for me."

"Dang, how he come up with that conclusion from our one meetin'."

"He peeped your character…. Now enough of that, wa'sup on the D."

"You serious, you'll take care of me fa' real," I asked, straddling him for a kiss.

"What I say?"

"You said you would."

"So it shouldn't be no mo questions then. My word is my bond."

"Well, how about taking care of me right now?" I insisted, pulling down his boxers to change the subject.

"Take care of you how?"

"With this," I replied, pushing his limp dick to the side.

"You sure you want some of this?" He asked, making it grow into a beast.

"I doooo," I whispered in his ear, getting off on his touch.

"I see you do. Damn, you're wet."

"I can't help it. I'm only gettin' it once a month. Shit, when you're not here my pussy be dying for some of you."

"That's why you need to come to Detroit. Then I could hit it everyday, a few times a day, if you want it like that."

"That's what I'm talking about," I replied, wrapping my legs around his waist. In his excitement, Alex started tenderly touching my body. "I love the way you make me feel," I moaned as he went from sucking my breast to eating me out. *Wooooooooo,* I thought. *Asia your ass is seventeen-years-old, what you know about getting your clit licked.* "Not a damn thing," I replied out loud.

"What you say, Boo?"

"I said that feels sooooo good."

14

"You like that?"

"Aw, yesss." I whimpered with my eyes rolling up in my head. Suddenly, Alex rose to his knees, lifted my legs even with my face, and slid inside of me.

"Wait, ain't you puttin' on a condom."

"A condom? Damn! You want to stop right in the middle of me tearin' this shit up?"

"Yeah! I ain't tryin'ta get pregnant."

"Do you trust me?"

"Yes."

"Do you love me?"

"Yes."

"Don't you know I hate rubbers?"

"Yes, but..."

"But nothing," he replied, cutting me off. "We always use condoms. I hate dem shits. Just let me feel you one time. I promise I won't get you pregnant. As soon as I'm 'bout to bust, I'll pull out."

"I don't know about all that. I ain't ever had sex without a condom before."

"You'll like it better. If you don't, I'll stop."

"What if you make a mistake?"

"I ain't gon' make no mistakes. If I do, then I'll pay for you to get an abortion."

"I ...."

"Shhhhhh," he whispered, slowly removing my hands from his chest. "Hold me," he tenderly whispered in my ear, attempting to put all seven and a half inches of his fat dick in me.

"Damn," I whined in pain.

"It don't feel good to you?"

"It hurts."

"Then relax, and I'll go slower."

"Relax. How am I supposed to relax?" I asked as my thighs shook like crazy. "Let my legs down some that might help."

Slower was exactly what he did. He grinded my sugar walls, talking in this soothing tone that only a hot piece of pussy could appreciate. Finally, I relaxed, and the love I made with Alex that day was something I'll never forget. Huh, prior to that evening, I never could comprehend what a nigga meant when he said, "I'll have you walking around in the daytime, looking for me with a flashlight." Well, after he finished, I had a better understanding. Like most young girls dating an older guy, I was whipped and ready to do damn near anything that man asked me to.

Chapter 4
Graduation

After getting my guts pumped to death, the room gave off the scent of hot sex. Neither of us seemed to care though. We laid up like two fools for the longest embraced in each others arms. I'd never been so obsessed with a guy before, but what loving Alex did to my mind, tripped me out. I thought I was stronger than the average old H.O.E, but the longer we dated, the more I learned that I was just as whipped and dumb for him as any old other chicken head.

"Baby, I got something for you," Alex rattled, easing out of bed with dick flopping everywhere. As he walked to the closet, Jaheem came on. "Aw shit, that's my jam," he stated, dancing.

"Boy, you don't know nothin' about Jah."

"I know I'm still feeling this cut."

"Why? It's old."

"So, it's the shit though. Plus he's tellin' you what a playa like me be thinkin' when I'm out grindin'."

"What's that?"

"*Just in case, I don't make it home tonight.......I love you, I love you,*" he sung in a tone only a woman that loved her man could appreciate.

"Boy, you don't sound nothin' like him."

"Shit, Jah wanna sound like me. I got my own flow."

"Keep dreamin'."

"Forget that, just know that I love you more than anything. Now do you want my surprise or not?"

"What is it?"

Alex walked inside the closet and pulled out a huge nicely wrapped box. "Here you go." When I tore off into the wrapping, I couldn't believe my eyes.

"Oh my God....... A Chinchilla fur jacket."

"Yep, anything for you, Boo."

"So that's why you got the room before you came and got me. You were hiddin' gifts," I teased, quickly coming to my senses. "Babe, I love it, but I can't take this home. My mom would know it's real. Shit, I can't afford nothing like this for myself."

"And."

"And if I take this to the house, my step-dads gon' automatically assume it came from you. He already hates you cuz he thinks you're a drug dealer."

"So what! Fuck that nigga, he don't like me and I don't like his ass either. I don't care if he knows it came from me? I can't help it that I can afford to buy my woman better gifts than he can buy his."

"I care. This gon' just cause drama for me."

"I ain't havin' that. I want you to have this coat, so do what you gotta do to make dat happen?"

"How about you keep it and whenever you come see me, bring it with you. I can wear it when we're together. Then when I move to Detroit, I'll get it from you."

"When you move to Detroit? So you've decided to come?"

"Yeah. As soon as I graduate, I'm there. Shit, with the kind of dick you're bringin', I ain't 'bout to let no dirty tramps come up with my man. Plus, you're buyin' furs. Shoot, I'd be a fool to let someone else have you."

"Damn!" Alex fussed, looking at his watch.

"What?"

"I got to get out of here. I'm s'posed to be back in Detroit by eleven tonight to make a drop. Boo, you and this good lovin' gon' get me reprimanded."

"Sorry. In the future I'll try to do a little less."

"You bet' not. If you like the way I bring these lavish gifts, you better keep workin' that shit like it's a 9 to 5."

"Yeah right, you better watch yo' mouth cuz that sounds like somethin' you'd say to a slut."

"Yeah right, nothin'. You know you ain't no hoe, so don't even trip. Yo' l'il featherweight butt better hit the showers 'fo I spank dat ass," he insisted, hitting my booty.

…◆◆◆…

When we made it to the house, Mom was just getting in from work. I got out of Alex's car and walked over to the driver's side to kiss him goodbye. As I leaned in, I noticed Mom staring us both down like we were on crack.

"Bye Pookie, drive carefully," I said, walking away.

"I will."

"Call me and let me know you made it home safely." Before he could reply, Rodney came storming out the house, raising hell.

"Asia, get that nigga away from this house. I already warned you once."

18

"He's leavin' now," I replied, as Al put his car in park.

"Naw……..No the fuck I'm not," he stated, opening the door. "Nigga, you got a problem," he lunged out, ranting at Rodney while I grabbed him and tried to hold him back.

"What you say boy?"

"Boy! I got yo damn boy. Nigga, I'm a man just like you…. I said is there a problem?"

"Yeah, I don't want yo ass near my house."

"As long as my woman's here, you gon' see me. And it ain't shit you can do about it."

"Oh yeah, punk ass nigga, there is something I can do."

"Well wa'sup," Al asked, inviting Rodney to a fight.

"I'm not about to go there with you. What you wanna shoot me?"

"Man, my heat's in my whip, I don't need shit to get at you dawg."

"I know how y'all drug dealers get down. Y'all gon' shoot a man first cuz you're heartless, and then play bad later."

"Nigga, Kool-Aid don't flow through these veins. I ain't got to hide behind no gun."

"Alex, get in yo car and leave now," I fussed.

"You better listen," Rodney hissed. "Now get the hell away from here before I call the police on your lowlife ass."

"On my mama, nigga if you keep talking shit to me, I'm gon' split yo wig."

"Boy, I'll fuck you up. Don't let this suit fool you."

"Don't threaten me, and I got yo, Boy!"

That last "Boy" was Al's breaking point. Alex pushed me aside, ran up on our lawn, and socked the hell out of Rodney. I tried to grab him from behind once they fell on the ground, but he was too strong. Mama, ran over to help, but got elbowed in the face as the men tussled around. Finally, Mama grabbed a stick off the ground and let Alex have it. *Wack,!!!!!!!* I heard the branch sound off, as it broke on his back. He jumped up like he was about to kick her ass, that's when Rodney grabbed him around his legs and he tumbled over face first. Our neighbor Mr. Davis came over with his gun, pointed it at Alex and talked him up off the ground.

"Nigga, I said get up slow. I got a l'il crazy in me and I'll send you and yo brains home in a bag. I suggest you go back to where ever you came from with all that nonsense. This is a respectable neighborhood and we want to keep it that way." Alex gave Mr. Davis the illest look, and then walked towards his car. "You got one minute to get in your car and go, then I'm calling 911."

Alex, aware of the fact that he had drugs in his car left without a word. He didn't want to deal with no police involvement or extra legal problems. More than anything, he didn't want Calvin in his ass about fucking off his drugs. Once Alex was gone, Mr. Davis started fussing me out.

"Asia, you should really be ashamed. Your parents deserve better than this. If you were mine, I'd kick yo l'il grown ass. Rodney and Zena give you the world and this is how you treat them?" *I know this old nigga better get out my business before I cuss him out*, I thought, mugging him on my way to the porch. "You disrespectful little shit. And unless you settle down, you'll continue to bring foolishness like this to your parent's home. You better be glad you ain't mine, cuz I'd put yo ungrateful ass out. Let you get a taste of real living and see how much you like that."

"Shut the hell up, Mr. Davis, I heard you the first time. Take yo nosey ass home," I stated walking into the house. Mama and Rodney were right on my tracks, still going off.

"Asia, I done told you about bringing them damn nigga to my house!" Rodney yelled. I didn't respond at first because he was right. He had told me not to have no "Lowlife, drug dealing punks" at the house, but Alex wasn't no "Lowlife."

Rodney and my mother hated Alex because they assumed he was a dope dealer. Yeah, he wore flashy jewelry, his clothes were stylish, and his 2002 Jaguar in 2001 could have been considered an expensive car for a teenager as well as a dead give away. But, I didn't care about following no rules. Hell, I was in love, so I didn't respect what neither one of them thought. Once mom started expressing what she felt about Alex, I was glad I was a few months short of graduating. As far as I was concerned, there wasn't anything she could say. I was a woman, too, so I couldn't be told nothing about my man or my business.

"Asia, you're making some bad choices right now. I wish you would reconsider dating this guy."

"Mom, you're judging Alex by his appearance. He's a nice guy. He comes from a good family," I expressed, lying something serious. I'd never met one person in Alex's family, so I didn't know what he came from, but it sounded good, so I ran with it. "You need to relax and allow me to grow up. Besides, all his nice stuff ain't come from drug money."

"Come on, Asia, do you think I was born yesterday. I know what street niggas look like. Your daddy was a thug. That's exactly why he went through half the shit he did. You better slow down young lady, or just like me, some of your choices are going to hurt you in the long run."

"Zena, Alex is not my daddy, and don't be slangin' my father's name through the mud like he ain't about shit."

"What?" Mama frowned.

"You heard what I said," I sassed, like I paid bills in her house.

"What the hell did you just say?"

"Dad has made some mistakes, but he has always been good to me. And for…" Before I could get the rest of my sentence out, Mom punched me so hard in my mouth that I saw foreign objects.

"Zena!...... Asia Prince, who the hell do you think you're talking to? You don't call me by my first name. I know you're a little short of eighteen, but I'm still your mother. This is still my house and you gon' respect me," she growled, spitting while she talked. "If you curse at me one more time, I'm gon' forget you're my child and kick your skinny black ass like a bitch on the streets. With all that just jumped off in my yard, you better be lucky all I did was punch you once. Next time you won't be so lucky."

"This is hopeless. You and Rodney are a joke. Oh, and just so you know, I'm moving to Detroit after graduation."

"What?

"You heard what I said," I replied, still holding my lip.

"What about college?"

"I'm going to stay with my daddy over the summer. I'm thinkin' about going to college in Michigan this fall."

"Your father and I need to talk about that."

"You don't need to talk about nothin'. I told you I'm movin' and that's my decision."

"If you keep talking shit to me, you'll be movin' today," Mom fussed, moving towards me like she was going to hit me again.

"That's fine."

"Does your daddy know you're moving to Detroit to be with a drug dealer?"

"I'm not going to be with nobody. I'm going to go to college, and spend some quality time with my daddy. I haven't told him I'm coming yet, but I'm about to call right now cuz I gots to get up out of here."

"Whatever, Asia, you'll be grown. I've done my part. I'm not going to stress about it anymore. I'm gon' tell you right now, these punk ass thugs ain't gon' treat you like you want to be treated. And they ain't gon' ever love you more than your family does."

"Mom, he already does love me more than y'all," I expressed, rolling my eyes.

"Asia, you just think he does. Your father didn't respect me for a long time, and I see you're about to make some of the same mistakes I did."

"Mom, I didn't have any kids in high school, you did. I graduated, you got a GED, you were out in dem streets, and I've stayed focused. If I make a few mistakes after high school, then I think I'm entitled to. That's what life and living is all about. Right?"

"Asia, get out of my face!" she disgustingly ordered. "I see with all the knowledge I've tried to lace you with, you still turned out to be a damn fool. Good dick and gifts don't confirm a nigga's love."

"Who said we're having sex?"

"Them hickeys all over your neck."

"Whatever," I stated, walking to my room.

After we had our words, I called my father to let him know I was moving to Detroit. Teretta answered first, so I spoke, and then asked for my dad.

"Hey, is my dad there."

"I think so. The last time I was downstairs, him and E were watching a bootlegged DVD. Let me check to see if he's still here." I held on while she yelled for Dad to get the phone. After a few tries, he finally picked up.

"Yeah," he answered like I was disturbing him.

"Yeah! Is that a way to answer the phone?"

"Butterfly?"

"Um hum."

"Hey, I thought Teretta said Ashley was on the phone."

"Ashley, who's that?"

"This little chick E hired to run the clothing store."

"Oh, what are you doing?"

"Watchin' a movie."

"Want me to call you back later?"

"Nah. Whas'up?"

"Ummm, I just called to talk."

"Talk! Talk about what?"

"What do you mean, talk about what?"

"Asia, you never just call to talk."

"Daddy, what is that s'posed to mean?"

"Usually when you call, it's for one of four reasons. One, you're mad at your mama and Rodney. Two, you want me to listen while you vent about how grown you are and how unfair everybody else is. Three, you want me to buy you something or you need some money. Four, you're on a pity party. Now which one is it this time?"

"Well, you're wrong today. I mean, you're kind of wrong. I am mad at Mama and Rodney, but I don't need any money. Actually, I was calling to tell you that I'm comin' to Detroit for the summer."

"That's nothing new," Dad replied, cutting me off.

"Well, if you'd let me finish."

"Oh, excuse me."

"I'm comin' for the entire summer, but I also want to try and get in a college there in Michigan."

"Here?"

"Yeah, is that a problem?"

"No, not at all. I'm just surprised. I thought you said you were going to Langston with your friend Nikki."

"I was."

"So what made you change your mind?"

"I don't know. I think I want to be closer to you. I miss you when we're apart."

"Butterfly, if you want to come and live with us for the summer, you're more than welcomed to. You know Teretta's pregnant, so you might have to walk lightly around here some days."

"Man, she can't be any worse than Mom, and she's not pregnant."

"I'm not touching that one."

"Okay," I laughed. "Anyway, I'm going online to start downloading applications for admission. When I decide where I want to go, I'll let you know."

"Sounds like a plan. Love you, Baby."

"Love you too, Daddy."

Chapter 5
Detroit

I flew to Detroit two days after graduation. My dad and our family left Chicago on that Wednesday, and I left that Friday. Dad and Teretta had just bought their new house in West Bloomfield, which I'd never seen, so I was excited about getting to the house to check out my new room. Usually, when I visited we stayed at my Grandma Bean's house, but after my aunt KeKe married Sam, Daddy rented Bean's place out and then bought him and Teretta a house out in the burbs. When I got in, Dad and Teretta picked me up from the airport and it was on from there.

My daddy owned three of the hottest spots in the city of Detroit, so our first stop took us to **Asia's Sports Bar**, which was named after me. Dad had made a lot of changes to the restaurant, since I'd last seen it, so I was impressed with its classiness. There were booths instead of just mix-match tables, and he had all sorts of antiques and framed autographed sports apparel hanging around.

"Dang, Daddy this is nice," I complimented, looking around at all the dope dealers chilling in the place.

"Glad you like it, and whenever you're up here, you better remember."

"Remember what?"

"If I catch you with any of these cats, I'm gon' nut the fuck up, and break my foot off in someone's ass. Probably yours first, since I've already warned you."

"Prince, lets go," Teretta intervened, saving me from my dad's threats. "Asia ain't been in Detroit a good ten minutes and you're already trying to run her off."

"I ain't trying to run her nothin'. I just want her to stay focused on college and her studies. I 'ont want her to make the same mistakes I made. I don't want no grandbabies and no excuses as to why she can't start college in August."

"Daddy, stop trippin'. Dang! I'm not thinkin' 'bout gettin' with no Ballas. I already know you ain't havin' that."

"Good and as long as you do, we won't have no problems in the future nor this conversation again."

This gon' be a long summer. I thought, walking out, pouting.

From there we went by **BEAN'S Spot,** which was jammed packed with tons of Detroiters looking for some good soul food. Right as we entered we ran into my Uncle Silk.

"Uncle Silk, how you doing?" I asked, excited to see him.

"Good, Baby Girl. And you," he paused, hugging me and speaking to Dad, but he kept walking, barely acknowledging Silk at all.

"I'm fine. Uncle Silk, I was looking for you at Graduation. What happened to you?" I asked, trying to ease the tension.

"I thought about coming, but P still isn't speaking to me. I didn't want to spoil your day with no bullshit."

"Do you think y'all gon' ever work through this?"

"Probably not, he's stubborn as hell. But no matter what, I still love you," he stated, reaching into his pocket to give me some money. "Here you go. Happy Graduation, you be good. I'm bout to get out of here `fo yo ignorant Pops tick me off."

"When will I see you again?"

"Don't know. I've been thinking about moving to Atlanta."

"Atlanta?"

"Yeah, I got a l'il female down there. She's ridin' me hard and wants me to relocate."

"Are you?"

"I'm thinking about it. I'm going down for a visit next week, and I'll decide after that."

"You still an old playa, huh, Uncle Silk?"

"Nah," he blushed as Dad walked out, ordering me to come on. "That boy is yo Grandma, Bean's son. Sometimes she was just as mean and evil for no reason."

"She was."

"Hell yeah."

"I don't remember that side of Grandma."

"Are you kiddin' me? Shit Bonita Prince was the meanest one in the family. And once she got a little liquor in her system, she'd cuss a nigga out on GP."

"I do remember her going off a time or two," I laughed.

"Yeah, I miss my baby. She was my favorite out of all my brothers and sisters."

"She was my favorite, too," I replied, looking out the window at Dads expression. "I bet Dad is goin' off now about me still being in here."

"That, or the fact that you're still in here kickin' it with your old Uncle Silk," he smiled.

"Silk, I'm gon' go outside and ask Daddy, P, you sho' you don't still wanna hang with old Eddie Cane," I mimicked.

"Girl you silly. What you know about the five heartbeats?"

"That was my favorite movie."

"You can tell you're a Prince."

"Why you say that?"

"Cause it was Daddy Ruenae's, GG's, Ants, Bean's and my favorite, too."

"Daddy likes it also. He watched it all the time after he came home from prison."

"I know, GG told me."

"Well Uncle Silk, I better go. Daddy's waiting. I'll be here until I start school. Hopefully I'll get to see you around."

"You will..... give me a hug. I'll catch up with you before I leave for Atlanta." I reached up, giving my uncle the biggest bear hug. And when I made it to the truck, Dad gave me the rudest cussing out I'd gotten from him in a long time.

"Don't ever keep me muthafuckin' waiting for that nigga again."

"Dad, he is our family."

"You heard what I said," he said real ignorantly.

I didn't say anything else. I just sat back because unlike Mom, Dad was real short and had flashbacks sometimes. I never knew what to expect and I was scared of him to some degree.

Dad whipped out that lot with much attitude, and we were off to *Top of the Line Fashions.* That was the clothing store Dad and E owned together. That place was packed with brotha's that had long money as well. As soon as I entered the store, playas were on me. I walked in talking major noise to Uncle Everett. Some old gangsta named Mauri that was about Dads age started trying to holla at me, and Dad 'bout went crazy.

"Umm, hey sexy l'il thang," he greeted, looking all down my shirt at my breast, cuz I was givin' much cleavage.

"Mauri, this is me," my daddy rudely responded.

"This is you? Damn, Prince, you got all the fine women. Man, I want to be like you when I grow up."

"Fool, this is my daughter, not my woman."

"Your daughter! Nigga, stop lying. You don't look old enough too have a daughter this age."

"I started slanging this big dick real young, homie," Dad said, grabbing himself.

"Nigga right! You just don't want it to get out that you're robbing the cradle."

"I ain't robbing shit."

"Well, niggga I do. Ain't nothing like the squirms of some tender trim."

"Yo, you better make sure you stay the hell away from this one."

"You serious."

"Hell yeah! This is my daughter, so do a double take cuz Asia Prince will get you an early check out date." Mauri smiled, but Dad didn't twitch. He pulled me in front of him and formally introduced me. "Asia, this is Mr. Mauri."

"Hello, Mr. Mauri."

"Uhhh, that's just Mauri," he said, grinning like crazy.

"Mau, yo ass gon' make me snap your damn neck man. I'm telling you Dawg, this is my child. She just graduated from high school, and I don't want to go back to prison today, so you better chill out."

"Man, you're serious?"

"You damn straight I am."

"Sorry Playa, I didn't believe yo' fly, pretty boy ass."

"It's all good," Dad replied, walking to the office.

I stayed out front talking to Uncle E for a minute, and then he finally went to the back as well. I was left alone with ole boy. *I wonder is this the Mauri Alex used to talk about that was so rich and down with Calvin Shaw. Naahh, couldn't be.* "You're a sexy muthafucka," he whispered as I looked at him like he was crazy. *He obviously don't know about Daddy's wrath.* Since I didn't want no drama for either one of us, when he started trying to talk to me again, I went on to the back, too. I knew my daddy, I knew he was crazy, and I figured he was closely watching my every move on them damn store monitors. Very few people knew about the hidden camera's, but I did, so I moved around. If it wasn't for the cameras, old Mauri would've gotten some play.

"Asia, I know that dirty old nigga was trying to talk to you, but I'm gon' tell you don't come up here tryin' to get involved with these lames."

"Daddy, I already told you ain't nobody tryin' to get with no drug dealers."

"Well, that ain't what your mother said. She said you got some little frail ass nigga down here that you got the hots fo'. She said something about the fight he had with Rodney and how he disrespected her, too. I wish a nigga would try me like dat. I'll break my foot off in that niggas ass," Dad hissed. "I don't know who he is or how he's living, but I don't want him around none of my shit. And he got one time to try me and I'ma let him know how a real one gets down. Come fall, you're going to college. If you want to date, I want you to find a nice nerdy nigga like your aunt Ke did. Find you somebody like Sam. Guys like that treat you right."

"Sam! Yuck. He's a lame."

"And that's what you need. Asia, Ballas ain't nothing nice, they get caught up in a lot of bullshit. Look at both of your uncles as an example. Ant and Ray fell victim to the game. Shit, when you think about it, I did, too. I want more for you than any of us had."

"Yeah, but I'm not trying to get involved in no trouble."

"You don't have to be lookin' for trouble in order for it to find you. Baby, sometimes you're guilty by association and it will get you caught up just as quick."

"Association?"

"Yeah, who you know, who you hang with, or possibly even who you are related to, which brings me to my next issues."

"What's that?"

"I don't care what or who, make sure you don't ever discuss our family or our family business with anyone. Asia, you never know who the enemy is. You can't trust your closest friends and sometimes your family. That's why I ain't got much kick it for Silk."

"Daddy, there you go tripping like Mama. Y'all all need to relax. I'm grown. I'm gon' make a few mistakes, so stop trying to protect me from the world. I'm smart, I know what I should and shouldn't do, and you ain't got to keep warnin' me everywhere we go."

"That's good to know, but you can't tell me what the hell I can do. I'm your parent, you ain't mine. Remember dat."

"So now what?"

Well, since you're so grown, seems like there's nothing else to tell you. But, I will say this."

"I knew that was comin," I sassed.

"You knew what was comin?"

"But I will say this," I mocked.

"Don't get smart," he frowned. "Like I was saying, and since you're so grown, no more hand outs for the entire summer. If you want anything, you're gonna have to earn it like adults do."

"Earn it!" I repeated with the most disgusted look on my face.

"That's right, earn it."

"How am I s'posed to do that?"

"Work."

"WORK! Work where? I know you don't want me to be nowhere washing no dishes, or running no rinky-dink cash register."

"You can go out and find a job or you can be a floor manager at the clothing store."

"You serious?"

"Dam straight I'm serious. Why wouldn't I be?"

"You're really tripping. You want me to work for real?"

"Asia, if you want money for the summer, you gon' have to."

"Man, you're trippin," I fussed. "Daddy, I see you suffered some serious side effects from spendin' all that time in prison."

"You better watch ya mouth. I ain't yo mama, and I ain't got no side effect from a damn thang. I just learned how to get *Hood Rich* off my hard knocks, and you better too."

"Okay, *Hood Rich,* but I think you're acting more like a Hood Rat," I replied, laughing.

"Yeah, I got your Hood Rat. Tramps that chase niggas for a come up or vise versa are Hood Rats. I ain't never jocked no bitch for what she had."

"Dang, Daddy, calm down. I'm just playing."

"Don't play with me. I'm a real nigga with real knowledge. Now what are you gonna do? Are you gonna work at the store or somewhere else?"

"Sheeeeesh," I sighed

"What's that about?" he asked real matter a fact.

"Nothin'," I pouted.

"By your actions, it seems like your plans were to be up here in the D actin' like a damn rat yourself?"

"I ain't no rat, so I guess I'll be workin', but can I work at the sports bar, instead of the clothing store with you and E."

"Ut'un."

"Please Daddy. You got to trust me at some point. I don't wanna work with you and Uncle E. If I was ugly that would be one thing, but men are gon' get at me, and I can't have the two of y'all breathin' down my back everyday."

"Good point. I'm gon' let you run the restaurant, but if I catch you slippin', you're movin' to the clothing store."

...♦♦♦♦...

Most often Daddy just gave me money, but to try to keep me out of the streets, he forced me to work. At first I wasn't feeling the employment thing, but after discovering that **Asia's** was off the chain on Fridays and Saturdays, I was hooked. Alex generally came up to the restaurant on the weekends because that's when my dad was the busiest at the clothing store. From time to time, Dad and Uncle E would fall through to grab a bite to eat or to check on things, but for some reason, he always told me when he was coming in advance. Though I tried to act like it wasn't necessary, I loved his heads up, because it gave me a chance to tell Alex to stay away. And since my dad always told me that 'Loose lips, sank ships, I didn't ask Alex about his family and in return, he knew absolutely nothing about mine.

Sometimes Mauri would tip in the bar throughout the week to say hi, and after a while we started getting kind of cool. I went out with him a few times, but after he tried to finger me in one of his limos, and Alex started sweating me about the time he was getting, I cut Mauri off with the quickness to avoid any drama.

...♦♦♦...

After being in Detroit for a month, I quickly discovered that I wasn't going to have as much time with Alex as I originally thought. Dad kept me busy and because of his threats, I kept Alex away from the store as much as possible. As bad as I missed him, I couldn't afford no unnecessary friction between my two favorite men. And though I tried to honor my father's request, Alex quickly grew tired of my Daddy and his demands.

"Asia, you're grown. Every place of employment entitles their employee's to a few sick days. Hell, tell your Pops you're not comin' in today and come hangout with me," Alex begged.

"Alex, my father is old fashion and strict. I don't know about anyone else, but my dad ain't havin' none of that. I need to continue working for the sake of keeping' the peace. Plus, my daddy is good to me, and I don't want to mess up our bomb relationship."

"Oh, I'm not good to you?"

"Yeah you are."

"Well then why don't you quit? If he doesn't like it, come live with me?"

"If I could, I would, but I just don't want any problems with my father. Besides, I kind of like workin'."

"What, you like workin'? Yeah Right! I bet some lame ass nigga that's been comin' in **Asia's** got yo nose wide open."

"Ain't no nigga got my nose wide open. Why you say that?"

"Because, you talkin' 'bout some you like workin', and I just gave you a chance to quit. Bitches ain't turnin' down opportunities to stay home."

"I ain't no bitch, and I like workin' for my father."

"Your father's a dictator, but if you want to work, keep workin'. I was hopin' you were gon' spend the summer with me before school started, but I'll work with whatever."

"What's that s'pose to mean?"

"It means, yo daddy is interfering with my time, so if I get me a part-time Boo on yo ass, I don't want to hear no lip."

"That's unfair to put me on a guilt trip. It would help if you were a little more supportive. I'd hate to be torn between the two men I love."

"Then choose up."

"What? I ain't choosin' between you and my daddy."

After seeing how my loyalty to my Dad upset Alex, I knew him not meeting my father was a good decision. Though Alex was jealous of Daddy, deep within, he knew I was doing the best I could regarding our relationship. Hell, with the pressure he was putting on me, Mr. DeMarques Prince would have hated Al just on GP.

Shortly after Al made his threats, I tried to pacify him. So weekly, after working long days, I'd creep out with him to make up for lost quality time. The only bad thing that came out of my spending more time with him was that I became exposed to a dark side I never knew existed.

The evenings we hooked up, I'd always tell my father I was hanging out with my girl Nikki to avoid hearing his lectures.

"Oh, and don't wait up. If we get in late, I'll probably spend the night with her, and then come home in the morning."

"Asia, you better call and let me know what you're doing."

"Daddy, I will," I'd fussed because he was always acting as though he didn't believe me. I guess I really couldn't be mad, I was known to lie."

CJ, Al's best friend had just moved back to Detroit from, New York. That evening, Alex picked me up and the three of us went out to some little bar off Seven Mile. We hooked up with some of his other boys, had a few drinks, and talked noise most of the night. While making small talk with CJ, I found out that he was on his way to college, too. He wasn't one who appeared to be on that thug living, so right away, I wondered what he had in common with Alex. The later it got, liquor consumed our sober minds. Suddenly, we were so out of control, the bar tender had to get on us.

"Hey, y'all gon' have to chill out some," he ordered.

"What you say?" Al asked.

"Chill out nigga, you heard me."

"Man, this is a bar! People come here to have a good time, talk shit, and get a fucking buzz."

"And I said chill out, not don't talk."

"Alex, let's go," I suggested, trying to prevent a bad situation from getting worse.

"Hell naw, I'm up in here wit' my niggas. Ain't no joke ass bartender 'bout to disrespect my gangsta. That fool don't know me like dat."

"Yo, Al, let's move around. Man, I'm one month short of college. I got this athletic scholarship, and I don't want nothin' to interfere with what I'm tryin' to do," CJ expressed.

"I'ma chill this time, but that nigga lucky," he stated, strolling out the bar walking like Tupac's replica.

"Asia, get up here and give Daddy some sugar," Alex insisted, pulling me towards him.

"Chump, you ain't my daddy."

"You ain't say dat a few days ago when I was up in them guts."

"Well, you ain't in 'em right now."

"As soon as I drop off my boy, we'll take care of that."

I ignored Al cuz he was drunk and tripping. After we dropped CJ off, he started feeling all over me. I could see his dick getting hard and the more he rubbed on my shit, the hotter I became. We headed to the flat he shared with two of his boys. I hated going there because privacy was always an issue. At times I could get kind of loud, so their presence affected my mood, and since Alex loved for me to talk nasty to him, so I quickly let him know it wasn't gon' be none of that. "If we go there, it ain't gon' be no moaning and shit tonight." That's all I needed to say. We busted a u-turn and headed straight for a hotel. While riding, I remembered I had not checked in.

"Hey, before we get to the hotel, stop me by the store. I need to buy some condoms."

"Condoms!"

"Yeah," I lied, trying to get him to stop so I could call my daddy.

"We don't need no condoms."

"Okay, well I still want to buy something to drink." Alex hesitantly pulled over, and I ran into the store. When I thought he wasn't looking, I slipped into a corner and into the restroom. I dialed Daddy's cell and as the phone rung, my heart raced. Finally, Dad said hello.

"Hey Dad, I'll be home late."

"Where are you?"

"Over Nikki's."

"You're sure spending a lot of time with her."

"Dad, I work almost everyday. I still got to socialize."

"Well, how are you getting' home?"

"She'll bring me," I fabricated. "Ut, as a matter of fact, she's calling me now." I lied. "Well, gotta go."

"Make sure you check in."

"I will."

I think Dad knew something slick was up with me. I say that because the more money Alex made, the more time I tried to spend with him to ensure that all his money got spent on me. I came up with a few extravagant pieces that Dad questioned, but my reply was always the same, "Man, I'm a Prince. I got expensive taste, and I work every week to get what I want." Dad couldn't argue with that. He, too, still had a love for expensive things, so we were on the same page about a Prince having expensive taste.

"Anyway back to the story."

Chapter 6
A Damn Fool

Before I could make it back to the car it started drizzling. I ran out with my head covered because I was trying to preserve my hairdo for a few more days and jumped in.

"Hey Sexy," I greeted, leaning over to kiss Al's spongy full lips.

"Hey, what took so long," he asked, grabbing my hand to place on his erection. "Are you ready for some of this?"

"Ready? I'm ready right now," I said.

"You want me to pull over? You know I'll tear it up in the back seat."

"Ut'un, keep drivin'. I got this, you just pay attention to the road," I insisted, pulling his dick out of his pants.

"What you doin"

"Just drive," I insisted, lowering my head.

"Aw…Damn!!!! I'm about to."

"Shhhhh," I replied, putting my fingers on his lips to prevent him from breaking my concentration. "You like that?"

"Hell yeah! Damn! I love you, boo," he moaned.

"You don't love me," I teased, sitting up.

"What you mean I don't love you?"

"If you did, you wouldn't want me slobbin on yo knob."

"You ain't sayin' that crack heads shit when I'm doing you."

"I was teasin'. Just drive."

Alex said something, but I ignored him and dialed Nikk once it registered that I hadn't called her to tell her my plans. That was my girl because she could relate to what I was going through with Alex and my daddy. She, too, had strict parents. Like me, she also dated ballas, was a gold digger to the utmost, and loved her man Terrell to death. Nikk understood the need to have a friend as an alibi, so she always covered for me. If my father called, she knew just what to say, and the tone in which to make it sound convincing. While I waited for her to answer, I smiled, looking over at Alex as he pouted after I'd teasingly told him he didn't love me.

"What's up, Chick?" She answered.

"Nikki, if my father calls, tell him I'm in the shower. After he hangs up, call me on my cell."

"I got you. What's up for tonight?"

"Me and Alex getting a room downtown at the *Zomni Hotel*."

"Damn, y'all doin' it like dat tonight? Shit, every room up in that bitch is hitting for $380 and up."

"I know, but my man got deep pockets," I bragged. "He ain't sparin' no expense to please his prize. Plus when he splurges like that, I reward him well."

"Reward him well?" She repeated.

"Hell yeah, I make both sets of lips talk to him in a manner in which only a dick can understand."

"Trick, you crazy," she laughed. "Let me get off this phone. Terrell's taking me to get some shrimp."

"He's comin' to the house?"

"Yeah."

"Where's your parents?"

"They went to check out my grandma in Miami."

"Okay, I'll hollar at you later. We're almost at the hotel anyway." I hung up and Alex chimed right in.

"Back to our conversation, what you mean I don't love you. Are you crazy, I'm in love with you?"

"How do you know you're in love?"

"Cuz I ain't ever felt this way about no woman before."

"Boy, you don't love anybody."

"Asia, all bullshit aside, I really do love you."

"You love me how much?"

"I know one thing, I'd fuck a nigga up behind you."

"Aw here we go on that jealous stuff again."

"I'm not gon' spoil our evening, all I'm gon' say is when you go to school, you better remember whose pussy that is."

"It's mine."

"It was yours, but the day you gave me some, it became mine. As a matter of fact, I've been thinking 'bout getting' my name tatted right above your hair line."

"Boy, stop playin'. I ain't getting' yo name tattooed on my pussy."

"Why not? You love me don't you?" he asked, looking crazy.

"Yeah, but not enough to be getting no tats."

"Well, you don't love me like you should then."

"We might break up one day, then what I'm gon' do with an Alex tat. My new man ain't gon' like that."

"New man! It ain't gon' be no new man. I'm gon' always be the only nigga in your life."

"Yeah right! Well, do you love me enough to get my name tatted on your dick?"

"Not my dick, but I'd get your name tatted on my neck."

"I'll believe that when I see it."

"Boo, you sound like you're doubtin' me."

"I am."

"What the hell you mean, you are?" He asked, looking crazy.

"I doubt that you'll ever get my name tatted on your body."

"Asia, don't ever doubt me. If I say I'll do something, I will," he insisted.

"Dang, don't get so serious, I'm playin."

"Don't play about nothin' like dat. You're my baby. If I tell you I'ma do somethin', I will. My word is my bond."

"You act like that's something serious."

"It is to me. Shit, that's all I've had all my life. If it wasn't for my word, there would have been plenty of days a nigga would've gone without. If I didn't grind, I would've been hungry and homeless, so my word means everything to me."

After seeing how my teasing sent Alex off the deep end, I changed the subject. "I sure can't wait to cuddle with you."

"I got some business to take care of, so we ain't about to be fuckin' all night like we usually do. When I leave to handle my business, I'm gon' drop you off at Nikki's. She can take you home."

"How long you gon be out?"

"As long as necessary!"

"When did you decide that you had somethin' else to do?"

"When you went in the store."

"What are you going to do?"

"You know better than to question me, I'm gon' do what I got to do, and when I get home, I'll call like usual."

"Naw, you might as well take me to Nikki's now. I'm not about to just give up the ass like a tramp, then get sent on my way."

"What?"

"You heard me, I said I'm...." Just as I was about to repeat myself, Alex cupped my face and firmly pressed his hands against my mouth.

"Shut the fuck up! Who do you think you're talkin' to?"

"Nigga, you better let me go. Don't ever grab my face like that again. Have you lost your damn mind?" I fussed, hitting him in his chest.

"Bitch, you about to make me hurt you," Alex yelled, whipping his Jag up in front to Valet. Two men approached the car, clearly missing our fight. Immediately the doors opened, which saved me.

"Welcome, to the *Zomni.* Are you staying tonight?"

"Punk! Don't do that shit again." I sassed, getting out of the car, ignoring the Valets question.

Alex was furious that I'd disrespected him. He snatched his backpack, and walked towards the entrance. Once we checked in, the attendant gave us our room key. I headed for the elevator. After the doors closed, Alex started talking crazy.

"As soon as we get to that room, I'm gon' beat yo ass for being disrespectful."

"My fuckin' daddy ain't ever put his hands on me, so I damn sure know you ain't 'bout to. I can't believe you're trippin' over some stupid shit."

"I ain't your daddy. But he should've spanked that ass and then you'd know that you always respect yo man."

"You damn sure ain't my daddy, so don't act like it. And for the record, I respect those who respect me."

"Okay, I hear you talkin' all that shit right now."

"Alex, stop fussin'. Damn!" I suggested, kissing him because I could see that he had become furious. "Baby, why are you so angry? You know I'm yours. Damn, I was only playing. You know I like to talk shit sometimes. Let's just enjoy our evening, okay. Sometimes I think you need Anger Management classes."

"I don't need no Anger nothin," then he kind of gave me this twisted smirk as though he was relieved to hear me acknowledge that I was sort of like his property. "Oh, so you were only playing. Well if that's the case I'm gon' let you slide this time, but you better not talk to me like that no more."

It seemed like everything was okay, but once we got to the room and showered, he snapped. I crawled in our King size bed, baring nothing but skin to make love to my man when that fool grabbed me around my neck and choked me.

"What's up with you?" he asked

"Alex, stop playing, you're hurting me."

"Don't disrespect me again, do you understand."

"Do I understand? Nigga are you on drugs?"

"I asked you a question, answer me, and don't repeat what the fuck I say."

"Okay, let my neck go, you're hurting me," I insisted.

Alex released my neck, tenderly kissing my forehead. He was quiet for a moment, then he apologized. "I'm sorry, Boo. I don't know what got into me. Do you forgive me?" I didn't say a word. "Baby, crawl up on top of me and give your man a kiss. I said I'm sorry."

"Alex, I don't feel good," I informed him, trying to ease out of bed. "Would you please take me to Nikk's house? I think I'm gon' throw up."

"Take you to Nikki's, you know I want some. What you mean take you somewhere?"

"I don't feel like fuckin'. I told you I'm sick."

"Since when have I ever fucked you? You know every time I hit that, I make love to you."

"Oh, my bad."

"You being sarcastic?"

"Ut'un."

"Good, and since you don't feel like fuckin', I don't want to fuck either. I know you tryin' to ration a nigga some sex cuz you mad I checked you about talkin' crazy to me."

"I'm not mad."

"Yes you are. I can tell by your body language. Any other time you'd be all on me."

"I said I'm ill."

"You're ill." He smirked in disbelief. "Asia, you'd be all over a nigga while you're on your period if I let you."

"What does that have to do with right now?"

"If you'll give me some when you're bleeding, then doin' it now shouldn't be an issue. But....... since you're mad, now all of a sudden you want to act like I can't touch you."

"I told you I'm sick."

"Yeah you are sick if you think I'm not hittin' that tonight. I paid damn near $300.00 for this room, now pull back that comforter and get in this fuckin' bed like I said."

I looked at him like he was a damn fool, but I didn't move.

"Come on. I ain't got all night, I told you I got somethin' else to do."

"I suggest you go do it then, cuz you ain't about to get none."

"You can't ration me what's mine. That's mine and you bet' not ever forget that," he demanded, pulling me into the bed and under him.

Without even allowing me to get wet or using any lubricant, Alex forced himself inside of me and took what he felt was enough to make him satisfied.

"Stop Alex, you're hurting me," I cried, but by that time, he was all the way inside of me. "Alex, stop," I screamed, which only irritated him more. He viciously covered my mouth with the entire palm of his hand, and kept pumping like a psyco.

"Whose is it?" he asked, forcing himself further inside of me, while carrying on like someone I didn't know. After he finished, I didn't move for several minutes. I'd never felt so violated, so taken advantage of, so ……..worthless before in my life.

"What are you cryin' fo?" He asked, kissing me. "Now that's what it feels like to be fucked. Better yet that's how rats are gettin' pipe laid to them everyday. Hopefully, after gettin' a ruff ride like that, you won't ever confuse the way I treat you again." I still didn't say anything, nor did I give him any eye contact. I was in shock, so I zoned out. "Asia, you don't have anything to say." Still no words could form in my mind or my mouth. "Oh, so you're mad. Boo, I'm sorry. Let me make it up to you later on tonight. I tell you what, I'll just make my run tomorrow. How does that sound?"

Sorry, nigga you just forced yourself on me and all you can say is "let me make it up to you." I don't think so, I thought, lifting myself off the bed to put on my clothes.

"See that's what pisses me off about you. One minute you on the next you off. Now you over there poutin' with yo no taking some dick ass and got the nerve to have a fuckin' attitude."

Chapter 7
Moving Out

I'll never forget that night. It was a long ride to Nikki's house, and I didn't say anything to Alex the entire way. Being in his presence had me on edge. I was literally scared to be around him. At the time, I didn't think I'd been raped, but I did consider filing a police report. Actually, I talked myself out of going for a number of reasons. First, I really just thought he'd put a little rough sex on me like he said, not to mention that I was certain that the police would make it seem like what happened was my fault. Secondly, Alex was on probation for getting caught up with major drugs on him right before I moved to Detroit, so he couldn't afford anything else on his record.

After getting through those first two weeks, all I had was two more weeks to go before school started. If I could get through it without giving in to Alex, I was home free, or so I thought. Right before I was due to report to school, me, Dad, and Teretta went shopping to get all the stuff I needed for my apartment. Me and Mom had made up, so she was going to come down to assist me with decorating. I thought with me being with Dad all summer, it was important to spread the excitement of my going to college around, so that's why I let Dad take me to get the things I needed for school. Plus, I knew he was sure to buy stuff, Mom wouldn't, so that's why he really got mall duty. While driving down Coolidge, I noticed Alex and that same girl from the restaurant stopped at the light. *For a nigga that claimed he loved me so much, he sure did replace me with the quickness,* I thought as Dad whipped into the parking lot.

For two weeks straight, Alex called, but I didn't make myself accessible to him. He repeatedly blew up my cell phone, left messages, came by the restaurant, and sent notes by Nikki. Once he realized I wasn't feeling him, he brought his sorry ass in for lunch with some high yellow, pretty bitch, trying to flaunt her in my face. I didn't give him the chance to dis me long, though. The fact that she was cute pissed me off, but the thought of her coming up in my place of business, really ran me hot more than anything.

After watching them out of the corner of my eye for as long as I could, I walked to the kitchen and remained there until they left.

"Asia, we're here," Teretta stated a second time because I didn't hear Dad at first.

"Wha'cha say?"

"We're here," Dad repeated, looking at me through his Versace sunglasses. "Butterfly, are you okay? You've been real distant for the past few weeks."

"I'm fine, just a little anxious about going to school and living on my own."

"You don't have to live on campus. You know you can stay at the house with us for the first semester if you want."

"Naaah, I'm lookin' forward to livin' on my own. I ain't tryin' to get caught up with all yo rules."

"My rules?"

"I'll be fine, I'm just nervous about living alone."

"Butterfly, as long as I'm paying for your education, I'll have a key to your apartment. So anytime I think I need to be in your business, trust and believe I will."

I didn't even feel like arguing with Dad. All I could think about was Alex and that girl. I couldn't help but wonder if she was being treated as wonderful as I had initially been treated or if he was buying her the same kinds of expensive gifts he once bought me. Dad tried to get me more focused on shopping, but who could shop at a time like that. My world was caving in on me, and another trick was chilling with my man. I wanted to tell Dad what I was going through because I needed someone to talk to, but he wasn't the understanding kind of guy, and I knew he wasn't about to feel sympathetic to my problems with no street nigga.

After going from store to store and getting everything I needed, from DVD's to comforters, Dad complained all the way home about the thirty-five hundred dollars he'd spent. *Oh shut up Dad, who wants to hear that shit right now. I'm dying over here and you don't even realize it. You're so caught up on what you spent that you're missing a golden opportunity to comfort your heartbroken daughter,* I thought, rolling my eyes at him.

Dad pulled up in the driveway unaware of my pain or thoughts. I got out of the truck, pulling bags out of the back seat, and also thinking about what a fool I was for feeling the way I did. I went into the house with the intent on keeping myself busy for the duration of the evening. No matter what I did, Alex kept coming to mind. I wanted to call and cuss him straight out, but instead, I kept finding other things to do to prevent myself from giving in to him. Surprisingly, I was able to hold out.

…◆◆◆…

In August 2002, my brother DeMarques Anthony Prince was born. That same week, I left for college. My Dad and Uncle E ended up helping me move. I arrived on the campus of the University of Metro Detroit looking like a million bucks. While getting my stuff up to my room, Dad and E couldn't stay focused. For some reason, whenever they were out getting my things, they had this "Dirty Old Man behavior," going on. That was very embarrassing, and it also grossed me out.

How the hell these old, shriveled dirty dick negro's gon' try to get with my classmates and Dad almost had a conniption fit when Mauri tried to get at me. "Dad, Uncle E, y'all are disgusting. Some of these girls are my age and younger."

"Yeah, and some are eighteen and older. Those are the ones me and E are looking for," Dad joked, giving Uncle E five. I looked at them like they were some real perverts. "Damn Butterfly, you act like your ole dude's a senior citizen."

"You're just like that Mauri cat. And just like he was too old for me, your daughter. These girls are someone's daughter too, and their daddy's don't want no old dicks chasing them either."

"Hush," Dad teased. "Shit, I might be in my thirties, but I ain't no old dick. All my shit still works, and I said you can't holla at older men. I don't care what other girls yo age are doing."

"Sounds like double standards to me."

"It is."

"Yeah, well you got a newborn at home with your wife. Don't forget that."

"It's okay for me to look as long as I don't touch."

"Well could y'all close your mouths, and stop acting like hounds. You and E are walkin' around here like two old dogs."

"Asia, get you some business," Uncle E replied. "I don't have any kids, so I can look. And for the record, I'll get with a tender, but she has to be at least twenty-three and mature. So, if you meet anyone in that age group that's fine as hell, let me know."

"Please…. Both of y'all niggas need to quit….and E what about Ashley?"

"Okay, we ain't gon' be too many more niggas. You and your daddy know how I feel about that word. And what about Ashley?"

"If you don't know, I'm not about to tell you."

"I don't know, and you don't either, so leave that alone."

"I will."

"Good, now get over here and give me and your pops some love. We `bout to be out."

Need I say that moving to college was a far greater memory than I ever expected. Thanks to my uncle and my dad, I was teased by the chicks on my floor the entire semester about being related to the "Fine ass flirty old men." "Yuck!"

Chapter 8
College

Freshman had a series of seminars going on for orientation week. The same day I moved in, there was a mandatory Date Rape session that all the freshman girls had to attend. I arrived early because I wanted to make sure I got a seat by the door. I planned to sign in, and slip out once things got started. Deborah Binkley, at one time was a Detroit Morning News anchor. Well she just so happened to be the facilitator of the group. She was an activist for women's rights, and traveled the fifty states, speaking to young females about gender specific issues. Mrs. Binkley was also the Dean over the School of Journalism. She was a well spoken sista, with an exceptionally broad vocabulary, so once she started talking, her opening question immediately captured my attention.

"What is Date Rape?"

I didn't know. A few hands went up, but not many. No one wanted to chance being wrong, especially considering that it was our first group gathering. "Well, date rape is when someone you know makes you have non-consensual sexual intercourse with them." *Non-consensual sexual intercourse! What the hell is that?* I thought before she continued with an answer. "That means you didn't want to have sex, but you were forced to do it anyway. The perpetrator could be someone you meet at a party or someone you love and trust, like your boyfriend."

Like my boyfriend, I thought. *That's exactly what Alex did to me.* Once I realized she was talking about something that interested me, I focused on her presentation.

"Date rape can happen to women of all ages, but young women between 15 and 24 are at the highest risk. Ladies, sexual assault is a crime. Whoever commits this act or however it happens, sex that you have not freely agreed to, is rape. And rape has nothing to do with love – it's about power and control."

Mrs. Binkley truly enlightened me. It was at that very moment that I realized I had in fact been raped. The sad part about her presentation is the fact that the more she talked, the more I recognized that I had all the signs of a victim in denial.

"Young sistas it's unfortunate, but date rape is much more common than you'd believe. Most people think of rape as being committed by a stranger or perhaps an attack in a dark alley, but date rape is actually much more common than rape by a stranger. Surveys have found that as many as 9 out of 10 women knew their attacker."

Side chatter immediately started between girls all over the room. After Mrs. Binkley quieted us down, she continued. "Rape is one of the most underreported crimes and because of a persons decision to keep it a secret, it's difficult to give exact figures. Date rape is often hidden because many girls and women who have been raped don't recognize the experience as a crime. They often think that because they knew their attacker, it wasn't actually rape, but I'm here to tell you, if you don't want to have sex and your friend or mate takes it, you have been raped."

This chick sitting next to me, named Kelly, distracted my attention. "Girl, I wish this trick would sit down and shut the hell up. Ain't nobody getting raped out here on this campus. If tricks wouldn't put themselves in a position to be raped, then it wouldn't happen. Bitches make me sick, acting like they so innocent after a brotha put a little ruff sex on 'em. Chicks know good and damn well when they go to a niggas spot at three o'clock in the morning, he don't want to play footsies."

"So you think it's okay for a guy to force himself on someone, even if she says no?" I asked.

"Hell yeah! My daddy told me years ago, if you got your stupid self up in a niggas house at 2am, what you think he wants. Surely not just to get his back rubbed and some kisses."

"But that may be all you're looking for or all you really intend to do."

"I tell you what, any sista that has that on her mind, please tell her to keep her dumb ass at home after midnight. Because at that time of night, coaches turn into pumpkins and boys turn into DICKS."

"Dicks?" I repeated.

"Yeah, **D**umb, **I**diotic **C**oochie **K**razed **S**talkers. Plus everybody knows that the freaks come out at night. Girl, pussy is so addictive that some fool's gon' catch a case behind gettin' his penis wet. That's why it's necessary to make chicks who just want to cuddle aware of the fact that coochie is a serious drug, and if they get caught up with a Coochie Addict after midnight, they're more than likely smoked."

"I can't believe you think like that."

"I damn sure do. Girl, ain't you heard Cardier & Caznova's new jam Azz and Titties."

"No."

"Well you better get wit the times Sis, cuz they puttin' it out there."

"Oh yeah, and what's that?"

"Nigga's want a see some ass shake, they want to see some titties."

"Yeah, but that's a song, and not every brotha is operatin' on that code of conduct."

"Shit, you show me a brotha that don't wanna smack it up, kiss it, and dick it down, and I'll bet my last dolla that that nigga's gay. Besides, every addict has his breaking point. Titty bar's are so addictive, they'll have dudes trickin' off major loot. Crack is so powerful, it'll make a hype steal from his mama and disown his kids. Heroin, is so lethal, it'll have a junkie sharing needles with a nigga that's HIV positive. Girl, then there's the Juicy. Good pussy's so off the chart that it'll drive a yssup fean so far over the edge that he don't even realize how caught up he is 'til he finds his horny ass on lock down for takin' the poo-poo."

"Okay," I replied to get her to shut her ignorant self up. Mrs. Binkley was coming to a close, and I was interested in what she was saying.

"Girls, in closing, I'd like to leave you with some statistics. Did you know that approximately one in four college aged women have been date raped or experienced an attempted date rape during her college years?" When she said that, everyone listened, including Kelly. "Eighty-four percent of the women who have been date raped knew their attackers. Women between the ages of 16-24 are four times more likely to be date raped than any other age group. Approximately ninety percent of date rapes happen with alcohol involved. In one study, approximately thirty-three percent of the men surveyed said if they could escape date rape without detection they would rape someone. Fourty-two percent of women who were date raped didn't tell any one at all about it. Twenty-seven percent of the women who were date raped didn't realize their incident met the legal definition of rape. Eighty-four percent of the men involved did not realize their behavior was date rape, and fourty-four percent of the women who have been date raped have considered suicide." Damn, I feel bad about what happened with Alex, but I ain't thinking about killing myself.

Mrs. Binkley's statistics were devastating, especially when she said the part about not telling anyone because I hadn't. Though, I think me keeping my incident a secret had more to do with fearing what my father might do to Alex, more so than being ashamed. Embarrassment was not the case. I realized that I had clearly put myself in a bad position and my father would have gone ballistic had he found out.

Chapter 9
Drama

After enrollment and a week of orientation, classes started. Following the Seminar, Kelly and I became pretty cool. Though I thought she was a straight nut, Kell was really fun to be around. She was the kind of sista that didn't bite her tongue for anyone. She said her father was a nigga in the game, and he taught her at a very young age not to take no shit off a brotha. Without us ever exchanging real family business, because we both knew better, I let her know that I was a product of a Big Tymer too, and Asia Prince wasn't bout to be on no foolishness either.

Kelly was a pretty l'il light caramel colored sista. She looked like she could have been Hispanic and African American, but she always let it be known that both of her parents were black. She had slightly chingy eyes, and was a stylish little, five-foot, four inch, bow-legged, motor mouth. Just a few weeks after classes started, half the females on campus hated her. That girl talked more noise than a little bit, and her attitude wasn't about nothing. That tattoo she had plastered right above her ass didn't help much either. Any trick proudly sporting a tat that said, *"The Bitch, Most Hoes Envy,"* was gon' automatically get hated on. So Kelly didn't stand a chance from day one. Since I thought I was half ass bad, I had her back, though. She knew if we had to run up on some tramps for trying to test our gangsta, it was gon' be on.

I think the two of us bonded so well because we had a lot in common. She was cute, I was fine as hell, and we kind of favored in appearance. What I loved most about her was that she'd call sista's out just because, and most of the fellas, simply adored her ghetto style. Kell had much game, too. It wasn't nothin' for her to put a tramp in check or let a brotha know her intentions. I knew from her demeanor that she was gon' keep me in some B.S., but I didn't trip cuz I knew how to spit game, and though I didn't go out looking for trouble, like my girl, I would handle mine if it came to that.

Right before enrollment ended, Nikki decided to go to U of MD with me instead of Langston. She ended up enrolling shortly after classes started, but with her being as intellectual as she was, she was able to catch up in no time. Now Nikk, she was out cold. Nigga's loved her because she was one of the prettiest sista's in the city of Detroit. She wore a bomb, sassy cut, and had real captivating eyes, which brought her face to life. She had perfect teeth, with deep dimples, shinny ass lips, and a winning smile. Huh, that girl gave niggas fever with that body of hers, too. She was bowlegged in one leg, had this sexy walk that sent brotha's hound doggin', stayed in something classy that was certain to fit her ass, hips, and breast like a glove.

Our apartments were sort of like dorms. I lived in 213, Kelly was in 214, and Nikki was right down the hall in 218. Man, some of our freshman adventures, regarding campus life are still unspeakable to this day. However, we were three Divas that thought we were the shit, brotha's jocked us like we were as popular as Super Bowl Sunday, and since we got hated on so much, we lived up to Kell's tat.

The third week of school, we had our first big beef and almost got sent home for the semester. Me, Kell, and Nikk were on our way to the café for lunch. This upperclassman named Sharonda and some of her girls call theyself gon' check us about this one football player named Raymond.

"Which one of ya'll bitches been kickin' it wit my man."

"Who you callin' a bitch?" I asked.

"And who's yo man?" Kell followed, with much attitude.

"Raymond."

"Raymond! We don't know no Raymond." Nikk rattled off.

"Well my girl Leslie told me that he was trying to get at you," she said pointing at Kell. *Aw damn, I should have known.*

"She's a damn lie, cause ain't no Rays been up in my spot. Does he go by another name."

"Yeah, Gibson." Kell smiled.

"I know him, but he told me he was single."

"Well he lied. I'm his woman."

"You can't be his woman, cause since I stepped foot on this campus, he's been wifeying me everyday."

"Well, you better move around or else."

"You ugly ass, muscle face, bitch, wha'sup." Before everything could even register, Sharonda ran up on Kell, and the seven of us squabbled like nigga's. Sharonda was a big girl, so I ended up banging the hell out of her head with my book bag. I had two thick hard cover textbooks in it and went to work on her crown. Officer King ran over to break us up, and when Sharonda was helped off the ground, there was blood all over her face from where Kell's diamond rings cut her up. Her girls didn't help much, but started popping off at the mouth while the police were there.

"Yeah we'll see later on tonight," Kell fired back. "If any of y'all want some, I live on the second floor in Perkins Hall."

"You better watch yo back," Sharonda fussed.

"Naw hoe, you better watch yours. Don't be mad at me cuz yo man like getting this," she said grabbing herself. "Grow some damn hair, get on Jenny Craig, and then he might want yo ugly ass."

"Ms. be quiet," the police fussed, trying to control the situation.

Finally when Kell wouldn't cool it, we were all carted to Student Affairs to meet with the VP.

....♦♦♦♦....

After we were fined and put on probation, a few weeks later Kell was right back up to her dirt again. We were chilling on a bench right outside our apartment and this fine brotha walked up.

"Ooooh shit, who is that?" Kelly asked, standing to get a better look.

"Damn, he's fine," Nikki confirmed.

"That nigga look like Nick Cannon to me."I said.

"And…. My point exactly. Nick is a fine muthafucka to me and so is he," Kell replied all in. "Dang, I wonder who he belong to?"

"That's the little star basketball player from Persian. He's a trip and all these hoes on his dick. He's in one of my classes. And at times, I think he's real full of himself." I confirmed.

"Why?" Nikk asked.

"Because the media swears he's going pro."

"Asia, you're lying. Tell me that's not Kerwin Phillips?" Kelly asked.

"Yeah, it is," I nonchalantly responded.

"Girl, I see why everyone's on his dick. Asia, you should be hollain'. I saw him pullin' up in a parking space last week in this platinum Lexus 330 SUV. I was wondering who he was, but I just figured his peeps had money," Kell confirmed.

"He tried to talk to me in class, but I wasn't feelin' him." I stated, discreetly trying to check him out.

"Bitch, you didn't try to holla?"

"Ut'un! For what? Kell, it's gon' be so many tricks on that nigga before midterms come up. I didn't even feel motivated to add my name to his hit list."

"Well he can add mine."

"Kelly, you're such a slut," Nikki teased.

"That's okay, as long as we both know it, then we won't have any problems. Besides, if I work this muscle on him just right, when he goes to the NBA, a trick like me gon' be right on his arm wavin' at y'all hoes."

"You're a trip," Nikki confirmed in disgust. "That's why we almost got kicked out of school last month."

"Naw trick, I'm about gettin' it how I live. Did you hear Asia say that the media believes he's going to the NBA?"

"Yeah, and your point is what? You know how many niggas the media says is going pro that don't," Nikk, gripped.

"My point is that when he goes, I want to be pregnant with his baby, and ridin' in the passenger seat of whatever he's drivin'. When he walks up here don't neither one of y'all try to holla. He's mine."

"Kelly, every chick on the yard is on his nuts," I reiterated.

"So what Asia! Every chick on this yard ain't got my skillz, and I'm gon' just tell you like my girl Beyonce, *I don't think he's ready for this jelly.*"

"You mean you don't think he's ready for that smelly."

"Aw Asia's, you ain't hatin' are you."

"No, I think you need to try a different approach and then he might give you some play."

"Nah, you take a different approach with your judgmental ass. And in the meantime watch a fly diva like myself get money," she insisted, moving towards him as he approached our building.

"Sup ladies," he greeted, doing a double take at me.

"Hey," we all chimed in together. Kelly wasn't wasting no time though, she immediately got on Kerwin.

"I'm Kelly," She greeted, shaking his hand.

"Sup, Kelly. How are you?"

"Fine."

"You are that," he flirted.

"Glad you think so, because my mission is to please, and the first thing I want to do is give you a small sample of what lovin' me could be like."

"Damn! You're bold." he laughed.

"There's no other way to be."

"Well, nice to meet you, but I'm not lookin'."

"Good, cause I'm not either." He grinned real big. "Well it's nice to meet you, too, Sexy. If you find yourself in need of company later on tonight, I'm in 214," she informed him, easing in his personal space.

"Okay," he laughed, turning to walk into the building.

"Kell, you're a nasty skank ho."

"Call me what you like, but you won't call me lonely. Asia, I ain't gon' be like yo butt. Huggin' pillows and stuffed animals at night cause I'm in need of a cuddle buddy, and Nikk, I ain't gon' bust you out. But I know yo business. I see you creepin' some evenings, and that's all I'm gon' say."

"Well' while you're attacking me, I know I won't be calling you lonely. All the dick I see running up in there these past few days is ridiculous," I hissed cuz Kell dissed me.

"Maybe so, but at least I ain't violating you in any way."

"And what Nikki is?" I paused, mugging her. "So what's your l'il secret, Nikk?"

"What?" Nikk asked, looking stupid.

"Asia, I know you ain't judging me. I just so happened to be one that loves getting mine. If you're uneasy about your sexual expression, that's on you. As for me, I lets a brotha know where I'm comin' from. If I want dick, I'm gon' say I want dick. If I want convo, then I'm gon' say that. And Nikk you know what I'm talkin' about."

"Hey that is between you and Asia. I ain't got nothin' to do with y'all's fight."

"Whatever, Tramp," I interrupted, fussing at Kelly.

"Ms. Tramp to you."

After Kerwin walked by, I was so embarrassed. I couldn't even believe what I was hearing.

…♦♦♦…

A few days passed and later that week, I saw Kerwin in class. He walked in the room and sat right next to me. He made small talk for the first few minutes and then shortly after the instructor walked in. She gave us this complicated group project, and just so happened Kerwin and I became partners. "Great, Kell is gon' swear I arranged this." I remember saying when our names were called. We exchanged numbers, and talked everyday for the first two weeks trying to pull our presentation together.

After three weeks, we were better acquainted and were becoming pretty tight, which Kelly hated, might I add? Just as I thought, she swore I'd gotten myself hooked up with Kerwin for my own benefit, but I knew I couldn't win with her, so I stopped explaining after a while.

"Asia, you think you're slick. Yo little skinny ass trying to come up with my man, but I got my eye on you." It was comments like that that stressed me out because if I wasn't anything, I was loyal to my friends. And once she expressed she was gon' be on him, it was a wrap for me.

While we were in the last week of our project, Kerwin came by my place to put the finishing touches on our assignment. He wasn't really focused on studying though. All he wanted to do was pressure me about why I wasn't trying to hook up with him. What I thought about him, and him this, and him that. Shoot, he talked so much about himself that after two hours of him

52

talking about nothing but Kerwin that fool had literally gotten on my nerves. *He's a loser.*

"Asia, why don't you want to give me no play?"

"Kerwin, you know I told you I just got out of a relationship. I ain't ready to be right back in the mix of things yet."

"Okay, I'm not gon' keep sweatin' you. Soon someone's gon' pursue me, if it's the right one, I'm gon' holla. I'm tryin' to give you first dibs on me, but you keep playin' a nigga off."

"I guess it'll be my loss then."

"You're right, it will be. So why you ain't feelin' me?"

"I can't really say. Maybe you're not my type."

"Come on, do you believe that?"

"I don't know what I believe."

"I think you're not feelin' me because I'm not thuggish enough for you. I bet if I was tossin' rocks instead of basketballs you'd be on me."

"Maybe so, but you're not, so we'll never know," I replied cutting him off.

Kerwin made it real obvious that he wanted more than a friendship, but I still loved Alex. I hadn't talked to him in almost two months, and was missing him like crazy. I felt like a fool, considering I'd actually been raped by him. And to know that the man I loved more than any other broke my heart, tormented me. While sitting there listening to Kerwin talk, I wondered if Alex missed me or if he had any remorse about what he'd done. *Maybe not. Asia, people like that don't have a conscience. The question is will you ever forgive him.* Thinking about the degree of love I had for Alex, I knew I would take him back without a doubt. That was scary to me. *Asia are you that weak that you can't do any better than Alex? Girl, you need to work through your self-esteem issues and move on.*

After zoning out for a moment, sadness started to dominate my mood. I didn't feel like working or company, so I rushed my project with Kerwin along and sent him on his way. I went to my bathroom, looked at myself in the mirror, then grabbed my keys before heading down to Nikki's apartment. When I walked in, Terrell, and Alex were sitting on the couch. I looked at them both and spoke. "Hey T, what's up?"

"You."

When I looked at Alex to speak, it was as though I'd seen a monster. I couldn't believe he was sitting in Nikki's place, especially since she hadn't mentioned that he was gon' be on the yard.

"What's up, Boo? Why you lookin' at me like that?" I couldn't reply. I was having a flashback and was speechless. "Asia, you ain't glad to see me?" He asked, smiling.

"No, that's not it. I'm just surprised to see you here."

"What's there to be surprised about? You know I've missed you. Hell, you ain't talked to a nigga in over two months."

"It's not like I thought you really cared. I've seen you around."

"You ain't seen me no where."

"Yes I have."

"Where?"

"I saw you right before I came to school on Coolidge with that same girl you came into the sports bar with."

"Melissa, that's just one of my girls, she ain't nobody for you to worry about."

"Oh, trust me, I wasn't worried."

"So why haven't I heard from you?"

"You know exactly why," I fussed, raising my voice.

"Calm down, don't do this here. Let's go to your apartment. I don't want these nosey niggas all in our business."

"Why not? You don't want them to know how you treat your lady?"

"Asia, stop! Let's just go and talk in private."

"Nah, I'll pass," I replied, remembering the manner in which he'd choked me the last time I "Disrespected" him. "What are you doing here?" I asked to change the subject.

"I was hopin' to run into you so we could talk."

"Talk! Talk about what?"

"Us. How much I've missed you. How much I love you, and how I want to be the kind of man you want me to be."

"Save it, Alex. I've never asked you to change what you do, I've only asked you to love me and treat me right," I replied, feeling myself getting a little emotional. "Nikki, call me once your company leaves. Terrell it was good to see you. Alex, have a good one," I stated, turning to leave.

"Sorry," Alex blurted out, as soon as I gripped the doorknob to exit. First of all, I couldn't believe he was apologizing in the presence of his boy, so I briefly paused. "Asia, I know I was wrong, but I promise I love you."

"What did you say?" I asked, trying to see if he'd repeat himself.

"I said, I'm sorry and I love you."

"That's nice to know. I'm sorry, too, but you still can't come by."

"What are you sorry about?"

"Alex, I'm sorry that our beautiful relationship came to this. I gotta go. I have a date," I lied, trying to make him jealous.

"A date? Why the hell are you going out on dates?"

"Don't worry about it."

"Don't worry about it! Damn, you've only been here for a few months, how you already datin'?"

"The same damn way you did two weeks after I didn't take your calls."

"Ain't that a bitch? Ut' un, we need to talk right now," he insisted, acting jealous.

"We can't talk tonight in person, but you can call me in five minutes, cuz I need to go to my apartment to get dressed."

Alex gave me this resentful stare, and watched me leave. After a few seconds, my cell phone beeped and it was him.

"Asia Prince, answer the phone. I know you hear that muthafucka ringing." He yelled on my voice mail after I kept letting it pick up. I sat on my couch looking out the window for like ten minutes. One message after another came in and I laughed at his desperate efforts. "Asia, answer the damn phone, we need to talk right now." Suddenly, my doorknob started shaking, followed by an angry knock. I was spooked by the way he pounded on the door, so I eased over to the peephole, looking without words.

"Who is it?" I asked, forcing some bass out behind my question.

"Asia, please let me talk to you," Alex whined. "You got me out here lookin' like a pussy, but I don't even care. Just give me ten minutes to spit at you."

"Alex, shut up! You're disturbing my neighbors. They're going to call the CA if you don't quiet down."

"I don't care. Open up."

"Okay, I'll come out to talk, but only if you promise not to do anything stupid."

"What?"

"Promise."

"I do."

Foolish me, I felt some real empathy for him. After he assured me that he wasn't gon' trip, I unlocked the door. As soon as it was slightly open, Alex grabbed me. At first I thought he was about to kick my ass, but instead, he held me like we'd never been apart. It tripped me out that he didn't seem to mind compromising his ruff-neck tactics for the sake of winning me over again. I ain't gon' lie, I liked him acting that way too.

"Now what's all that noise about?" I asked, pulling my apartment door up to keep him from entering.

"Asia, I don't know what got into me, but I'm sorry. If you forgive me, I promise I'll do better."

That was the first time Alex ever made such a plea to me, but in time it would become a phrase highly used in his apologies.

"Alex, you scared me. I don't think you realize that you got some serious control issues."

"Boo, ain't nobody ever loved me like you. My mother was a crack head, my father was on lock down all my life, my grandmother's the only person I've ever had and she's dying. No one else in my family has ever reached out to me. Yeah, I'm a thug, but baby, I got feelings just like the next man. All I want is to make you happy. Tell me what I gotta' do to get you back and it's done. If you want me to stop hangin' 'til all hours of the morning, I'll do better. If you want me to cut off all the chicken heads I fool around with, it's done. If you want me to get my GED and get in school so we can have a real future, I'll do that, too. Just tell me, and Baby, like that, it's done."

"Alex, I want you to stop thinking you control me. I'm a grown ass woman, I'm my own person, and I don't need or want nobody trying to tell me what to do. If I'm your lady, then I'm not sleepin' with no one else. But I ain't about to get my shit tatted up just to let you know that my stuff belongs to you."

"That's cool. I was trippin' that night. I don't know what came over me. I think you doubtin' me started it and things got out of hand from there. But I promise I won't ever go there again."

"And how do you explain raping me?" I angrily whispered.

"I didn't rape you."

"Shhhhh, quiet down, yes you did rape me. Alex, I said I didn't feel like fucking and you took it anyway."

"Asia, you're my woman, you're s'posed to give me some when I say so."

"No, not if I don't feel like it."

"Okay, you're right. I don't want to argue. I should have respected your decision. If I raped you that wasn't my intention, I just wanted you to see first hand what hoe's get treated like. That way you'd know I didn't think you were one. Maybe I shouldn't have been so aggressive. I apologize. You know I ain't never had sex with you like that before."

"Alex, you were wrong. You violated me, you hurt me, and you did something awful to our relationship."

56

"Boo, don't talk like that. I love you, and we can work it out. You'll see what you mean to me. I'll show you that I am still that charmin, dapper nigga you met in T-Bell's Party Store."

Like most young foolish girls in love, I forgave Alex. I don't think it was the speech about him proving his love, more so than his look of loneliness and sincerity. I knew that I was the only one in his life that loved him, and he truly meant a lot to me.

"Alex, I love you so much," I confirmed, resting my head on his shoulder.

"Boo, I don't want us trippin' like this again," He suggested, kissing my hand.

After we finished talking, I was sort of uncertain about inviting him in, so we sat in my hallway for the longest in silence. We both knew with as long as we'd spent making up, Nikki and Terrell had already gotten busy a few times and were probably knocked out.

"Man, it's late. I have class in the morning, so I better go."

"Yeah, what time is it?"

"3:45 in the morning."

"Damn, we've been talking for a long time."

"Yep, almost six hours."

"Asia, you think sittin' out here all this time was worth it?"

"What?"

"Do you think we'll get back on the level we were on?"

"I don't know. I really can't say."

"I guess time will tell," he sadly replied.

"Yeah, I guess so. Well, I'ma 'bout to call it a night," I yawned.

"Already?"

"Yeah, I am. What are you about to do?"

"I guess since I rode out here with Terrell, I'll sleep in my car until him and Nikki get up."

"Your car," I repeated a little concerned about the temperature. Suddenly, it registered that I was still s'posed to be playing it hard. "Okay. Take care. Do you need a blanket?"

"Naw, it's only a few hours before day break, I'll cut on my heater and be fine."

"Boy, it's October, you gon' freeze."

"So let me spend the night."

"That's not about to happen. I know how you are and you know me. As soon as we close the door, you'll touch all the right spots, say all the things I love to hear, and have me naked in a matter of minutes."

"You don't miss this?" He asked, grabbing himself.

"Goodnight, Alex."

"I guess that means no?"

"Um, hum."

"So, you gon' let me sleep in the car?"

"That's right."

Alex looked at me like he couldn't believe I was about to let him sleep out in the cold, but I sure did. Hell, I knew I was a fool for forgiving him in the first place, but I didn't have to act like one by allowing him to spend the night minutes after making up. At first, I won't lie, I felt a little bad about sending him to his car. I thought about calling him back a thousand times, but I kept praying for strength and endurance. Thank God He showed me favor, because I didn't break and it sure felt great.

Chapter 10
Love Ain't No Joke

Throughout the month of October, Alex and I rebuilt our relationship. Although we were talking a little more than we had been, I still tried to take things slow. A few days before Halloween, Kerwin and I had lunch with my dad at **BEAN'S Spot**. That chump was on his best behavior. I think that's why Dad liked him so much.

"See Asia, you need to keep hanging out with this cat. He seems like a nice young man for you."

"He's a'ight, but every female on the yard is on 'em. I ain't got time for no womanizer or no womanizing. Right now, it's all about my books and maintaining my grades. I probably won't get me a boyfriend until my sophomore year. You know me and my girls trying to get high GPA's, so we have something to work with later."

"That's good you're trying to graduate academically prepared."

"Graduate! Pleeeease, Dad, you know I'm gon' be a Delta next year."

"Delta! You tryin' to get into some lame Greek organizations. "

"Lame? Did you hear me say I want to be a Delta? Man, Delta's are the cream of the crop. That means I got to show up at their informational with a 3.8 or higher. This Delta, named Tajma told me if I'm tryin' to do the Crimson and Cream, I got to come correct. Daddy, the Delta's don't play. Shoot, Nikk, and I got to learn their Five Point Thrust, and everything."

"Five Point what?"

"That's some stuff you ain't even ready for."

"You're right. All that Greek madness is foreign to me, but as long as your grades are tight, I got you."

"See that's what I'm talking about. I knew you was gon' break bread for me to pledge."

"Just make sure your grades are what I expect."

I cut Dad off because we needed to get back to campus. Right before leaving the restaurant, Kerwin invited him to come check out one of his games.

"Man, have Asia call me the next time you play and I'll be there." *Dad's acting like a bitch, I know he ain't jockin' ole boy too. I'm gon' have to tell him about that later.* Suddenly, Dad interrupted my thoughts with a kiss on the cheek.

"See you Daddy, love ya."

While getting into Kerwin's truck, I noticed Alex driving by. He must have noticed me, too, because when I glanced out the rear window, he was busting a u-turn. We drove off, but got stopped at the light. Within seconds, Alex pulled up. I looked over at him, only to catch him making eye contact with me. *How twisted,* I thought as he winked then waved with this evil smirk on his face.

"Who are you waving at?" Kerwin asked.

"My ex."

"Alex?"

"Umm hum."

"Since that nigga wanna be all up in my whip, let's give him something to see."

"Boy, he's crazy. I ain't teasing him like that."

"Yeah, and so am I."

"Ker, you ain't no beasty nigga. Al will break you off."

"Break me off," he laughed, "I can see you underestimate your boy."

"No I don't, I'm just tryin' to prevent some BS from jumpin' off." The entire time we sat, I hoped there wouldn't be any controversy. Seconds later, the light changed, and Alex sped off.

Once we got back to the campus, Kerwin dropped me off in front of my apartment.

"Call me later."

"For what?" I asked with attitude.

"So I'll know you're alive. If that nigga is as crazy as you say, he might pop up and kill yo ass for rollin' wit a real G."

I slammed the door, and switched up to the main entrance, throwing ass all over the place. I knew Kerwin was checking me out, so I gave him something to look at. Once I made it into the building, Alex walked up behind me.

"Hey, Boo."

"Hi," I replied with trembling in my voice.

"Who was that simp you were with at the restaurant?"

"My friend, Kerwin."

"Where do you know him from?"

"Here, we have a few classes together."

"Is that who you were going out with the other day?"

"Nah, we're just cool, nothing more."

"Good answer, 'cause you were about to have me jealous."

"Jealous? Boy, please. I'm not tryin' to be with anyone," I smiled, thinking his behavior was kind of cute. "I didn't even see you when I was walking in. Where did you come from?"

"I was sittin' on the bench right by the door, waitin' on you."

"What if I hadn't come straight here?"

"Then I would have been waitin' for you at Nikki's."

"You about to trip, aren't you?"

"Naw, I'm cool. I wanted to see you. We talked about hookin' back up, so I was makin' sure I still had a chance," he expressed, kissing me on my hand.

"You so crazy."

"Only for you though."

"Do you want to come in?"

"Oh you gon' let me in today?"

"I guess."

"You know I do," he stated, moving to the side to let me go ahead of him.

I was shocked that Alex didn't trip like I expected. I know it took everything within to keep his composure. I suspect he was trying to prove to me that he was a changed man. Controlling his temper that day got him off to a good start.

We talked and sat listening to a slow jam CD for a while. He made a few jokes about seeing me earlier that day with Kerwin as I tried to play it off. He swore seeing me with another man wasn't his motivating factor for the u-turn. I knew he was lying, but I didn't want to spoil the moment, so I didn't address it. Suddenly, after about forty minutes into our visit, Alex got up.

"Where you going?"

"I'll be right back. I gotta get something out of my car."

My gut told me he was going to get some sort of peace offering for me, so I practiced acting surprised. "Aw, Baaaa...beee, thanks," I rattled, jumping around the room, looking like a fool. *Gurl be serious, you know you real corny sometimes.* "Wow, thanks, Boo-Boo," I said a little more discreetly before the door opened and he walked back in.

"Asia, what are you doing?"

"Being' silly," I laughed, embarrassed about being caught. "Wha'cha go to yo car to get?"

"This," he replied, holding up a bottle of *Chris.*

Aw, damn is that it. I can't believe this negro got me acting straight stupid over some drank. Nigga where's the bling, a nice fur, how about a pair of them badass Alexia Dondo Boots that just came out? Anything besides this crap.

"Boo, we gon' have a toast, and then get wasted tonight"

"A toast for what?"

"A toast to our future."

"What's all that about?"

"I don't wanna be without you, so here's to a new beginning."

"A new beginning?"

"Yeah, I want you to be my lady."

"Yo lady?"

"Boo, I don't ever want to see you with another nigga again. And, I most certainly don't want to think about one getting my shit."

"Oh, is that right?"

"Yeah, it is, so what you got to say about that?"

"I'm speechless. I mean, how you gon' try to get all romantic on somebody out of nowhere?"

"Is it workin'?"

"It might be," I replied, smiling real big.

"Well, if that's the case," Alex paused to get down on one knee, "Asia Prince, would you be my lady again?"

I kept looking and taking my time to reply, expecting some kind of gift to follow. I mean that chump was down on one knee. However, once I realized a blingish item wasn't part of the question, I had to turn him down.

"Alex, you don't know about being in a real loving relationship."

"What's that shit s'pose to mean?"

"I mean, I love romance."

"I'm not romantic?"

"Not the kind of romantic I'm talking about."

"What?"

"I mean, being with a romantic guy is something I've always dreamed of, but never really experienced."

"Asia, haven't I done all kinds of nice shit for you."

"Yeah."

"Haven't we always made good love?"

"Yeah but!"

"But what, besides that one incident?"

"Yeah, you have."

"So what are you talkin' about?"

"Alex, men need to learn that intimacy for a woman starts way before bedtime. Woman love to be adored. We want to be told that we're beautiful first thing in the morning when we're still in head rags and bed clothes. Men and most certainly young men don't even realize that women yearn for verbal and emotional affection way more than they do physical."

"So I don't tell you I love you and make you feel special?"

"I see you have a lot to learn. Alex, all I'm saying is when a woman is into her man based on the fact that he's loving her right emotionally, everything else falls into place. When you see that dick and gifts don't represent love, you'll see what I mean." I paused, giving Alex eye contact and then continued. "Baby, I know we'll hook back up in time, but we're not ready right now."

"Not ready! Why not?"

"To be honest, I'm not quite ready to be tied down. I like the fact that we're dating, but I don't want any strings."

"You don't want no commitment because of that nigga I saw you with earlier today?"

"No, he doesn't have anything to do with my decision."

"You a damn lie."

"I promise he doesn't. And if you about to start."

"Asia, I ain't gon' force it, when you're ready for a real one, get at me," he replied, cutting me off.

"I agree Alex, we shouldn't force it."

"Well, what you want to do until you make up your mind?"

"I don't know."

"Can I at least hold you tonight? It's been a minute since we've cuddled." I paused thinking about how good it once felt to be held in Alex's arms.

"That sounds harmless, I guess we can do that."

I knew once we went there, we would probably end up getting busy, but I wanted to show him that he couldn't manipulate me as well as convince myself that I could hold out. As soon as Alex pulled me up off the couch towards the room and gently lowered me on the bed, I started talking to myself. Next thing I knew, he had stripped down to his boxers and was holding me. As Jesse Powell's, *Baby It's You* softly played in the background, the mood was set. Alex removed my shirt and then my pants. When he went to pull off my panties, I grabbed his hand. He slowly lowered his face next to mine and eased towards my ear, Softly he started singing to me, putting much emphasis on the part that says, *"Gonna make a change in my life, starting here today."* His approach caused me to start reminiscing. Once he tenderly wrapped me in his arms, I was able to recall the things about him that initially made me love him.

I pushed away, grabbed Alex's hands, and slid them down my breast. It had been so long since I'd felt him inside of me that I honestly got off on his touch. When I couldn't take any more, I eased my hands inside his boxers, sliding them over his ass, and down to his knees.

"Damn girl, my Sean John's got you gone, huh."

"I don't care 'bout no Sean John's, just shut the hell up and make love to me," I whispered, as he rolled over on top of me unfastening my bra.

Hot and soaking wet was only a brief description to explain where I was sexually. Before I knew it, Alex was deep inside of me, banging the hell out of my walls like a Punk-rocker on a set of new drums. We went at it like two freaks. I mean, I couldn't believe how we were carrying on. Here we were, getting' it like porn stars. Alex most certainly caught me off guard when he flipped me over on all four, and tossed my salad like a professional chef. I thought he was about to hit it doggie style, but when I discovered that he was licking my ass, I flinched cause it tingled. But I can't lie, for a new experience, I was loving every bit of it. That shit made me feel sexy and nasty at that same time. "Relax, Boo," he insisted, slowly dragging his tongue across the crack of my ass once again. *Now who he been with for the past few months that's done turned him out like this. Some old freaky ass trifling trick done taught him a l'il som'in, because he surely wasn't eating ass before we broke up.*

After I got past feeling kind of nasty, I got use to a wet, floppy tongue grazing across my duke-shoot and loved it. From that day forward, it was a weekly requirement. I also have to admit that it was the best encounter Alex and I ever had. The love we made that day most certainly moved our sex life to a whole different level. Shit, for the record, it was a session that would go down in history as one I ended up saving for future chats with my girls. On a more serious note, there is no way to deny it, after a session like that, Alex had me back under his spell. Though I tried to play it off, I was weak behind him. Hell, love ain't no joke, and what I felt for him over shadowed my own willpower.

Chapter 11
Hit and Run

By November, Alex and I were seriously dating again. We were going out to dinner, movies, professional basketball games, shopping sprees, and having a simple kind of fun, which we'd never really experienced. My girls were getting a little jealous about the time I was giving him because it broke up our trio and the girly stuff we did as a group. Since Nikk and I were friends before college and our men were as well, we occasionally did things together away from campus. Kell, would get mad about that, too and cuss us out because she didn't have a steady man. And on some real shit, at times I was kind of leery about having her around mine. Not because she did anything to me directly, but just because I didn't trust females like her period.

Some days we'd sit around and talk about our men and Nikki always checked me about speaking to loosely around Kell about my sex life with Alex.

"Asia, you know Kell's a slut. She's the kind of tramp that'll holla at yo man with the quickness."

"You trippin'. Kell is out there, but she ain't going out like that."

"Okay, you heard what I said."

"Plus with as hard as Alex worked to get me back, he ain't goin nowhere anyway."

...♦♦♦...

A few weeks before Thanksgiving, we all went to Pookies Pool Hall to kick it. That's when Alex taught me how to shoot darts. After a few drinks and talking much noise, by the time the evening ended, my game was on point.

Nikk and I teamed up against the boys. We played about twenty games, and they drank at least seven rounds of Crown. Once they were blitz, Nikki and I won every round.

"Man, I'm done," Terrell slurred, putting his darts back in the glass.

"Me, too. Let's go," Alex insisted, grabbing his leather Pelle Pelle.

"Y'all chumps just want to break camp cuz we spanked dat ass."

"Asia, you and boot mouth Nikk are some real lames. Get to the car. Ain't nobody tryin' to hear that B.S. We let y'all win."

"Al, you a little ripped. Let Asia drive," Terrell insisted.

"Man, I'm straight."

"That's cool, but I'm followin' you to the campus to make sure."

T jumped in his kitted up Denali, cranked his beats, and pulled off. We drove for about five minutes before coming up on a red light at Joy Road and Greenfield. Alex was driving a little fast, so he was a minute ahead of Terrell. We came up on a red light, stopped briefly, and suddenly out of nowhere, this hype ran up on us, pointing a gun at Alex.

"Get out the fuckin' car," he ordered, sliding his finger on the trigger. Alex looked at him, acting like he was about to get out.

"Renzo," I stated shocked to see my aunties daddy trying to rob us. Before he could reply, a horn sounded off, scaring that nigga. He tried to run, but this black Denali sped by, knocked him about twenty feet, and kept going.

"Bitch ass nigga, you won't try to carjack another muthafucka no time soon!" Alex coldly yelled. "Asia, you know that nigga?"

"Yeah," I answered with watery eyes.

"From where!"

"That's my auntie's daddy."

"To bad for his simp ass," Alex snapped, opening the door. As he was getting out, a passerby pulled up and stopped.

"What happened?" He asked, pulling his phone from his ear.

"Damn! Man, my girl and I got caught at this light. Ole boy just came out of nowhere screaming for help. After that a grey Pathfinder rolled him over and kept going."

"Did you get the tag number?" He asked, making his way over to the body.

"Ut' un. The lights were off."

"Damn! This is the third hit and run this week."

"Fa'real?"

"Yeah, this shit is getting to be ridiculous." He paused. "Sorry about that, I'm Lieutenant Jeffery Williams. I'm gonna need you to stay and make a statement. I got a unit on the way."

"Man, I don't mind making a statement, but I'm gon' be honest. I've been drinking," Alex replied, walking behind him. I got out and followed because I wanted to see if Zo was dead.

"Relax, I ain't concerned with you. This homicide right here is my priority. Did the young lady with you see anything?"

"I don't know."

"Has she been drinking?"

"A cooler, but she's not ripped like me."

"You need to let her drive after we're done."

"No problem, Sir.

He didn't have to say another word. I was gon' make sure I was behind the wheel. Once we made it to the body, I looked over at Zo and felt sick to my stomach when I saw his face. His head was split right down the middle to his nose, and there was blood all over. His legs were twisted in all different directions like a dummy, and I could tell just about every bone in his body was broken. *Dang, T must have hit him a lot harder than I thought. Half of his face looks torn off.* Leaning in a little more to get a better look, I thought about Kell's comment about addicts, *"A heroin addict will do anything when he's chasing his high."* The saddest part about her comment is that Zo's fix for that night cost him his life.

"Miss, I need you to back up." Lieutenant, Jeff Williams insisted. "I don't want you to contaminate the crime scene. Evidence could be anywhere. Actually, you both need to go back to your car. Someone will be over to question you shortly."

"Okay." When we made it to the car, Alex shut the car door, and drilled me to death.

"Did you hear what I told the Po-Po's?"

"Yeah, but..."

"But what?"

"That dead guy is my auntie's daddy."

"Fuck! I heard you the last time. Why you keep tellin' me dat?"

"Because."

"Shit, Terrell's stupid ass! We'll talk about that later. Just make sure you got the story down. Don't say nothin' about him tryin' to jack us and don't say nothin' about a Denali." Alex paused, looking at the fear that registered on my face. His expression became serious. "Boo, don't say shit at all if you don't have to or we might look suspect."

Once all the officers started arriving, I became real scared. I just knew I was gon' slip up and say something I wasn't supposed to. When questioned, I told them the exact same thing Alex did. Though we were at that crime scene late as hell explaining, our story did come across very convincing. I believe the one thing that helped us more than anything was the fact that Renzo had an extensive criminal record and everyone knows that drug addicts, ex-con's, and menaces to society don't get no justice.

We made it to the campus about five o'clock that morning. Alex and I went straight to Nikk's apartment because they were blowing us up while we were still at the accident. As soon as we made it through the door, Nikki started with a hundred questions.

"Damn, what took so long?"

"A police officer pulled up right after y'all turned and started askin' hella questions. He made us stay. Why did y'all keep callin'? Common sense should have told you somethin' was up." I stated, pissed off about being pulled into some bullshit.

"Naw, the questions is why didn't y'all pull off?" Nikk fussed.

"Bitch, we didn't have time to pull off."

"Y'all should have called to say what was up then."

"What if the police got suspicious and started checkin' phone records? Once they discovered that y'all was blowin up Al's phone, it was gon' be a wrap. Terrell's truck gon' get checked, the po-po's gon' find damage, and the next thing we know, them damn forensic muthafuckas checkin' out his shit. Like that, our secret's out. Then guess who's goin' to jail with him.... all of our black asses."

"Forget all this arguing. T, let's make moves," Al insisted, putting on his jacket. "Boo, I'll see you later."

"Where, y'all going?"

"To clean the truck. We got to see what's up wit it and if push comes to shove, scrap it."

"Okay, call me later."

I was a little irritated with Terrell and Nikki. I couldn't believe what he had done. The more I thought about it, the more I realized that after lying with Alex, I was aiding in Terrell's crime. *I'm just as guilty,* I thought as my morals came crashing in on me. I felt beat down as I envisioned the look on Renzo's dead face. Yeah he was a hype, but he had a family and friends who cared about him. Most importantly, he was my favorite aunt's sperm donor.

"Nikk, I'm gone."

"Okay, call me later."

I left her apartment seconds behind the guys. With as high as they were, I knew Alex was tired. Nonetheless, his loyalty to his boy took precedence over me and his rest. Sad to say, but T's truck ended up having enough damage on the hood to concern Alex. After leaving the carwash, they took it to the chop shop. After they told us what happened with the SUV, we all vowed that none of us would ever talk about that night again.

Chapter 12
Thanksgiving

Since it was November and what I call *Fur Season* in Detroit, I asked Al to bring my jacket to the apartment.

"What jacket?"

"Don't play. You know the Chinchilla you bought me earlier this year."

"Oh, the one you had goin' back and forth to Chicago?"

"Yeah, the only one I have. What did you do with it?"

"It's in storage."

Yeah right nigga, "Well, can you bring it to me?"

"I'll go pick 'em up later this week."

"Do you think you can pick it up before Thanksgiving? I'd like to wear it for the holidays."

"Yeah, I'll get it later this week. Just remind me."

"Okay."

For some reason, I ended up reminding Alex about that jacket at least twenty times. He always had some kind of lame excuse as to why he hadn't made time to pick it up. I figured he'd either given it away for some collateral or he gave it to the l'il redbone he was jockin' so hard after we broke up. Whatever his reason was behind not getting me the coat, he never clearly made me understand. All I know is Thanksgiving came, and Asia Prince wasn't rocking no fur with her holiday outfit.

Thanksgiving morning, I woke up to a screaming baby. That was the second thing that messed up my weekend. The only reason I decided to stay with my dad and Teretta in West Bloomfield instead of going back to Chicago was because Mom wasn't cooking and Rodney was still a little mad at me. I was irritated about both issues because I hadn't had a home cooked meal since graduation, and I was craving some Garrett's Popcorn.

"Good morning," I grumbled, walking into the nursery, rubbing my eyes.

"Hey Butterfly, did little Ant wake you?"

"Yeah, how do y'all get any sleep around here with that brat?"

"Brat, if that ain't the pot callin' the kettle black."

"What?"

"He ain't no worse than you."

"Pleeeeee...ease. He's runnin' the dang house."

"Get me a diaper out of his drawer and stop complaining for once in your life."

"Dad, you're changin' diapers?"

"Yeah, I changed yours. I remember one day you shit all over everywhere and Bean wouldn't help me. I was so pissed off with your grandma. Had it not been for Ke, you would have stayed nasty."

"Why wouldn't grandma change my diaper?"

"Because she was a stubborn trip. Bean had her own way of doin' things, plus she was gon' show me that you were not her or KeKe's responsibility."

"Why you say that?"

"Bean didn't raise me or your uncle Ant, but when you were born, she called herself teachin' me about parental responsibility. She wouldn't baby sit, she wouldn't let Ke baby sit, and every chance she got to give me hell, she did. Sometime she was just mean for no reason at all."

"You miss her, don't you Dad?"

"Miss who?"

"Bean."

"Yeah. I miss the hell out of her. We weren't real close when I was young, but while I did my time, some days she was my sanity. Over the years, Bean became my girl. She showed me an unconditional love I might not ever be able to tell you about."

"What you mean?"

"She did some real risky shit for me to prove her love."

"I already know. Mama told me about some of y'all ghetto stories. When I was young, mama use to say that grandma was foolish over you just like she was."

"What stories did she tell you," Dad asked, appearing somewhat irritated about how much I knew.

"I know about grandma sneakin' them drugs into the prison. I know about her jumping on the guards to defend you. I know about her going to jail, being on probation, and them fines she had to pay along with the community service she done for that incident, too."

"Your mother told you all that?"

"No, actually I overheard her tellin' Rodney. Right after it happened, she was expressing how glad she was that I wasn't with grandma. She said had I been, she might have kicked Beans ass."

"Yeah right. Bean would've put a beat down on Zena. Your mother knows Bean wasn't the one. Babe, Bean had a mean streak that kept our family in controversy. She'd cuss out anybody. And when she got a little Henn in her system, it was straight embarassin' how she carried on," Dad laughed. "Zena knew better than to test Bean."

We talked a minute longer, but the scent of holiday breakfast, dominated our special moment.

"Ummm, I smell somethin' good," Dad expressed.

"Fa-shizzo."

"What," Dad frowned.

"Dad, I said fa' sho. You're gettin' old. I'll see you downstairs,"

"Yeah." I walked down to the kitchen to Teretta slavin' over a hot stove.

"Goooood Mooor….ning," Teretta sung, making me feel welcomed.

"Good Morning. I'm hungry, what you cooking?"

"Turkey bacon, pancakes, turkey sausage, cheese eggs, grits, and orange juice."

"Yuck, what's with all this turkey?"

"You know your daddy don't eat no pork."

"So! That don't mean everybody else has to eat like him. Shoot, I hate rubbery imitation turkey stuff. Bacon and sausage were meant to come from a pig. If it ain't pork, it ain't real breakfast meat to me."

"Asia, are you down here complaining now," Dad fussed, walking into the kitchen. "First you were upstairs naggin', now you're doing it down here."

"All I said was just because you don't like pork, doesn't mean that everybody got to eat turkey meat. Shoot Dad, its Thanksgiving, we gon' get our fair share of turkey this whole dang week."

"I'm the king of this Casa. When we're at your apartment, then I'll eat around whatever you serve. If I don't like what you have, then I'll get what I like or not eat at all."

"So are you suggestin' that I do the same?"

"Nooooo! Would I do something like that?"

"I know you're not trying to be sarcastic?" I fussed, rolling my eyes.

"Asia, just sit down and eat before you get your daddy started. I don't feel like hearing his mouth."

I looked at Teretta like *who you think you talking to.* Instead of continuing on and getting doubled teamed, I let it go. As the holiday parade played on the flat screen that was mounted to the kitchen wall, I sat pouting as I watched all the festivities. *Dang I wish I was there,* I thought, catching an eyeful of Detroit's fine ass mayor.

"There go the mayor. That boy be styling, with his sexy self."

"Yeah, he got mad flava, but he ain't got your old dude beat."

"Dad, are you kiddin'. You mean you ain't got nothin' on him. Besides good looks, he's the youngest mayor of any U.S. major city in our nation. You can't fade him. Besides, I bet you he ain't forcing turkey meat on his family for breakfast."

"That just shows how brilliant you are, Einstein. Think about his name, Kwame M. Kilpatrick, and then ask yourself if he eats pork."

"Just because he has a unique name doesn't mean that he's protesting pork. Shoot, with all the V.I.P. gala's he's getting' invites to, I know he done sucked down a pork sandwich or som'em."

"I'm not going there with you." Dad smirked, ticking me off. I was about to tell him something, but our debate was interrupted by the doorbell.

Bong Bong Bong Bong…..Bong.. Bong.. Bong.. Bong. "I'll get it," I stated, getting up from my seat. I ran to the door like a little kid, expecting it to be my Uncle E, but it wasn't. "Heyyyy…Aunt Ke…… Sam! Why y'all didn't tell nobody y'all were comin' we would have rolled out the red carpet?"

"We wanted to surprise everybody."

"Come on in," I insisted, fanning my hands. "Daddy, Aunt Ke and Sam are here." Daddy came rushing out the kitchen like he'd hit the lottery.

"Ke, why you didn't tell me you were comin'?" he asked.

"Sam and I wanted to surprise you. Plus, I had to see my nephew. I didn't want to see another e-mailed photo. I had to hold this boy in my arms and kiss on his fat cheeks in person."

"Are you hungry? We just sat down, y'all want to join us?"

"I'm starving," Sam quickly blurted out, not allowing my auntie a chance to respond. "What you eating?"

"TURKEY…." I sarcastically replied.

"P, you're my kind of man. That's all me and your sister eat."

"Yuck. That's a shame."

"What's a shame?"

"You and Aunt Ke have been brain washed, too. Sam I thought you were much smarter than that. I guess all that jet fuel at N.A.S.A got you trippin."

"Huh!"

"Man, ignore Asia. She woke up on the wrong side of the bed this morning. She's been fussin' since we crossed paths. Come on in the kitchen and fix yourself a plate."

Sam walked into the breakfast-nook, spoke to Teretta and washed his hands. I looked at him in total shock as he piled tons of food on his plate.

"Why you looking at me like that Asia?"

"Sam you said you don't eat pork, but you got all that food on your plate. So you don't want to die from pork, but it's okay to die from a heart attack."

"A heart attack?"

"Yeah, that's what you gon' have once you become obese from eating so much."

"Girl, shut up," Dad ordered. "Go sit in the den or something."

"Daddy, I'm only playin'."

"Well, you're getting' on my nerves."

"Teretta, you gon' let him talk to me like he's crazy?"

"Hey, I'm staying out of that."

"Yeah, okay. I thought you had my back."

"Ut'un, I got to live with Prince once you return to school."

Now that move reminded me of my mother. That's the exact same thing my mama did to me when Rodney and I would argue. Teretta kind of pissed me off, so I grabbed my plate and took Dad's advice. I went and sat in the den.

I stayed in there pouting for the longest, but no one seemed to care. My family all sat around the kitchen table talking and laughing. Dad and Ke were catching up while Sam and Teretta talked to each other. The baby was asleep across Aunt Ke's lap, and I sort of felt left out and a little jealous. Daddy and my aunt always gave me lots of attention. I guess since I was living in Detroit, I had gotten somewhat old to him. And I was always Aunt Ke's favorite, but she was more thrilled about the baby. *Dang! She could at least ask me about school, how I like living in Detroit, anything. She so busy making a fuss over little egghead that she forgot about her favorite niece.*

A few hours after eating, I didn't smell the delicious scent of pies, greens, dressing, nothing, so I wondered what was up with dinner. Finally, after another hour, I had to go investigate.

"What's up with dinner? I don't smell no food cooking."

"Ke and Sam are going to his mother's for dinner and we're going to Teretta's parents."

"Dad," I whined, thinking *I don't want to go to nobody's house.*

"What now Asia?"

"Why you didn't tell me y'all weren't cookin'. I would have gone home or made other plans. I don't want to go be a third leg."

"You're my child. There's not a place I'm goin' that you're not welcomed."

"I don't want to go over there. I wanted to eat with you here."

"That ain't gon' happen."

"Well, I want to go home then."

"Call your mother, and then call the airport. Let me know how much the ticket cost, and I'll send your ass home," he impatiently fussed.

"Dad, who do you think you're talkin' to like that? I didn't raise my voice at you, so don't raise yours at me," I lashed back, walking up the stairs to go use the phone in privacy.

"Prince, since Asia waited 'til the last minute, a ticket to Chicago is gonna be high," Teretta expressed.

"Baby, I don't care. Asia can take all that whining to the house."

I couldn't believe Daddy said that. *He's picking that trick and his new baby over me,* I thought, without saying anything. Though my feelings were hurt, I stretched out in the floor and called my mother.

"Happy Thanksgiving," Mom answered.

"Hi Ma, Happy Thanksgiving to you. What are you doing?"

"Getting ready to go to Shirley's. Everybody cooked a dish and we're having dinner together this year."

"Oh, I didn't know you weren't cooking."

"I told you I wasn't cooking last week, I guess you weren't listening."

"Maybe I didn't hear you. And I sure didn't think you were gonna eat at someone else's house."

"Well you said you weren't coming home, so I made other plans. Why you sound so upset?"

"Because Daddy was going to fly me home to see you."

"Well, come go with us to Shirley's."

"Nah, I'll pass. You know Shirley's daughter, Lavern gets on my nerves with her skinny self."

"Asia, you're being petty."

"Ut'un, you know we've had beef every since, her man tried to talk to me."

"Okay, well y'all need to work it out. I gotta go. We were about to leave when the phone rung. Enjoy the holiday. Tell your daddy and yo step mama, hello."

"Yeah right. I ain't got no step-mama."

"Oh lawd. Teretta must have pissed you off."

"Not really."

"Asia, I've been your mother all your life. I know you. You're not getting your way about something, so you're pouting."

"Happy Holidays, Mom, I got to go," I stated, cutting her off.

"Okay, bye," she nonchalantly replied.

I didn't know what I was going to do. I wasn't welcomed at home, I didn't want to go with Dad, Nikki had gone out of town with her parents, and.... *Wait, I can call Alex,* I thought, feeling relieved.

"Hello."

"Hey Alex."

"Hey, Boo. Happy Thanksgiving."

"What are you doing?"

"Lying around, I ain't got shit else to do."

"Why didn't you go have dinner with T and his family?"

"Didn't want to," he sadly replied.

"You sound real sad. What's wrong?"

"I don't know. I guess I get tired of always bein' by myself on holidays. I ain't got no family, and my girl picked hers over me."

"Ut'un. I'm about to go back to my apartment. My dad and his family are goin' to his baby's mama's house. I don't know them people like dat, so I ain't goin'."

"You want me to meet you at your apartment later?" he asked.

"Yeah, about five, I've gotta get me a ride."

"Okay. Call my cell when you're on your way."

We hung up and I went back downstairs. "Dad the flights are expensive," I lied, trying not to reveal that Mom had plans also.

"So are you going with us to Teretta's parents?"

"Nope, I'm stayin' here. I might go to Nikki's house and eat with her and her family."

"How are you getting there? You need me to drop you off."

"Nope, Nikk said she'd come get me."

"That's fine."

My Aunt and Sam left about four that afternoon, and Dad and Teretta left shortly after. At first, I thought he might take his truck, but they ended up leaving in Teretta's Benz. Once I was sure they were out of the neighborhood, I called Alex.

"Alex, I'm on my way to the apartment."

"Okay, I'll be there about five thirty or six."

I grabbed Dad's keys off the counter, got this mixed CD out the player in my room, and headed for the garage. From the hills to the hood, niggas and tricks alike were trying to see who was rolling the Cadi Escalade. I cranked Dad's beats up to the max and bumped *Who's Loving These Freaks* by Stormy. I bobbed my head and rapped along with the CD as I attracted attention all the way to the campus. Dad's tint was mobbed out, and his winter rims were just as clean as the Spreewells he rolled in the summer. Good thing no one could see inside. That way, even if someone spotted his truck, they wouldn't necessarily know it was me driving. Right at 5:15, I pulled up on campus. There was no sign of Alex. I snatched my things out of the passenger seat and headed towards the building.

I was in desperate need of a store run, but Dad only gave me money to grocery shop every four weeks. Though I still had to the end of the month to go, I fished around in my freezer 'til I found something. Our choice was a frozen enchilada dinner, with chili sauce or a pack of frozen pizzas pockets. *What a selection for a Thanksgiving dinner,* I thought. *Well I guess it's better than nothing.* "At least we got each other," I stated, looking at the clock.

Once I finished picking out our holiday meal, I looked at my watch. It was after 5:45pm and Alex still hadn't made it. Before I knew it six and then six-thirty passed. I started blowin' up his cell. 6:39 no answer, 6:50, 6:55, 7:00, 7:25, and so on. "Alex, where the hell are you." I screamed in the phone, looking out the window. When nine o'clock passed, I concluded that Alex wasn't coming. Considering it was so late, I knew Dad had probably beat me home. I threw on my brown coach boots, put on my chocolate brown leather jacket, and grabbed my purse. As I was locking my apartment door, someone came up behind me and covered my mouth.

"Open the door, and get your ass inside right now," he demanded, with a object in my neck.

"I have money if that's what you want. Please don't hurt me," I begged as loud laughter suddenly followed.

"I have money, just please don't hurt me. Girl you're a wimp."

"Kerwin," I yelled, hitting him. "Yo punk ass play too much."

"What's up kid? Why you out here on the campus for the holiday?"

"Mindin' my b'iness."

"You expectin' someone?"

"Alex was s'posed to have dinner with me, but was a no show."

"So what you about to do now?"

"I'm about to head to my daddy's house. You want to follow me and hang out for a little while."

"Nah, I ain't tryin' to sit up with you and your family."

"What's that suppose to mean?"

"You ain't about to be my woman, are you?"

"So."

"I thought you were ready to give in, but I see you're still not tryin' to hear from a winner like me."

"Nope, not right now. What are you doing here?"

"Gettin' me a change of clothes for tonight. I was about to pull out the lot, and saw your light on."

"So you're stalking me," I teased.

"Hell naw! I came by to say wa'sup."

"Chump don't be poppin' up at my spot. My man will have a fit if you stop by and he's here."

"How he gon' know?"

"Boy, you can't even sneak in a visit with all that cologne you got on right now. Alex will fall up in here, smell your shit, and go nuts."

"I told you once, I ain't worried about yo nigga. And if he was into you like he should be, you wouldn't be up here spendin' Thanksgiving alone," he insisted, easing up in my face to kiss me.

"Kerwin, what are you doing?"

"Trying to see if you have soft lips."

"All you got to do is ask and I can tell you that."

"Just let me find out for myself?"

"I don't think so. Come on. I'm out," I insisted, pissed off about Alex not showing. "So are you gon' come by my dad's or what?" I asked, needing an alibi just in case he was home.

"You're on your own tonight. I'm 'bout to get with a few of my partners, so I'll see you Sunday when we get back on campus."

"That's cool," I replied, looking sad. Kerwin walked half way down the stairs and stopped.

"What's wrong?" he asked.

"I don't know, for some reason I feel bad as hell."

"What are you upset about?"

"Man tis the season to be jolly. It's Thanksgiving, I'm lonely, and all my people stood me up for someone else. My dad has his new female and their son. My mother is with her family, my girl went with her parents out of town for the holiday, my man was a no show, and I'm standing here talking to you, when I should be somewhere celebrating."

"Shit, peace out then," he replied, offended.

"Boy, shut up, I don't mean it like that. I'm sayin' holidays are meant to be spent festively with family and friends, but don't nothin' feel festive about today to me."

"Oh, I ain't your friend?"

"Yeah, but that's still not what I mean."

"Asia, you're making me depressed. Shit, I guess unhappiness is contagious. I'm 'bout to be out."

"Holla," I replied, locking my door.

"Do you want to hang with me tonight?"

"Are you serious?"

"Yeah, I'll be a gentleman. I'll pick you up around elevenish."

"Call me on my cell when you're on your way. I gotta get this truck back home before my dad misses it and nuts up."

"You stole your dad's truck?"

"Umm hum."

"Damn girl, that nigga got you gone. I don't know about picking you up from the crib."

"Why you say that?"

"I don't want your ole dude trippin' on me."

"Dad's feelin' you. Like I said, call when you're on your way."

"At least one of y'all Prince's know a real nigga when they see one."

Kerwin and I walked out together. I called the house to see if Dad was there, but didn't get an answer. I called his cell to get a feel for his whereabouts and he was still at Teretta's parents.

"Hey Dad, when are you comin' home?"

"I don't know. Why?"

"Just asking. I'm goin' out with Kerwin. He's pickin' me up about eleven, so I probably won't be here when you get home."

"Okay, make sure you call and check in. You know nigga's gon' be acting a fool tonight."

I got to the house, relieved that I didn't have to come up with a lie about using Dad's truck. I took myself a quick shower, threw on this clean fitted *Baby Phat* hookup, and sprayed myself down in some Tiffany perfume. While I sat in the den waiting on Kerwin, I called Alex about five more times. "Alex you better have a damn good excuse for standing me up," I fussed, leaving a message on his voicemail. As I was hanging up, the doorbell rang. Before heading out through the garage, I grabbed my purse, coat, and then set the alarm.

When I got an opportunity to take a real good look at Kerwin, I saw something in my homie that I'd never seen before. I don't know if it was the fact that I was lonely or that he was really sexy, but whatever the case may have been, I was feeling him.

"Damn! Boy you got it goin' on. I ain't never looked at you and thought you were the bomb, but you got real sex appeal," I commented, meeting him in the driveway.

"I've always been on my shit, you just ain't never noticed because you're to busy sweatin' the wrong kind of balla."

"Say what you want, I ain't even about to go there with you."

"You don't have to. I already know I'm right."

"Are we gon' argue the entire evening or are we gon' have a good time?'

"Asia, you're the one who insists on arguing. If you wouldn't try to debate about everything, we would get along better."

"Okay. Let's start over."

"Cool."

"Damn! Boy you sure got it going on," I laughed, as he opened the door for me.

"Get in," he replied, grinning as deep dimples and beautiful pearly whites brought his radiant smile to life.

The entire way to the Motor City Club, I lusted. I had never looked at Kerwin and wanted him, but I did that night. It was crazy for me to be feeling him sexually like I was, because he was the one person I confided in about so many things. I don't know if it was his ball cap or his outfit that turned me on most, but whichever, I was feeling him.

"Asia, I'm gon' valet, that way you don't have to walk so far."

"Why you tellin' me?"

"Because, it's fifteen dollars, and you gon' pay half."

"What? Nigga, you cheap."

"Hell, I ain't no drug dealer. Every dollar I get, I earn from an honest days work."

"Work, I didn't know you worked."

"Sure do."

"When do you have time to work with basketball practice and games?"

"I ain't talkin' about no physical labor. I'm talkin' 'bout puttin' my Mack down."

"Mack?"

"Yeah, my convo."

"Convo! Nigga please. Ain't nobody on campus payin' you for all that bullshit you be spittin'."

"That's what you think."

"Who? Name one person that's paying you?"

"Come on now. Asia, you know half the rats on the yard payin' me."

"Rats like who?"

"Like Rachel, Darshel, Sweetie, Precious, Leslie, and yo' girl."

"Leslie, who? I know you not talkin' 'bout uppity, big nose, ugly, Ms. Thank She Fine, Leslie with them jacked up goddess braids."

"Sure am.."

"Ain't that a trip, you know she be trying to act like she's all that with them big ass ankles that could brace a leanin' house."

"I don't care about her ankles. Yeah, she be trying to act all classy, but I know different."

"What you know?"

"I know she be hummin' on a playa's balls and suckin' my Johnson like a pro. The other day, she was suckin' a nigga's toes with ice cubes, then had the nerve to ask for a kiss."

"What! And you gave her one?"

"Hell naw, but she is the kind of freak niggas like."

"Boy, you know nigga's talk. I heard she's doing one of the football coaches, and some of those frat boys."

"So I don't care. It ain't like I'm making her my woman."

"Yeah, and rumor has it that she's on Dean K's nuts for an A."

"You ain't even got to tell me. I already know fa'myself."

"So she's a rat like that?" I asked.

"She's a rat trying to be on the DL and so is yo girl."

"My girl who?"

"Kelly."

"Kelly! Hell naw."

"I'm not lying. She broke me off tonight right before I came to your house."

"Oh you're a straight slut. That's why I knew better than to holla at you. And Kelly, always fakin' like she so hard. I knew that tramp was a carbon copy."

"I don't know about a carbon copy, but she gives good head."

"A blowjob ain't got shit to do with keepin' it real."

"We can sit here and argue forever. All I'm gon' say is that you need to dig off in that fake ass *Baby Phat* bag and get seven bills."

"You're serious?"

"Yeah I'm serious. Why wouldn't I be?"

"Because."

"Because what?" He asked, looking crazy. "You ain't my woman or my date. What we got goin' on here tonight is like being out with one of the homies. Homie!"

"I got your homie," I said, throwing seven dollars at him. "I bet whoever just got out of that phat stretched limo didn't make their date or their homies pay part of the valet tab."

"I bet whoever rented that bitch could afford to splurge and seven bills wasn't an issue for 'em either. I ain't got money like that, plus no romance, no finance."

"Whatever cheap nigga, and for the record, my purse ain't no knockoff. This cost me some grip."

"You mean it cost yo daddy some grip."

"Who the hell ever, it's still not fake."

Chapter 13
The Club

Kerwin had a little clout everywhere, which is why we walked straight to the front of the line.

"Kerwin Phillips is in the house tonight! What's up my nigga?" A bouncer yelled, greeting him with much love. "Is this you, Dawg?"

"Nah, she playin' a nigga to the left."

"You better get on him. My man 'bout to be doing big thangs."

"I'll pass. We're cool like he said, but thanks for the tip," I smiled.

"Go on in, my man. Have a good time, and tell Money Mike the first two are on me."

We moved our way through the crowd without ever being searched. *Damn! I could learn to like this. I see VIP with a nigga of status gon' be some serious shit.*

"Ker, how they riskin' their liquor license on you?"

"What you mean?"

"You're eighteen. This joint is for twenty-one and over. Can't neither one of us drink legally."

"Correction, you can't drink," he suggested, holding up a fake ID. "I can drink whatever I like, but I don't drink alcohol. I'm a real athlete. I ain't impairing my mind or my body with that poison."

Here we go again, I thought, rolling my eyes. "So I guess you don't eat pork either? Huh, brother Ishmeal?"

"What you say?" He asked because by then we were deep inside the club and the music was humping.

"Nothin."

We found our way to the table Kerwin's boys had reserved and pulled up a few extra seats. Four of his homies were already there and two were on their way.

"So you doing it like that there tonight?" His boy Joe asked.

"Nigga, who is this pretty lady wit ch'ou?" another uttered.

"Dawg, she's available. This my homie Asia," he smiled.

No he didn't just tell all these black ass niggas that I'm available. Shoot, they bout to be on me like a dick locked on a piece of ass. I'm gon' kill him as soon as we leave this club if any one of them end up sweatin' me all night.

"Oh, Asia. This is Steve, Weary, Joe, Kevin, and my boy Dave."

"Sup Asia," they greeted.

"Hi." I replied, wondering who was gon' get his bid in first. "Is the club crackin' so far?"

"It's straight," Dave replied. "We were waiting for some fine women to show up."

"Fine women?"

"The pickings are real slim. It's a bunch of beast out tonight. Or all the pretty ladies, gettin' cock blocked by their ugly home girls." *How this nigga gon' be choosy up in here, looking like a mixture of Zilla Gorilla, Beetle Juice, and Sam I am,* I thought, laughing.

"So that's causing you not to have a good time."

"Nah. Women just make the night what it's s'posed to be."

"Oh, I see. Well, where do you know Kerwin from?" I asked to change the subject.

"Two years ago, we played ball together at Persian."

"Cool, so what college do you go to?"

"I was at Michigan State."

"Was?"

"Yeah, I got drafted after my second season."

"Drafted like in the league?"

"Yeah, somethin' like that," he smiled. *I bet he's thinking him mentioning his status is gon' influence my thoughts.*

"Something like that? What do you mean?"

"I'm jokin'. I play for the Bucks."

"Wow, you play for the Bucks. So why are you in Detroit?"

"It's the holiday. My family's here. We didn't have a game, so I came home."

"That has to be an exciting life."

"It's cool. Some days the lifestyle is very fascinating, and some days it's not. As an individual who's always in the public's eye, you have to be very careful. When the media is talkin' about Dave Roberson, I want them to be focused on the positive shit. I don't want the world trying to be all up in my business."

"I know that's real. So what do you think about Kobe?"

"No comment. We play ball against each other and I'm going to respect his privacy."

I really respected Dave after that. Most often, niggas always hatin' on each other, especially when you're on top of your game like Kobe was. He got points from me cuz he didn't bash Kobe while he was down. And because of his thought provoking conversation, we talked most of the night.

When I finally decided to take a restroom run, I realized that we'd been talking for about an hour. It was almost one o'clock in the morning and I hadn't danced or anything. Obviously the company is exactly what I needed because I didn't even realize that Alex still hadn't called. I bumped into Leslie in the bathroom and she was sloppy drunk. *Umm speak of the devil, I* thought, looking at her like she had shit on her face. *Watch this fake bitch try to speak to me cuz I'm up in here looking like a million bucks.*

"Wha'sup Chick," She greeted.

"Hey," I replied, making my way around her to exit the ladies room. *Don't try to act like we're cool. You know I ain't feelin' you like that.* As the door shut behind me, there was no remorse about my behavior. *She's a damn trip. How she gon' be all on my tip and she just had me and my girls beefin' with Sharonda and her click a few months ago.*

...◆◆◆◆...

On my way back to my seat, I noticed this familiar face. It was that little pretty trick Alex was all on when we weren't talking. I stopped and watched her for a moment. *Umm, that rat ain't got shit on me,* I concluded, wondering what Alex saw in her to begin with. Right when I was about to return to my seat, I noticed her walking to her table. Immediately, I wondered if he had stood me up for her, so I watched her. Instead of sitting in her seat, she sat on some dudes lap. His back was turned towards me, so I really couldn't tell if it was Al or not.

I kept looking, and looking, and looking because I wanted to make sure it wasn't Alex. My snooping paid off. After standing there for about five minutes, Miss Thang and her date headed for the dance floor. I grabbed my mouth in shock when I focused in on the two of them. Alex's girl was out partying with Terrell. *Oh, this hoe is a slut, too. I know he was delirious when he tried to make me jealous with her.* "I'll be damn," I whispered, watching T bump and grind all over that hoe. *Nikki would die. Hell, Alex would die if he knew his boy was out kicking it with his bitch.* Or at least I thought he would until I saw Alex making his way out on the dance floor holding Kelly's hand. *What the hell is going on? I should go out there and beat that slut down.* As I stood to make my way over to them, Kerwin bumped me.

"A, why you standin' here with that look on yo face?"

"What?"

"My boy Dave is feeling you. He wanted to know if it was okay to holla at you. What should I tell him?"

"What do you mean, what should you tell him?"

"You know, do you think you gon' ever let a brotha like me in or should I let my boy spit at you?"

"Huh!" I asked, clearly not listening to him.

"Who are you looking at?"

"Look," I said, guiding his face in the direction of Al and Kelly.

"Hell naw!"

"Can you believe that she's with him?" I asked.

"Naw, because she rushed me off tonight, talking about her family was all going to the movies together."

"When she was rushing you off? Rushing you off from where?"

"We hooked up for a minute tonight. I had to get my money and my little homie had to get paid, too."

"You got busy with that tramp before we hooked up?"

"Hell naw! She slobbed on my boy to help me release."

"Yuck! I don't give a damn about that. I want to know what she's doin' with my man."

"She gets around, so ain't no telling."

"Why would she do this? She knows how much I love Alex."

"You know she ain't got no loyalty."

"That punk stood me up on a holiday to go out with her."

"Maybe she gives better head than you," Kerwin teased.

"I doubt that."

"Asia, you suck dick?"

"None of your damn business. This ain't the time or the place to be actin' stupid."

"So what you gon' do?"

"Beat that hoe down for violating the code," I stated, walking towards the dance floor. "They all out there skinnin' and grinnin' to *Step to This*, let's see how *Clean* she thank she is when I pop her in the back of her damn head with this bottle." Kerwin grabbed me around my waist and pulled me back, causing a slight scene.

"Don't put yourself out there like that over no nigga or no bitch."

"I know, but damn. We're s'posed to be girls. How she gon' do this to me?"

"Asia, I've been tellin' you that..."

Suddenly, I couldn't even listen to Kerwin. I zoomed in on the four of them as they returned to their table. I could see they were getting ready to leave. It killed me as I watched Alex help Kelly put on her coat. *She got on my fur, too. Aw hell naw, it's gon' be some drama tonight.*

"Kerwin, do you see that?"

"See what?"

"That bitch got on my coat."

"She's got yo man and she's wearin' yo gear, too."

"You think that's funny?"

"Nah, I don't. I think that's what you needed to see."

"You sounding like a hater right now."

"Nah, I just don't think you should worship no man. I don't care who he is."

"Well you sure don't mind no tricks on your tab jockeying for you."

"Forget it. Let's change the subject. I don't want to talk about yo man or yo coat."

"What?"

"I wanna know how she gon' suck the life out of my dick, drop me a few hundreds, tell me she'll call me after she get in from the movies to come back for part two, then show up in the club with another nigga."

"Oh you got jokes."

"Naw, I'm hot about your man gettin' my scrilla. It's messed up that she out in your coat looking just as good in it as you do too. But the real killa is that she'll be up in your face on Sunday like she ain't violated yo trust?"

"Shut up! Let me go, this ain't funny to me."

"I ain't 'bout to let you go out like this."

"Why not, shit, she ain't gon' mind?"

"Well, you're way classier than that."

"So I'm s'posed to ignore what I just saw?"

"For right now you should. Don't let no gutter bitch have you makin' moves based on her actions. You're in control of this situation. You can make smart moves or you can go over there, show your ass, and possibly cause a fatal scene."

"What?"

"Asia, you can leave here with some dignity and sleep this off or you can cause a scene and possibly get embarrassed. You know both of them are ignorant as hell. And if that nigga get out of line, me, you, and all my boys goin' to jail."

"Jail?"

"Yeah, Alex gon' disrespect you, I'm gon' beat his ass, Kelly gon' try to fight you, my boys gon' intervene, and once that happens, we're off to jail."

"That's true."

"Okay then let it go for now and stop fightin' me."

"You're right. I'm gon' let it go for now, but when I get home I'm gon' deal with this."

"Smart choice, Baby Girl."

As painful as it was for me to see Alex out with another woman, I took Kerwin's advice. Though I wasn't in the mood, Dave tried to push up on me right before we left.

"Dave, it was nice to meet you. Hope to see you again real soon. Maybe when you're free again, you can come to one of Kerwin's games."

"Maybe so. Can I get your number?"

"Sure," I stated, grabbing his hand to write my number in his palm.

"I could've just programmed it in my cell."

"Yeah, you could have. I'm different. I bet you're programming a lot of numbers in that phone. If mine is that important, you'll take the time to transfer it after the fact."

"Dawg, you better be on this one or I'm snaggin' her from you."

"Nigga please," Kerwin stated, leaning in to show him some love. "Man, we out."

"Us, too," Dave replied, putting on his Mink coat and hat that matched.

Dave and his boys walked out with us and jumped in the limo Kerwin and I had earlier argued about. After I got in Kerwin's truck, tears uncontrollably fell from my eyes. Suddenly, he grabbed my hand and tenderly stroked my fingers to sooth my pain. I didn't say anything all the way to my dad's house. I just sniffled and repeatedly wiped my eyes. When we pulled up, Kerwin walked me to the door and gave me the most sympathetic hug.

"Good night, Sunshine. I hope the morning brings about a new glow for you."

"Good night, Kerwin. Thanks for letting me hang out."

"Anytime, yo."

Chapter 14
About Kelly

Maybe Alex knew I was hot with him because, I didn't hear from him for the rest of the weekend. I tried to call him a few times, but he never answered his phone. I'm sure he figured I was angry with him about standing me up, but since he hadn't checked in, it didn't seem as though he really cared. That Sunday, Dad took me back to the campus.

"Butterfly, are you alright?"

"Yeah, why?"

"I don't know, I guess you seem a little down. Are you still mad at me about Thanksgiving?"

"I'm fine. I think the stress that comes along with finals is taking a toll on me."

"Are you sure it's not Teretta and Little Ant?"

"Naaaaa, my lows have nothin' to do with them."

"Well, what is it then?"

"Dad, I don't feel like talkin' about it."

"You know that there's nothing we can't talk about?"

Yeah right, except for me datin' a street nigga, I thought before replying. "I know, I said I'm fine."

"Okay, but if you need to talk, I'm here."

"Thanks. Are you coming in?"

"Nope, not unless you want me to. I promised Teretta I was gonna put lights on the house for Christmas. E's supposed to come over and help me. Can you believe that we're putting lights up?"

"Heck naw, that's like Larry and Curly trying to drive."

"Get out. We got way more sense than the three stooges. You sure know how to steal your Dad's joy."

"Like you really care. Dad as long as you have your new son and your new little woman, you aren't hardly phased by me or my comments."

"I sense a little jealously."

"Good."

"Good! Well why are you feeling that way?"

"I've never really had to share you before. When I visited you with that Carrington chick, I could claim my territory and you were all about me. It's not like that anymore."

"Butterfly, you don't have to claim no territory with me. I'll always love you no matter who's in my life or how many kids I have."

"That's nice to know," I stated, half believing him. "I'll see you later in the week."

"Okay, love you," he stated, leaning forward to kiss me on my forehead.

I wrestled my things into my apartment, dropping everything in the middle of the floor. As I walked to shut the door behind me, my phone started ringing.

"Hello."

"Boo." Once it registered that it was Alex, I became totally quiet. "Boo, I know you're mad as hell at me, but I've got a good explanation. I was on my way to your apartment on Thanksgiving and I got pulled over. I had a few bags of weed on me. Once the police searched my car, they also found my gun. Next thing I knew, I was in the back of the squad car on my way to jail."

"Why didn't you call me to bail you out or get a bondsman?"

"I tried to call you."

"You a lie. You know you ain't tried to call no damn body."

"Okay, I didn't directly call, but I asked T's cousin to hit you up for me."

"Okay, whatever. I'm busy, I'll call you back."

"Busy doing what?"

"I was walking through the door when the phone rung. I dropped my things in the middle of the floor, so I need to clean up this mess."

"I know you, you don't believe me, do you?"

"Hell naw I don't believe you."

"I can tell because any other time we'd talk, but you ain't got much for me right now."

"Alex, I said I just walked in. I'll call you back."

"Call my cell, I'm about to move around."

"That's fine."

I hung up, mumbling the entire time I was putting up my things. Once I finished, I rested in fetal position on my couch, feeling sorry for myself. *I had one hell of holiday break* or so I thought. I knew Alex was lying, but I almost wanted to believe him because his story was just that convincing. I didn't bother to call him back at all. Instead, I called Kerwin. Talking with him was always so soothing. What I liked most about him and our friendship was that he always made me laugh about something. Once we got to talking, Kerwin could tell I was feeling down and immediately tried to make me feel better.

"You sound terrible. You still trippin' about your boy?"

"I don't know. I think I feel stupid."

"Why? You handled the situation didn't you?"

"No."

"No! You ain't check 'em?"

"I should have, but I didn't. Alex called and I played stupid. I should have kicked that bitch's ass at the club. How she gon' be my girl and she's fucking my man?"

"Let's change the subject."

"What else is there to talk about?"

"Why don't you come over?"

"Come over and do what?"

"Watch a movie?"

"I'll come over, but I don't want to watch no movies. I'm hungry, let's go get something to eat."

"I'm not hungry."

"I am, so go with me."

"I'll think about it."

"Boy, whatever, I'm on my way."

I hung up the phone, grabbed a ball cap, and threw on a jacket. Kerwin only lived a few buildings away, so I knew it would only take a minute to walk over. Suddenly, there was a knock at my door.

"Coming!" I yelled, thinking he'd come to pick me up. When I opened the door, Alex was standing on the other side.

"Hey, Boo, where you going?"

"Out," I coldly replied.

"Where are you going?"

"I'm about to go study with some of my friends."

"Call 'em and tell 'em you ain't comin."

"What! Why would I do that?"

"You haven't seen me in almost five days."

"So, you didn't think about that this weekend."

"Boo, I told you I was in jail."

"Alex, I don't want to talk about it, just like you called T's cousin, you could've called me."

"No I couldn't."

"I don't care and I don't want to discuss it. Whatever happened is fine. I'm going to study, so get at me later."

"I drove all the way out here and you sendin' a nigga home."

"Alex, you don't have to go home, you just got to leave here."

"Come on let's talk," he suggested, trying to hug me.

I pushed him away right when Kerwin was coming up the steps. Alex looked at him as if he were sizing him up.

"What's up," Kerwin, greeted, walking past us to knock on a door a few feet from mine.

"Hey Man," I spoke, sensing him assessing the uneasiness in my face.

"What's up with that nigga? Is that who you were going to study with or was he really coming over here?"

"I had on my jacket, a cap, and was on my way out. I don't have to lie. Maybe you're questioning me because you're guilty about somethin'."

"Forget it! Asia, can I come in or what."

"Come back later," I stated, closing the door behind me. I'll be back in a few hours."

"Where am I s'posed to go 'til then?"

"I don't know. Go to Nikki's."

"I ain't goin' there without T."

"Fine, well go to Kelly's then."

"Kelly," he suspiciously repeated. "Kelly! What the hell am I gon' do over there?"

"I don't know, you tell me," I yelled back, walking down the stairs. Alex followed me out of the building, trying to get me to stay. "Alex, leave me the hell alone. I'm about to go."

Finally, he got the message and walked over to his car.

"Asia, do you want me to drop you off somewhere?"

"For what? So you can sit outside and try to stalk me? That's okay. I'll walk."

"Why you want to walk? You must be up to something."

"If I am it's my business, ain't it."

"Girl, you on some bull tonight."

"Alex, I'm not about to go there with you. I said I want to walk, and I'm going to walk. If I'm up to something it's not any of your business, so beat it. Go do what you do."

"Fuck you, Asia, you're trippin' hard," he expressed, closing his car door.

I wasn't even moved by Alex's outburst. I watched him pull off and slowly started walking towards Kerwin's complex. As soon as he was out of my sight, I called Kerwin on his cell, informing him to meet me there.

"My complex, why you want me to meet you there?"

"Just come on and I'll tell you later."

"I'm on my way."

I stood by a tree in front of his building until I saw his head lights. Suddenly, I noticed him creeping up on me, and couldn't help but wonder what he was doing.

"I know you sold out?" he insisted, yelling out the window.

"Shut up, Kerwin. No one has time for that."

"I'm not lettin' you in 'til you admit that you got weak on dude."

"Kerwin, stop playin' and unlock this door or else."

"Or else what? This is my whip," he expressed, unlocking the door.

"Why do you play so much?"

"I was just trying to make you smile."

"There's nothing to smile about, you know crazy ass Alex just left here trying to make me believe he was locked up for the weekend."

"I don't care about that nigga. You should have told him to move around. I know you're scared of him, but he don't put fear in me."

"Yeah, I hear you."

"Asia, seriously, are you scared of him?" Immediately this stupid expression took over my face. I was a little afraid of Alex, but I didn't want Kerwin to know that.

"Boy, naw I ain't afraid of Alex. My daddy would snap that sucka's neck if he did anything to me."

"Based on his actions, I think he's easily provoked, and if you stay with him, he's going to kill you."

"You're probably right, but I really do love him."

"Asia, how can you love a nigga that you're afraid of? That doesn't make any sense to me."

"I know, but he's my first love, so it's kind of hard to shake him."

"So what it sounds like you're saying is that what he did to you this past weekend was okay."

"I don't know."

"That means yes."

"Kerwin, you don't know what it means."

"Why you gettin' so defensive, you can't handle the truth?"

"Yes I can. I'm just not in the mood for this tonight."

Kerwin went on and on for a while, until I finally started to ignore him. We ended up going to White Castle's to get some of those soy burgers. He wasn't big on red meats, so he ordered about seven little chicken sandwiches.

"I knew you were a damn Ishmeal."

"What?"

"Forget it," I stated noticing Melissa. That was the little red-bone I saw T with in the club. This time she was out with some Balla who drove a H2 on spinners.

"There are too many sluts in the world."

"Who you talkin' about?"

"That Melissa chick from the club."

"She's bad," Kerwin lusted.

"Boy, she's selling pussy too."

"Why you say that?"

"She's too mobile and she's ugly."

"Naw, I'm gon' disagree with you on that one. She's far from ugly. Shoot, I ain't gon' lie, if I wasn't your boy, I'd be on her."

"Well, that just goes to show that you ain't got no class either."

"You ain't got no damn class, if you did, you wouldn't be with a nigga you scared of."

For a second I ignored Kerwin, because one thing I knew for sure was that he was a hoe too. Then finally I couldn't help myself.

"Boy you ain't no better. You get around just like the next nigga."

"Yeah, I do, but if you were my woman, I'd be all about you."

"How I know that?"

"Because I told you so. One thing about me, I'm a one woman's man when I make a commitment."

"Yeah right."

"Yeah right my ass. Try me and you'll see."

"Shut up," I lashed out.

"Naw, you shut me up," he teased.

As Melissa was walking out of the restaurant, she noticed me and gave me this bitchy smirk. *I know she ain't about to come over here and say nothing to me.* But yes she did.

"Hey, don't I know you from somewhere?"

"Naw, you sure don't," I replied real bitchy.

"Yes, I'm sure I've seen you before."

"Maybe you saw me at my sports bar."

"What's the name of it?"

"Asia's."

"Yeah, I frequent that spot, so it's possible that I saw you there."

This slut got me messed up. She better get out my face right now before I snatch that fake Li'l Kim outfit off her ass. I thought without responding to her comment.

"Were you the cashier there."

"Bitch, don't play me. What the hell do you want over here?"

"Excuse me, bitch, who you calling a bitch."

"You tramp," I roared, approaching her with a bottle of ketchup in my hand. "You know damn well you saw me at the sports bar," I confirmed, shooting the red paste all over her. She ran up on me and before I knew it, I had a hand full of yacky weave all in my hands. Kerwin grabbed me, but I wasn't letting go and once he gave me a solid yank to get us unhooked, I wasn't letting go, so her track came right along with me.

"Asia, chill," Kerwin fussed, grabbing my purse off the bench.

"How this tramp gon' play me?" I asked in my defense. "She knows who the hell I am."

"Be quiet, and let's bounce." I looked over at Melissa, and she was on her cell. I figured she was calling Alex, but at that point it didn't matter.

"If that's Alex, tell that nigga yo weave need replacing too, you slut."

Kerwin, got me in the car and tried to calm me down.

"Why would you do that?"

"I don't care about no image. How this hoe gon' play me? I ain't the one. She better recognize that right damn now."

"I'm sure she does."

"Good that means the next time she see me, she gon' check that fake ass weave at the door, or it's coming off again."

"You do got a little Tommy Hearns in you," Kerwin laughed. "Where you learn to squab like that?"

"Shut up. You was trying to make me get beat down, grabbing me like that. You should have grabbed her, so I could steal that gold digger in the face one good time."

"Relax, Rocky the round is over. You're the undesputed, One-Rip Weave Removing Champion of the world," He teased, humming the rocky theme song.

"I guess Alex will be at my place waiting."

"I'm not worried about him."

"If you say so."

"Why you be trying to play me like I'm a weak ass nigga?"

"I don't."

"You do, but you better ask somebody," he insisted.

Once we made it back to campus, I noticed Alex walking into my building just as I expected.

"There's your boy. What you wanna do? Do you want me to walk you in or do you want to chill at my spot for a while?"

"Do you mind if I come over?"

"A little, I'm s'posed to have a booty call jumping off after midnight, but let me call and see if I can cancel."

I'd been playing like I wasn't feeling Kerwin for so long that I actually believed that. Well that is until he mentioned that he had a booty call and I sensed some jealously on my behalf.

"Who you tryin' to go screw?"

"None of your b'iness."

"I thought we were homies, but I see you're keepin' secrets from your girl now."

"No secrets, I know it'll hurt your feelings if I tell you who it is."

"No it won't. Tell me."

"Kelly."

"Kelly! How you gon' get with that slut after you peeped her in the club this weekend?"

"Asia, Kelly's a chicken head, but she's also a pretty face. Like I said I ain't tryin' to make her my woman, but she is somethin' to do on days when I'm in need. I don't love her, and I most certainly don't care about seeing her out with yo man. Kelly knows where she stands with me. She knows she's a booty call. She respects the boundaries of or thang, and I like that."

"So why you keep goin' back?"

"No strings attached, and she likes to do some freak nasty shit to me that only the king of playboy can relate to."

"Oh so she's bringin' orgasms like old dudes getting' at the Playboy Mansion?" he cheezed real big. "Yeah Right! Give me a break."

"She might not be on that level, but she's bringing it."

"Fuck her! Don't tell me nothin' about that girl."

"You're the one who asked. See that's why I didn't tell you."

"Save it," I insisted, getting out of his car.

I made it to his apartment and it almost shocked me to see how much of a neat freak Kerwin was. *Now that's very out of character for an athlete.* I guess that particular quality about him never stood out to me because most of the time we spent together was in class, talking on the phone, eating, or at my place studying. It had just dawned on me that I'd never been in his apartment.

"Make yourself comfortable," he suggested, lifting his phone to his face. "Kelly, somethin' came up, I'm not gon' make it." He paused to listen, then replied. "I don't know how long it'll take. I'll holla at you tomorrow." She obviously didn't want to accept that, so she asked him another question. "I said, somethin' came up, if you want to hook-up tomorrow, call me, if not, see you around," he fussed, closing his flip phone.

"No strings, huh? Don't seem like that to me."

"Damn, I don't see why she thinks she deserves an explanation."

"Well, I understand."

"How?"

"She givin' you the ass, so that's why she feels like she does."

"That's all she's giving. We get down and then I send her on her way. I don't ever make her feel like there's more to us than a fuck. Ain't no kissin' no huggin', no convo, no nothing after the nut."

"Umm humm."

"I'm serious."

"Save it."

"That's real talk."

"Oh so you gon' tell me you get yo skeet on, then bounce?"

"Yeah, pretty much."

"Damn, you're a cold brother. All I can say is that I'm glad we're homies."

"Come on."

"Where are we going?"

"Just follow me."

Kerwin, walked back to his bedroom and I followed. As I looked at all the framed autographed photos of various athletes hangin' on his wall, my attention was distracted as he pitched his ball cap on a hook. *Wow his family must have some money, too,* I thought because I didn't know much about Kerwin's parents, but after seeing how he was living, I wanted to.

"Kerwin, tell me a little about your family."

"Tell you about my family for what?"

"No reason in particular, I was makin' small talk."

"There's not much to tell."

"Well it seems like there is."

"Why you say that?"

"Because look at you. You drive a Lexus SUV, you're a big name in the city as far as sports, your place is real cute, and you've got style."

"Dope Dealers have style too, but that doesn't change the fact that they do what they do to survive. For all you know my place may not have anything in this world to do with my parents."

"Well that's what I'm trying to find out."

"Not tonight. You're my girl and all, but I'm not one for tellin' my family business."

"Okay, I respect that. Maybe one day you'll tell me."

"And maybe one day I won't."

"Maybe you will."

"Maybe...."

"Okay Kerwin, that's fine. When you're ready to tell me, I'm interested in knowing."

We went back and forth with senseless bickering for thirty minutes. "Damn, Asia. It's almost three o'clock. I better get you home."

"Don't worry about it, I'll walk."

"That's not even an option."

"Why is it not an option?" I asked, easing forward to kiss his lips. I could see shock in his face, so to play down my actions, I grabbed my coat.

"Wait a minute, what was the kiss about?"

"I appreciate you. Your support today was what I needed. I have some things to deal with, regarding Alex. Your conversation helped me realize that."

"Not to sound like a hater, but I hope you gon' drop that nigga."

"Thanks again, I'll see you tomorrow in class," I stated, without answering his question.

As I walked from Kerwin's building over to mine, I could see him watching me from his living room window. *Alex must have checked to see if I was home, and then left,* I thought, entering my building because I didn't see his car in the parking lot.

Chapter 15
Call 911

I called Kerwin to let him know I'd made it in, but he didn't answer either of his phones. I stood by my door peering out the peephole like a peeping tom, waiting to see if I saw him come up the stairs to go to Kelly's apartment. Three minutes of waiting and looking got me an eye full, but it wasn't Kerwin. Kelly's door creaked open and out fell Alex. He was fixing his pants and slobbing her down with one last good night kiss. *Hell Naw! Hell Naw!................ Hell Naw! These fools done lost their damn minds. How he gon' come to my place of residence with this bullshit?* I flung open the door and stormed out.

"What the Hell is going on! Kel, have you lost your mind. I should crack you in yo damn mouth."

"Nah, I should crack you in yours." That's all she needed to say, I ran up on Kel and punched her so hard, I know she saw stars. She tried to fight back, but Alex pushed her to the side.

"Asia, chill out," Alex yelled, grabbing me by my hair. "I've been by here three times tonight. If you were on top of your game like you s'posed to be, then Kelly wouldn't be puttin' it down."

"Fuck both of y'all," I screamed, swinging at Alex. He pushed my hands down and gripped my neck like he was palming a baseball. "Let me go, I can't breathe you sorry bastard."

"Stop tryin' to jump bad then. You can't kick my ass. You need to take your l'il frail butt back in dat apartment foe I put in work. It ain't like you didn't know this was gon' happen."

"Get yo hands off of me," I struggled to speak because it felt like Alex was trying to break my neck. I know my face was turning red from limited oxygen, but Alex still wouldn't let go.

"I've wanted to do this since I saw yo ass out with that nigga some time ago. You think I'm a sucka or something? You givin' my pussy to that nigga?" He paused to wait for a reply. After none was given, he chocked me harder. "I know you hear me. You better answer....." he fussed, slightly releasing some of the pressure.

"I ain't fuckin' nobody," I replied, looking at Kelly who hadn't said anything in my defense. Finally, the door next to my apartment opened and it was Chawntese our dorm RA.

"Punk, I called 911. You got about one minute and then yo black ass is going to jail. Our hall monitors have you on video assaulting her, not to mention that you're trespassing because visitation hours are over. I suggest that you leave while you still have a chance."

"You suggest. Bitch, you need to mind your own damn b'iness. This between me and my woman. I don't give a damn about you callin' no police. By the time they get here, she gon' be dead anyway. Neither one of y'all don't know who you dealin with. If you don't want no problems, you better go back in yo apartment and shut the damn door'," he ordered, holding me by my arm.

"Let me go," I insisted, since the RA was in the hall.

"Shut up and let's go."

"I'm not going nowhere with yo crazy ass. You not about to take me out somewhere and kill me."

At that point I didn't have anything to loose. I started fighting Alex with everything I had. Kelly, somewhat spooked, I believe, went back into her apartment and closed the door. Alex punched me in my mouth and blood went gushing out everywhere. Immediately, I could feel my lip swelling like an air mattress. The next thing I know I had a fist in my side, and he was trying to force me down the stairs. By the time we made it down the first three steps, Chawntese had gone into her apartment and came back with a can of mace. Out of nowhere, she sprayed liquid all in Alex's face and mine too. He bent over rubbing his eyes, and I ran up the stairs coughing something fierce. Right then, Kerwin came up, noticed Alex trying to grab at me and went off. Kerwin yanked Alex up by his neck, and socked him so hard, spit and blood gushed out of his mouth as his teeth chattered. I was draped over the top step, so Chawntese pulled me into my apartment and locked us in.

"Nigga, how you gon' be over here hittin' on a woman. You want to fight somebody, fight me," Kerwin fussed, punching Alex in the jaw once again.

"You dead," Alex assured Kerwin, trying to fight back.

"Nigga you know where to find me. If you got a problem I'm right here everyday."

We were only in my place for a few seconds before there was a tapping sound echoing off my door. "Campus police, open up." I went to the door, lookin' like I'd been in the ring with Tyson. My face was bruised, my side was sore, my eye was black and rapidly swelling. I had scrapes and finger imprints on my neck from Alex choking me, and with all that, I was still scared to file a report on him.

"We've apprehended two young men in the hallway. Someone said one of them assaulted you. We're going to need you to make a positive ID and a statement."

"Okay," I responded, crying. I followed the officer out into the hallway and identified Alex.

"Yes, he's the one that did this to me officer," I confirmed, barely making eye contact with him.

"Asia, don't do this to me."

"Shut up!" I yelled, turning to walk away.

"Baby, I'm sorry. I was just trippin'. I thought you were fucking this nigga. I let my jealously get the best of me."

"Shut up, Alex. Fuck you! You don't care about nobody but yourself," I screamed, looking him dead in his somber eyes.

"Ms., please reframe from arguing with the suspect."

"Asia, you know I can't get caught up with these charges."

I ignored Alex, then turned once again to walk away. I knew he was on probation for getting caught with a bunch of drugs on him. As a matter of fact, Judge Horton told him if he came back before him anytime soon, he was gon' make sure he had time to think about his actions. *So be it, after the way that dirty bastard did me that nigga can serve the rest of his life and I wouldn't care.* I walked back into my apartment and closed the door behind me.

Chapter 16
Kerwin

After I locked myself in for the night, the only person who got in to see me was Kerwin. That's because shortly after everything jumped off, he called once he finished up with his police report as frantic as ever. "Are you okay, I'm on my way up?" When his call came in, all I remember is that I was so relieved to hear his voice. I was in a lot of pain, I couldn't call my family, and needed someone to be with me. My parents couldn't find out what transpired for anything. I knew they wouldn't be sympathetic to my situation, and my dad was certain to nut up on me because I'd gotten myself involved with such a looser.

When Kerwin knocked on the door, I stood behind it and slowly pulled it open. My apartment was dark, but the lighting from the hallway allowed him to capture a glimpse of my face.

"Shit, I can't believe that sorry nigga did this to you? Aw, hell naw Asia, I'm bout to get with ole' boy. He gon' pay for this. It's not cool to fight a lady. My mom's man did the same thing to her, until he finally killed her. I ain't with that."

"Kerwin, don't get involved."

"What the hell you mean don't get involved. I'm already involved. I beat that nigga down, so you know he gon' want to square off with me."

"I can't believe you fought him."

"You're my girl. I told you this was gonna happen. I know niggas like Alex. That's why I tried to get you to leave him alone."

"Well I didn't and I don't want to hear no I told you so. Lock the door and come in, if you're coming."

Kerwin, locked the door behind him and followed me to my room. He pulled back my comforter, fluffed my pillows, and then helped me ease into bed. I was so sore, I literally whined for over an hour.

"Asia, do you want to go to the hospital?"

"Ut'un. I'll be fine in the morning, just give me an icepack for my face."

"You need to let me call your father. I think someone in your family needs to know what went down just in case something happens to you throughout the night."

"Somethin' like what? Man, it was only a fight."

"That doesn't matter. Haven't you heard of people dying after they've been beat up?"

"Yeah, but I'm fine. Just get the ice like I asked and let me worry about when to tell my family."

"Yo, what's up with that? You snappin' on me like I did this."

"Sorry, I'm just in pain, and mad as hell about all of this."

After I apologized, Kerwin went and got me a baggie full of ice and wrapped it in a face cloth. He sat on the side of the bed, nursing my wounds for the longest and before I knew it, I was knocked out.

My alarm went sounding off at seven in the morning like always, but I knew I wasn't leaving my apartment. I rolled over looking for Kerwin, and there he was, snuggled in a chair, in the corner of my room, with covers pulled over his head. The sun was beaming through a space in my blinds right down in his face, so I guess that's why he'd taken shelter under the blanket.

"Kerwin!" I yelled, only to get no reply. "Kerwin!" I yelled a second time and there still was little to no movement.

"Yeah."

"Could you get me a glass of water?" I mumbled because my top lip felt as big as a ducks beak.

"What you say?"

"Water, could you get me some?" Kerwin, uncovered his face, stretched to revive himself from an uncomfortable nights rest, and peeled his body out of the chair.

"Damn!" he expressed, looking so compassionately at me.

"What?"

"Babe, you look bad."

"Just get the water."

"Sure, right away, Boss." When he returned from the kitchen, he also had aspirin in his hand. "Here, take these. You're gonna need them. Once your muscles settle and you recover from being in shock, you're gonna ache like hell."

"I already ache like hell."

"Well that means these are right on time." I opened my mouth then he plopped the pills on my tongue. I reached for the glass of water, slightly tilted my head to move the medicine to the back of my throat, and swallowed.

"Thanks."

"You're welcome," he replied, tenderly moving my hair from my face.

"Are you going to class today?" I asked.

"You want me to?"

"No."

"That's all you had to say. I'm here."

"Oh, and it's that easy?"

"Yep, for you it is."

Kerwin stayed with me that entire day. He catered to my every need and treated me like such a princess. With the degree of tender affection he gave while taking care of me, one would have thought I was his woman, not his home girl. Before he left that Tuesday morning to go get dressed for class, he fixed me some breakfast and jotted down a copy of my schedule so he could pick up my work.

"Asia, I'll be back in a little while. If I can, I'm gon' go by the classes we don't have together to see if your professors will let me pick up your assignments."

"Okay. Take my key. That way I won't have to get up when you come back."

Kerwin grabbed my key off the dresser and headed out. Seconds after he was gone, there was a knocking at my door. I knew Kerwin had the key, so I was certain it wasn't him. As much as he liked to play, I knew at that point in my life, he wouldn't make me get up. When I headed for the door, I yelled "Who is it," a few times, but no one responded. *I know Alex isn't out,* I thought, easing my face forward to look out the peephole. *Kelly, Oh ut'un. What does she want.* Once I saw her face, I didn't bother to answer.

"Asia, I know you're in there. I just wanted to say I'm sorry and see if you needed anything." *No this back stabber didn't say she's sorry.* I eased away from my door and walked back to my room, never bothering to answer.

I made sure I spent the first few days after the incident in my apartment. Nikki came down to check on me that next morning, but I didn't let her in either. *I know that sorry trick heard me screaming for dear life last night, but didn't want to get involved out of her loyalty to Terrell,* I thought, looking her dead in her eye out my peephole. I didn't want her or anyone else to see me in the condition I was in. I knew females and I knew how much they talked. There was no way I was going to give Nikki a sneak peek at me so she could go back down the hall and tell Terrell what a hot mess I looked with my two black eyes and swollen fat lips.

Chapter 17
Friend or Foe

Some of everyone was talking about my little altercation for weeks. With as much discussion as Asia Prince was getting about the ass kicking I'd taken, I was so surprised that the apartment manager or one of the school officials didn't come by to check on me or call my parents. Once my swelling went down, I decided to return to class. To hide the after effects of two black eyes, I rocked this pair of Cartier sunglasses my father had gotten me until they were damn near played out.

Nikki tried to come around and be all up in my face, talking about how concerned she was for me, but I just kept it real.

"Bitch, where were you the night Alex was kickin' my ass, and I screamed out in pain until the RA came out to save me."

"What, Chawntese had to come out?"

"Hell yeah, and thank God she did," I confirmed as she tried to pretend like she didn't understand why I was so angry. That was just her style though, trying to run game, but most certainly on the wrong damn person.

"Asia, I didn't hear you."

"Nikki, I got you. I know you didn't want to get involved because Terrell's was down there with you. He probably told you to mind yo own business and because you so gone for that nigga, you followed his instructions."

"Not true."

"Well, if I'm yo girl, why didn't you come help me out?" Nikki started looking crazy, and refused to respond.

"Exactly! Just what I thought, you can't say nothin' because you heard me."

"I promise I wasn't here."

"Where were you then? If you can't tell me, get the hell out my face because as far as I'm concerned we're not the friends I thought we were."

"Asia, don't do this."

"You ain't no better than Kelly. And the sad part about it all is that we been girls way longer than Kel and I."

"I know. That's why I wouldn't dis you like that."

"Whatever. You need to get out my face and move around."

Nikk walked on to class. I could tell she wanted to come up with a logical explanation as to why she couldn't tell me where she was that night, but I wasn't giving her an opportunity to manipulate me. *Such as life, if she's s'posed to be so loyal to me and my home girl like she claims, she would have come correct.*

The same day, Nikk and I had words, there was also a basketball game on campus that evening. There was no question that I was going to be front and center. Kerwin was starting and nothing was gon' keep me from supporting my boy. I walked up in the gym after the first ten minutes of the game, and all eyes shifted from the players to me. I already felt awkward being at the game alone, so the stares made me extremely uncomfortable. I usually sat way up in the bleachers with my girls, but since I was by myself, I sat right behind the team. Immediately, Kerwin noticed me and winked, motioning with his mouth, "Hey beautiful." For some odd reason, I blushed like I was his girl and then quickly looked behind me to see who else might have seen him.

Kelly was about twenty rows up from me, and waved when our eyes met. *No she didn't just try to taunt me. I see right now I'm gon' have to beat that trick down real good before it's all said and done.* Suddenly, my thoughts were interrupted by the buzzing of the game clock. I turned back around and tried to enjoy the game. As we took the lead, I cheered, I screamed, I cheered, and screamed some more. By the time the first period was over, the score was close, but we were in the lead. My boy had twenty points and seven assists. I don't know if those were good stats, but I was proud of him.

While watching the halftime show, my cell started vibrating. I looked at the ID, but it wasn't a number I knew.

"Hello," I answered.

"Hey Boo."

"Alex!"

"Yeah, I see you decided to come out and participate in yo' nigga's activities tonight. Hope you're enjoyin' the game."

"What are you doing here, you've been banned from the campus?"

"CJ on the other team. I thought I'd come out and support my boy, since I hadn't seen him in a while. You miss me?"

"Screw you! "Lose my number, and don't ever call me again!" I ranted, hanging up in his face. I immediately started scanning the crowd to locate him because I was too spooked to leave the gym alone. I also figured after hanging up on him, he might become angry or call right back. I was right. My phone started vibrating.

"What!"

"I'm sorry about the other day and in spite of what you think, I really do love you."

"You sick ass psychopath, you don't know what love is. Get you some help and stop harassing me."

"Asia, I am sorry. Just accept my apology before you hang up. That way I know you at least forgive me."

"I don't forgive you, now stop callin' me! And it better not be any problems after the game or else."

"Or else what?"

"Try me and see."

"I ain't here on no nonsense. I got more respect for CJ than that."

"Goodbye."

"Wait."

"What?"

"You know I'm gon' have to do some time. They found drugs on me at the police station that night."

"Sounds like a personal problem," I stated, hanging up again.

Because I was afraid, after hanging up on Alex a second time, I dialed the first five digits to my father's cell number. After considering what my dad might do or say in his fit of rage, I immediately hung up. I sat forward on the bench with an uneasy look on my face, waiting for Kerwin to come back out.

Suddenly, the announcer came on, "Everybody on your feet. Here comes our Tigers." My mood was ruined, so I stayed seated while the crowd went nuts. I could hear women screaming Kerwin's name and making comments about him. *Please, he don't want none of y'all,* I smirked. But since I wasn't his woman, my smirks didn't raise one eyebrow.

Once the opponents came back out, I immediately noticed CJ. Actually, I' saw him before the game and thought he looked familiar, but because I'd only met him once, his face didn't jog my memory until Alex told me why he was there. I didn't know if CJ was going to try to start something with Kerwin after I realized who he was, so I was on pins and needles from the start of the second period until the game was over. CJ pushed and shoved Kerwin a few times, but fortunately no fight broke out. The fifteen minutes that made up that half, seemed like an eternity. Once it was over, the players shook hands, and before Kerwin went to the dressing room, he told me to wait. He didn't have to worry. I had no intention on leaving that gym without him.

As he made his way to the locker room to change, I stayed in my seat. After some minutes the gymnasium started to thin out. Kelly, who appeared to be waiting for the area to lighten up some, came down the bleachers with Leslie who was now her new best friend.

"What's up, Asia?"

"Not you."

"I see you're still pissed about me and Alex."

"Nope not at all. I see you stoop to all levels when you feel like you need to take care of Kell's needs." I frowned, looking at Leslie.

"I really don't care about you going behind me. What I'm salty about is that we were girls and you showed me what kind of hoe you really were when he was beating my ass."

"Hoe, let's not go there. You knew what I was about from day one."

"You're right, but I thought kickin' it with me would refine your rat ass a bit. Oh, but I see I was wrong."

"How you gon' refine me? Bitch, please. You can't be serious."

"I was, but I guess it takes more than poison to kill some rats."

"You're a rat too."

"What do you want Kelly?"

"Just to say for whatever it's worth, I'm sorry. Sleeping with Alex wasn't personal, it was business."

"Yeah, you are sorry, and I hope your business was worth our friendship." I said, getting up to go meet Kerwin who was coming through the door. "You ready," I yelled, winking at her because I knew she wanted him.

"Oh, so that's how it is, Asia?"

"Not at all. The difference between me and you is that me fuckin' around with Kerwin ain't business, it's personal." *Now tramp, how you like a little taste of your own medicine,* I thought, walking away.

"Kerwin, so that's how it is?" Kelly, asked as I met up with him.

He didn't even acknowledge her. Once I was by his side, he cupped my hand in his and led me out the building. While walking to his SUV, Kelly and her girl looked on hatin'. *Had Kell been as nosey as I was, she would have learned long before today that Kerwin and I were hanging out on some cupcake shit. A peephole can expose you to a lot of things. You just got to use it to your advantage.*

Right before I got in the truck, I noticed her making her way over to Alex and C.J., who were a few feet away talking. I don't think he got a chance to see me, but I hurried myself into the truck before she got something started. *Ump, so she knows C.J. too,* I thought as I caught a glimpse of him warmly embracing her. *So Alex had C.J. around all his women, not just the main one. Damn shame he had me out there looking like a fool. Men make me sick, grinning in yo face like they all about you, and then they be on some real BS. I can't stand niggas, they some sorry dogs.*

"So, what you think about your boy tonight?" Kerwin asked, pulling out of his parking space and smiling like a kid.

"What I think about what?"

"Don't trip. What you think about my game?"

"I mean, you got mad skillz. I think you did real well for your last game of the semester, and I know when it's all said and done, you're going to the league."

"I think I'm gon' go after this year."

"What! Boy, are you crazy? I think you should get a degree first."

"Degree! I ain't gon' need no degree. Girl, I'm gon' have so much money it's gon' be a shame."

"Well, that's my opinion. You asked, so I told you."

"Naw, I didn't ask you what you thought about me going to the league, I asked you what you thought about my game."

"You can't ask a woman to speak on part of a question without thinking she ain't gon' give you her complete outlook on the rest of the conversation."

"Yeah, I did."

"Newsflash! Boo-Boo, ladies just don't operate like that."

"Naw, you just don't operate like that. There are some females who will only answer what you ask them."

"Do you like women like that?"

"Not really. I like women like you," he replied, leaning forward to kiss me on the forehead.

"That spots reserved for my daddy. He's kissed me there all my life."

"So what about here?" he asked, kissing my cheek.

"Nope, that's my Uncle E's."

"Well right here bet not belong to nobody with as much time as I've put in over the past few weeks," he replied, tenderly biting my lips.

"They might," I smiled as he kissed me.

"Whatever, they bet not."

I never told Kerwin about the call from Alex that day. I didn't want to get him involved or stirred up. I knew with as close as we'd gotten, he'd be trying to fight my battles. With Alex being the kind of nut he was, I didn't want to put Kerwin in that position again.

...♦♦♦...

The following week was finals. Kerwin and I studied together like always. However, after spending all that time together the week he nursed me back to good health and the kiss he put on me the week before, my feelings for him were starting to change. Staying focused on just our friendship became very hard. I knew I wasn't ready for a relationship, but I didn't want anyone else to have him. Kerwin tried to talk about us being together a few times, but I refused to go there.

"When we come back from winter break, you gon' be my woman?"

"Winter break is a whole month. When I come back to Detroit, you'll be chasing some new hottie."

"The only hottie I want is you. You're so different from all these other females out here. I'm crazy about you, Asia. If you give me a chance, I'll show you what a woman really deserves from her man."

"I don't want to be with anyone right now Kerwin. Plus, we're so cool, if we go there, we'll only destroy our friendship."

"No we won't. See that's the problem with so many relationships now. People don't become friends before they become lovers. They jump each others bones, fuck like rabbits for a few years, and then when it's all said and done, they discover that there's no real substance in their relationship."

"That may be true, but we're way too cool. I know all your dirty secrets and you know mine. I know you like to tip out, get yo dick sucked from whoever, and be out all hours of the night pushing up in somebody."

"I told you too much, huh?" he asked, laughing. "Yeah, well, I know about you creeping around with that old ass nigga Mauri that you met in your father's store, so what's up with that."

"I told you that?"

"Umm, humm."

"Yep, see, that's why we'd never trust each other."

"Let's just see what happens and go from there. I'd treat you right, if you gave me the chance."

"What makes me any different from any ole other piece of meat on the yard?"

"You got the complete package, and I'm feelin' you."

"What's the complete package?"

"It's different for every man, but for me. I love a woman with sex appeal. She's got to have personality, some class, be intelligent, have some pretty legs, thick thighs, ass for days, a beautiful face is a must, understand the importance of love, and be about her b'iness."

"So why is a beautiful face a must?"

"What nigga do you know in college that cares about much more? Asia, I got game, much sense, major contacts, a fresh ride, and I'm bout to have long money. The only thing I'm lacking is a fine woman that I can love to make my ticket complete."

That was the way our conversation ended that night. After we finished studying, Kerwin spent the night, but instead of trying to get some of my goodies, he made love to my mind. That chump pulled me up under him, tenderly cuddled me, which is just what I needed, then told me all the things I wanted to hear. He was doing just what I had once told Alex he needed to do, allow himself to establish an intimate relationship with my intellect not just my   P-hole.

"Asia, baby, there are days when I leave you and can't sleep because you invade my thoughts. One thing I'm not gon' ever take for granted is you and what we share. If I could have things my way right now, you'd be mine. Take your time, get to know me. I'm not going to apply any pressure, just don't make me wait too long because eventually, I'll grow impatient." he whispered, pulling me closer. "Then I'm going for the next cutie that gets my interest."

"Oh, and who is that?"

"Leslie," he laughed.

"That slut ain't even about to keep your attention. Once all your NBA homies catch a glimpse of that big nose, they gon' tease you for the rest of your life about not only havin' an ugly chick, but also for havin' one whose ankles could be mistaken for a ham hocks."

"Shut up," he laughed, snuggling into the pillow I was lying on. *Umm, this boy is so soft. Damn he smells good, too. Asia, girl, if you don't get on this man and let him be a part of your life, I'm gon' slap you myself.* **Don't listen to your heart Asia, it's being vulnerable right now. Who are you trying to kid? You know you ain't ready to be in love again, move on,** my brain insisted.

"Asia, did I tell you how sexy you were with your blood shot eyes."

"Shut up. That's not funny."

"I wasn't trying to be funny. I was paying you a real compliment."

"Oh, so you think my black eyes are gorgeous?" I asked, feeling special.

"Nope, not at all," he grinned.

"Thanks for your honesty, but that's still not funny with your ignorant self."

"Don't play, you know it was kind of funny."

"No it's wasn't."

"Sorry, Smoochie face, give me kisses," he teased.

"Ut'un, that's so gay. Get out my bed," I demanded, wrapping my arms around him.

Chapter 18
Can't Get Enuff 2003

When I went to Chicago for Christmas, Kerwin and I talked everyday until I was due back in Detroit. I had a flight booked to return on New Years Eve, but my father and Teretta were going out that night. I called Kerwin to let him know I needed a ride, so he ended up getting me from the airport. Fortunately, he'd just gotten back in town himself from a basketball tournament in Ohio, so he didn't have any plans for the evening.

"You sure you don't mind picking me up?"

"Asia, it's Tuesday, I ain't tryin' to party on no Tuesday."

"Kerwin, you'll party any day."

"I might party if you weren't comin' home, but I'd rather see you, if that's okay."

"It is," I quickly answered because I'd grown sweet on him over the break.

"So what you want to do tonight?"

"Surprise me. Let me see how creative you are."

"Surprise you?"

"Yeah, surprise me. Anything you plan, I'm wit it."

"Right you are."

"I'm serious. Sometimes I'm very spontaneous. Everything I do ain't always planned. So like I said, surprise me."

"Well Asia, I only got a few hours to plan one hell of an evening, so I gots to go."

"What you gon' do?"

"None of your business."

"Bye silly."

I got off the phone with Kerwin and hurried Mom along. She was trying to be all in my video, but I didn't provide her with much information on my college heartthrob. All the way to the airport, she was trying to pump me for info so she could go back to tell my dad, but I wasn't talking.

"Thanks for the ride. I'm glad I got to see you guys. I was really missing your cooking."

"If you miss us so much, why don't you try coming home a little more often? I still love you, and Rodney has also forgiven you for the little incident that happened right before you left."

"Oh, here we go. Thanks for the ride, Mom. See you this summer," I responded, getting out of the car.

I think my blunt response saddened Mom a little, but I couldn't feel real sympathetic for her at the time. I guess it was a phase I was going through. The so grown phase, you know, a college student, slash teenager who still couldn't be told anything. I wasn't that out cold though, so before I went to check in, I walked around to the driver's side of the car and leaned in to kiss my mom.

"Love you so much, Mommy. I know in time, we're going to be tight again."

"Yeah, sometimes I hate you ever grew up."

…◆◆◆…

When my plane touched down at Detroit Metro, it couldn't pull up to the gate fast enough. I unfastened my seatbelt long before the plane stopped and as soon as the seat belt light beeped, I sprung up out of my seat like a woman on a mission. Down the terminal, to baggage claim, Kerwin stayed on my mind. *Umm, I see this nigga got in yo heart over the break. You weren't s'posed to let your guard down like this and now you're about to be caught slipping,* my brain fussed……*But……so what,* my heart confirmed after a slight pause, *he makes me feel special and that's what I like.*

I got to the carrousel, snatched my first bag, and when I went to reach for my second one, a hand rested on top of mine and pulled with me.

"Got it, let go," Kerwin insisted.

"You're late. How you gon' let me get here with no one to greet me?"

"I didn't."

"Yes you did. When I got down here you were no where to be found."

"I stood right over there by the restrooms and watched you look for me. I wanted to see if you were as anxious to see me as I was to see you."

"How does observing me tell you how anxious I am?"

"Because if you look, and look, and look that means you really want to see me."

"So was I doing that?" I asked, grinning.

"You already know the answer," he replied, kissing me.

"Who said you could kiss me in public?"

"Your smile did."

"My smile?"

"Yeah, it was flirtin' with me."

"You say some crazy stuff."

"Good, get that big bag and come on." He insisted, walking off with the smaller of my two.

"I know you're playing," I fussed, struggling with the heavier one.

"Say you missed me, and I'll take it. If you don't, then a homie like me will let you pull the biggest bag cuz I ain't got nothing to prove to my Dawg."

Ooooooo he thinks he's so smart. I can't stand him. "Okay, you're right, I missed you," I admitted.

"That's what I thought," he teased, grabbing the other bag as well. I followed Kerwin out the door, and then he came to a screeching halt.

"What you stoppin' here for?"

"Just wait and see. Part one of your surprise begins now. Close your eyes."

"Close my eyes. Man, I'm not closing my eyes. I don't trust you like that."

"Dang Girl, be quiet for once and close your eyes. You always want to argue with someone."

"No I don't."

"See there you go."

I briefly closed my eyes and when I opened them again, there was a stretched Bentley parked right before me. The chauffeur was standing tall with the door already open and his hand extended to assist me in the car.

"Wow Kerby, is this a Bentley?"

"Yep."

"Man where you get the money to rent a car like this on the biggest holiday of the year?"

"Don't be all up in mine, just enjoy yourself. You deserve it."

"I can't believe this."

"Well, get used to it. I'm gon' make you my woman and when I do, this is how you gon' be living everyday. As soon as the commissioner puts that hat on my head, Baby this is us."

"I'm not even bout to act like you takin' me to the NBA with you as your woman, but if you say so, I'll play the role for tonight."

"Get in and stop talkin' before you kill the moment," he fussed.

I laughed, easing myself into the car because I didn't know what else to do. *A Bentley, Damn, I know I said surprise me, but this boy went all out.*

"So do you like my surprise?" he asked, interrupting my thoughts.

"Yes! I feel so special," I answered, watching the driver put my bags in the trunk.

"You are."

"So how did you get this? Did Dave rent it for you?

"Why you think Dave rented this?"

"He's the only one with long money that could afford something like this for us."

"You're wrong. Some Alum from the university got it for me."

"Alumni, yeah right."

"Seriously, Alum take real good care of star athletes."

"For real! I didn't know that."

"Why should you. You ain't got no kind of skillz to ever find out."

"That's what you think."

"What kind?" He asked, scooping me in his arms.

"I can show you better than I can tell you."

"So show me."

"You want to take me on one-on-one?"

"Hell yeah," Kerwin admitted, pushing me back with his body to kiss me.

"You didn't ask me for a kiss," I stated, interrupting him.

"You told me to surprise you, right?"

"Umm, yeah."

"Well let me do me, and stop all that damn talkin'." I could feel my legs shaking like crazy. I hadn't been close like that with any man but Alex. "Baby, relax, and try to enjoy the evening."

"I am relaxed."

"No you ain't. I feel you shaking."

"You do?"

"Yeah, and you know what?"

"What?"

"I want to make love to you so bad."

"What!" I quickly asked, leaning forward.

"You heard me, I said I want to make love to you."

"We can't go there. We're friends. I tell you everything. Besides, you know too much about me for us to venture there."

"That's what's gonna make us good for each other. You know me and I know you."

"I don't know about that. I'm nervous about this already."

"Why? I make you feel good when were together, don't I?"

"Yeah, but you're my boy. We're like brothers and sisters"

116

"Nah, we ain't no brothers and sisters, but with the way I feel about you, I'm prepared to be homie, lover, friends."

"But,"

"Shhhh, Asia, who cares about being homies these days? Hell, I don't."

I started laughing because he was so serious. That boy was really trying hard to talk me out of my decision to maintain our friendship. I relaxed, trying to go with the flow, suddenly, his cell chirped. *Damn, what a life saver.*

"Hello." He answered some what irritated. "Oh, hey Steve, what up, yo? I was gon' call you tomorrow to wish you a Happy New Year.... Yeah, I'm out with this little bad honey celebrating the holiday..... Is she fine? Man are you kiddin' me, Asia Prince is the baddest female on the yard... Oh yeah, my grades were tight.. Okay, I'll be looking for it.... Yeah, I might try to make a few games after our season ends. I'll let you know, I might want to bring my girl. Will that be cool?..... Okay. One."

"Who was that?"

"Steve Burtt."

"Who is that."

"He's like my mentor. We've been friends every since I played in one of his summer leagues."

"Is he a coach at one of the schools here?"

"Nah, he's the head coach for the And1 Street Basketball Franchise."

"Um....Stop lying."

"I ain't got to lie. What I'm gon' lie for?"

"To make a sista think you all that."

"You already know I'm all that, so why I got to stunt?"

"You don't, so why he call you?"

"He wants me to come out to a few games. I told him I would if I could bring you."

"Me?"

"Yeah, will you go?"

"Are you serious? I ain't never been on no trip with no guy before."

"Well get ready to be exposed to some real fine shit? So you want to go?"

"I'd love to," I replied, thinking he might really be feeling a sista after all. "Kerwin, where are we going?"

"Just ride. I got everything all planned. If I tell you, I'll spoil the surprise, and then I'll have to kill you."

Just ride might have been the ideal thing for him to say, but it was torturous to me. I was like a kid when it came to surprises. I didn't do well. I looked over at Kerwin a few times, then scooped his hand into mine to tenderly massage his fingers. *I wonder if he thinks he's gon' really get some tonight? Shoot, if he kisses me like he just did one more time, I might just have to give in. Naaaaaaaah, I better stick with my "No" because he don't realize how good my stuff really is.*

"Asia,"

Don't he know if I give him some of the kitty cat, he'll be walking around here purring like Sylvester and stalking me like my name is Tweety.

"Asia," Kerwin repeated, interrupting my thoughts.

"What," I jumped, "You scared me."

"We're here."

"We're here! What's this?" I asked, gawking at a building I'd never seen before.

"Just get out. Harold we'll be in here about three hours. I'll call you when I'm ready to be picked up." Harold helped me out of the car. "Thanks Man, here you go," Kerwin stated, giving him a tip.

I was a little hesitant about going into the building, but once inside, I was amazed. There were candles everywhere, and a long hallway, which led to a set of French doors.

"Is this someone's house?" I asked.

"Umm humm."

"Whose?"

"Mine."

"Sure it is."

"It is. This is Dave's house, but while he's out of town, I live here on the weekends."

"Shut up. This is the bomb."

"You like it?"

"Hell yeah. But..............," I paused.

"But what?"

"If we're so cool and talk about everything, why you didn't tell me about this place."

"I don't tell you everything."

"I see you don't."

"Only the important things."

"Good answer, Slickster."

"You don't tell me all your business, do you?" he asked.

"Almost."

"Almost is not all, so we're even."

We went back and forth with that for as long as we could. Finally, Kerwin told me to close my eyes. Once I did, he led me the rest of the way down the hall. We made it to the double doors then stopped. I could hear him twist the handle and wanted to peek, but I went along with the program for a change. Once it was opened, we started to move. We walked a little further and stopped once again.

"Okay, open your eyes."

"Oh my God……….. Kerwin, are you for real?" I asked, hugging him.

There was an elegant table next to this super king sized bed. *Damn this mug is like a bed for Shaq.* On it sat a card, a nicely decorated box, some roses, and a bottle of champagne. A lavish teddy was also draped over the chair that only a highly paid bitch could appreciate. Shoot, I knew it was expensive because of the designer's name. It was one I couldn't even pronounce, but most of all, I knew it cost some grip because the price tag was still on it. *$400.00, Shiiiii…t. Ain't no way in hell I'm paying that kind of money for something that's gon' cover a coochie for every bit of fifteen minutes. For this kind of money, that dang piece of cloth better make my stuff smell April fresh and it better self clean after my man gets him some.*

"Open the box, Asia," I heard a voice fading in to suggest. I opened the box and went nuts. It was a diamond necklace, with a matching bracelet. "Merry Christmas, you like it?"

"Do I like it, are diamonds a girls best friend?"

"I'll take that as a yes."

"Oh Kerwin, this is so nice. Thank you so much," I said, looking a little funny.

"No problem, what's wrong."

"Man, I feel so bad."

"Why? You don't want your gift." *Are you stupid,* I thought.

"No that's not it. I don't have a gift for you. I didn't know you were going to get me something for Christmas."

"Baby, I didn't get you this gift to necessarily get something in return. But if you want to give me something, you can be my lady for the evening."

"Be your lady? Are you for real?"

"Very."

"Oh, I don't know about that Kerwin. I'm just not ready."

"It's just for the evening. What's that gonna hurt?"

"I'm not ready."

"Not for one night. What's it gon' hurt?"

"I…"

"Okay, I'm not gon' beg. I don't want you to feel pressured, but you gon' keep telling me no, and I'm gon' be on a new mission."

I knew Kerwin was right. I also knew I didn't want to see him with anyone else. *Quit playing Asia before you lose on this one.* I tried to talk some sense into myself, but for some reason, my ego wasn't listening.

"With all your credentials, I know you got tricks throwin' it at you every day. Like I said, I ain't ready, so I guess I'll deal with you jettin' on me when that happens, but for now, I think we better go."

"Go," Kerwin repeated, easing up on me. "If you don't want to be my lady, that's one thing, but we're still homies, so we might as well make the best of this night."

"Best of what?"

"This," he said and pushed a button. Doors started moving, floors started revolving, and before I knew it, a fireplace with two burning logs appeared, along with a jumbo Jacuzzi in this oversized bathroom. It was so big that it looked like a mini house itself. *Damn!!!! Dave living like this, ugly or not, I should have been on that brotha.*

"So what's all this?"

"It's your surprise. You like it?" he asked, putting on a song he had his boys Cardier and Caznova do just for me called *Can't Get Enuff.* "I had two of my boys from the block make this song just for you. They finished it up in the studio about an hour before I picked you up." *Damn I'm getting songs made just for me, too. Oh Asia, you're a Bad Mama Jamma.*

Kerwin, pressed the repeat button and started in with the words of the song…. "*Ooooooo Baby, O….I can't get enuff.*" I couldn't help but smile as he continued. "*Shorty, I can't get enuff of your style, and your whole profile, you got me vexed off the way that you smile...*" I looked at him cheezin' from ear to ear. This man had gone all out for me. I never experienced anything like it, which is why I was confused and wondered if I was doing the right thing. He was so charming, but I wondered if I should resist him for the sake of our friendship. When I looked at those delicious juicy lips of his, it was a wrap for me.

"Come here, Sexy" he whispered, moving his head in this sensual manner. "Let me hold you." I zoomed in on that bottom lip a second time, which was as enticing as juicy ripe strawberries. *Umm, I could bite off into that,* I lusted, licking my lips and moving towards him.

"Yes?"

Kerwin, tenderly stroked my face, allowing his hands to flow from my brows, softly down my cheeks, past my lips, over my shoulder, to the sides of my breast, down my waist, my hips, my thighs, around to my ass, and up my back again. *Lawd this man is turning me on. I have never been so passionately touched by anyone in my life. But I can't be feeling this way.*

"Asia," Kerwin, mumbled in my ear.

"Huh."

"I want you."

"Huh," I repeated as my eyes rolled up in my head.

"Get in the Jacuzzi with me," he suggested, biting my cheek.

At that point it didn't take much. I pulled off my sweater and jeans, stripping down to my sheer panties and bra. I walked over to the Jacuzzi, taking off my undergarments in route and stepped up, and then down into the bubbling water. I smiled as I caught a glimpse of Kerwin's face. Once he realized that I was coming out of my gear, he locked in on my gap and studied it like a hawk. I guess he thought I wasn't going to honor his request, but there was no denying it, his charm had won me over.

Shortly after, he got butt ass naked in a matter of seconds. I watched him walk towards me and damn near swallowed my tongue after realizing just how big and thick his dick was. *Shoot, he's flopping around here like Mr. Ed with his horse dick. I know he don't think he about to drive all that up in here.*

"What'cha looking at?" he asked. I was too stunned at what I'd seen to reply. He made his way in the water and I think the way the bubbles formed around my breast turned him on. Before I knew it, my titties were in his mouth. He sucked and bit down on them causing me to flinch. I could feel my coochie getting hot, when suddenly this wet, gushy, slipperiness immediately took over. Kerwin, rubbed his finger across my cat, delicately swooshing his fingers around on my clit, and then inside my vagina.

"Ohhh, Baby," I moaned, pulling him towards me because I was ready to feel him deep thrusting me. Finally, he straddled me, feeling somewhat passionate. Cupping my face with his Mandingo power, Kerwin eased his soft tongue in my mouth, kissing me hard. *This nigga actin' like there's no tomorrow. Umm, Umm, there should be a law against a man making a woman feel so good. He got to hurry up and get some of this before I scream.*

Out of the water I came as my body was propped up on the side of the Jacuzzi. Kerwin bit inside of my thighs, nibbled down sort of hard close to my vaginal lips. Once my legs started trembling like crazy, it was then that I realized he was about to eat me up like an exotic Caribbean fruit. He grabbed my frame, flipping me over on all four and propped me up on the ledge. Delicately grabbing my ass cheeks, he slowly spread them apart, then rubbed his finger up and down my crack. *I hope he don't think he about to pound off in there. That's an exit only hole.*

"Damn, Asia you're wet. *Seems like you're ready,*" he mumbled.

"I am, baby," I moaned, hunching my back because he buried his face in my ass. *Oh hell-to-da-naw. I know this nigga ain't eating my ass. Damn... I thought only Alex was up on nat. Ut'* I jumped. *Is that his tongue up inside my dook-shoot. This boy's tongue feels like a wet, thick suppository. Dang, I kind of like it though. Shi....t, this nigga got to love me fa'sho to be licking my ass like this,* I thought, getting mad when I realized that my adversary might have been his tutor. *Freaky ass Kell must have taught him and Alex about dat there move cuz they skillz are to similar when it comes to this.* Suddenly juices slid down my leg. Kerwin, rotated his body, lifted my legs to his shoulders, and put in some serious work. *Ummm, it's about to go down like that? Right here in the Jacuzzi. I think I'd prefer the bed over this. Shut up, Asia, and just go with the flow,* my conscience fussed. *You was up in her freak nasty just a second ago and now you trying to get all conservative. Tramp please.*

"Huuuuuuu," I gasped for dear life, digging my nails in Kerwin's back. "Ooo Kerby," I whispered as he eased deep inside of me. Banging my walls like an African Drum, he beat, and beat, and beat, and beat. "You ready to cum?" He asked. I tried to answer, but he was so big that I repeatedly gasped for air like I was asthmatic. For the longest I tried to tell him how good he was. But at times, I couldn't get nothing out. "Oo.... Ker... tha... fee," I moaned as farts, erupted out of nowhere due to the air slithering inside me from each of Kerwin's long strokes. Shoot, by the time we finished, my lips were dry, my mouth was dry, my stuff was worked out, and Kerwin had brought it so tuff that he had me walking around slow and gapped legged for the rest of the week. *Hell, That's what I'm talking about. Kerwin better watch out cuz from this point forward, I'm claiming him. Alex ain't gon' ever stand another chance after today.*

That following Friday morning, I had to be in court for Alex's sentencing. He'd already gone through his preliminary stuff and was about to hear his fate. Kerwin went with me. Alex looked over at us with his cold eyes a few times, but I don't particularly know what he was thinking. However, if looks could kill, I'd be dead.

"Jury, have you reached a verdict," the judge asked.

"Yes."

I knew Alex was going to serve time for probation violation, but he also went down for assaulting me. Alex was sentenced to serve five to fifteen years. At first that didn't seem like enough time for all that he'd done, but after considering the fact that any kind of isolation, which exceeded five minutes, is cruelty to anyone, I was satisfied with his punishment.

"Asia, I was always about you," Alex yelled, being led away in shackles. I flipped him off, trying not to give him much eye contact because I knew his sad eyes would make me feel bad for him.

Chapter 19
Eye For An Eye

In mid spring 2003, basketball season ended with Kerwin stat's off the chart. He was a super star at the college, and once talk about him going to the league started to spread across the city, gold diggers of all ages were on him tuff. That got on my nerves since the two of us were dating hot and heavy. I remember right before he went to the league, we were at a Camouflage Party. I was looking hella cute on my man's arm in my Cami hook-up and the females were hating. I was giving the party goers much cleavage as I rocked the cut up Cami jacket, which stopped right below my breast. It had these stylish buttons I'd special ordered from the fabric store, and my fitted low riders had nigga's mad thirsty. This one tramp walked up on Kerwin as if I was invisible.

"Ain't you Kerwin Phillips?" she asked, grabbing his dick right in my face.

"Yeah," he grinned, peeking over at me to see if I saw what she'd done. As she leaned in to whisper something in his ear, I was furious. *I know she seen us walk up in here hand in hand, so she knows he's with me,* I thought before getting ignorant.

"Back the hell up," I growled, pushing her face away from his ear. "You ain't 'bout to disrespect me like dat."

"Asia, chill," Kerwin insisted. As I looked to respond to his comment, she, grabbed my jacket, ripping off the two little buttons that held my breast secure, and tits went spilling out like a stuffed sack of potatoes. Brotha's got an eyeful that evening, Kerwin was a little embarrassed, but by the time they got me up off of that chick, she was wishing she'd stepped to someone else's man.

"How you gon' come up in here and blow your cool like that?" Kerwin asked.

"How you gon' let that bitch disrespect me like that? Do you know her or something?"

"We used to mess around in high school."

"So is that why you let her disrespect me like that."

"Taylor is out cold like that, but she knows I ain't got nothin' for her. Besides, I was about to handle the situation."

"Yeah right you were. That's why you looked over at me like you did when she grabbed your dick, right?"

"You didn't give me a chance to say anything, Tommy. You just got ill and came in swingin'."

"Tommy?"

"Tommy Hearns, come on now babe. He's one of Detroit's very own."

"I know who he is," I sassed. "I do got a mean right hook?" I bragged, smiling.

"Sure do baby. I ain't never gon' tick you off," he teased.

"Shut up. Nothin' like this bet not ever happen again."

"I was about to tell you the exact same thing, roughneck. If you gon' be my lady, you gon' have to be that lady I fell in love with. Shoot I don't want no snag-a-tooth woman."

"Snag-a-tooth?"

"Yeah, you keep scrappin' like that and one day you might get stole on."

"Whatever. Boy, I'm a Prince. I thought you already knew."

"You're a lady as well, and I want you to act like one."

Kerwin and I snapped on each other a little about that incident, but in the end we were back to ourselves in no time.

...◆◆◆◆...

So much had happened over the months and of all people to be missing, I was missing my girl Nikk. To be the bigger woman, I thought I should go on and end the beef between the two of us. And, since I had really started the fight to begin with, I thought I should be the person to resolve it.

Late one Friday evening, I walked down to her apartment. As soon as I reached the door, I could hear *In Da Club* playing. *Damn, that is my jam, 50 came wit it on that jont',* I thought as I started shaking my shoulders to her music. I was carrying on like I was in somebody's club and before I knew it the door slowly opened and there was Nikk standing on the other side.

"Asia," Nikk screamed, jumping. "What are you doing?"

"Girl, missin' you."

"I was on my way to the dumpster, come in. I'll go later." I walked in feeling silly, so to break the ice, I made small talk.

"So what's up Sis?"

"Not much."

"Girl, this is my jam you're bumpin'?"

"Mine too," she replied, smiling.

"I'm sorry," I confessed, reaching out to hug her. "I've missed you so much."

"Me too. And I heard about you breakin' a hoe off at the Camouflage Party," she laughed. "What was that all about?"

I told Nikk what happened, and that was the icing on the cake.

"Girl, if I had been there, old girl would have gotten the beat down of her life."

"Oh, she did."

"Yo, I heard you decked her," Nikk responded, pausing to look at me. "Girl, I'm so sorry. I've really missed hangin' with you."

"So did I. Girl, we're like sisters," I insisted. "Let's promise not to ever let things get so out of hand like this again."

"I promise, sis." Nikk and I apologized like women and were back on point. I know that's very rare for females, considering that we're catty as hell and as stubborn as mules, but I'm glad we were able to look over the BS and be about our bonding again.

Nikk and I caught up on lost time. She never told me what she was up to the day I got my face smashed, and since it was so long after the fact, I really didn't want to know. One thing that did come out during our visit was that she and Terrell no longer kicked it.

"What!" I yelled. "Girl, I didn't think you and him were ever gon' break up."

"Well he was tippin' with some tramp named Melissa, so I fired him. If he wants her that bad that he got to sneak, then I suggested that he just be with her."

"So you a'ight?"

"Naw, I ain't. You know I loved that boy. All he did is make me bitter. From this point forward, there's no more loyalty to one man. I'm 'bout to get my slut on."

"What?"

"I'm 'bout to do like niggas do."

"What's that?"

"Get me about three or four cuddle buddies and do what I do."

"And what's that?"

"Asia, come on, you know your girl. I'm bout to get P.A.I.D."

"You better hope your butt don't get a S.T.D."

By the end of the semester, Kerwin and I started discussing the NBA draft once again. Most of his boys, including Dave wanted him to go to the draft. Steve and I wanted him to finish college. I know Steve was thinking more about his future if professional basketball turned out to be short lived, but my reasons were all about me. I figured if he left before I was close to finishing school, he'd go on to whatever city, get him some real eye candy, and forget all about little ol' e me. I knew some of the prettiest females found their way to the waiting area outside the locker rooms after every NBA game. I know because I saw it for myself. Kerwin and I went to some of Dave's games, and a few of the And1 games, and after the clock stopped, the lights dimmed, and the crowd scattered, pretty ass groupies came out the walls like roaches to get them a baller.

"I'm going Asia, this might be my only opportunity. The league is hungry right now for some fresh faces, and if that young cat LeBron James from St. Vincent is getting ninety-five million dollar shoe contracts, hell, imagine what your man gon' get when it's my time to shine."

I didn't sweat Kerwin about his decision. I let him rattle on about what he was gon' do and moved on with our conversation.

"All I got to say is this, when you blow up, it bet not be no late night nothing going on, cuz the only thing open after three o'clock in the morning is a bitches legs or the hospital. You shouldn't be up in neither one of 'em because both gon' interfere with my money."

"With yo money?"

"Yeah, I heard what you said to me on New Years Eve."

"What I say?"

"You said when you make it big this is how *We* gon' be livin'."

"Yeah, but you said you wasn't with that."

"Boy please. That was then, this is now. You weren't getting my goodies on a daily basis back then either."

"Well if it's gon' cost me like that, what's up on an advancement?"

"That'll cost you one Lexus SUV when you get your signing bonus."

"Baby, it's worth all that to me."

"It is?"

"Sure is," he smoothly confirmed, unzipping my jeans.

Kerwin and I were about to make some serious love, but the moment was interrupted. My phone started blowing up. One call after another, and it just wouldn't stop. I looked over at the ID and was pissed. *Daddy, what does he want?*

"Who the hell is it?"

"My father."

"Damnnnnnn…Answer it." *Dad would call at this time and kill my little hour of passion. Dang, I was about to put in some major work. After I answer this phone, I know its gon' be a wrap for the romance.*

"Hello."

"Asia, what the hell's going on?"

"Daddy, what you talkin' about?"

"Has some nigga been smackin' you around?" He yelled. "Is it that ball player?"

"Daddy, what are you talkin' about?"

"One of my customer's daughters said she lives in your building and some guy jumped on you. The only guy I know about is that ball player." I immediately started shaking my head no, but Daddy was to mad to reason with. "Was he the nigga that laid hands on you?" He asked, pausing to wait for my answer, but no words would form. "If he is, I'm gon' break my foot off in his…." *That's just why I didn't want him to find out.*

"Daddy, just chill." I fussed, wondering, *Who's been telling my business and got things blown out of proportion.*

"Asia,"

"Huh."

"Did you hear my question?"

"Yes."

"Well then answer me. Was that the nigga that hit you?"

"No."

"You said that kind of fast. I think you're lying. I'm on my way to that campus.

"For what?"

"Because, I'm 'bout to kill a nigga today."

"Daddy, you need to calm down."

"Calm down my ass. You need to tell me who's been smacking you around or I'm going to jail tonight." *My father is a fool. He is, he is, he is,* I thought as he raved on. "I told you when I came home years ago don't put me in a bad position. I ain't toleratin' no mess from no niggas, NBA or not, I don't give a damn. If a chump put his hands on my kids, he got to deal with me."

"Daddy,"

"What!"

"Where are you?" I asked when I heard his car door shut in the background.

"About to walk into your building right now, so open the door."

128

"Kerwin, my father's outside and he thinks you beat me up. What should I tell him?" I asked, covering the phone.

"Shit the truth. I don't want no problems with your Pops. Him and I are boys and I'd like to keep it that way." Suddenly, we were interrupted by a banging on the door. "Girl, get your panties on and talk to me later."

"Okay, fix the bed," I whispered, as Dad banged louder.

"Asia, open this door right now."

"Coming!" I yelled, making my way to the living room. I opened the door and Dad came storming in like he'd lost his mind.

"Who the hell's been hitting you?"

"Dad, nobody, would you please calm down."

"Calm down my ass. Answer my question."

At that point real fear consumed me. My dad had been upset with me before, but I'd never seen him that angry. I sat on the couch and motioned for him to sit next to me. However, his preference was to stand, so I went on and told him what happened to prevent him from killing Kerwin who was coming out of the room.

"Hell naw. Who is this Alex, and where does he live?"

"Dad, I dated him for almost three years. Mom tried to tell you about him when I first moved here last summer, but I kept him away from you."

"I ain't talking about the past. Where is he now?"

"He's locked up, so it doesn't matter."

"Oh yeah it matters. I'm gon' get that punks cap twisted back. I'm gon' make one call and I promise you he'll be dealt with. Don't nobody put they hands on you without having to face some consequences." Kerwin stood in the doorway of the kitchen, propped up against the wall. He was just listening and agreeing at first, and then suddenly Dad jumped on him. "And man where we're you when all this was going on?"

"Daddy, he," I was about to explain, but he cut me off.

"Asia, I can speak for myself," He responded. "Prince, I came right after he'd jumped on her. I had a l'il scuffle with dude, and then took care of Asia for over a week. I told her to tell you, but she was afraid you'd react just like you are."

"You came after the fact?"

"I came as it was going down."

"Why didn't you deal with that punk ass nigga? You must have been scared."

"Naw, I'm no coward. He got a few scars on him to remember me by. I was gon' get with that nigga again, but I couldn't get suspended from school. And I ain't seen him since, because he's been locked up. I had intentions on dealing with him, but the courts beat me to it."

"Well thanks for looking out for my baby girl, but next time make something big happen or call me and I will."

Dad stayed and fussed for about another hour. He made it clear that he was gon' get the word to his inside connects and get Alex hit for what he'd done. I knew a jailhouse ass kicking wasn't even compatible to the one he'd given me, but every person knows the little saying, "An eye for and eye and a tooth for a tooth," in his case it was gon' be a beat down for a beat down.

Dad must have talked Alex up because shortly after our conversation Alex sent me a letter.

April 15 2003

Asia,

What up doe, Boo. I just wanted to drop you a line to express that there are no hard feelings. I got caught up, and as a result of my behavior, I'm reaping the consequences for my poor choices. I don't know what came over me that night, maybe jealously. I do want you to know that I am very sorry and I still love you more than anything. Kelly don't mean shit to me. She was nothing more than a piece of ass who gave me one hell of a blowjob. I wish you the best. Maybe when I get out we can talk about ways to resolve our differences and be together again. I know you're mad right now, but give it some thought.

Much Love,
Young Al

This nigga sound like a real damn fool, I thought, pitching his letter into the trash.

Chapter 20
Years Later

Kerwin did go on to the league in 2003 like he said he was. He wasn't one of the first seven picks like he expected, but he still went in the first round. *"Cha-ching"* is all I kept thinking. I know a first round draftee gets money and that was good enough for us. A month after the Commissioner hooded him with a Detroit Piston's ball cap, he came through for me like he said he was. My baby went out and purchased me a candy apple red Lexus 300 SUV. At first he joked about giving me his, but once he saw that it wasn't so much about the money as it was about the love I had for him, he wanted me to have nothing but the best.

His first season with the league went well, but his second was off the hook. When the Lakers came to play in Detroit, our fans did what they do best. They got the visiting team off their square. I'd say the Lakers came to play ball, but so did the Bad Boys, and they put an ass kicking on L.A. that they're probably still talking about to this day. That's right, Detroit went on in 2004 to win the NBA championship and mad love from their fans once again.

Oh yeah, Me, Nikki, Dad, and Uncle E were up in the stands cheering like some damn fools. "Do it, Baby. Do it," I'd scream as Kerwin put moves on his opponent.

"Ref, come on dude, can we get a foul," Daddy would fuss when things didn't go Kerwin's way.

By the end of the game, I'd yelled so much that I literally went horse. Fortunately, the Lakers just couldn't hold the Pistons that year, and though Kerwin was fairly new to the team, he got a sufficient amount of game time, which made him feel as though he contributed to the win. When the Commissioner handed over the trophy, my man was front and center along with all the other Big Tymers, getting his shine on, too.

While I was standing there cheering on Kerwin, Dad noticed one of his friends from prison.

"B Holmes!" he yelled. "What's up?"

"Just maintaining."

"Man it's good to see you. You're looking like a million bucks," Dad stated, acting as though he was really sincere.

"Yeah and I'm feeling like a million buck thanks to you. Man the day they let me walk out of that prison, I could only think of how you saved my life. I thank God everyday that you didn't kill me."

"It was all I could do, considering all you did for Ant before and after he got killed."

"Hey, Ant was like a brother to me and my nephew's father as well. I had mad love for that cat."

"How's Ant's son doing anyway? I haven't seen him in a few years."

"He's good."

"Great," Dad sadly replied. "Tell him if he needs anything to get at me."

"I will and I'll tell him you asked about him."

"Please do, and tell him to call me anytime."

"Okay." Byron said, noticing Uncle E as he turned to walk away. "E, What's up homie," he yelled.

"Just enjoyin' the game. They played some ball tonight, didn't they."

"Yeah, the Bad Boys showed up."

"Sure did."

"Hey, I'm gon' get out of here. Y'all take care."

"Man, you take care." Uncle E waved.

"You do the same and get at me sometimes," Byron suggested, walking down the steps.

Dad and E watched that man walk completely out of the arena. I wondered what that was all about, but when I was about to ask, Uncle E, shook his head no. Since he knew Dad best, I figured he better understood Dad's expression than I did, therefore I respected his suggestion and let it rest.

That evening there were all kinds of VIP parties going on in the city. I just knew Kerwin would ditch me to hang with the fellas, but I guess real love kept him focused. Club 313 was hosting the official after party, so Kerwin and some of the other players reserved all the tables in VIP. Our limos pulled up in Valet and once we got out, fans went nuts. They were cheering, screaming, and asking for autographs. I was in disbelief. Kerwin grabbed my hand and pulled me through the small crowd that slipped under the barricades. I immediately grabbed Nikk's hands because Dad and Uncle E were able to fend for themselves. Right before I entered the club, I noticed Kelly and Leslie front and center, acting like the trick ass groupies they were.

"Hey, Kerwin," Kell screamed, "What's up on a few VIP passes." I looked at her like she was crazy.

"Nikk, did you just hear that scank?"

"Asia, let it go. Kelly ain't even worth it. We doin' it big tonight Boo. She's hatin. Don't let her get you off yo shine."

Nikk was right, but I wasn't gon' just ignore her disrespecting me. *How she gon' acknowledge my man and play me like that?*

"Naw, ain't gon' be no passes for you tonight. Wait in line like the common niggas." I expressed, entering the building all draped on my mans arm.

Club 313 was off the hook that night. We made it to VIP and popped the bubbly all night long. Everyone had a little buzz goin' on and the evening turned out to be a hit. A few of us went down to the dance floor and partied like there was no tomorrow. Nikk was dancing with my dad to *White T, by the Franchise Boyz,* and I had to do a double take on them because he was all on her ass like he was our age and she was loving it. She was giving him way too much for me. *Ut'un, they trippin' now. Liquor or not, these niggas have gone too far,* I thought, mugging Dad. He looked over at me like mind my own business. I wasn't having that though. *Dad is sixteen years older than Nikki. That's way too old for her. Besides, he got a woman at home.* My mouth couldn't stay closed any longer. I bounced around to Nikki and leaned in.

"What are you two doing?"

"Dancin', what it look like?"

"Foreplay."

"Asia, get out of their business," Kerwin insisted, after hearing Nikki's response.

"Ha Ha," she replied, sticking her tongue out at me.

Ooo, just wait, I'm gon' tell her something tomorrow, I thought, smiling at her because she knew it was gon' be on. I didn't even trip after that. Hell we were there to celebrate. Dad might not have meant anything by his dancing, but seeing him all on my girl grossed me out. When the evening ended, we left just as we came, to screaming fans who showed major love to the Motor City Bad Boys.

After we dropped everyone off, Kerwin made a call, informing someone that we were on our way. *I wonder who he's talking to.* But I never asked because he sometimes got offended when I was in his discussions. I also knew that in a matter of time, I'd find out anyway, so why start an unnecessary dispute for nothing.

When we made it to the house that evening, the driver pulled up to the front door. Kerwin got out first, and then helped me out like always.

"Thank you, Baby," I stated, kissing his lips. "I'm so proud of you. I know this is one of the greatest days of your life and I'm so glad I was a part of it."

"Me too. I told you when I made it to the league, it was gon' be all about you and me."

"Yeah, but I didn't believe you."

"Shhhhh," he whispered, covering my lips with one finger. Kerwin, scooped me into his arms and carried me in the house straight towards his room. "Let me show you how much I love you," he whispered, pushing open the slightly cracked door with his foot. He sat me on his bed, which was covered in one hundred dollar bills and rose pedals. "This is a sample of what my bonus is going to look like after this win," he teased. I looked around the room, quickly noticing that they created a trail for me to follow. I slid out of bed, following the path and found myself standing at the bathroom door. There was a card attached to the knob which instructed me to read before entering. I read the card and followed the instructions.

Stop here. Take off all of your clothes. Leave on your thong, cuz it's sexy and also one of my favorites. Twist your hair up in a ball, you know the way I like it. Lick your lips as you lift your arms to pull your hair together. Do you feel sexy? Shake your head yes because you better. Now slowly open the door and enter backwards. No peeking. Make sure your eyes are closed. I know how you like to cheat. Take twenty steps forward, and then stop with your back facing me. Think about how good I make love to you as you count to fifty in silence. Now do one of your l'il nasty erotic dances for me. Bend over, let me see it. Um, it's lookin' juicy. Open your eyes. When you hear my voice, turn around and walk towards me without saying one word. No talking. I don't want to ruin the mood cuz this is my night. That's right Baby, it's all about me, and I want things to go 100 percent my way. When our eyes meet, wink at me. For no reason in particular, just because your man got mad game, and played his ass off for you tonight. I always see you rootin' for me from the stands. That turns me on, too. Now walk towards the Jacuzzi. Kneel down on the satin pillow, which I've placed on the first step. Once you get there, I want total submissiveness and I will take over from there. Remember, no words until I give you the sign.

I love you.

Your Bad Boy

Kerwin

For once, I followed his instructions to a T. When I kneeled down, I was right between Kerwin's legs. He was sitting on the side of the Jacuzzi, looking down at me with such an intense look.

"Hey Beautiful. I went out of my way to do all of this for you this evening because win or lose, you are always in my corner. You're one of the best things that's ever happened to me. Asia, when I come across something good, I just don't want to lose out in the end. I've seen so much heartache in my life, sometimes I don't feel like I deserve all this. You, this house, these cars, my career, hell anything." He paused for a moment to tenderly rub my face. I guess, after admiring something in my eyes that captured his attention, Kerwin leaned forward, pecked my lips, and proceeded with what he was saying. "Asia, I played my ass off tonight. I wanted that championship ring so bad, but most of all, I wanted to win it for you. I saw you over there cheering like crazy for me and it pushed me even more. Baby, I didn't want to let you down. You know something else?" I shook my head no. "I also wanted to win in memory of my Mom. I know that's shocking to hear because I've never talked about her, but that's because her death has always been so painful for me. I blamed myself for her death for a very long time. We were out shopping one evening for my first day back to school. I was about to start the eighth grade. And I was so hype because my moms had finally agreed to let me play basketball. She'd always been so focused on me gettin' my books that sports was never an option. We came home and while I ran next door to show my boy Craig's my new Jordan's, Mama's sorry nigga beat her so damn bad. When I walked up to the house, I knew I didn't leave the door opened when I left. I guess in dudes rush to flee, he didn't even bother to lock my mother in. I walked passed the kitchen and could faintly hear my mother calling me. 'Call 911,' she begged as blood rushed out of her mouth and nose. I guess when I first came in I was in shock, so I didn't realize how bad off she was. I scooped her in my arms and pleaded with her to hold on. 'I'm tired," she cried before closing her eyes to die with me cuddling her." Tears rolled down Kerwin's face, but he continued. "My mother never dated men that beat on her until she dated old boy. I think after her and my pops split up, she needed something in her life, but she looked in all the wrong places and it cost her everything. Asia, I miss her so much. Tonight, I wished like hell she was sitting out there with you and your family," He smiled, wiping his tears. "You know what else? She's never seen me play one game, and you'd think I'd be used to it by now. But every big event in my life that she can't be a part of reminds me of what I lost. That's the main reason I'm so thankful for you. Every big event that happens in my life from this point forward reminds me of what I've gained, a precious gift. Asia, you have been the one person in my life that has provided me with some consistency, and I'm grateful for you. I haven't loved for the last six years, not even God, but you helped restore that in me, and I hope we never stop growin' as a couple." *You stopped loving God..* I tought as he obviously read my expression. "God took my mother and I never understood why, so I've been angry with him. I know that sounds crazy, but it's true."

Tears fell from my eyes like a heavy rain. I could no longer keep my emotions in check. I was only able to stay quiet for as long as I did because he asked me not to speak. However, due to his compassion, it was a very hard task once I considered all he had to say. Kerwin reached over and grabbed this small gold platter off the counter. It was covered with a stylish matching lid. I figured it contained some sort of food or fruit he planned to feed me, so I tilted my head back and opened my mouth.

"What are you doing?" He asked, flashing them pretty teeth on me. "Did I tell you to open your mouth?" I shook my head no. "See, there you go tryin' to take charge of my moment," he smiled. Since I still couldn't talk, I smiled too. He removed the lid and I immediately zoomed in, searching for some grapes, some orange slices, strawberries, or something fruity. Instead, there were two chocolate cover strawberries, and between them sat something that looked like a ring box. Kerwin opened it and that's when this seven karat platinum diamond ring jumped out at me. *My LORD!!!* I thought as my eyes stretched wide open. I'd never seen a stone so big. *Damn! This nigga is the truth.*

"Asia, will you marry me?" I stayed silent, trying to still follow his initial instructions. "Did you hear me?" I shook my head yes. "Well, why don't you reply?" I shrugged my shoulders. "Damn, say something. I just poured my heart out to you and you're speechless."

"You said you were going to tell me when to speak."

"When I asked you to marry me that was your cue."

"Oh."

"And since when have you followed my instructions anyway? I expected you to start talking long ago," he teased.

"Forget that, did you say will I marry you?"

"You heard the question."

"Are you serious?"

"What?"

"I mean, yes," I answered, hugging him. "But it'll have to be after I graduate."

"I wouldn't have it any other way. Your Pops ain't gon' kill me," he replied, grabbing my hand." I was so anxious to receive that phat rock Kerwin bought, I dang near shoved my finger in his eye. After he slid it on my ring finger, I couldn't help but hold my hand out a few times to admire the radiant bling. *Shoot, Real Big Tymers do it Real Big. My man gots to be one of 'em fa' sho cuz this rock is serious. Thank God, angels dwelled in the midst of my storm and helped me to come to my senses while I was dealing with that fool Alex. And I'm so glad I was blessed with a new man and a second chance to see what real love is supposed to feel like. Shoot, Asia had you stayed with Alex, girl you probably wouldn't be here today to experience all of this good love .*

Need I say our evening ended with some serious romance? Nah, I didn't think so. Any sista in her right mind gon' make sure she rewards her king very well for a gift of that magnitude. But, so he'd know how really special he was to me, I got up early that following morning and went to the corner store and bought up all 20 of the newspapers they had left just because. Then I rushed back to his place before he got up so I could post papers all over the house. I didn't mind doing it though because it allowed me to showcase just how proud I was of him and his victory.

Chapter 21
Pillow Talk

The Pistons went to the championship again in 2005, but the Spurs came up with the win and my baby was heartbroken for weeks. I consoled my Boo like a good woman's supposed to. Instead of going out with my girl, I stayed around the house with Kerwin trying to make him feel good and help him escape his agony. At first nothing was working, so I'd suggest little things for us to do.

"Hey, let's read."

"Read... Read for what?"

"I thought it might get your mind off of your loss."

"I don't want to read."

"I got some good books," I teased, waving one in his face.

"What you got?"

"*Kiss by Betrayal* by Kelvin King. It's Erotica," I smiled.

"Why I want to read Erotica when I can make my own?"

"Well sounds like a plan to me."

"You don't want none today."

"I want some everyday."

"Why is that?"

"Glad you asked."

"Why's that?"

"Cause ...*Sex With You is Like...like a pocket full of dope....and I ain't worried `bout a damn thing.*"

"You silly," he laughed. "That's the song I always sing to you. Get off Marques Houston's nuts? If you gon' sing what sex with me is like, I want some original shit like I be making up for you."

"Chump, I got original stuff, I was just trying to *See You Smile Again*," I sung.

"Okay for BBD," he nonchalantly teased. "Come over here and give me some of dem lips," he demanded, puckering up.

I know we sound crazy, but me and my man had fun like that. I must admit that the loss was hard on him, but the support I provided always helped him get through the tough times. Once his moping came to an end, he was back to himself and we were at it again. When I think about the way I ended up falling in love with Kerwin, it kind of amazed me that I initially tried my damnedest to only be his friend. We turned out to have real chemistry, and I'm so glad I took a chance on him.

With us, there was just never a dull moment. And with that in mind, all I'm gon' say is that two spontaneous people make a bomb ass couple. Our relationship was simply at its best. After being engaged for a year, and living in separate homes that entire time, Kerwin decided that he wanted to wake up to me everyday, so he suggested that I move in with him and I didn't hesitate to accommodate his request.

During the summer of 2005, I moved out of my apartment on campus and into Kerwin's place with him. I believe that was good for us as a couple. I say that because prior to my move, we were homies, lovers, and friends who had good sex. However, afterwards, we became homies, best friends, thick as thieves, loved each other to death, and got busy everyday like lab rats. We were hooking up two, three, and sometimes four times a day. We'd do it in the bathroom, backyard, living room, on the stairs, um that was my favorite, and in the closet. I remember we were on our way to Chene Park to hear Kem in Concert. *A Matter of Time* was blowing up the airwaves and my baby had gotten us tickets. While in route, Omarion's song *O* came on. Can't one person in the world say that wasn't the jam. Anyway, my baby eased up in my ear nibbling and the next thing I know he was talking my language.

"*Let me tell you, girl. O o o o o o o,*" he sung. "*You make a nigga want to get involved, wanna hit dem draws....*"

"Baby, stop sucking on my ears like that, you makin' me horny, I whispered, sliding off my panties.

"Damn, you want some right now in the back of the limo?"

"Ummm' hum."

"What about the concert?"

"Forget the concert, I'm ready to be on something else."

Hell, that was all I needed to say. We got down in the limo like we were home in bed. By the time we finished, our clothes were a mess, considering that, we skipped out on our plans and had Harold take us back to the house.

...♦♦♦♦...

That following fall, Kerwin started his third season. While he was touring, I developed a l'il fetish for reading *Hood Lit.* Nikk's cousin,

Nardsbaby was a member of a book club and started me to reading. She had me hooked on some good books, but my girl in my Biology class, named Hot told me about her online book club called coast2coastreaders. I checked out their site, got hooked, and joined. They were reading about four titles a month, so my new habit was getting on Kerby's nerves. Shoot, I remember around Christmas 2005, the group was on this book entitled *Brooklyn Jewelry Exchange by Meisha Holmes,* I was so caught up on the freaky tales in that book that I almost jeopardized my home. The first time I ever saw Kerwin seriously upset with me was when I didn't make his game against the San Antonio Spurs on Christmas Day nor did I watch it on T.V. They were playing at the Palace, so he called me a few times before the game, but I wouldn't answer. Later that night, he came in talking noise.

"Sup with you and all these booty tales," Kerwin teased. "You missin me that much while I'm away," he asked stroking his dick.

"What? Yo sex ain't that bomb."

"I know you a lie. You be on a brotha too tuff as soon as I hit the crib for me not to be all that. I know one thing, you better not ignore my calls again."

"I'm sorry, and you can trust and believe my reading about sex ain't nothin' like feelin' something inside of me."

"Put that book down and come let me hold you."

"Wait?" I teased, easing my foot across his. "I just got a few more pages."

"Forget that book. I'm ready for you to *act right, show me som'thin, back it up....*"

"*Put it on me,*" I chimed in. "What, you know about that new Jamie Fox."

"I know *I'm gon' tear dat pussy up* like Jeezy," Kerwin cheezed. "I'm feeling both of them cuts."

"Me too."

"Good, then you already know so bring it on over here so *I can make it do what it do baby.*"

"That's not how the song goes."

"So what! You know I like to make up my own l'il lines."

"Naw, it's more like you don't know the words."

"And."

"Forget what you on, get the dick on swoll. This nigga Malika in this book, got me hot."

"You so naaaa…sty," he smiled.

"Only for you."

"Well you still ain't getting off that easy, the next time I call your phone you better answer."

☺ ..... ☻

I'm happy to say that my book addiction didn't keep me out there to long. In spring 2006, I graduated from the University of Michigan Detroit with a Bachelors degree in Social Work. Prior to graduation, Kerwin talked about how he didn't want me to work once I became Mrs. Phillips. He decided he wanted me to stay home and travel with him, but after four long years of college, I thought I should put my degree to use. Sitting around the house, and gaining a bunch of weight was never a plan for my future.

Anyway, right after graduation, my family threw a big Bar B Q for me at the house. Some of everyone was there, my mom, Rodney, and my sister came out. Dad and Teretta, Uncle E and his date, Nikk was there solo on creep mode trying to get chose as usual. Some of the employees from Dad's three stores came out, Dave, and a few other NBA players stopped by with their dates, and Steve Burtt flew in for the day. Though Steve was initially Kerwin's mentor and coach, I'm glad Kerwin befriended him at that basketball camp in New York. He was one of the few men Kerwin had mad respect for. And because Steve was so instrumental in helping Kerwin get into college, he promised him that during the off seasons, he would continue to pursue his degree. And over the years, Steve grew to simply love me like a daughter-in-law, which is why he took off from his And1 tour to fly in and celebrate my day with me.

Oh our neighbor Mr. Cheeks was there also. Mr. Cheeks was a rich old contractor. He was responsible for building some of the greatest sites in the city of Detroit. That man had money to burn and was friendly with his paper. Nikk sack chasin' tail was flirting something serious with him, too. Hell, after hanging out with me and Kerwin for the past few years, she craved niggas with money more than she ever did. My girl was throwing butt all over the city. She had turned into a straight rat on a mission, and wasn't gon' stop 'til she landed herself a millionaire. I started recapping all her money makers who made booty call and tripped out.

Damn, Nikk's already messed around with Dave, Sean, and JR. All them niggas playing in the NBA. She's getting down with Ferrad, Terryonto, and Big Boy, three of the hottest ballas in the game, and now she trying to add an old ass sugar daddy to the list. You hoe, work your money maker. Now when yo dumb ass get caught up by the wrong Big Tymer, that's gon' cost you a possible beat down fa'sho. After peeping Nikk for a minute, I went into the house to change into something more comfortable. Nikk followed me in so that's when I took a moment to ask her about her behavior.

"Fool, what do you think you're doing?"

"Wha 'cha mean?"

"Why are you trying to get on Mr. Cheeks? Girl he's damn near a hundred. You gon' fool around and get nats messing around with his old ass."

"I holla at older men."

"I know you ain't got with no dude more than five years older than you, so none of them count."

"Yes I have."

"You a lie. What older man you been with that you ain't told me about."

"Your father."

"Bitch, don't play. You'll get yo neck snapped, talkin' 'bout you fuckin' my daddy."

"I'm serious."

"What?" I paused, looking at her in complete shock. "Slut, you better be playin'!"

"I'm not. We been kickin' it for a few years."

"You better be lyin."

"I'm not."

"Why you ain't never tell me?"

"I didn't think I needed to. Plus, I knew you'd bug out."

"You damn skippy. How you gon' get with my father? You s'posed to be my girl! How you let some shit like that happen?"

"I always thought your dad was hot. Hell, you know he's sexy. I've been digging him every since you introduced us."

"But he's got a wife and a child."

"Your dad wasn't tripping, so why are you?"

"Nikk, he lives with his woman, they're a family, you be up in his wifes face all the time, what you mean, why I'm trippin?"

"So, and your point is what. Do you know how many niggas live with they woman and tippin'?"

"No, but I'm sure you do. It seems like Kelly rubbed off on you. How could you do that, your parents raised you better than that? What if a home wrecker was tippin' out with your ole' dude?"

"Girl, do you know how many affairs my father has had? Men cheat. Shit, my mother was tippin' out on my father, too. It's life, get over it, Asia. Shit happens."

"Nah, shit don't just happen. You got to do a little more work to be creepin and getting dicked down by my daddy."

"Don't go judging me. You ain't no different than me. Before Kerwin, you were chasin' money too."

"Who?

"Alex, Mauri's old ass. Not to mention that he's your daddy's boy. Try explaining that to him."

"You told him about Mauri?"

"Hell Naw! So he can kill him?"

"Besides, we only went out two times."

"And…"

"And I didn't give him no ass, or break up his happy home."

"So what. I'm just pointing out that you're no angel."

"Umm, I'm gon' have to watch you around my man."

"Girl please. We're girls, I wouldn't do that to you. That's a major violation in the Home Girl Code of Ethics."

"So is fucking your girl's dad, but you did that."

"That doesn't count unless he's married to your biological mother."

"I can't believe you just said that."

"Why not? Teretta is not yo mama, so why you care."

"It's the principle."

"Those were made to be violated.

"That's why I don't trust you."

"Yeah, I'm sure I'm gon' sleep with yo man. Come on Asia, give me a break."

"So when did all this go on between you and my daddy?"

"The night Alex jumped on you was the first night I hooked up with Prince."

"Prince, oh so y'all on a first name basis?"

"Asia, hello…..we were fucking. You think I'm gon' be in bed getting' boned by your dad talkin' 'bout some oh hit it Mr. Prince? Girl, come on. Once he started bangin' this, we were no longer formal."

"I can't believe you would do my father. That's so nasty."

"Well, it's not to me. And for the record, he's got mad skillz," she grinned, lifting her hand to give me five. I looked at her like she'd lost her mind.

"What!"

"Yeah that's right, the nigga brings it."

"YUCK!!!! That's way too much information. Are y'all still…"

"Sometimes."

"Oh, hell naw. So were you the one that told him about Alex jumping on me?" Nikk went quiet. She looked away with guilt all over her face, so I asked her again. "Nikk, I said were you the one that told?"

"Asia, pillow talk will have you confessin' every damn thing."

"So what all did you tell?" I asked, rolling my eyes. "I could kill you. My father was about to beat Kerwin down behind you runnin' yo mouth."

"I told...." Nikk paused because we were disturbed by a knock at the door.

"Who is it!" I yelled.

"Baby, it's me."

"Oh' come in."

"What are you doing?" Kerwin asked, easing up behind me to hug my waist. "When are you coming back out? Everyone's looking for you, plus I got a surprise."

"Okay, well be out in one minute."

"Hurry up," he insisted, leaving the room.

"Back to you," I turned and angrily said to Nikki. "Just what all did you confess while you were getting your guts dug out?"

"Promise you won't be mad at me first."

"Girl, you didn't," I rattled, afraid that she let the cat out the bag about the murder of my aunt Ke's daddy."

"I did, but I knew he wasn't going to tell anyone, especially not on you. He didn't even care anyway. He said that's what his sorry ass get. Renzo, that is his name, right?" She asked.

"Yeah."

"Well that man did something to your dad that he is still bitter about."

"That doesn't matter. You weren't s'posed to say anything. Nikk, suppose that story about Zo gets out. We covered up for those fools, which makes us just as guilty. That man was my aunt's father. Suppose she finds out?" I fussed.

"Terrell's deserves to be locked down. He's ruthless for doing that shit anyway."

"Right, and say he finds out you told and comes for us due to your loose lips."

"Asia, you're spooked for nothing."

"You and Terrell are no longer together. He won't think twice about killing you. Nikki, you don't mean shit to him anymore, not to mention that you're messing around with his rivals. Girl you're crazy. I pray to God you're not telling anyone else during your pillow talk about that night."

"Asia, stop trippin' and let's get back outside."

"I don't believe you told. Damn, ain't you ever heard, *Loose Lips Sink Ships?*"

"Yeah, your dad said that to me the night he made me promise not to tell you about us."

"So why are you tellin' me then?"

"I didn't tell you the night it went down."

"Some things you're not ever supposed to tell. And some things are meant to be taken to your grave. Everything you just shared was dirt worthy and should have accompanied you on to glory."

"We're girls, it's nothin' wrong with me tellin' you."

"I see you don't understand the slogan, but I'm gon' tell you now, you better find out what it really means and shut up 'til you do. Pillow talk will get you put to sleep on a permanent basis for real."

"I ain't trying to here what you talkin' about right now Ms. Prissy."

"What?"

"You heard me, forget all that, and since you say Mr. Cheeks is too old for a diva like me, what's up with the sexy chocolate."

"Who, Steve?"

"Yeah...Girl, he's my kind. His smile is gorgeous. I could do some things to him. You know, lick that bald head while he's putting in work."

"Nikk, he don't want you."

"Girl, I'd grab that head and..."

"Stop it... You're makin' me sick." I teased. "I'm sure he's taken, and if he wasn't I know he don't want no rats."

"I got your rat. Yo daddy liked it, you hater."

"Hater... Girl pleeeease... My daddy went 16 years without no sex at all. He's still recovering from limited nuts."

"Naw, this body drove him crazy."

"That might be right, but he didn't know any better."

"From the way he eats it up, I beg to differ." I reached over and slapped Nikk on her back so hard, her eyes watered. "Ouch, don't hit me like that again. That stuff hurt."

"Don't talk to me about my daddy eatin' you out again and I wont."

"Okay sorry, well since you don't want me doing DeMarques, you think I could get a formal intro to Steve?"

"No," I screamed, pushing her out the door.

Chapter 22
Gifts

Once we returned to the backyard, *Family Reunion* by the O'jays was blaring out of the stereo. I walked out by the pool and sat in between Kerwin's legs on a lawn chair. He wrapped me up in his arms and kissed the back of my neck. Clearing his throat, he got everyone's attention, and all eyes were on us.

"Turn that music down," he ordered as Dad lowered the volume. "Baby, we're so proud of you. These three envelopes have something special in 'em for you."

"For me?" I asked, being sarcastic.

"Yeah, pick one."

I immediately started looking at each of the envelopes which all had very dainty packages to go with them. I didn't know which to pick, so one of my grammar school chants came in handy. *My mother told me to pick this one.* I'd selected envelope number two, which went with this crimson and cream box with a huge gold bow.

"Awwwwwwww, Asia that's the one," Nikki confirmed like she knew what was in each one.

"Okay, wait Baby, before you open this, let everyone else give you their gifts first," Kerwin interrupted.

"There are more gifts?" I asked, being silly.

"Hell yeah, Chick," Nikki, responded, shoving her gift at me. I unwrapped it and out of the box I pulled this hot nighty.

"This is so you."

"I know," she replied.

Next, Dad and Teretta gave me their gift. It was the biggest box I received that day. I ripped off the bow, then the paper like a *Jazzy Little Five-Year-Old*. When I dug off into their package, I gasped as it registered that they'd gotten me a full length mink coat, which still had the tag attached.

"Dad $12,000 dollars, you know you're good for letting a nigga know what you paid for something." Dad ignored my comment.

"I know it is summer, but you had such a fit about Teretta getting one, so now you got one too."

"And Asia, your daddy got that coat on sale," Teretta interrupted.

"Shoot, it is eight hundred degrees now, I can't even wear it."

"I know Ungrateful One. Just put it in storage until it gets cold. Then around October get it out for the winter. It'll still mean as much then as it does now," Dad fussed.

"It's beautiful. Thanks Daddy.... Sorry."

"Butterfly, you're just being yourself. It wouldn't be you any other way."

Mom and Rodney bought me two nice suits, with shoes and accessories to match.

"Thanks Mom, thanks Rodney, they're beautiful."

"I'm glad you like them, Asia. I know our taste is very different, and we can't compete with your dad, but we wanted you to have some nice professional attire for Co-America."

"Mom, it's cool. I knew you were going to keep me humble with your gift."

Laughing, Mom replied, "Yeah, you had me worried for a minute, but I'm so glad you proved me wrong."

"Okay, Zena. Don't go getting' all mushy on me," I sassed.

"Baby, I am proud of you. I know we've had some hard times over the years, but you've always been my girl. My tough love was only done with the intent of making you a responsible woman," Mom confessed, tearing like crazy.

"And Mom, I thank you for those hard times because they made me a better woman. Your firm guidance kept me grounded."

"Okay, Damn! This is starting to sound like a funeral. Next," Dad stated, moving us right along.

Uncle E was next, "Okay Baby Girl, here you go." I opened Uncle E's card and it was full of money, seven Benjamin's to be exact. Dave gave me a nice diamond watch, Steve gave me two airline tickets, and Mr. Cheeks gave me an all expense paid five day vacation to a resort in Maui.

"Aw Chick, I know me and you on them tickets and that resort like Stella and Whoopie, right," Nikk asked.

"Nope, I'm taking my man."

"Should have known," she mumbled. Finally, I was back to Kerwin's box.

"Well, I know ain't no puppy in here." I teased, opening the box. "Huh," I gasped, grabbing a set of keys up in my hand.

"What are these to?"

"Wouldn't you like to know?"

"Yeah, I really would."

"You'll see next week."

"Next week! You're going to leave me hangin' for a week?"

"Yep."

"But today is my day."

"No Baby, everyday is your day. I'd give you the world twenty-four, seven."

"Awwwwwww, with words like that, what's a sista to say besides, see all y'all later? Me and my man got business."

Everyone laughed, but Dad's smile stood out most to me. He had a glow about himself that was unexplainable. I gathered from his look that he was pleased with my mate. Kerwin, was not only a Big Tymer and a Big Baller on some positive, but he loved me. For once in my life, I felt good about loving a man that wasn't on some thugin.

"That's our cue to leave. Let's go Teretta," Dad insisted.

"Damn Asia, how you gon' just kick us out like that?" Nikk asked real irritated.

"Easy, it's going on eight o'clock and I've been with you since last night and everyone else since early this morning. I want some time for me and my man. So PEACE OUT B'a!"

"I got your B'a."

"Nikk, come here," I said. She eased over by me looking silly.

"What?"

"If you that lonely, go home with Mr. Cheek's rich butt and let him dig you out. He can probably use some good young coochie tonight anyway."

"Yeah, he might appreciate this fresh, wet ocean of temptation."

"Wet and ocean it might be, but it's far from fresh."

"Ask yo daddy," she whispered, laughing. "I didn't find that funny at all," I fussed, pulling a handful of her hair in my hands before yanking the heck out of it. "I already warned you once."

"Ouch!"

"Shut up and get out," I joked, pushing her away from me.

"Yeah, I better hurry, I might be able to catch the coach, I know he gets lonely on the road up in them hotels."

"I doubt it. I done told you once, he don't want you."

"We'll let him be the judge of that," she sassed, switching through the gate.

....♦♦♦♦....

A week later, I was sitting around the house, watching one of those stupid reality shows. The phone started ringing, but because I was all in, I didn't want to be disturbed, so I ignored it. Suddenly, it started ringing off the hook.

"Hello," I answered clearly irritated.

"Damn, I've called five times, what's up with that."

"Hey Babe, sorry, I was watching TV."

"And."

"Dudes and Dames got a good show on today. This man just caught his wife in bed with a couple of their friends."

"I know all females love drama, but don't ignore the phone."

"Shut up! What you want anyway?"

"I'm serious. It could be an emergency. I told you that already."

"You're right, sorry."

"It's okay. Get dressed, Daddy got a surprise for you."

"Daddy, since when did you become my daddy?"

"The first time you let me in."

"What?"

"New Years of 2003 you don't remember telling me to 'Hit it Daddy' when I was inside of you."

"Boy, bye. I'll see you when you get here."

"No I'm not comin', I'm sendin' Harold. He's supposed to pick you up about eight."

"Okay."

"Okay, my butt. Be ready! Time is money."

"I'll be ready. Bye."

"Bye."

I showered, got dressed and was waiting when the limo arrived. I peeped out the window, immediately noticing that our normal limo driver wasn't the one walking to our door. Instead, it was this medium built, dark chocolate, sexy dude who introduced himself as Barry.

"Sorry, I know you were probably expecting Harold, but he's ill today."

"Oh, what's the matter?"

"He's been having chest pains, so his doctor made him take a break. Actually, I'm his grandson. My granddad's been running our family limo business for years. He told me to make sure I took really good care of you. So if there's anything I can do, please don't hesitate to let me know."

"Okay. Well give me one second, let me get my purse."

After grabbing my things, we headed for Detroit Metro Airport. I thought I was meeting Kerwin at some nice restaurant or a fine club, but instead, I was transported to the front door of Desoto's International Airlines. There standing right out front was my man and a skycap with four Louis Vuitton Bags. I couldn't help but smile from ear to ear because Kerwin was always hitting me up with bomb surprises. I quickly slid my little sexy self out of the limo and over to my Boo.

"Hey," I smiled, wrapping my arms around him.

"Hey to you," he mumbled, kissing my nose. *This man got me weak. He better marry me like he said, or I'll be stalking him and his new boo.* "Who's this?" He asked, pointing. "Where's Harold?"

"Sup Man, I'm Harold's grandson, Barry. I'm his back up driver. It's rare that granddad is ever sick, but when he is, I fill in for him."

"That's good to know. Tell the old guy I said get better and we'll see him when we get back."

"Yeah, I will," he paused. "Excuse me Mr. Phillips, I know it's not good to harass clients, but do you mind giving me an autograph for my son Duke?"

"Not at all," He replied, pulling out three fresh hundreds and signing one of them.

"Thanks man."

"No problem. Come on Pretty, we got a plane to catch."

We made our way inside, got cleared, and walked down to gate 13G. I couldn't believe that we were on our way to some exotic Island called Mindego. *Where the hell is that,* I thought without asking because I didn't want to appear ignorant. We had to fly to Florida that night, and the following morning we caught a private jet to the Island. Once we arrived, I was in disbelief. I'd never seen anything so beautiful before in my life. I couldn't believe what I was seeing. There weren't many people there nor was there much that resembled city living, but if you wanted to get away, it was the place to be.

After exiting the plane, we finally made it to the end of the tarp. Waiting to pick us up was this old man in an odd looking ride. I can't even describe it, but it was like nothing I've ever seen. We were transported to this elegant home in a gated area that stood on at least seven acres of land. Being that I don't know a thing about land surveying, it really could have been more or less, whichever, it was a lot. It wasn't no super sized home like rich niggas generally buy, but it was one of the biggest on the island. Kerwin said it was about ten thousand square feet. All I knew is that it was far more home than we needed to be vacationing in.

"This is it," he said.

"It… What's it?"

"Our summer get away."

"Get away! Out here in the middle of nowhere?"

"Yeah, you like it."

"I'm speechless." *Hell-to-the-naw, I don't like it. It's in the middle of nowhere and I'm a city girl,* I thought. "It's beautiful."

"Good, that means I did my job," he grinned.

"This house has to be expensive, can we afford this?"

"We, what you mean we?"

"You heard me chump," I teased, hitting him.

"We're leasing. I wouldn't buy us a home way out here."

"So what made you pick this location?"

"I thought it would be a nice place to get married."

"Married! We can't get married without my friends and family."

"I know."

"So why you talkin' about getting' married here then?"

"Everybody knows Mrs. Phillips," he whispered, kissing my forehead. "They're coming for the wedding. I had Nikk call around 'til she found you the best of everything you needed to make our day a hit. There's a consultant waiting in the study to assist you."

"Consultant! Are you serious?"

"Very."

"Where is the study?"

"Why don't you go find it?"

"I would, but I don't know my way around this house."

"Well, let me call someone to show you the way." Kerwin flipped out his phone and dialed some numbers. "My lady needs to get to the study. Can someone come show her the way?" Much to my surprise someone quickly arrives.

"Daddy! What are you doing here?"

"I came to show you to the study."

"I know that, but what are you doing here?" Dad grinned, but said nothing. I couldn't believe my eyes. I'd only dreamed of being catered to in such a fashion, but here my man was making my dreams a reality. "Kerwin, had I known the key in the box I picked belonged to a house as beautiful as this, I would have probably picked a different one."

"Why?"

"Because I don't know if I'm ready for all of this."

"Either way the outcome was gon' be the same."

"Why you say that?"
"Baby, all the boxes had the same gift."
"Awwww, you're smooth."
"Naw, you're so nosey, so I got to always be thinking."
"Whatever."

Chapter 23
The Surprise

I don't want to go into all the details, but I had a very small wedding with close friends and family in attendance only. It was a beautiful thing, but I'm glad that two days after we were married, everyone left. I say that because my father and Nikki stressed me out sneaking around the damn house the entire week. I think Teretta became a little suspicious of them, but she never caused a scene. She was way too classy for that, and out of respect for the occasion, I think she preferred to wait until they got home. After observing my daddy's behavior, all I hoped was that I never grew old to my man.

I guess daddy was falling into that typical married man syndrome. You know the saying, "*Wifey getting' old, ain't acting right, gon' find me some young pussy that's still good and tight. Feed her some B.S., spend a little doe, and make her trick ass my personal little hoe.*" *How wack! Humph, old niggas kill me trying to always flatter these young women. Dad know he need to cool it before he have a heart attack, and Nikk, better chill before Teretta beat her down*, I thought, making it my business to think of ways to keep me and Kerwin's love alive forever.

Kerwin and I stayed on the island an additional two weeks. During those fourteen days, I promise we broke in every section of that house. My sex drive was off the chart, so if that nigga slightly brushed up on me, I was ready. Before I knew it, we'd turned the place upside down. We got busy in the kitchen, living room, closet, bathroom, shower, Jacuzzi, pool, the backyard on the lawn chairs, and the dining room table. Huh, the dining room, I got to tell you about that. That was the most exciting place we'd ever made love. Seconds after eating, we found ourselves sprouted out all over the meal making real passion happen. I remember Kerwin and I were sitting teasing each other over dinner. The next thing I knew he was sliding his fingers up my legs and across my girl. I gasped and closed my eyes cuz a sista was feeling good. Once I started getting wet, I knew he was gon' flip my l'il frame in the air and get his chomp on. That was one of his best skillz, aside from basketball. Sure enough that's exactly what he did. Kerwin lifted me out of my chair, tenderly placed me on the table, romantically eased up my skirt with his teeth, which I loved, and relaxed in his seat to enjoy dessert. I could feel his fingers crawl my inner thigh. They felt so good, creeping up my legs that I snickered a little as he slid my thong to the side. He lowered his face and damn near flat lined me when his tongue flopped on my clit. The coolness from the ice he'd been eating was comforting. I pulled my legs closer to my chest, allowing him to get at it a little better. When I was about to cum, I didn't want to make the ugly erotica face, so I relaxed my cheeks, and had the damn nerve to try and cum pretty.

It was all I could do to control the jacked up looks a bomb orgasm brings. So the better it got, the crazier I looked, until I just told myself, *Guuurl forget it.* I palmed Kerwin's head, forcing his face to the right spot, and then I locked my legs on his dome, moaning in sheer pleasure.

"I can't breathe, let my head go" he mumbled, seconds after trying to force my legs apart.

"Stop whining and get some of dis," I demanded, taking off my bra.

Kerwin, stood to his feet, slid me to the edge of the table, and made me respect every inch of meat his six-foot, five inch tall butt was packin'. We made love 'til I was sore. I know he dumped hella sperm in me, cuz he wasn't 'bout to use no condoms and pulling out was a high school move. Finally, I had more than I could take. I had to throw in the towel.

"Cum," I begged.

"Nah, I ain't ready," he replied, getting his.

"We'll I am," I whined.

"Stop complaining with yo' can't take no dick self." *Now I done heard that line before. What's that about? Maybe I can't take too much, but let this nigga get a little hole and see how long he can take it,* I thought before saying just that.

"Nigga you get a hole and let me ram you. Let's see how long you last?"

"I gives, not receives," he teased, smacking his tongue. "I'm about to cum," he wimpered, wiping the sweat off his face on my belly. "Look at you, you got rice and gravy all in your hair."

"That's because you didn't give me a chance to move the plates."

"Nah, that's cause you was running away from my man right here," he insisted, grabbing himself. "He had yo' l'il frail butt on spook."

"Whatever."

"Oh, so he didn't."

"Ut'un."

"Quit lying, and since you can't tell the truth, we gon' see tonight."

"With as sore as I am, if you think you gettin' some mo, you on crack."

"Yeah, just what I thought. You can't take all this," he bragged, walking to the shower.

Even though I quit, that turned out to be the best session we had the whole time we were at Mindego. Yeah, I know I sound real raunchy, but I don't care. Ain't nothing nasty about a husband and wife doing what it takes to please each other and keep their marriage alive. I know we was sinning prior to our marriage, but that legit love, was more bomb than I ever imagined. Don't judge me. All I'm gon' say is that more people should try it, and maybe the divorce rates would decline.

…♦♦♦…

Once we landed in Detroit, Barry was waiting on us. Kerwin signed a few autographs for fans, and then Barry hurried us into the car.

"Thanks man, where's Harold?" Kerwin asked.

"He's still not well. Looks like I'll be driving for a while."

"With the way you handled the fans that's cool with me."

"Yeah, Granddad's been drivin' for a lifetime, so he needed this break."

"Yeah, Harold's my man. He's never late, he's dependable, and I'm gon' use y'all company 'til he can't drive no more."

"Well I hope you stay with us after that. I'm next in line for the family business."

"Is that right?" Kerwin asked, laughing.

"So how was the trip?" Barry asked.

"Nice. Man, I got me a little wifey while I was out of the country," he expressed, kissing me.

"You got married! Congratulations."

"Thanks."

…♦♦♦…

When we pulled up in front of our house, I looked it up and down, thinking *this doesn't even seem to compare to the massive crib we just left.* Once we got settled in, and got to carrying on like newlyweds, the romance was better in the D than in Mindego. Afterwards, I showered and crawled into bed. Kerwin sat in his office for a while, talking on the phone, and later walked into our bedroom with a crazy smile on his face.

"What you smiling so big for?"

"You know I'm going into the last year of my contract. My agent is working on some big things for me."

"Big things like what?"

"Possibly a new team, if necessary."

"I don't want to leave Detroit."

"What! Baby, come on. You know we got to go where the money's at. So who ever is payin' the best, that's where we'll be."

I guess he told me. Needless to say, Detroit kept Kerwin, and I was glad about that.

Chapter 24
CMB Mobile

Days after making it back to the city, I was up in *Top of the Line* visiting. I was flashin my ice for a couple of chicks that worked in the store when Mr. Mauri and some trick name Rock Candy stopped by. I looked her up and down and immediately the song, *I'm in love with a stripper* came to mind 'cause that what she put me in the mind of with her hoochie mama gear on.

"What up doe."

"Mau, it's all you baby."

"Man, you got them aqua gators in yet?" Before Dad could reply, he stopped to salivate over Mauri's woman.

"Yeah, they're here. They came in last week," he answered, undressing old girl with his eyes like she was the badest bitch, he'd ever seen. "Where you been, we ain't seen you for a minute?"

"I'm trying to open up a few new clothing stores, so I've been running between Chicago and Cali getting' my grind on. Then I got my little Eye-Candy up in Brooklyn, so right now I'm back and forth to New York, getting' my cup-cake on." I looked at Ms. Rocky smiling like she was into Mauri and immediately read her vibes. *Eye Candy, ummm, this fake trick up in here skinning and grinning like she feelin him, she know good and damn well, she's a rat.*

"Yo, Ashley, go get that order from the back for me," Dad asked.

"P you lookin' a little hard at my prize," Mauri, cunningly smiled. "Keep looking and I'm gon' have to burn yo eyes out."

"What? Man get out of here befo' I.."

"Here you go," Ashley stated, cutting him off.

"That's gon' be two-G's.

"Damn, you going up on yo prices?"

"Nigga inflation ain't just making gas prices go up."

"I see. I guess I'm gon' have to get some of my money back from you on them tables this weekend."

"Yeah right, I'll be in Greektown at the Casino, just bring yo lucky charm with you," Dad suggested. *Give me a break Dad, you on her jock a little to tuff for me.*

"Lucky fa'sho. Ain't that right Rocky?" She gave off this little uppity look that most gold diggers sport and I immediately knew I wasn't feeling her. I knew I wasn't jealous because when I went out with Mauri, there was no chemistry, but how was this chick gon' come up in my spot acting like she was all that.

"Maybe sometime when my l'il lady's in town, Asia you and Rocky can hang out." *I don't think so. She ain't even on my level,* I thought forcing a smile.

"Sure, Mr. Mauri, I'd love to kick it with Rocky," I lied. He walked out, thinking he had it going on, and I gave Dad this ill look and walked to the office.

"What!" Dad asked like he was innocent.

"You're a slut."

"What? I was just being polite."

"You simped out. I know my man can't be around you."

...◆◆◆...

In January 2007, while Nikk and I were out shopping, we ran into Alex and Kelly at the mall, and I thought I'd seen a ghost. The closer we got to them, the clearer the image of Alex became. Kelly was pregnant and between the two of them was a little girl who looked to be right at a year old.

"Asia, is that Alex and Kelly?" Nikk asked.

"Yeah."

"What we gon' do?"

"I don't know, but if she says one thing, I'm beating her down."

"Well I got Alex."

"Fool, you can't beat that nigga."

"Girl, I know, but I'll shock his ass with this, and have him foamin' at the mouth like a wild dog," she laughed, pulling a tazer out her purse.

We were destined to cross each others path, with the make up of the strip we were walking. I didn't want Nikk and me to end up in jail, so we detoured into a clothing store to avoid them. Within seconds, Kelly walked in behind me, acting like she was shopping. Alex stayed out in the Mall, so either way, we were going to run into one of them.

I looked around in the store for a minute, but instead of just hanging in the store, looking stupid, I opted to exit. As soon as we walked out, we ran right into Alex.

"Asia. How are you? Long time no see," he cheerfully greeted.

"Yeah it has been," I replied, trying to move on.

Alex slightly blocked my path, and continued talking. "Sup Nikk, you still looking good."

"Hey Alex," she grinned.

"You heard from T?"

"Hell naw! Why he gon' call me?"

"Y'all were a couple at one time."

"Not no mo. And forget about T, what's up wit that?" she asked, pointing at Kelly.

"Shit a nigga needed an address to parole to. My grandmother died while I was in prison and I didn't have anywhere to go."

Umm, in that letter he wrote he said she wasn't nothin' more than a piece of ass that gave good head. Nigga's be on some BS.

"So y'all an item now?" Nikk asked, interrupting my thoughts.

"We got a kid and one on the way."

"That's not what I asked you. Plenty of men got babies by sistas, but they ain't no item."

"Yeah, somethin' like that," he answered, shifting his attention back to me. "Asia, you sure are lookin' fine. What you been up to?"

"Alex, don't stand here talking to me as though the last time we saw each other we were on good terms."

"I know, I'm real sorry about what happened. Asia, I was young, foolish, jealous, and a boy in so many ways."

"A boy, so are you sayin you've grown up."

"I'm a man now. Prison taught me some harsh lessons about life, which is why I apologize from the bottom of my heart about all that went down."

"Okay, take care," I rudely responded, walking away. Nikk, just kind of stood there frozen in her tracks. "Girl, come on!"

"Asia, let me talk to you," Alex insisted.

"Ut'un, that sorry, pregnant Bitch of yours is wobbling over here, you better go on and tend to her or it's gon' be some shit."

"I'm gon call you. Is your cell number the same?" I looked at him like he was crazy, then pulled Nikk away.

"See you Alex, tell your boy I said hi," Nikk yelled, as I yanked her shirt by the collar for speaking so jolly to the enemy. We made it a little ways down the mall and I let Nikk have it.

"How you gon' stand there and hold a full fledge conversation with that nigga after what he did to me?"

"Asia, the man apologized, you ain't got to be his woman again, but it's okay to be sociable. And don't forget I was cool with him too. Damn, we all got history. I could see if I said something to Kelly."

"Alex and Kelly are in the same position as far as I'm concerned." Suddenly my cell phone vibrated, interrupting me. I had an incoming text. "That's Alex textin' me."

"What he say?"

"Just checkin 2 C if your # changed. By the way, U looked so Sex-C. Can I call U 2 nite?"

"That fool ain't over you. Damn, I can't believe he hit you up while he's out with his woman. Asia, that's a real dirty nigga. You better beware of him."

"I don't know why you're so surprised, it ain't no more scandalous than when Kelly hooked up with him."

"Reply then. Entertain his wack ass a little and pay her back."

"Are you crazy? I'm married."

"So, I didn't say sleep with the man, I said entertain him."

"Naw, I'm gon' pass." I insisted.

"What! Why you looking at me like that?"

"I just realized that you got some real issues. Tramp, you ain't no good. How you gon' sit up in my house, hang out with me and my man like you our damn child, then tell me to cheat on him. Would you tell yo mama to cheat on yo daddy?"

"Hell yeah, if I could benefit from it."

"You foul. Wait 'til I tell Kerwin about you tonight. He gon' kick yo' ass out the family."

"You better not tell him nothing. I don't want to have to cuss him out."

"Naw you don't want him to cuss you out and then ban you from our spot. He'll take away your power. Then you ain't gon' be able to pass out your cheap, watered-down pussy coupons to the elite nigga's no more."

"That ain't gon' happen."

"Girl, Kerwin's exposed you to over half the heavy hitters you know. If he bans you, your coupons will only be good in the hood again. And you know you don't want no broke Johns up in that black gold."

"You so right, and since you put it like that, forget entertaining Alex. He ain't worth getting us both caught up," she laughed.

Nikk was a fool. We both gave each other five, cracked up, and continued our little shopping spree.

...♦♦♦...

I dropped Nikki off about eight and made it home around nine. When I got in the house, I noticed Kerwin was back from their away game that I opted not to attend just because I'd gotten a little burned out on the frequent traveling. His Range Rover was backed in the driveway and parked as if he'd gotten out in a hurry. I made my way into the house, hands filled with bags, and walked straight to our room. I could hear the shower running, so I quickly undressed to get in before he got out. As I approached the bathroom door, I could hear him talking, so I stopped and listened for a moment.

"Oh you were watching the game today. Yeah, we put in work. Chi-Town wasn't ready for the Bad Boys tonight. I agree, a nigga was ballin'." He paused to laugh. "I gots to, in this business, if I don't produce, they strip my dignity, and whip my ass by benching me. Then after the season, they'll trade me like a slave." He paused, and laughed again. I eased forward to see if I could see him. Immediately, I noticed him looking at himself in the mirror. He was smoothing down his mustache and I guess looking for flaws on his skin. *This nigga is so on his own nuts.* "I don't know if I can get out tonight. My wife may have something special planned, if not, I'll swing by and give you some time."

At that point, I became territorial. I walked into the bathroom, grinning as though I'd just come in.

"Hey Baby, when did you get here?" He smiled, looking me up and down from head to toe.

"Hey, I missed you," I stated, easing into his arms, trying to hear someone talking. He kind of pulled back to prevent that from happening, then gestured for me to wait one minute.

"Okay man, my beautiful wife just walked in. I got to go." He paused. "Yeah, that's cool. I might get out tonight. Holla back." Kerwin pitched his cell on the counter, and grabbed me. He was standing draped in a towel with this mischievous smirk on his face.

"Hey Devil," I greeted.

"Devil! What kind of name is that?"

"One that's probably fitting for the look you have right now," He grinned. "Are you up to something tonight?" I asked.

"Nope. I'm in for the evening. I'll be hanging out with my baby," he affectionately mumbled, nibbling on my breast. "I want some of you. You think I can have some of my wife tonight without any interruptions?"

"Um hum," I responded. Kerwin picked me up, carried me into the shower, and forced me against the wall. He looked me passionately in my eyes and kissed me.

"I love you Mrs. Phillips, you're my baby. I couldn't think of any woman that would've made a better wife. Plus you're sexy and finer than a mutha." *Um hum, this chumps feeling guilty.*

"What's that all about?" I asked.

"Nothing, I missed you and I love you."

"I love you too."

No words existed after that. Only moans sounded off in our shower for the next twenty minutes. Once we dried off and made it to the bed, like a fool, I told Kerwin about seeing Alex in the mall.

"Did that nigga say anything?"

"Yeah, he tried to speak, asked me if he could call me sometime, and talked with Nikk for a minute."

"When he get out of prison?"

"Obviously he's been out for a while."

"Why you say that?"

"Cause him and yo girl got a daughter that's walking and a second baby on the way."

"My girl?" He asked puzzled.

"Kelly."

"Damn! He got out and hooked up with her?"

"He said he needed a place to parole to and she was his ticket."

"Why you know all that?"

"That's what he told Nikk while I was standing there."

"Oh, that nigga better not try no dumb shit or he gon' regret it."

"Boy ain't nobody thinking about Alex."

"You ain't got to be thinking about a nigga for them to be thinking about you."

"Okay, let's change the subject," I suggested, hugging him. "Babe, ain't nobody gon' mess up what we got. Like Bobby and Whitney baby, *We got something in common.* Babe, we were friends long before we were lovers. It's gon' always be like that cuz I ain't having it no other way." I looked over at my husband, who was asleep. *How this nigga gon' go from raising hell to knocked out in a matter of seconds.*

...◆◆◆...

Around three o'clock in the morning, I was awakened by a rattling sound. Once I came to my senses, I realized that it was Kerwin's cell. I slid out of bed, trying hard not to disturb him. By the time I got to the dresser to answer, the call had already gone to voicemail. I looked at the screen, noticing that there were three missed calls. *Three missed calls! Who the hell is calling at this time of the morning and what's so urgent that it can't wait until tomorrow?*

With questions like that, my women's intuition was going berserk. I walked to the front of the house, sat on the couch, and called the number back.

"What's up, I thought you were coming over?" A woman immediately asked.

"Who the hell is this?" I ranted.

"Who is this?"

"Wifey!"

"Wifey?"

"Yeah, bitch, didn't you just call my husband?"

"Yo husband?"

"Kerwin?"

Realizing she'd just been called out, she abruptly hung up in my face. I called the number back two or three times, but old girl didn't answer. I stormed my ass into our bedroom and threw Kerwin's cell phone at him.

"Damn!" he yelled, springing up, with his hands gripping his face. "What the hell is wrong with you?"

"You got another bitch!"

"What!"

"You heard me! You got another woman on the side. I know you do and you can't lie. She's been blowing you up all night and I called her back on your phone."

"What are you talking about? I ain't got nobody."

"You're lying."

"What I got to lie for. I said I ain't seeing no damn body, and that's what I mean."

"You're a lie! Look….. Look at your phone and tell me with a straight face that you don't know who that number belongs to." Kerwin looked at his phone and laid his head back on the pillow. The nervous smirk on his face made me believe he was lying.

"I know who it is, but she ain't nobody." I walked towards him screaming like a maniac.

"What you mean she ain't nobody?" She some damn body since she thinks she can call you all hours of the morning," I fussed, punching him.

"Asia, don't hit me no more. Calm down or get back."

"Calm down! Calm down! Ain't no calming down. You get the hell up and talk to me." Kerwin, nonchalantly sat up in the bed. He fluffed his pillows and leaned up against the headboard.

"Baby, come here," he requested, tapping the bed next to him. Tears streamed down my face as I tried to imagine my husband being with another woman. "Asia, she's nobody. I met this chick a few months ago at Fishbones. I was having lunch with Mr. Cheeks, Uncle E, and your pops. This female kept staring at me, then finally came over and asked for an autograph. I signed the back of one of my business cards because she didn't have any paper. I left and didn't think anything about it. I dropped your dad and E back off at the clothing store, and while I was driving home, she called."

"What the hell did you sit up and chat with her for? You know groupies be on the prowl. You ain't crazy, when you gave her that card, you knew her trifling, gold digging ass was gon' call out of curiosity."

"No I didn't."

"Give me a break. I ain't stupid."

"I know you're not."

"So why you trying to make me think that you gave a fan your personal information, without thinking she wasn't gon' call to see if it was legit?"

"I."

"I my ass. I think you wanted her to contact you. If not, you could've gotten some paper from the waiter or signed a napkin."

"Baby, do you want me to finish or are you going to go off on another tangent?"

"You act like I'm supposed to be okay with this."

"Naw, I knew you'd be pissed if you ever found out, but she don't mean nothing to me. I love you. You're my muthafuckin' wife. I don't care how many pretty faces I come across, and I do come across many. My heart belongs to you, which is why I come home everyday."

"Why you conversatin' with other women then?"

"Just talking, but talking is innocent."

"No talking leads to other things."

"Asia, I come home every night like I'm supposed to. Hell, the only thing talking can lead to is what ever I allow it to lead to, and I don't have any plans on gettin with that woman."

"So I can talk to niggas and it's okay with you?"

"Hell naw! Niggas don't respect another man like that."

"Bitches don't either. So as of today don't talk to her again." Suddenly, he scratched his head like he was considering my comment. "Kerwin, it's not an option. As a matter of fact, I want you to call her right now and tell her not to call you anymore."

"What!"

"You heard me. If she ain't nobody, like you say, call her now." To appease me, he called, but just my luck, she didn't answer the phone. "Well that's fine, we'll call her first thing in the morning. And if she can't be reached, I'm changing your number."

"No you're not."

"What you mean, no I'm not?"

"Just what I said?"

"Just what you said," I repeated, pissed off.

"Yeah, I'll let you have your tangents, talk your shit, fuss about this, think your running things most often, but you're going too far. You ain't changing my cell phone number. I've had this number for years. People from the block, some of my family, old friends, and so on have this number. You ain't changing shit. Now I said I'll call the girl and tell her not to call anymore, but you can't control who I talk to. Even if you changed the number, if I wanted to talk to someone bad enough, I'm gon' do it."

"That's fine," I replied, before grabbing my robe to leave.

"Where are you going?"

"To the Guess Room?"

"You mean the Guest Room."

"That too."

"What? Why are you sleeping in there?"

"Because I **guess** until you get back in husband mode, one of us is a guest in this house."

"You're trippin'," he insisted, rolling over to go back to sleep. *Oh and he don't care that I'm mad as hell either. That slut is more than just a phone buddy. How he gon' play me?*

I flipped Kerwin off and slammed the door behind me. Once I got to the other room, I couldn't sleep. The thought of him being with another woman drove me over the edge. I laid in bed for about twenty minutes before my conscience drug me out of bed and forced me into our computer room. I pulled up CMB Mobile's website, and changed all Kerwin's information. After I got all the information changed over, I logged on and checked his records. Immediately, I noticed that there were frequent calls made to this 493 number, which was programmed in his missed call log. *Oh my God, 168 minutes, 120 minutes, 98 minutes. Ut'un, this nigga is talking way too much to someone to be a married man. I'm gon' kill him. Better yet, I'm gon' run a trace on these numbers.*

I printed myself a copy of his last seven phone bills damn near using up every drop of ink in our little bubble jet printer. *This is ridiculous, first thing tomorrow, I'm calling Miles at Office Max and have them deliver me a real printer.* By the time all the sheets printed, I was sleepy. I put the pages up in a safe place and called it a night.

Chapter 25
That's Life

For fourteen days, I talked back and forth with Nikk about the incident that occurred that night. I'd calmed down some, so I thought about not checking the numbers. Nikk, thought I was a fool.

"Asia, what the hell you mean you ain't callin' dem numbers?"

"When you go looking for somethin', you're sure to find it. When I printed that log, I was a hurt wife grasping for answers. For two weeks I've had time to think."

"Annnd"

"And, I don't think I should play myself like that."

"Are you stupid? Asia, you're starting to sound crazy. What happened to yo' gangsta?"

"What? Nikk you sound so stupid. Fool I'm not a gangsta, I'm a college graduate, and a wife."

"College grad or not, if you let this pass, you're stupid."

"Why you say that?"

"Cuz you got the evidence right in your hand. Why wouldn't you call?"

"I don't want to put my business out in the streets. I don't want to call and find myself talking to someone who thinks she's Kerwin's top bitch. I know how y'all groupies are."

"What! Who the hell you callin' y'all groupies?"

"Nikk, I don't want to cause no controversy in my marriage behind some tramp looking for a good time and a pay day. And I don't mean this as no dis, but you fall into that category too."

"How you figure?"

"Girl, stop playin'. There are so many camera phone video's of you going around. You think these nigga's capturing shots of their nut skeeting all over yo face and ain't talking it up? Girl, you just a piece of easy ass. And you better chill on that, cuz they putting you out there bad."

"What you mean?"

"A few of them ball players told Kerwin that you goin' raw. That is a lie, I hope." Nikk had this puzzled look on her face that gave her away. "You dirty trick. I know you makin' them nigga's strap up?"

"Not always."

"What? Nikk, come on. You don't really know these niggas. What's up with that? You trying to get pregnant?"

"Asia, don't judge me. I ain't the one sleeping with yo man."

"I just can't believe you're that grimey."

"Well, I can't believe you're that weak. So we got some shit in common. Don't we?"

"Naw we ain't got a damn thing in common."

"I beg to differ."

"Well I don't. I'm very different."

"Asia, how you figure we're so different?"

"Nikk, I bet you could meet someone as insignificant as the team's camera guy and you'd give him some just on GP."

"Asia, screw what you talking about. Let's get off of me, Mrs. Too Nice Sometimes. The topic at hand is you. If you don't want to call that hoe who's violating your marriage, give me the phone log, and I'll call for you. Shit, we need to be runnin' up on old girl's ass like Mary J did in that *It's a Rap* video on Blair Underwood. Oh and by the way, I ain't fucking no lame camera man because he can't afford my time, conversation, or this pussy."

"You've got issues."

"Yeah, I do. They're called *Rent, Gas Bill, Car Note, Food, Lights,* and *Accessories*, Baby."

"No, they're called hoing."

"I like to think of my weakness as getting paid for a service. What you call yours?"

"My what?"

"Your weakness."

"I call it my business, and that's exactly why you're not about to be in the middle of it. I'm gon' shred this log and then make up with my husband."

"You're so weak. It has to be that NBA money that has you talkin' so ignorant," Nikk griped in discussed.

"Shut up home wrecker."

"Asia, in this day and time when you got a chance to bust your man cheating, sistas ain't ignoring the facts. Hell, they checkin' shit in and taking hostages. Ya'll ain't got no Pre-nuptial agreement either. Girl, do you know you could have half of all his money and move on to the next man?"

"What most sistas are doing is on them. This is me and I love my husband. I don't want his money. I want him."

"You want him and you suspect he's cheating on you?"

"Yeah, did you hear me say I love my husband, not his money?"

"No way I'm hearing this BS from you," she hissed like an angry snake. "Weak, that's what you are!"

"My grandma Bean always told me to be careful of the serpant. She said they grin in yo face like they're your best friend, but really envy you."

"Girl please, you ain't got nothing I envy. I'm just lookin out."

"Well if you want to know so bad call yourself," I insisted, throwing the sheets at her.

"Oh don't you worry, I'm gon call. And whatever I come up with, I'll be sure to keep it to myself."

"Yeah, you do that."

"What's that s'posed to mean?"

"You know exactly what it means, Big Mouth," I paused, "better yet, give 'em back. You ain't 'bout to be pillow talkin' my business with DeMarques Prince."

"Girl, I haven't seen your daddy in about a month."

"You're sick."

"Heffa please. If you could kick it with a sexy married man, you would too."

"I do kick it with a sexy married man. My own."

"Well I ain't even 'bout to go there with you. These sheets of paper tell me that your husband like adventure like yo daddy."

"Get out!"

"What!"

"You heard me. Get out!"

"Asia, I was playin."

"Well, you said the wrong thing today."

"But girl, I was only teasing."

"Well, my pain ain't no damn joke," I confirmed, walking towards my front door.

"Wait, before you put me out, are we still going shopping tomorrow?" I slammed the door in Nikk's face, and then returned to my living room to admire the sunset. I tried to figure out where I'd gon' wrong, but I had no answers. I'd been a good wife. Therefore Kerwin's shortcomings couldn't have been a result of something I'd done wrong.

I was desperate for some answers, so I got the phone log, and dialed the number from that night.

"Hello," this sensual voice answered.

"Hello. Who is this?"

"Who is this, you called me?"

"I'm sorry, I was trying to reach Chrice?"

"Wrong number."

"Okay, thank you."

Then just as politely as she answered, she hung up. "Okay, no problem."

I dare not call back and tell her that I was Kerwin's wife, so I let it go, about two hours later, I tried one other frequently called number and got a voicemail. *"Hello, you've reached the right number at the wrong time. This is Taylor, please leave a message and I'll be sure to get back with you. Beep…"* *I know this ain't the tramp that felt him up all in my face at the Camouflage Party. I know he said the other girl ain't nobody, but what's up with this.*

Chapter 26
Social Services

Almost four weeks had passed and I was still barely speaking to Kerwin. I had grown bored with staying home, and since I wasn't traveling to the games, I was ready to put my college degree to work. Out of the clear blue, I got up one Tuesday morning and decided to go to the Michigan State Employment Building to finally take the Social Workers exam. After being a pampered woman for so long, convincing myself to actually work a real nine to five was tearing at me something fierce.

I walked in and there was Leslie. She was a receptionist, a damn snooty one for that matter. I half spoke and told her my purpose for being there. She directed me in the right direction, and I proceeded with my mission without thinking twice about her. There was no stress about not studying in advance because passing the test was not the real challenge, however, working everyday was.

Two days after testing, the Department of Human Services granted me an interview and offered me a job. I was excited because the only job I'd ever had was at my dad's restaurant. But I ain't gon' lie, I was appalled and almost died when they told me the monthly salary. *Shit $1900.00, I spend that kind of money on shoes alone each month,* I thought, turning up my nose. *What was I thinking when I led myself to believe that a Bachelors degree in Social Work was gon' get me paid? Hell, I must have been on one of my save the world missions when I picked my major fa' sho. I could always go back to managing one of Dad's businesses, but then again, I need to get me a job for myself. How in the world do people make it on a salary like that? We need some better laws cuz that's a shame.*

"Mrs. Phillips.... Are you okay?"

"I'm sorry. I drifted off for a second. What did you say?"

"I said, are you interested in the position?"

"I need to speak with my husband before I give you my final decision. Can you give me until tomorrow, I'll get back with you then."

"Okay, I'll keep your application on my desk until, say, five tomorrow evening?"

"Perfect."

I knew Kerwin was going to have a fit about me going to work, especially considering that I'd been home living his dreams out with him all this time. He loved me being wherever he was while traveling at one time, but somewhere down the line things had slightly changed. I couldn't help but wonder how I'd grown old to him so quick, but it was my intention to get some kind of answers. If he wanted to play ignorant, I was gon' have to pull the old Asia Prince out on him and get his butt back on track.

When I made it home, I tried to ask him about his thoughts on me workin, but he wasn't hearing me. Because of the way he was playing me, my spirit was real vindictive. And since I was still upset with him, I really didn't care what he thought about me going into broken homes as a millionaire to fix other peoples problems. So without further thought, the next day, I accepted the job and started working that following week.

As expected Kerwin was livid about me working, but after going back and forth with him for a few days, he accepted my decision.

"Don't get out there and forget that you're married to a star athlete."

"You're so full of yourself lately. I don't know where you come off with this new found arrogance, but I don't like it one bit."

"Yeah, well I can't say that I care much about what you think since you didn't honor my opinion about you working."

"Fine, I've got to see a family late this afternoon, so don't look for me until after seven."

"We got a game tonight. You're not coming?"

"Nope! For what?"

"For support."

"Get Taylor or one of your other hoes to sit on the side line and boost your ego. I'm done being rotated out with your other bitches."

"What?"

"You heard me. And soon as I get myself together, I'm leaving yo sorry ass."

"You ain't goin' nowhere. All this money you got access too, you think I believe you're leavin' me."

"Nigga, I had money before you. My father was a millionaire way before you ever saw long money."

"Well I got him now."

"Fuck you." I yelled, snatching my car keys off the counter.

"Who you talkin' to like that?

"You."

"Naw, you ain't talkin' to me, the last time I checked, I was the HNIC up in here."

"You were, but since you're not the man I fell in love with. You get treated like any other lame ass nigga."

"Why am I so different now?"

"You tell me. All I know is I saw your phone bills, and I know you got a sidekick," I yelled.

"You don't know a damn thing."

"Your phone bills don't lie."

"Asia, tell me you didn't," he paused, clearly furious with me.

"I did. I printed your bills from the past three months and all I got to say is fuck you," I screamed, slapping him.

"Naw, fuck you, crazy ass bitch!" he launched back, grabbing my hands as I went to slap him a second time. "Look, you're on some BS. You don't invade my privacy like that. I don't do it to you and I want the same respect in return."

"Ain't no privacy when you're married."

"Well it is in this house," he paused, holding his face. "And you got one more time to hit me like that, and I'm gon' hurt you."

"Yeah, and my daddy…"

"Shut that Daddy shit up. I got mad respect for you. I don't put my hands on you, and I expect the same in return. You heard what I said, now try me. I swore that I'd never hit a woman after what happened to my moms, but if you hit me again, it's on."

Kerwin had this cold stare like never before. I read his sincerity and figured I better go on and leave before our situation got out of control.

"Get rid of your groupies, or you gon' be a single man," I fussed, walking out the room.

"You ain't goin' no damn where like I said."

For the months that passed, the late night calls, my working, and the constant fighting kept real bad vibes brewing between us. Kerwin stayed away when he wasn't playing ball, and I was shopping and eating like a pig with the little $1900.00 I made. Before I knew it, I started gaining a little weight, and feeling somewhat self conscience about my body. I tried to talk with my dad about it, but he wasn't any help.

"Butterfly if you see it's a problem, work on it. Don't no nigga want his Halle Berry to become a Miss Piggy."

"Daddy, you're so cold. Is that what happened with you and Teretta? She didn't keep that model figure after she had the baby, so she wasn't the one any more."

"She's my wife, but I'm a man first. Though I love her to death, pretty faces and sculpted bodies capture my attention and bring out the dog in me."

"So is that why you doin' Nikk?" I asked, shocking him.

"What you say?"

"You heard me. I know about what you two are up to and I think it's sad and trifling."

"Who told you?"

"That don't matter. How can you do that to Teretta?"

"Butterfly, it's not personal."

"So if Kerwin tipped out on me cause he's quote "A man," is that going to be okay with you?"

"See there you go turning the story around and makin' this discussion too personal."

"Answer the question. Do you think it's okay for Kerwin to cheat on me?"

"Naw I don't think it's okay. However, as a man, he may find himself slipping a little, but not intentionally. Baby, you new millennium women make it hard to be loyal. These low riders y'all wearing with all your ass hanging out is driving bortha's over the edge. Y'all to sexually explicit in all aspects of life, ya half naked in the grocery stores, malls, clubs, work, while you're checking the mail, shoot anywhere. Women just don't believe in covering up anymore. Y'all don't leave much to the imagination, and for a man with raging hormones that could be lethal."

"So because women dress sexy, are you telling me that it's okay for my husband to cheat based on that example?"

"No, I'm not saying it's okay. I'm saying that due to all the sexual explicitness in society today, sometimes we aren't in control like we need to be."

"Forget it!" That topic with Dad was hopeless. He was a slut and not a good person to seek advice from. I decided to allow Kerwin to have his moment, do his man thing, and I went on and made the best of my new career.

....◆◆◆....

Seven months after I took on my position, I don't know how, but Alex and Kelly crossed my path once again. I couldn't believe that Alex and Kelly became a part of the system due to a nasty domestic dispute. *Karma...*

hum, got a way of making you wish you would have done things differently. Anyway, the day I was scheduled to see them for their initial visit, I'd forgotten about my appointment and hadn't dressed my best. There was no way I was going to their place looking average, so I decided to stop by the store to buy a new pair of shoes and a much sexier shirt. I originally had on a pair of sneakers, a polo style shirt, and some jeans. *How cheesy,* I thought, whipping up in a mini mall parking lot to get my shop on. I bought this cute frilly shirt to go with my jeans, some sexy slide in shoes, with a low heel, and a bottle of Tiffany perfume. I freshened up my make-up, fixed my ponytail, and headed to their house.

When I arrived, I quickly grabbed my things, sprayed myself down with way to much perfume, and headed for the door.

I stood on the porch anxiously tapping my foot, suddenly Kelly's face appeared in the door.

"Asia," she stated in shock.

"Kelly," I repeated, being an ass.

"What are you doing here?"

"I've been assigned to your case."

"What? I can't believe you're working a job like this with your man playing in the pros. Things must not be so well at home."

"Yeah, well they are. Can we get on with it, Kelly? You know I called yesterday to schedule this appointment. I'm here for your home study. If we get started right now, it'll only take about an hour."

"I didn't realize that was you." *Yeah, well I knew it was you.* "Come on in," she apprehensively suggested, moving to the side.

I walked in kind of scanning the room. When I got a glance of their Flea Market furniture and the way they lived, I suddenly found myself celebrating within. It quickly registered that nothing in their house could remotely come close to my standard of living, and losing Alex was a good thing after all. *So this is how I would have been living had I turned up with Alex. Hell naw, I wouldn't have lived like this cuz my daddy wasn't gon have that.*

"Asia can I offer you something to drink," Kelly asked, interrupting my thought.

Yeah right so you can poison me, I don't think so. "No thank you," I quickly replied.

We sat looking at each other for a second in kind of a blank stare. Finally, I had to ask her why she'd slept with Alex.

"Kell, we were girls, how could you sleep with my man, then watch him beat me down and not intervene."

"Asia," she sighed. "I've thought about that day and what happened between us for so many years. I've thought about what I could or should have done differently and I'm sorry."

"Sorry, just tell me why. Forget sorry."

"Asia, the day you introduced me to Alex, I wanted to tell you that I already knew him, but we were already cool, and I didn't want to mess up our friendship. Alex and I used to kick it back in the day, but once he saw that we knew each other, he made me promise that I wouldn't tell you."

"Well where and when did y'all meet? And why didn't he want you to tell me. You were someone from his past?"

"No, I was still kicking it with him when you and I met in college. Neither of us knew it though."

"Huh?"

"When Al and I hooked up, I knew he had a girlfriend, I just didn't know it was you. And by the time I found out, him and I had long history."

"So you knew he had a woman, but you didn't care?"

"He told me he had someone in Chicago, but he was always on me so tuff, I mean he was jockin' me so hard that I gave in to his persistence and became his other woman."

"It didn't bother you to know that you were his B woman?"

"You assume I was his B, but as far as I'm concerned, you might have been his B. I believed I was his A or at least he treated me like I was. Asia, Alex broke so much bread on me that if I was his B woman, it surely didn't feel like it. That nigga bought me jewelry, designer bags, clothes, shoes, a fur jacket, and kept my pockets on swoll. I mean right before school started our freshman year, he was with me everyday for about three weeks straight."

"Yeah because we broke up."

"Y'all broke up?"

"Yeah, long story," I said in intense thought. "Then that explains how you came up with my fur coat"

"Your fur coat! Alex gave me that jacket in a box with the tags still in the pocket."

"They were originally on the coat, but when he gave it to me, I pulled them off and put them in the pocket."

"So you tellin' me that we were sharing furs too."

"Yep," I smiled, feeling a little vindictive.

"Shit, we were sharing more than just coats then, because there were days when Alex would be on campus, leave your apartment like he was going home, and when you were on your way to class, he'd come get in bed with me."

Dirty Bastard, I thought before saying just that. "Alex gets on my nerves. He wasn't right and he knew he wasn't right. But that's how life is and you came up with everything in the end, so you were the better woman I guess."

"Asia, you think a nigga cares about being right when he's given the opportunity to have his cake and eat it too?"

"Well, you should know since you made it possible for him."

"If not me, then it would have been someone else."

"So where did y'all meet?"

"He used to move dope for my daddy before he was murdered."

"Who is your daddy?"

"Melvin Daniels. He and Calvin Shaw built a drug empire together. No one ever knew he was my daddy because my mother always feared for my safety."

"So did he know he was your daddy?"

"Yeah, but all my life, he made people think I was his niece."

"His niece! Why his niece?"

"I don't know. My mom always said he was one that was into way more dirt than the city or the law gave him credit for. But no matter what, he always loved me and made sure I had the things I needed."

"So Melvin was your daddy? Alex idolized him and Calvin. I see why he was trying to be all in good with you."

"What!"

"I'm not saying that as a dis. I'm saying considering the way Alex loved Calvin and Mel, it doesn't surprise me that you two ended up together. I think you gave Alex a sense of connection to two people he loved more than himself."

"Alex loved me then, and he loves me now for the same reasons," she hissed. "My daddy ain't got a thing to do wit it."

"Don't get so defensive, I believe he does love you now, but I'm saying he probably didn't as much at first, but with time you won him over."

"Anyway, let's move on. This ain't why you're here."

"Fine," I snapped, pulling my paperwork out of my briefcase. "Is Alex here? I'll need to ask him a few questions as well?"

"No, but he's on his way home."

At that point, my demeanor shifted as I had a flashback. *No this rat bitch didn't just sit here and say a fur coat wasn't all we shared. How she gon' be girls with me, sleep with my man, and make the shit seem like it was okay.*

To keep from kicking her skinny tail right up in her own house, I got back on task quickly.

"Kelly, let's get these forms filled out now and when Alex gets here, he can do his part."

"Okay."

"Tell me a little about the incident that occurred the day you and Alex got arrested."

"What you need to know?"

"Anything pertaining to the incident in order to help me assess where I need to start with your court ordered family therapy."

"I don't know if I want to openly share my personal business with you like that."

"You don't have much of a choice. We can get this home study completed or I can forward a note to the judge tomorrow, informing him that you were non compliant."

"I think I want to work with someone other than you."

"That's fine, but if there was someone other than me, you'd have them. The system is strained right now, and so is personnel. You got to go with what they give you or deal with the consequences later for refusal of services."

She sat in silence for a moment, then she finally spoke.

"I caught Alex messing'around. Saddest part about the entire story is that he cheated on me with an eighteen-year-old. I was so angry when I confronted him, that I jumped on her too. Here this nigga was driving around town in my car with our two kids and his bitch. That man is twenty-six years old. What is he gon' do with a bitch still in high school?"

"That's ridiculous," I uttered, giving my opinion when I wasn't supposed to. "So how come in the police report the statement is written as though you two were fighting here."

"We were. When Alex came home, I started hitting him as soon as he walked through the door. I immediately punched him in his face, ignoring the fact that he was holding my baby, and when he went to block my swing, she fell out of his arms. That probably restrained him to some extent, but he still managed to punch me in my chest and face, before checking on her. My neighbor called 911, and when the cops arrived we both went to jail."

"And the kids went to the shelter."

"Not at first. Alexis had a bruise on her cheek from the fall, so they took the girls to the hospital to be checked out and then to the shelter."

"So what do you think you and Al need to make this go away?"

"The judge ordered parenting classes, family therapy, and individual anger management sessions. I'm going to do whatever I need to do to get my kids back."

"Good, I'm glad to hear you say that." Finally, I looked at my watch, noticing the time. "Shoot, two and a half hours have already passed us by. It doesn't look like Alex is going to make it. I guess I'm going to have to speak with him next time."

"Okay."

"For the record, could I get a contact number for him?"

"Um, sure, I guess so, it is 555-1733."

"I'll call you some time soon to set up my next visit," I said, rising to my feet.

"That's fine."

I left the house that day thinking, *Kelly was lucky someone heard her screams for help. Had they not, Alex might have killed her.* He was a very different person when enraged. Sometimes he was so out of control when got angry that he looked like the devil himself. I knew God spared my life both times he attacked me. I just thank Him that I wasn't stupid enough to stay. So many women get warning signs, but they often ignore them. Alex's actions forced me out of his life, and there was just no way I'd ever go back. The only thing I couldn't understand is why our paths were crossing once again. Time has a way of exposing answers and that's exactly what it did for me.

Chapter 27
Alex

After working closely with Kelly and Alex for about three months, I finally told Kerwin. Considering my past with them, I kind of felt guilty that it took me that long.

"So what does that mean? Are you and him creepin' around?"

"See there you go being silly. Why would I sneak around with him when I have you?"

"Cause lately I been slippin' when it comes to home. And I know first hand my wife gon' stray before she goes without."

"That's a real ignorant comment."

"Ignorant it might be, but true. I see it happening all the time."

"You see what happenin' all the time?"

"Infidelity."

"So what's your excuse?"

"Who said I'm cheating?"

"I did."

"Well provide me with some facts and then you can accuse me of something."

"What about all those calls on your bill to that Taylor chick?"

"Did it show me and her having sex?"

"You're trying to be funny."

"No I'm not, all that says is that we spent time talking. That's still not cheating. So until you can prove that fact, keep all that lip service you spitin' to yourself."

"Who you think you talkin' to?" I paused staring him down like he had me twisted. "What is with you Kerwin? Am I not sexy to you anymore? Do you not love me? What?"

"Yeah I love you. You just be talkin' to much shit. That gets on my nerves. You need to learn how to be a little more submissive sometimes."

"Submissive!"

"Hell yeah, I said submissive. You're so busy trying to run the house that you forget I'm the king of this here palace."

"So my controlling personality ain't turnin' you on anymore?"

"Naw. It was cute before we got married, but once we started livin' together, you should have toned it down a bit."

"So is that what happened to us?"

"Is what, what happened to us?"

"My bossiness pushed you away." I smirked. "And if that's the case, did you get yourself someone you can run over now."

"What?"

"You heard me, do you love Taylor now?"

"See there you go again. I'm done."

"Nigga it ain't over until I say so," I fussed, pulling his arm.

"Asia, have a great day at work. I've got some runs to make."

I looked at him in clear disgust. *How this punk gon' just cut me off in the middle of our argument and try to walk out like I don't matter?*

"Whatever, Nigga!" I yelled, pissed about him dismissing me. I guess he caught a glimpse of my expression cuz he stopped and walked back towards me.

"What you say chump?" he smiled.

"You heard me," I repeated with a trembling lip, trying to hold back tears.

"Give me a kiss," he cunningly requested with puckered lips, and then a glowing smile that made me remember what we once shared. "We're better than this, Baby, I'm tired of fighting. I was just talking shit cuz I'm frustrated. Asia. I love you. I love who you are and your bossy personality. I'm sorry about tripping lately," he stated, resting his head up against mine. "I got a lot of pressure on me. Got some things going on in my life that I really don't want to talk about right now, but as soon as the season is over, I promise I'm gon' take you on one hell of a vacation and we gon' make up."

"Make up?" I repeated.

"Yeah! You know be like we used to be, laugh, talk, play, and make love all day long like old times."

"You got things going on in your life like what?"

"Things I don't want to talk about right now, but again, as soon as the season ends, we'll talk."

I wanted to keep prying Kerwin for information, but I knew if I did he'd get mad and then we'd argue again. I accepted his suggestion to talk about things at a later time, then left for work.

Once I pulled into the parking lot, I whipped up in a spot close to the main door. As I sat organizing my things to carry into the building, I was startled by a familiar voice.

"Lookin' mighty fine this morning, pretty lady."

"Thank you," I responded, looking up.

"I've been callin' your office for the past two weeks. Why haven't you returned any of my calls?"

"Alex, I don't need to return personal calls."

"Why not?"

"First of all, you're my ex, secondly, we ended our relationship on bad terms, thirdly, you're one of my clients, and finally, I'm married and not at all interested in you."

"You don't think it's good to mix business with pleasure?"

"Sure don't."

"Good, me either."

"So why are you here then?"

"Cause, I wanted to see you without Kelly's ass all up in my face casin' my every word."

"What?"

"Asia, I miss you," he confessed, looking desperate. Baby, I fucked up. I fucked up bad, but I still love you more than anything and anyone."

"Alex you are the past, and I'm on to bigger and better things. You're happy, I'm happy, and our lives took us in opposite directions. I have no hard feelings about that. Actually, I wish you and Kell the best."

"I believe you, but Boo, I'm going through it. I miss the hell out of you. I miss the way we made love, I miss our long talks, I miss your pretty smile," he suggested, stroking my face, "I miss the way you said my name when I was putting it to you. Shit, Asia, I miss you."

"I'm sorry Alex. I'm not interested."

"Boo, if you give me one more chance, I'll prove to you that I can be a better man."

"Alex, you're still on that same old nonsense."

"What nonsense?"

"It really doesn't matter. I'm married, you have a family, and I'm on something else. I don't want to be with no damn drug dealer anymore. That played out for me long before I graduated from college."

"Oh, so you think you're better than me."

"Absolutely not. I didn't say that."

"Well it sounds like you did to me."

"Well, that's because you're not listening. I said I'm on something else."

"What does something else mean?"

"I'm on something and someone that's productive and able to assist me with moving towards goals that take me to the next level in my life?"

"I'm productive, and I could move you in that direction."

"Yeah right. Boy you can't even maintain something as simple as a 9 to 5. You think runnin' dope is the only way you can make it. I've got too much to sacrifice for ten weeks of excitement cuz I know we wouldn't last much longer than that."

"Asia, I introduced you to so much back in our day. You can't even fix your mouth to tell me that you didn't love being with me."

"Yeah you did show me things I was ignorant too, but I'm older now. The things that fascinated me back then, don't anymore. Alex in case you haven't noticed, I'm a woman. I'm not a sixteen-year-old looking for adventure or some roughneck to help me rebel against my parents."

"I know I ain't got bread like yo man. I can't buy you all that high dollar shit you've grown accustomed to, but I can offer you love and happiness."

"No you can't."

"Why can't I."

"Because it's impossible to give me something I've already got."

I looked in Alex's eyes, noticing his expression. For the first time in years, I saw the man I met in T-Bells as a teeny bopper and felt some compassion for him.

"Alex, thanks for dropping by, but I'm not interested. Duty calls. You have a great day," I insisted, forcing my way past him.

"Asia, I'm not going to go away that easy. We've got unfinished business."

"Our business ended the day you slapped me around like I was a fucking rag doll," I growled, putting distance between us.

"Everyone makes mistakes," he replied, looking pitiful.

I simply ignored him and headed into our building. I usually made a pit stop by the restroom before going to my desk to make sure my makeup and hair were in order, but that particular day I had to stop to take five minutes of self-talk. As the door slammed behind me, I found myself looking at the woman in the mirror. I questioned myself for a moment. *Asia, why did you even entertain that man's conversation? Girl, are you really over Alex or do you just think you are?* Suddenly, I wiped my face to redirect my thoughts, but Alex wouldn't go away. *There wasn't any real closure for us, Right?............ Umm, Ms. Thang, who are you kidding. The day Alex blacked your eyes and made your lip five sizes larger than an elephants ass should have been closure enough. Get your house in order and reclaim your marriage. The simple fact that you're considering him once again is real scary. You're lonely, missin your husband; therefore you're vulnerable. Get it together before you make a real big mistake.* "I will."

My conscience was right. I had to be a damn fool or desperate as hell for some affection to be missing Alex's abusive ass. I wasn't either of the two, so getting' it together was a must. *What could he really offer me?* I knew for a fact that he was still abusive. Shit, I was the worker on his domestic violence case with Kelly. It didn't take a brain scientist to decipher that he hadn't changed much since his prison tour. So why was I even thinking about the conversation we had to any degree? *Asia, Asia, Asia, get your mind right. Girl, you are really trippin',* I thought, walking out of the restroom.

....◆◆◆◆....

By the time I'd made it home that evening, my mind was made up. I was going to work out my situation with my husband, and get our lives back on track. *Hell in the past we'd had such a bomb rapport, so why allow another woman to take my prize. If I'm slacking in some areas of my relationship, I'm gon' find out today and do my best to get our life back on track.*

When Kerwin got in that evening, I'd prepared dinner, set our table, lit a few candles, and put on R. Kelly's greatest hits CD. *Honey Love* echoed throughout the room when Kerwin entered the house. *"There is something that I want from you.....ri...iii...ght now,"* I sung, walking up on him for a kiss.

"Give me that yummy lo....oove," he chimmed in.

"Right now ..right now," I finished up laughing. Suddenly the song changed. Kerwin gripped me tight and dipped me.

"I feel soooooo..... freaky tonight, better bring yo body here baby" Kerwin sung, lifting me to carry me to our bedroom. I smiled and teared at the same time because we hadn't played or sung together in so long. I'd really missed being close to my husband and something as simple as us singing songs together like old times exposed just how much we'd lost. "Asia, what's wrong, Baby?"

"We've been tripping for too long."

"I agree."

"Kerby, it's just been a while since we've kicked it like this. I've missed our friendship."

"Yeah, me too. Come here and let me hold you."

"I cooked," I expressed, moving towards him in my biker shorts and fitted T-shirt.

"Um' I knew something smelled good. What did you cook?"

"I cooked baked chicken, spinach, yams, dressing, and rolls."

"Sounds good, but that's not what I smell."

"What you smell then?"

"You."

"Oh," I snickered, leaning my face into his chest. "Baby, I love you so much. I wish we could be like we used to be. You were my man, my best friend, my lover, my confidant, my homeboy, my..."

"I got you," he replied, cutting me off.

"So what did I do wrong? Where did I fall short? What made you want to get out there and be with someone else?"

"Asia, you're a good woman. I can't take anything from you. You've been good to me, good for me, and my number one lady for sure. What we're going through is about me, not you."

"What does that mean?"

"I'm the one that's trippin'. You're still beautiful to me, I still love you very much, but I'm a man."

"That sounds like an excuse to me."

"I don't want nobody but you."

"So why you out there then?"

"Sometimes men take good women for granted. We can have the best thing going on in our lives and one little distraction can have us off track. I'm no angel, but I promise I love you and I don't want nobody else."

"So that still doesn't explain the need for another woman."

"Babe, we hooked up our first year in college. Sometimes I don't think I got a chance to experience all of the non-financial perks that come along with being in the league. I mean I didn't get them out of my system before we got married."

"Perks?"

"Yeah, shit that comes along with being a professional athlete that's not in the contract."

"Like...."

"Come on, Baby, don't make me say it. You know."

"What women in every city! Groupies! Life on the creep. No commitment or strings to anyone."

"You asking me or telling me?"

"Askin'."

"All of that if you want me to be honest and then some."

"So what do you suggest we do? Do you want a divorce?"

"I want you."

185

"I'm sorry, Kerwin. You can't have the ***Best of both worlds***. R Kelly and Jay Z can attest to that. With all the money they had, even two of the greatest in the industry saw it just wasn't realistically possible."

"They ain't got shit to do with this discussion."

"Not really, but I was just showing you that money don't predict a perfect world in any person's life. What those women see is your money, and what they think you offer them. If you were broke, half of them hoes wouldn't even want you."

"Yeah, back then they didn't want me, but right now I'm hot, and they all up on me."

"And, your point is what?"

"Why not live a little?"

"Fool, did you just hear what you said to me?"

"Asia, I was only playing," he laughed. "Mike Jones already lettin' a nigga know how it's layin' for a brotha once he come up. I told you I want you. That's what I mean."

"So how do we fix our relationship?"

"It was never broken. You were just trippin' Ma."

"Naw, you were until you found out yo dirt wasn't on the DL."

"Okay, let's change the subject. You cooked a nice dinner, you're lookin' very sexy in dem bikers that's hugging my monkey, and I'm focused on home. So can we enjoy the evening and start over from here?"

"Start over from here how?"

"Let me show you."

Kerwin turned, acting as though he was rewinding. He walked out of the room, and then re-entered singing, "*I feel soooooo freaky tonight, better bring yo body here....*"

"*Sex me... Sex me, Baby....*" I chimed in, laughing.

Chapter 28
Asia Stop Playin

That was the one thing that I always loved about Kerwin. We made up easy and he kept me smiling. After that evening, Kerwin and I were back on track and life in the Phillip's household was going well. He ended up changing his cell phone number, got rid of Taylor, I guess, and focused more on home. I never thought it was in me to be the kind of woman to forgive a cheating soul mate, but I figured if I could forgive a domesticly violent, psycho rapist, I could surely forgive the man I vowed to love a lifetime.

Seven months had come and gone and Thanksgiving of 2009 was quickly approaching. I was still working my job with the state, but had gone part-time to travel with my man again and run interference on tramps trying to come up. The Piston's played an early game at home for the holiday, so afterwards, family and friends came over for dinner. Mildred, the cook from Bean's Spot prepared the meal and that sista threw down. She had so much food on the table that the thought of eating it all made me full before I ever fixed myself a plate. Daddy and Teretta were the last to make it to the house, so as soon as he hung up his coat, he came into the family room talking noise.

"Dawg, you were spankin' that ass tonight. I don't know why Latrell Thomas thinks he can hold you. Nigga my son-in-law can't be faded," Dad roared.

"Yeah, but for a rookie he got mad game. I'd give him about two more years in the league and he's gon' be a serious household name," Uncle E assured Dad.

"E, get out. How you gon' be in my son's house jockin' another nigga. In this Casa, he's the household name."

"Yeah," I chimed in, giving my man his props. "And he's gon' be a Papi too."

"What you say?" Daddy asked.

"You heard me, Kerwin's about to be a daddy."

"Asia, stop playin," Kerwin insisted.

"I'm serious." Kerwin looked at my expression, realized I was serious and went ballistic.

"Aw Damn, y'all hear that. I'm bout to be a father," he cheered.

"Congratulations Son," my father expressed, being crunchy.

"Not a little Kerwin in the family," Nikk sassed from her seat.

"Dawg, you bout to be a daddy," Dave repeated, dapin Kerwin in excitement.

"Hey, what about me? I'm going to be a parent too. All y'all around here jockin' him like he did this by himself."

"Sorry, Butterfly. I'm so happy for you," Dad assured me, getting watery eyed. "I remember when you were a baby. Man your mother used to get on my nerves. One time your mama left me baby sitting while she went to the beauty shop. She was supposed to be back by two to pick you up and was a no call, no show. Me and my boys, Chew and J had plans to go to one of the biggest skating parties of the year at Detroit Roller Wheels, but yo mama left me hanging. Even though I loved you, Daddy sitting wasn't a priority. I had my own agenda and you came second." Dad paused for a brief moment, affectionately looking at me. "Once I went to prison, I learned the value of what I'd lost as a father and since the day them cell bars shut on me, I ain't stopped. That's why it was always about you while I was locked up. I knew I couldn't give you much, but I could always give you Daddy. Butterfly, I'm so glad you loved me in spite of my inadequacies." Suddenly, he paused and turned to Kerwin. "Man, you better love my grandchild to no end or else."

"You don't have to ever worry about that. Man, I got so much I want to share with my family that loving my child won't ever be an issue for me."

"Okay…… Leeeeeeeee…..eeeeeeeeets eat," Mildred yelled from the dining room, cutting us all off before we got to sentimental.

"I'm gon' always love my wife and our child. Ain't nobody got too ever tell me about the importance of having a family. No better person to appreciate having someone to call his own than a person who went most of his life without. Growing up with no parents or siblings helped me understand the value of having a wife, great in-laws, and a child."

"Good, cause you mess over Asia and.."

"Daddy, stop it," I fussed

"I'm serious," Dad insisted.

"Man, I ain't scared of you," Kerwin teased. "You know I got all that yard out there if you want some of me," he informed Dad, grabbing him around his neck.

The two of them horse played all the way to the dining room, and I loved it. My dad always liked Kerwin, seems like he and I turning out to be an item worked out for the both of us. See that's why a woman should keep the household family drama between her and her man. cuz if she doesn't, once she decided to forgive him, the family keeps hatin' him 'til the bitter end. My family never knew Kerwin and I were having marital problems because I'd learned from Mama and Rodney that you keep things like that to yourself. I'm glad I followed my first mind. Had I not, that particular day could have been much different.

We all gathered around the table to bless the meal. Once we joined hands, Dad said the prayer. "Lord, thank you for this meal, the hands that prepared it, the stomachs that will take it in, and the sewage it will pass through once digested..... Amen."

"Chump, what kind of prayer was that?" E asked.

"My granddaddy was always long winded with his prayers. I always said when I came together for my family meals and I was a granddad, I wasn't gon' keep my grandchildren waiting like Daddy Ruenae kept us waiting."

"Well, ain't no grandchildren here today."

"Yes there is. She's in my baby's stomach and I'm practicing."

"You a fool," E laughed, hugging Dad.

"Let's eat!" Dad insisted, raising the knife to carve the turkey.

That was one of the most festive holidays our family spent together in a long time. When we were wrapping up, Kerwin and I walked my dad, Uncle E, and Teretta out. "Thanks for having us. Butterfly, when you were a newborn, you were so beautiful. You were a real brat, but you were my brat. I'm so glad I didn't do something evil to you like I wanted to the day you shit all over me." Dad laughed. "Had I, I wouldn't feel as happy as I do today. Once that baby comes, you make sure you keep lovin' your husband as much as you do today. After you deliver, he's going to need some extra attention for a while. That's how you ensure that your marriage doesn't encounter any issues regarding the new addition to the family."

"I won't, Daddy," I replied, respecting his fatherly advice as well as wondering just where that statement came from.

Then once I started to think about it, I answered the question for myself. I remember asking Dad after Nikk revealed their secret, what happened with him and Terretta that caused him to go outside their marriage for satisfaction. I guess this was his way of discretely answering my question.

"Ker, don't ever be so jealous of our baby that you go else where lookin' for love."

"Girl, are you kidding me," he replied, grabbing me around my waist from behind to massage my still flat tummy. "It ain't nothing out there that's gon mess up my happy home again."

Chapter 29
Dr. Clifton Henry

When I was thirteen weeks pregnant, Kerwin accompanied me to my first real doctor's appointment. Dr. Henry came in singing some song called Midnight Fantasy that tickled me to death.

"Doc, what are you singing?" Kerwin asked.

"Man some song I wrote back in my college days at Langston."

"Cliff, you went to Langston? My cousin went there," I interrupted.

"Yeah, I was on the football team."

"I can't imagine."

"I don't know what you're talking about. Shoot, I was the campus star. Took home the money from all the talent shows, too" he smiled.

"Talent shows?"

"Fa'sho. I would sing a few songs and the girls went crazy."

"Songs like what?"

"I had this song called, Time for Dinner."

"What was that about?" Kerwin interrupted.

"Man, ask me when the wife's not in the room."

"Whatever I'm not green," I fussed.

"I guess. Kerwin, you better get on her man," he teased. "She's a feisty little something since she got pregnant."

"Anyway," I said, rolling my eyes. "Did you know Langston has a real strong Alumnus here in the Motor City."

"I didn't, but that's good to know. Maybe I can look up a few of my old honeys."

"I can't imagine any of them wanting to still see you."

"That's cause you don't know a thing about Miami Sex Appeal."

"My man is what you'd consider Sex Appeal," I expressed.

"I ain't about to argue with you today, Asia. How are you and this little big head baby getting along?"

"Doc, you better be glad we're cool."

"Why you say that?"

"Cuz I can't see myself paying nobody all this money that's dissin' my child and my wife."

"Man, you want to hear the baby's heartbeat?" he asked, ignoring Kerwin.

"Yeah."

"Asia, lay back."

Kerwin eased up beside me, placing his right hand on my stomach. Once he heard the little thumping of our baby's heart for the very first time, his eyes got a little watery. I'd never seen him so emotional. I mean, he was a sensitive man, but not a crying one.

"Damn, I can't believe that this is a part of me. I wish my mama could be here to see this."

"You about to be a daddy," I sung, puckering my lips for him to lay one on me.

"Hey, hey, cut all that out. That's how you got in this predicament in the first place," Cliff teased.

"Come on Asia, Doc's hatin'."

"Naw, I just don't want you to get pregnant again before you deliver this baby."

"Man, are you sure you got a degree in medicine?" Kerwin asked, helping me down. "Baby, where did you find him again?"

"And make sure you pay the receptionist on your way out. Kerwin, don't forget about the gym tomorrow. And don't come with no excuses about why you can't lift either."

"Yeah, yeah, yeah, we out, nigga."

"Nigga! Nigga, Asia, see how your man talks to your doctor?"

"Both of y'all need to stop. Let's go Kerwin."

"See you in a month, Asia. See you tomorrow Kerwin."

My doctor and Kerwin were childhood friends from the block. Cliff attended Cass Tech, a school for the academically elite, before moving to Miami to finish his senior year. He thought he was going to the University of Maimi, so he was trying to get residency. Whenever the two of them got together they always carried on like they were brothers, but while I was pregnant, it got on my nerves. Cliff was a Family Doctor, not an OBGYN, but I ended up using him because he had been my primary care physician since Kerwin and I got married. Though Kerwin sometimes joked about him seeing his wife's goodies that really didn't matter to me, he was a great doctor and there was no one I trusted more with my child's precious life than him.

...◆◆◆◆...

Kerwin dropped me off at home and went on to practice. I didn't even bother to go into the house. Instead, I headed straight for work. I sung all the way to my job like I was in concert, bumping this throwback jam by *Charlie, last name, Wilson.*

Soon as I pulled up in my spot and entered the building. I made it as far as the elevator still singing, "*I was wondering, if I could take you out, show you a good time....,*" and out of nowhere popped Alex.

"*Here is my number, so you can call me,*" he joined in. "Yeah that was the jam, wasn't it?"

"Umm, hum," I replied, getting on the elevator, smiling.

"Hey Boo, I saw you on my way out."

"What are you doing here Alex?"

"I just got out of court. They dismissed all the charges and closed our case."

"Great. I'm happy for you and Kell."

"I see you're about to be a mommy," he stated, rubbing my belly like my baby was his.

"Yeah, Kerwin and I are expecting."

"You look beautiful pregnant. I always knew you would."

"Thank you."

"You know this baby should be mine," he expressed, making full circular strokes on my tummy. I flung his hand down.

"Please don't touch me like that," I lashed out at him.

"Why, does that make you uncomfortable or do you realize you miss my touch."

"I don't appreciate it."

"I love you," he smirked. "And have I ever told you how sexy you look when you're scared. I can see fear all in your eyes. Do I make you nervous? You know I could pull this emergency button and stop this elevator? Then you'd be forced to talk to me." *Is this nigga bout to try and rape me or something talking like that?*

"Not at all," I replied with comfidence. "I just don't want you touchin' on me." Finally, I made it to my floor, and the doors opened. "Well, I guess this is me. Congrats on getting your case closed. Have a great week."

"Asia, I'm not going to pretend like I don't miss or love you."

"Alex, I told you before I was done and that's what I mean."

"Come on Asia, I know I haven't done right, but just let me take you out one last time for your birthday."

"Ut'un," I firmly insisted, letting my no, mean no. "I don't think so. We've been living separate lives for a while, so we need to leave it like that. Goin' out with you will cause friction in my home."

"Boo, please! I'm beggin' you. I'm missin' the hell out of you. Besides, I already got your gift."

"Yeah right you got a gift for me. I know how manipulative you are."

"Asia, did I say I have a gift?"

"Yeah, but you said a lot of things that turned out to be lies."

"Why I got to lie about a gift though."

"I don't know. Why did you lie about half the shit you lied about in the past that was just as dumb?"

"It seems like you're trying to make me mad, but I'm not gon' even trip with you today. I'm a changed man."

"That's what you always say," I replied all frowned up. "Bye Alex," I responded, pushing the button for floor one as I exited the elevator.

"Asia, you'll see me again real soon." *This nigga is crazy. I know he ain't about to start harassing me on the job,* I thought without responding to his comment.

I walked into my office, immediately noticing a package on my desk. It was nicely wrapped in some expensive turquoise paper, with a shiny turquoise bow. *Um... a gift from Kerwin,* so I rushed to open it. A card was attached, so I read it first.

Asia

I knew you wouldn't agree to dinner, so I'm one step ahead of you. I just wanted you to know that we all make mistakes that we grow to regret later in life. I fucked up, but I really do need you. I hope we can at least be friends?

P.S. Good Luck with parenthood. And diamonds are a girl's best friend. I always wanted you to give me a daughter, if you don't have a girl, return the bracelet and get my little nigga something nice.

Al.

Alex was this close to my desk without anyone noticing. I was shocked. I grabbed the box to open the gift and once I did, I was floored. It was a gift from Tiffany's. Enclosed was two diamond bracelets, one for me and one for my baby. *This fool is crazy. How is he gon' refer to Kerwin's son as his little nigga. And where did he get the coins to afford such a gift. Alex ain't ballin like that... is he?*

Alex wasn't fooling anybody with his lavish gifts. I learned from him early on that the expensive material things he gave me meant nothing more than what they represented at the moment. I don't care how nice a gift is, when a woman ain't being loved right, there's no joy....and no peace. In spite of what most men think, a sista don't care about pricey shit while she's weathering a storm in her relationship. All the money in the world ain't gon' make an unhappy sista want to stay with no psychopathic man that's kickin' her ass. And once she get a taste of a new Romeo, she most certainly ain't trading in her Prince to get back with no toad.

Alex had become a little to spooky acting for me. I didn't know how to read his demeanor, which was scary. I didn't understand his motives or why he was suddenly harassing me. However, after our encounter in the elevator and the gift, I was uneasy about him being in my presence. *I'm not going to take any chances, when I go back to see my Dr., I going on medical leave.*

That evening when I left work, Alex was waiting outside. While putting my things in my trunk, I looked up and he was standing before me. I jumped because he startled me.

"Hey Boo," He greeted with this creepy expression.

"Alex! What are you doing here again?"

"I can't stay away. I need to talk to you."

"Talk to me about what?"

"Us."

"Alex, there is no us. Hell, there ain't gon' never be no us."

"But I..."

"What part of there ain't gon' be no us don't you understand."

"Look," he shouted with evil in his eyes. "You owe me."

"I don't owe you shit."

"Had it not been for you, I wouldn't be on parole."

"You were jail bound prior to our incident, so don't try to blame me for your situation."

"You're right."

"So leave me the hell alone then, Alex."

"I'm sorry for yelling. I'm just angry because you won't give me the time of day. I'm trying so hard and it's frustrating to know how bad I want you and deal with you ignoring me the way you do. Did you get my gift?"

"Yes, and since you mentioned that, thank you, but I can't keep it," I expressed, reaching into my bag to hand it to him.

"Naw, you keep it. One day you're going to know it was given out of love."

"We'll I gotta go. Take care."

Before pulling out of the lot, I watched Alex walk over to his BMW SUV. I wanted to make sure he was gone before I ventured home. I didn't want to check my mirrors, only to discover him trailing me. He, jumped in his whip, and zipped off, bumping *Gotta Make My Money*. He had Stormy's jam on full blast. When his truck was out of sight, I called Kerwin.

"Speak."

"Is that any way to answer your phone?"

"Yeah, what up?"

"I'm going by Nikk's and then I'll be home."

"Okay, don't be out to late. When I finish up, I want to come home to my two favorite people."

"Why's that so important today?"

"It's always been important. I hate coming to an empty house. Plus, I got a surprise for the baby."

"A surprise, what kind of surprise?"

"If I tell you then it won't be a surprise, now will it?"

"It ain't for me so what difference does it make?"

"It's for you and the baby."

"Well maybe I should come home now."

"Naw, go see Nikk, and I'll see you later."

"Okay, love you."

"Love you, too."

"Hey!"

"Yeah."

"Let's go to church this weekend."

"Church! Where did that come from?"

"In all the years that we've been married, Kerwin, we ain't never been to church."

"Good point, so why go now?"

"If we're going to be parents and live like a happy family, I think we need to find us a church, let God be a part of our lives, and raise our child with some Christian principles."

"I'll think about that. I still got mad beef with God about my moms."

"So you don't want to go to church?"

"It's not that, it's just that I've been mad at God for so long for allowing my mother to die. I know I've been blessed since, but I don't think He'll forgive me for the kind of neglect I've sent His way over the years."

"Well my great grandma, GG always said, He's a forgiving God. She said so often people, sinners that is, struggle in their walk with God because they got issues. Issues that keep them down, but if we just allowed Jesus to help us get back up on our feet, we could conquer a multitude of things."

"Okay, I'll think about it. Gotta go, Coach is walkin' in."

I hung up, thinking Kerwin really has it out for God, but as good as God had been to him, I couldn't understand his long term bitterness. It wasn't for me to figure out either, shoot, I had my own shortcomings to deal with. Finally, I made it to Nikk's, so I called her and told her to open the door. As soon as I walked into her house, I pulled out the gift from Alex.

"Bitch, that is tight as hell. Kerwin loves you?"

"Not Kerwin."

"Not Kerwin! Asia, you messing around?"

"Hell no! Girl, Alex left this on my desk today."

"Daaaa…yum! That is tight."

"It is nice, but I can't keep this. I can't take this up in my house and explain to my husband how I'm accepting pricey gifts like this from my ex."

"So you want me to keep it."

"What! You sound ig'nant."

"Well you said you can't take it home. Shit, I might as well take it off your hands. It don't make no sense for it to just sit when I got a few outfits I can rock with it."

"Yeah right." I sarcastically replied, before being interrupted by a familiar face.

"Sup, Booty Face," the gentleman greeted.

"Terrell," I stated in shock. "Who you calling booty face?"

"Nigga yeah, Terrell," he replied with his ignorant self. "Who did you expect? You act like you saw a ghost."

"I did," I replied.

"You can't speak to a nigga?"

"Yeah, sorry, how you doing?"

"Livin'. By the looks of it I'd think you ain't know Nikk and I were back together."

"Noooo, that's not it at all," I lied because she hadn't said one word to me 'bout them hooking back up. "I'm just shocked to see you."

"So how have you been, Ms. Asia?"

"Good. Thanks for asking."

"Nikki I'm 'bout to be out. Call me some time this evening and we'll hook up for dinner and go to the casino."

"Okay."

I looked at Nikk like Scank-trick. She knew the look so well, so I didn't even have to tell her what was on my mind.

"Asia, I already know what you gon' say, so save it."

"I'm not going to say anything."

"I didn't tell you because I knew you were going to think I was dumb. But in all honesty, I missed him. T was my first love. We got history, you know," she asked, looking for my approval. "And in spite of our separation back in the day, we broke up on good terms."

"I'm not going to say anything. If he makes you happy, you're a grown ass woman. All I'm gon' say is I hope you ain't still fucking around with my Daddy and you get him caught up in this nonsense."

"Your daddy, ain't fooled with me since last year. He said he was going to focus on getting his home right after you gave the, 'I'm pregnant speech, and he ain't messed wit me since."

"Good. You was on some home wrecking shit anyway."

"Whatever you think. All I'm gon' say is a chick gotta do what a chick gotta do. Asia, I got to get it how I live. It's hard out here. Getting paid don't come easy, and the rent is due every month."

"Getting laid don't come easy either. Your integrity is a costly price to pay for some dirty dick and a few dollars."

"You call it dirty dick, I call it gettin' dinner."

"Yeah, but Nikk, you ain't got nothin' to show for it in the end."

"Who cares about the end, I'm living for now. When it's all said and done, I can't take none of this shit up in here with me. So I'm going to enjoy life until it's my time to bust Hell wide open."

"Well that's a good thing. At least you know."

"What?" Nikk asked.

"At least you're not in denial about the fact that you're goin' to hell."

"And so are you, why you up here judging me?"

"You need to get a job, Nikk. And for the record, I won't be up in hell with you."

"Naw, what you need to do is get a life and get out my business."

I thought it was a damn shame that Nikk had the kind of mentality she had. Actually, I really couldn't understand where it came from. Nikk came up in a healthy two parent home. Her mother was a college educated woman and her dad was too. They lived in a nice up scale community in Detroit, and her daddy bought himself a new Cadi every two years like it was as cheap as buying a pair of shoes. Nikk, didn't want for much in college because her parents paid her way after she turned down her scholarship to Langston. I couldn't understand what had become of her. I know we'd both made some bad choices in men when we were young, but for some reason, I grew up and realized that I wanted more for myself. Nikk was still on the chase, so that's why I had to leave her behind.

With us being the best of friends, I hoped she would get it together before she found herself seriously regretting something. Her behavior was too self-destructive. I worried because at the rate she was sleeping around, she was on the verge of adding some letters to her name that weren't degree related.

Chapter 30
Long Time No See

When I went back in for my monthly check up, I had Dr. Henry put me on medical. I could have easily quit my job and not thought twice about it, but to some extent I enjoyed having a career. I only took off as early as I did to prevent Alex from harassing me, but once I had the baby, I intended to return.

Seventeen weeks into my pregnancy, I had become a home body. With twenty-three weeks left until D day, I had to find something to do to keep myself occupied. Kerwin worked out on a regular basis, so a few days during that first week I was off, I went to the gym with him.

"Baby, what do you suggest I do while you work out?"

"Walk the treadmill, it'll help you stay in shape."

"So what are you insinuating? Are you trying to say I'm fat?"

"Not at all," he quickly replied.

"Un' hum."

"You're sexy, wit' yo plump self."

"Think so?"

"Hell yeah, and since you're carrying my little seed, you're even sexier," he commented, patting me on my butt.

"I'll be in here waiting until you finish," I informed him.

"Don't be flirting."

As ugly as I felt, he surely didn't have to worry about that. I walked the treadmill for five long minutes and was quickly out of breath. *Maybe you should try the bikes. Girl, you know you're out of shape.* With all the heavy breathing I was doing, the bike was going to simply make it worse. I scooped up a magazine and found me a seat by the pool. I was posted up right next to the towels and this steam room, so I was sweating up a storm. I pulled my chair away from the door and sat down to read. By the time I was half way finished, CJ came walking out the steam bath, dabbing sweat off his face. At first I wasn't going to speak because he was Alex's friend and I didn't know how Alex had portrayed me to him, or what to expect. However, once we made eye contact, he found his way over to my chair.

"Hey Asia," he greeted, bending over to peck my cheek.

"Hey, Man. Long time, no see."

"Yeah, I haven't seen you since the game that one night."

"I know," I responded, uneasily.

"So I hear you're married."

"Yeah."

"Good, you seemed like a real nice person when we met. I always wondered how Al got you in the first place."

"You know when you're in love, you don't pay attention to a persons faults until they become a problem for you."

"I agree. Well to bad for him."

"What are you doing now?" I asked, being nosey.

"Oh a little of this, a little of that."

"Do you come here often?"

"Nope. My girl told me I was uptight, so I came here to relax."

"Umm, well don't let me interrupt."

"It's cool. I'm glad I saw you. I'll have to tell Al we bumped into each other."

"Please don't. That boy is on something."

"What`cha mean?"

"I mean, he's acting strange. He talkin' about some he loves me, but when he had me he treated me like shit."

"Al was young, he didn't know what he had in you. But, Asia, he did really love you."

"Well, he didn't act like it. Now I don't want to be bothered and it seems like the fool is stalking me."

"Stalkin' you? My nigga ain't stalking you," he laughed. "When Al first got locked up, he called me everyday crying about losing you. He begged me a few times to touch basis with you, but I wouldn't. I told him to give you some time and if ya'll were meant to be, once he got out, you'd realize it and take him back."

"Well we don't," I quickly confirmed, hoping he'd tell Alex exactly what I said.

"Hey, it was good to see you. I'ma get out of here. You take care, and again, it was good to see you."

"You too."

Now as crazy as this sounds, I had the nerve to find some pleasure in hearing CJ say Alex cried over me. Why would that matter at all to me if I was, over him? I couldn't figure it out and didn't entertain it to long either.

"Hey, Mrs. Phillips, you ready," I heard this voice ask.

"Yes."

"So get your stuff and let's go," Kerwin insisted, helping me up.

Once I was up and could see into one of the weight rooms, I saw Alex. I couldn't believe it. *What is this nigga doin here?* While I was praying that Kerwin did not see Alex, a real uneasiness gathered in my stomach. It's hard to describe what I felt, but I grabbed Kerwin's hand and wobbled out of the gym as fast as I could.

"Slow down before you fall."

"I'm trying to get out to the truck, suddenly I feel sick."

"Sick, sick like what?"

"Just quizzie."

"Well slow down, before you blackout," he fussed, helping me get into the truck.

Kerwin tried to entertain me with small chatter about this and that. I slightly ignored him at first, trying to make sure we were not being followed.

"Asia, did you hear me?"

"No, I'm sorry, what did you say, Babe?"

"I was saying that coach got me under a lot of pressure. That new cat, Roy Henderson's trying to take my spot."

"Take your spot how?"

"Baby, every year a new draftee is always trying to jack a nigga for his position. When I was the new kid on the block, I had to let the veterans know that I had game. Now I'm in a position where I'm the vet, and the rookies are challenging me every season."

"So what, you don't think your game is up to par?"

"Are you serious? Hell yeah! My game is still on point, I just ain't never really had to work so hard to keep it."

"Welcome to life. With age, time changes, some of the things you used to do, you don't do as well anymore. In time, your season is going to come to an end, and you're going to have to pass the torch."

"Thanks," he sarcastically responded. "You don't know the kind of pressure I'm under."

"So tell me, so I can understand."

"Okay, listen. The need to win causes a lot of pressure on the coach and the team, which can at times be overwhelming. Asia, it's all about the dollar. The more you win, the more fans you have, the more fans you have, the more money the team makes. The more money the team makes, the happier the owners are. Babe, everyone wants their time to shine. Roy's going to make more money if he can up his value, so right now he's jockeying for my position. I'm a guard and so is he. I play 35 minutes a game, he plays 15. I know and so does everyone else that I am better than him. Not to mention that for what our team is trying to do, I am the better fit as well."

"Why are you the better fit?" I asked, playing devils advocate.

"What do you mean?"

"What makes you the best fit for the team?"

"Asia, I've been playing in the league for years, I understand the business, not just the game."

"Wooo!" I stated, grabbing my belly.

"What?"

"The baby just kicked me."

"Are you serious? Let me feel."

"Okay, put your hand right here."

"That's right, daddy's baby. Kick mommy for giving your daddy static."

Chapter 31
It's a Boy

At twenty-one weeks we found out we were having a little boy. My God you should have seen Kerwin's face when he discovered that he was going to have a son to play basketball with. I remember while we were doing the ultrasound the nurse was trying to show him our son's family jewels. Kerwin couldn't make out a thing at first for nothing in the world.

"Seems like you're only good at locating balls that bounce off a rim," the nurse stated.

"Yeah, and my own since they've been with me all my life," he replied, grabbing himself. I gave him the silliest look after his response. I couldn't believe his reply.

"Honey! Don't talk to people like that."

"Man, did you hear what...'

I bumped him because I was highly irritated. "Honey, chill out please!"

Once we left the doctors office, Kerwin fussed about the way I spoke to him in the presence of company. I wasn't feeling him, which is why I defended myself all the way to the truck.

"Asia, I don't care what I say, you don't check me in front of no damn body."

"It wasn't that serious."

"It was to me. Baby, did you hear what I said?"

"Yes."

"Fine, now get in the damn truck."

"Get in the damn truck! I don't know who you think you're talking to, but you don't order me around like I'm some bitch off the streets."

"Don't act like one then. Just get in the truck like I said."

"Like you said? Boy, you almost made me tell you something."

"Look, I don't want to argue out here in public. You know I ain't the average nigga and they'll have me on channel seven's news tonight, talking about, 'Star athlete beats up wife in parking lot.' That's all I need for my image to be shot to hell. So please get in the car."

I could see why Kerwin didn't want our little simple dispute to be out there like that for spectators to observe, which is why I got in the truck.

"Can you help me, please?"

"Oh, two minutes ago you were talkin' shit, now you need a nigga to help you," he joked.

"Yeah Chump, and soon you gon' wish you treated me better. Just wait 'til we get ready to have this baby, I'm gon' pay you back."

...♦♦♦♦...

With my pregnancy, I had mood swings like crazy. Most often Kerwin didn't understand why my hormones were all out of wack or why I didn't want him jabbing dick up in me, but I told him to try carrying around a little person that stayed up in his rib cage, bumped the heck out his spine, kept him pissing, made all his joints hurt, and kicked the hell out of his area. Then try to tell me he wouldn't feel any different. I guess my example helped out some, because on the nights he was in town, he'd rub my feet, my back, and my belly until I fell asleep instead of getting him some.

"I love you, Asia Phillips," he'd always whisper to me before scooping me and the baby up under him for closeness.

Chapter 32
Cousins

About two weeks after we found out we were having a son, Dad came by to take me shopping. I think he was more excited than Kerwin was at times. Aside from treating me like a fragile priceless artifact, he about drove me crazy being over protective. While we were walking in the mall, we went into almost every store there was for kids. Unlike most men, Dad loved to shop. Actually, shopping was one of his obsessions. I don't know if it was him being deprived for all the years he was incarcerated or what, but he was a shop-aholic.

As we were coming out of *Saks Fifth Avenue,* we bumped into Carrington. I immediately noticed her, but Dad tried to play it off cuz she had him so gone at one time. She immediately walked over to us, grinning at Dad with all thirty-two of her pearly whites showing.

"Oh my God, Prince is that you?" She asked, making her way towards us. "You better get over here and give me a hug," she insisted, forcing her big titties and a bunch of overexposed cleavage towards Dad. He casually eased in and gave her this lame hug that kind of tickled me.

"Carrington…. Wha'sup, baby. How you been?" Dad replied, backing away from her.

"I'm good. I can't complain."

"You're looking just as gorgeous as ever." *Crunchy… Now come on Dad, don't let her see that you're still a sucka.*

"Thank you. I'm trying to keep my school girl figure," she snickered. *Umph, this counterfeit trick need to give me a break,* I thought, fake smiling at her, remembering how at one time her hugs were more satisfying for Dad than hugs from anyone else. "So Prince, how have you been?"

"Real good. I can't complain either. Just out shopping with my baby girl."

"Oh my………Is this, Asia?"

"Um hum. Hi," I greeted, kind of rudely cuz I still wasn't feelin her.

"Girl, you have grown up to be quite a young lady and you're so beautiful."

"Thank you."

"I see you're expecting."

"Yeah, it's a boy," I replied as Dad grinned with much pride.

"That's right, I'm 'bout to have me a second little nigga."

"Prince, you're still so cool. You haven't changed one bit."

"Carrington, I've changed, but some things about me will always be the same."

"Let me guess what the main one is." Carrington sugguested, trying to remember. "Umm, you'll always be real, right" she flirted.

"Carrington, you being sarcastic."

"No, I just remember our last encounter… I suppose you kept it real that day too, huh Prince?"

"You sound like you're still mad. Are you?"

"No, I'm not bitter, but I still haven't forgotten about that one little incident. I've spent a lot of time reflecting over it for years."

"Have you?"

"Sure have."

"And so what did you come up with."

"Prince, there have been many times I have thought about the manner in which you loved me, and then I wondered how I let you get away."

"Look, I meant no harm. As a matter of fact, let me apologize to you about that again." *Um, seems like I missed something,* I thought, bobbing my eyes back and forth from Carrington to Dad.

"No apology needed. E said I got what I deserved."

"Damn straight you did at the time, but I feel bad about that now." I looked at my dad trying to figure out what they were talking about. "Oh and by the way, how's India?"

"She's great, getting grown, testing limits like Asia used to."

"You're gon' have your hands full then, cuz Asia still does."

"I already know, India told me the other day she was ready for a boyfriend."

I could see where Daddy and Carrington were headed, so I cut in. "Well, Daddy, we need to try to get back on this shopping. I know you and Carrington could stand here and reminisce forever, but we need to get going, my feet are starting to hurt."

"Yeah, I guess we better. It was nice to see you again Carrington. You take care."

"You too, and don't be a stranger," she suggested, writing her home and cell number on the back of her business card.

"Damn, I see you made Regional Manager with the pharmaceutical company."

"Yeah," she grinned.

"Congrats. I always knew you had it in you," he paused for a minute to reflect. "Well gotta go, be good," he suggested, kissing her on the cheek.

Yuck, Dad is still kind of soft on this old uppity chick. Right as we were about to make our departure, I noticed Nikk and Terrell walking by.

"Hey, Chick," Nikk greeted, rubbing my belly."

"Sup, Miss Thang. Hey, Terrell."

"Carrington, what you doing out here?" Nikk asked.

"Shopping."

"What have you been up to? How's Uncle Chris and your mom?"

"Great."

"Hold on," I interrupted. "You two are related?"

"Girl, first cousins." Nikk answered. "Our fathers are brothers."

"Small world," Daddy joked. "E never told me that."

"Why would E say anything about us being related?" Nikk asked.

"E is so much older and has never met Nikki. He's my mother's nephew, and Nikk's on my daddy's side of the family," Carrington clarified.

"Carrie, how you know Asia and Mr. Prince?" *Oh, so he's Mr. Prince now. Wait 'til I get her one-on-one,* I thought butting in.

"Nikk, Daddy and Carrington kicked it back in the day."

"Oh, so you got jokes. Trick, you know I'm calling you tonight," she leaned over and whispered in my ear. I cracked up laughing because she knew exactly what I was insinuating. *Dad had ran through both of them gold diggers and was still with the woman he loved.*

"Okay. Daddy we need to leave. I'm s'posed to meet Kerwin later this evening. You know he gets back tonight."

"Carrington, again it was nice to see you. E and I still have the stores. You should come by and visit some time."

"I will."

I don't think that's a good idea. Daddy knows he's on some bullshit, inviting that woman to the store. And I told him just that once we walked away.

"Why is that such a bad idea, Asia?" Dad asked.

"First of all you got mad playa genes in your blood. Secondly, you're a hoochie. Thirdly, you on some big time infidelity stuff right now, and Fourthly, you're a dog."

"Thanks for speaking and thinking so highly of your old dude, and how you figure I'm a dog."

"Man, I think you're the greatest dad, but you're a sorry companion. You have no loyalty to your wife. Teretta is a good woman, and she loves you. She don't put you through no drama, she takes good care of your son, and she's always been nice to me."

"I agree with everything you've said."

"Well then if that's the case, why do you cheat?"

"Baby I told you before a man could have a great woman. She could be beautiful and loving, like my wife, but we'll still tip out. Hell, she could be doing everything he wants her to do and more, but if the right kind of temptation crosses our path, our little head take over and most times it leads us astray. There are a few men that can resist the challenge. I ain't one of them, and the nigga's that can are some pussies."

"So if someone was trying to holla at my man and he resist, then he's a pussy?"

"Hell naw, he's wise."

"He's wise? But you just said."

"I know what I just said," Dad replied, interrupting me.

"Explain, don't just leave me hanging."

"He's wise because you're my daughter."

"Daddy, you need help. I don't get you. It's cool for you to mess over women, but it's not okay for someone to mess over the women in your family."

"That's right, now change the subject b'foe you make me mad."

Men are shallow. "Hey, I got a question."

"What's that?"

"What you think about the fact that you were banging off cousins from two different generations?"

"Shut up. Girl, you shot out. I'm not going there with you," he laughed.

"Yeah, let's talk about that for a moment. On some real talk, why did you sleep with Nikk?"

"I made a bad decision."

"You sure did, but you got to give me more than that. I mean, why do men act now and think later."

"You gon' let me finish or do you want the floor?"

"Finish, dang."

"Nikk is real sexy. I was attracted to her body, her face, and her spunk. For an old dude like me to conquer a young sista like your girl, well, it did something for my ego. Being with her reminded me of my day. Shoot when your dad was a shorty, the girls loved me. I was all that and then some. I guess getting with her reminded me of my past. Butterfly, she made me feel young again, but most of all being with her allowed me to relive my youth and portions of it that I missed out on. Things were going well between us until she told me she was pregnant and she wanted me to leave my family."

"WHAT!!!!!!!!!!!!!!!!!!!! You got her pregnant."

"I fucked up and slept with her one time without a condom."

"So when was she pregnant?"

"Right before you."

"Before me! What you mean before me?"

"You told us you were pregnant in November."

"Yeah."

"Nikk was pregnant in August."

"So what did she do with the baby?"

"At first she threatened to keep it and tell Teretta."

"What! She was gon' tell Teretta?"

"She said she was, but I didn't sweat it. I told her to get an abortion." Dad, looked over at my expression. "I was gon'pay for it, send her on an all expense paid trip for some recovery time, and give her a little extra money to splurge."

"What? Daddy, you got that girl pregnant and then forced her to get rid of it?"

"I didn't force her. I suggested. Hell, I wasn't bout to leave my family for her, and I ain't never wanted my kids spread all around."

"What other kids do you have besides P and me."

"None, I'm saying from the time I got you, I ain't wanted no bunch of babies mamas."

"You're a real trip, and what kind of extra money were you gon' give her?"

"Like four thousand dollars."

"Dad, I'm real disgusted with you. I can't believe Nikk killed that baby, but I am glad y'all decided to terminate that relationship."

"Yeah, I wasn't about to sacrifice my home. I love coming home to Terretta and my little man."

"Wait 'til I see Nikk."

"You can't say anything."

"Why not?"

"I promised her I wouldn't tell you."

"So why did you?"

"Because you're my Butterfly."

"What does that have to do with anything? You also told me loose lips, sink ships."

"Yeah, but I know I disappointed you, and I want to let you know that sometimes people make foolish decisions, but when we find ourselves, it's important to admit your wrong doings, ask for forgiveness, and make things right. So I apologize."

"Apology accepted. Now lets go into Childrens Fashions right quick, there's about two thousand dollars worth of stuff my baby needs from his granddaddy. And I know if his Auntie Nikki could get four G's, he's good for at least half. "

"You're always competing," Dad teased, hugging me around my neck.

Dad spent about fifteen hundred, and once we finished shopping, we headed to the car. While I was throwing my things into the truck, my cell started ringing.

"Hello," I answered.

"Asia, you're sure looking pretty today. I see you and your Daddy are out shopping for the baby. So what are you having?"

"Alex, don't call me, and if you keep stalking me, I'm going to put a VPO out on you," I whispered to prevent Daddy from hearing.

"A Victims Protection Order is a little much, don't you think. I only called to tell you how nice you looked."

"You're a stalker. This is my last time warning you."

"Asia, you need to...." I didn't even let him finish, I just slammed the phone closed in his face.

"Butterfly, you wanna grab a bite to eat before I drop you off?"

"No, I'm just ready to go home."

"Who were you talking to?"

"You heard me?"

"I didn't hear what you were saying."

"It wasn't anybody, just my ex."

"Why is he calling you? Weren't you just telling me what a dog I was?"

"It's not like that Dad. He calls from time to time, but there's nothing going on between us."

"It better not be, my son-in-law is a fine young man. I don't want you to mess up like me."

"Oh, you don't have to worry about that," I confirmed.

...◆◆◆...

When we pulled up in our driveway, it was getting dark. I pushed the remote to lift the garage and Daddy let me out. I looked around my driveway because Alex's call made me uneasy.

"Daddy, you want to come in?"

"Naw, I better get home, but call me if you need something. I'll bring this big stuff back to the house tomorrow. I know if I take it in tonight, you're going to be trying to put it up."

"Okay."

Chapter 33
Family Connection

I made it in the house, turned on all the lights in most of the rooms, and put up the little things Daddy and I bought. Once again my phone rung, and once again I answered it.

"Hello."

"Asia, listen to me. I'm not stalking you. I'm trying,"

"Alex, who the hell do you think you are? I told you once, I don't want you, and I'm not interested, and leave me alone. You're a sick, twisted bastard. You need professional help," I screamed, hanging up. My phone rung again a few more times, but I ignored his calls.

About two hours later, I noticed the limo lights coming up the driveway. *Yeah, my baby's home,* I thought, wobbling to open the door. I quickly made my way outside, and slowly down the steps to the end of the walkway. I stood there for a second, before the door opened, some skinny guy got out of the front passenger side.

"Hey, who are you?" I asked.

"Why?"

"Well…..la.. maybe because you're on my property." Suddenly, Barry got out making his way over to the passenger side.

"Good evening, Asia. How are you?"

"I'm doing well. I'm anxious to see my man. Who's this guy," I asked, pointing.

"That's my cousin, Recardo. Sorry 'bout dat, he was being silly."

"For a minute, he had me nervous, but don't worry about it. How's your granddad?"

"He's good," he replied, opening Kerwin's door.

I eased a little closer to greet my man, and became very puzzled. The man in the car was not Kerwin, it was CJ. Immediately, I became spooked because I thought Alex was up to something.

"Where's Kerwin," I asked, trying to stay calm as I backed up.

"He'll be here shortly," CJ replied. "Now how are you and the baby doing?"

"Great," I answered, fearing that no reply would tick him off. "CJ, why are you here?"

"I came to pay you a long overdue visit."

"What?"

"I brought someone to meet you."

"Who? And why would you come to my house? Did Alex put you up to this?"

"Ut'un, someone else."

"Who, Kerwin?"

"Naw, he did," pointing to this well dressed, handsome brotha with an odd tattoo on his neck, but a familiar face.

"Who's he?" *I asked, thinking he looked familiar.*

"I'm your Uncle," the gentleman smoothly replied.

"My uncle? I don't see how that's possible. Both of my uncles are dead."

"Asia, it's been a long time since we've seen each other."

"Do I know you?"

"Yeah, I met you some years ago at Big Fellas." I looked at him like he was crazy, I'd only met one person there and he was dead. "I'm Calvin Shaw," he confirmed, as an indescribable chill overcame me.

"Calvin Shaw, Alex's, Calvin Shaw who died years ago."

"Yeah, so many thought, but I'm alive and well." I grabbed my stomach out of shock. "Are you okay?" I just looked.

"Asia, can we go inside so you can sit down? My father wants to explain," CJ suggested.

"Your father? Oh, hell naw, I don't think so. Barry, get them off of my property," I defensively demanded, fearing for my life. "And where's my husband?"

"You want me to put her in the limo, Cal?" Recardo asked.

"Nah, Dude, let's just go before we upset my pretty little neice."

"You sure, man you know it ain't no problem?"

"Yeah, I'm sure. No need to do this now. My points been made." Calvin expressed.

"What point are you talkin' about?" I asked, mugging him.

"Asia, like CJ said, this visit is long overdue. Please give Prince my regards when you speak with him again."

"Does he know you, too?"

"Tell you what. Just tell P, I paid you a visit today. He's not going to believe you at first, but tell him I said 4357 and he'll know it's really me."

"4357!" I repeated, suspensefully.

"Yeah, he'll know exactly what it means."

Just like that, he nodded his head, blew me a kiss, and closed the door with his cold eyes. I didn't like the way he looked at me one bit. I knew from his stare that 4357 didn't mean anything good for daddy. Recardo, looked like he wanted to kidnap me even after being advised to leave me alone. Barry jumped back in the limo like wasn't shit going on and pulled off. As I headed towards the stairs, I was shaking like crazy from our encounter. Just as I hit the top step, I saw headlights coming up the driveway. I tried to move a little fast to get in the house just in case they changed their minds. As I took a second glance, I realized it was the lights from Kerwin's Range Rover, so I waited for him.

"What are you doing out here?" He asked, getting out of his truck.

"I was looking for you," I lied. "I'm glad you're home, the baby and I missed you."

"I missed y'all too," he expressed, scooping me into his arms to carry me into the house.

"Aren't you going to get your things?"

"Nah, I'll bring them in tomorrow. I just want to cuddle with my baby right now."

"Sounds like a plan to me. You don't know what kind of day I've had."

"Well tell me about it," he suggested.

"Naaaaah, I'd rather cuddle, too."

That evening my husband eased a great deal of my stress. By the time we showered together, laughed a little about Nikk being a gold digger, and briefly talked about Kerwin's away game, I got in bed and zonked out.

....♦♦♦....

That following morning, as soon as Kerwin left, I called my dad.

"What did you say, Butterfly?"

"Get over here now!" I yelled.

"Are you in labor?"

"No."

"Well you must be cause you hollering at me like that."

"I need to talk to you about yesterday."

"Baby, I'm at the store right now, can I come by later?"

"I need you to come by now."

"Well, I can't leave. Come up here."

"I'll be there as soon as I get dressed."

"Okay, I'll see you in about two hours," Daddy joked.

"Real funny. You'll see me sooner than that."

"See you when you get here."

Once I got dressed, I sped over to *Top of the Line* to see Dad. I parked half crazy and rushed into the store wobbling.

"Dad, in the office now!" I demanded, not bothering to stop and speak to anyone. He was standing at the counter talking to Uncle E, but followed my request with the quickness.

"What is it!" he frantically inquired.

"Who the Hell is Calvin Shaw?"

"What?"

"You heard me, who is he?" I yelled at the top of my lungs.

"I don't know a Calvin Shaw," he replied, shutting the door.

"Well he seems to know you."

"Why are you asking about him?"

"He came by my house yesterday."

"WHAT!"

"You heard me. He came by my house, talking about tell you..."

"Hold on," Dad interrupted. "You said he came by your house. That's impossible."

"Why is that so impossible, you just said you didn't know him?"

"I know what I said."

"So that means you lied?"

"I didn't lie."

"What do you call it then?"

"Hey, look! I said I didn't lie, I just didn't tell the total truth."

"What's the truth, Daddy?"

"I know he was a drug dealer and years ago I heard he was found dead floating in the lake. Someone's playing a dirty trick on you."

"No Daddy, he was very much alive and he told me that he was my Uncle."

"That nigga said he was yo what!" Dad yelled.

"You heard me."

"What did he say?"

"Five seconds ago you didn't know him, now his conversation with me seems real important."

"Don't be so damn smart for a change, just answer the question."

"He said that he was my uncle, his visit was long overdue, and for me to also tell you 4357." Dad's mouth immediately fell open and he turned extremely pale. All of a sudden, he was at a loss for words. I couldn't quite make out what he was thinking, but I could tell that there was more to the news I delivered than I was aware of. After minutes of silence, I tried to revive my dad because his demeanor was as if he'd died. "Daddy, are you okay?"

"Yeah. I need to talk to E," Dad stated, getting up. "I'll be right back."

I watched Dad walk out the office and then observed him and Uncle E on the monitors as they talked at the counter. Dad seemed frigid, and highly irritated. He was right up on E talking a hundred miles a minute. *What's that all about? I wonder if Dad's in some kind of trouble with this guy.* Suddenly, E walked towards the office and Dad followed him in, slamming the door behind him.

"Nigga, I told you we should have handled that shit ourselves," E fussed. "Now we gon' be watching our damn backs. Man, my life been carefree for the past few years, so I suggest that we get this issue handled A-Fuckin-Sap."

"Nigga, I know!" Dad fussed back. "You think I'm cool with that bitch popping up at my daughters spot? Hell fucking naw I'm not. I wanna know how he even found out where she lived, how long he's been watching her, and most of all, what the hell he wants."

"So we gotta do what we gotta do then."

"Ut'un, E, I'm not bringing Asia into this."

"Bringin' Asia into what?" I asked, interrupting them.

"Nothin," Dad snapped off.

"P, I swear if you don't tell her, I will," E, hissed.

"Tell me what?"

"Nothing, Butterfly. E, shut the hell up, Man."

"Tell her!" he yelled.

"Asia, go to my house now."

"Dad, no disrespect, but with the way y'all carrying on, I ain't going no damn where, somebody in here 'bout to tell me somethin'. I got a stranger that's s'posed to be dead showing up at my spot, talking about some we're related, and you think I'm going home."

"I said go to my place."

"Ut'un, I got nigga's that once worked for this Calvin Shaw stalking me. My family could be in jeopardy. Daddy, if you think I'm leaving here with nothing, you're crazy."

"Asia, what you talkin' about? You pissin' me off."

"Better to be pissed off than pissed on. Daddy, I don't care. I want some answers right fuckin now."

"Watch yo damn mouth. I'm still your father."

"Well, I'm grown and both of y'all are on some BS with all this lying."

"We ain't lie about shit. I just ain't tell you all there was to know."

"Then that's a lie."

"No, that's called selective sharing to protect the innocent."

"Fuck all that right now." E said. "Asia, how did he say he found you?"

"He didn't have to say, I knew for myself."

"What you mean?"

"Barry, our limo driver brought him."

"Barry! P' don't we know a Barry?"

"Asia, what does he look like?" Dad asked, cutting us off.

"He's a chocolate, well dressed brotha. His grandfather owns Jones Limousines. His granddad's been ill, so Barry's been driving us around for a while."

"Bullshit. Harold ain't sick. He was in **Bean's Spot** the other day, eating some fried chicken and greens. That nigga Barry done set us up, P. You paid Barry's bitch ass some serious money to do a job that he didn't do. That nigga and Recardo was probably on Calvin Shaw's payroll when we hired them to do that hit."

"What! Daddy, Uncle E………… What are y'all talking about?" I asked, looking at them with clear shock in my eyes. "Tell me y'all didn't have something to do with Calvin Shaw's death."

"Asia, we…." Uncle E tried to explain, but Dad cut him off.

"Fuck that nigga," Dad yelled. "Butterfly, he killed my brotha, and I paid some grimey muthafucka's to do what I should have done myself."

I couldn't believe what I was hearing. I was upset, the baby was turning flips and kicking the shit out of me, and I couldn't take anymore.

"Daddy, I can't believe you would step to a Big Tymer like him right after you'd just gotten out of prison. You and Uncle E weren't even on that man's level."

"What the fuck you say? How the hell you know so much about this nigga?" Dad asked, grabbing my arm like I was one of his women.

"Daddy, stop! You're hurting me."

"You heard me," he repeated with clinched teeth. "How you know this nigga?"

"I was dating one of his runners before I moved to Detroit."

"That's who Zena was talking about and yo lying ass said it wasn't nobody."

"Who cares about that? Don't try to turn this around on me."

"Asia, you were sleeping with the adversary and brought his ass back into existence."

"Daddy, I ain't the one that had loose lips. I never said nothin' to Alex about our family."

"Shit, you didn't have to say nothing. Did he know I owned the sports grill, clothing store, etc?" I looked on speechless with bucked eyes. "Nuff said. You ain't never been ready for this kind of game, that's why I told yo ass to get you a nice nerd like Sam."

"I got one."

"Yeah, after you got with the devil. Now his ass is coming back to haunt us."

"You act like I knew about this Shaw nigga. I didn't. If you weren't so secretive, then I would have known better."

"I warned you, but you didn't listen. I wasn't threatening you so much because I was trying to put fear in your heart. I was trying to let you know that this lifestyle wasn't for you due to the circumstances."

"How I know it was a warning, if I didn't know there was a real problem?"

"Don't get smart. All I know is now we got to wonder how Calvin plans to retaliate against us. If he killed Ant his own damn twin, he ain't gon' think twice about you, me or anyone else for that matter."

"Twin! What! Uncle Ant had a twin? Why wasn't he in any of the family photos?"

"Long story, wrong time. I'll tell you that one later." *There Daddy goes with his damn secrets again. If he would have been open and honest from jump, we wouldn't be in this situation,* I thought before saying just that.

"Well if you would have…"

"Asia, P, lets try to calm down. There's no need to go pointing fingers. We all made some mistakes here. What we need to do is come up with a game plan and get ready for his next visit. He's surfaced after all these years for a reason. And he wouldn't go to Asia's house, just on GP," E said.

"So what, are we just s'posed to wait for that nigga to surface again?" Dad asked.

"P, what else we gon' do? Hell an hour ago, we didn't even know the cat was still living. You don't know how to reach him, do you?" Dad looked pitiful. "Exactly, so we wait it out."

"And when he comes out blastin' on our asses then what?"

"We don't have any options. And stop talkin' like that in front of Asia and the baby before you spook 'em."

And wait it out is just what we had to do because Uncle E was right, none of us knew how or where to find Calvin Shaw.

Chapter 34
Baby Shower

June 3, 2010 I was twenty-five years old and thirty-two weeks pregnant. Mama, Teretta, Aunt Ke, and Nikk threw me a baby shower. I don't know whose great idea it was, but we had a ball. My biggest surprise is when Nardsbaby and a few of my home chicks from my book club surprised me. I remember Hot, Glam, Virgo, Scorpio, Mz.Crys, Greeneyes, Shyste, Mskiki, Kathyj, and Rayamon came walking through the door, bearing gifts. I screamed like a maniac because I hadn't seen them since the Harlem Book Festival in 2006, and I knew my reading sista's came from near and far to be with me at such a special time in my life. They ain't fall up in my place with them l'il cheap ass gift bags for baby Phillips neither, which was just a sign of the love they had for me.

The men were also allowed to participate, which made the party more exciting for me. Some of the players from Kerwin's team sent their wives or girlfriends to represent them, and of course Mr. Cheeks, Dave, and Steve weren't going to miss one of our family celebrations for nothing. Nikk, brought Terrell, who seemed to fit in for a change, while Sam, Dad, Rodney, and Kerwin complained the entire time about having to participate.

"Y'all need to stop it. This is Asia's day and we're going to make it the best for our first grandchild," My mama fussed. After she got onto them, they kind of came around. It was one of the best times I ever had in my life. We played games, we ate food, the men complained, we laughed, we opened gifts, the men complained, I read cards, joked about the baby being just like his daddy, and the men complained more until it literally ended.

Finally, we wrapped up the shower thang and people started leaving. The wives, girlfriends, and my book club members were the first to leave. Then Steve, Mr. Cheeks, and Dave left together, talking about they were on their way to *Da Wing House* to get some buffalo wings, *Yeah Right,* I thought, winking as I envisioned all the uncovered tits and ass that greeted you at the door in that place. Finally, Mom, Rodney, Daddy, Teretta, Aunt Ke, and Sam left. Nikk and T stayed to help me put the baby's gifts in his nursery.

Well Nikk helped out some. Terrell and Kerwin sat in the den, watching television.

"Nikk, I'll be in there to help you as soon as I use the pottie," I expressed, wobbling down the hall to the master bathroom.

"Okay, but you know I can do this, Asia. You might want to take it easy. Today has been real busy for you," she stated, dragging bags in the opposite direction to the babies room.

"Girl naw, I want to help."

"Okay, I'll save you all the easy stuff to put up."

When I get back, I'm gon' ask her about being pregnant by my dad. I want to know why she didn't tell me. I know she's gon' get all amped up, start talkin' noise, and probably make me want to fight her stupid ass. Oh well, if we girls, we'll get through it.

Once I made it to the restroom, I stayed in there all of three minutes. While pulling up my pants, I heard my bedroom door shut. While washing my hands, I yelled, "Honey, is that you?" No one answered, so I thought I was tripping. When I walked into the room, I suddenly noticed these dark eyes that I knew so well staring at me. I damn near jumped out of my skin.

"Hey, Boo."

"Alex, what the hell are you doing in my house? You better leave before I call the police."

"You can't call no police, I cut the cord, see," he expressed, showing me the cut wire.

"What do you want?"

"I just want to talk to you."

"Talk about what?"

"How much I love you."

"How the hell did you get in here?"

"Terrell, let me in. I've been trying to follow you home for months, but you were always on that detour stuff. The day you were with your dad, I almost made it here, but I was too many cars behind, got caught at the light, and that nigga drives fast."

I knew it. I knew I shouldn't have let Nikk bring him to my house.

"You're sick, Alex. You need help."

"I'm not sick, Asia. I'm in love."

"You don't stalk people you love."

"If you only knew why I was doing this, you'd understand. See that was always your problem. You never really knew me. Hold on, let me show you something," Alex suggested, pulling up his shirt. I focused in on this Jail House Asia tat that had blood drops and a knife sticking through it. *So this fool was really serious about getting a tat. I knew it.* I got back on task, totally ignored his tattoo and continued.

"You're right, I don't understand and if you don't get out of here, I'm gonna scream."

"Asia, if you do that, everyone in here is gonna die," he insisted, pulling his gun out of his waist. I jumped, grabbing my stomach. "Just relax. You gon' go into labor early. I don't want nothin' to happen to you and my little nigga."

"Your little nigga."

"Here, come over here and sit down," he insisted, helping me to a chair by the bed. I noticed my cell phone tucked down in the side of the chair and made a mental note. *Gotta grab that if he takes me out of this room.*

"Alex, please leave. Don't do this," I begged, with tears streaming down my face. "You're scaring me. I don't know why you can't let go. You've moved on."

"See that's the problem. You think I moved on. You're the only one that's moved on. You're the one that left me for that lame ass nigga, but I never stopped loving you."

"Yeah after you raped me on one occasion and kicked my ass on another. I bet you did love me."

"We had good times, too. Don't act like I was all bad."

"I'm not saying that."

"Whatever you're sayin' there's no time for it. I need you to trust me and do what I tell you to do."

"Trust you? Are you stupid? You've broken into my house and now you want me to trust you."

"Boo, something's about to go down."

"Something like what? What are you talking about, Alex."

"Asia, you need to…" As he was trying to explain, I heard Terrell's voice.

"Yo, Al where you at? You handled that yet?"

"Shhhhhhhs," Alex whispered.

"Trust you… You sorry Bastard," I screamed.

"Asia, be quiet."

"I will not be quiet. Nikk, Kerwin, anybody, we're in here!" I yelled. "Help me!"

The door came flying open after being kicked with force.

"Bitch, shut up! What's up with all that damn screamin'." I've never been so scared, but I felt real fear after looking in Terrell's eerie eyes. *Is this the same man that just finished partying with me and my family,* I thought, before he stated fussing again. "Nigga why you ain't tied her up yet? I took care of everyone else and I told you to get her. I knew I should have done her myself, pussy whipped nigga."

"Man, she's pregnant."

"You think I give a fuck about that. Here, get her ass tied up," he demanded, throwing some tape to Alex. "Then bring her in the den with everyone else." When Terrell, turned and walked out of the room, I knew I was dead.

"Asia, I'm not here to hurt you. You have to trust me, Boo, remember I told you I loved you. Terrell's on some ill shit. He's been talking about killing you and Nikk for the past two years. That's why I've been kind of watchin' you. At first I thought he was bullshitin, but he called me last night and said it was a go. I didn't want nothin' to happen to you, so when he asked me if I was down, I told him yeah."

"Killing us for what?" I paused and before he could answer, I interrupted. "I know he ain't bout to kill me over that hit and run shit?" I asked, panicking. "Alex, I never told anyone. I never said a word. It got out, but not because I told."

"Asia, quiet down, he's gonna hear you. We know Nikk was runnin' her mouth. But I ain't here for her. Now just let me tie you up like he asked. That might be the only thing that saves your life. I won't put the tape on tight. I promise."

"Don't put it on at all. Let's just pretend like I'm bound. I'll walk to the front with my hands behind me. You know T ain't that sharp."

"We could try that, but I don't want to take no chances. You know that nigga is crazy and he might kill me. Then who's gon' protect you?"

"So you gon' tape me up?"

"Yeah. I got to."

"Before you do, will you at least get me some water, I'm thirsty."

"Where?"

"Get it from the bathroom." Alex looked real puzzled at me. "I promise I won't try anything."

"You better not." As he walked over to the sink, I quickly grabbed my phone and slid it in my pocket. Once he came back with the water, he held it up to my mouth for me to drink.

"You straight?"

"Un, hum. Thank you."

"No problem, now lets do this." Alex walked up on me and loosely taped my hands behind me as promised. "Now wiggle your hands. Do you think you can get them out if necessary?"

"Yeah."

"As soon as I sit you down start working your arms a loose. Give me a little time to try to talk him down. If he acts like he's gonna try something, then and only then, fight like hell cuz at that point you ain't got much of a choice."

"What about you? What are you gonna do?"

"What ever I can to help you, and only you, everybody else is on their own, especially that hoe ass husband of yours."

"Alex, you can't let Terrell kill Nikk or Kerwin."

"Kerwin, fuck that nigga, I just might kill him my damn self."

"You can't."

"Why not? They don't mean shit to me."

"But they mean something to me. Kerwin's `bout to be a daddy. You've got to help us."

"Damn, Nigga! What's taking you so long to get the hell out here?" Terrell screamed.

"Here I come, hold tight!" Alex yelled….. "Asia, lets go."

As soon as I made my way into the den, I immediately noticed that Kerwin's wrist and legs were bound, and his mouth gagged. I gasped as tears uncontrollably fell from my eyes because I knew he would be defenseless at that point. "Sit her fat ass over there next to her girl," T ordered. I sat next to Nikk, and she was shaking like a baby. She had a fat lip and a slightly swollen eye. Tears were streaming down her face, and her lip trembled. I think at that moment, she not only feared for her life, but also realized that she'd made some real poor choices. And as a consequence of being a gold digger, she put more than just herself in jeopardy with her carelessness. When Nikk brought Terrell along just to make him think she was all about him, we all paid a heavy price for her game.

"Oh my God, Nikk are you okay?" I helplessly asked, hurting so badly inside for her. "Terrell, you asshole, why are you doing this? What have we done?" At first he ignored me, as he pulled blankets into the den and cut the phone cord behind the television. "Terrell, you heard me, why are you doing this?" I asked a second time.

"Asia, shut the fuck up. I can't concentrate on my next move with all that damn talkin? Nikk's ho ass been giving my pussy to a simp I've beefed with forever. She's been fucking my brains out, getting info during my pillow talk and taking it back to that nigga Terryonto."

"Baby, I ain't been with nobody, but you," Nikk whined.

224

"Bitch, shut up! Shut the hell up! I told you when we hooked back up that you better not fuck over me…. You broke the rules."

"Terrell, I promise I ain't been with nobody," Nikk cried, pleading for him to believe her.

"I don't believe you, nasty tramp ass bitch, if you ain't been with nobody why my boy Remrock tell me he saw you the other day rollin' with Terryonto's ass. You know me and that nigga got major beef. You know that nigga think he the man. And here you are giving up my shit to him, trying to get me set the fuck up."

"Terrell, I promise I ain't said a word to nobody. I don't even get down with no damn Terryonto like that."

"You lyin."

"Baby, I love you," Nikk, insisted as T turned his back on her. "Terrell, look at me," she begged, but he didn't. He kept right on spreading out blankets, so she continued to try to get in his head. "I promise I'm not lying. Who said they saw me with Terryonto?"

"Remrock."

"I swear I haven't been with him." T turned and slapped Nikk in the face as she pleaded for him to believe her. She grabbed her face and cried out in pain as blood ran from her mouth.

"Nikki, didn't I just tell you to shut up?" he asked with an empty cold stare.

"Un'hm," she nodded, crying even harder.

"Then that's what I mean. If you say another word, I'm gon' fuck you up."

"T, chill," Alex insisted. "You said you was gon' just scare Nikk and Asia, and take this home wreckin' nigga out for me," He reminded Terrell, pointing at Kerwin. "That's the only reason I agreed to come." *This dirty nigga said he came to save me. Now I don't believe him,* I thought, anxiously trying to wrestle my hands free from the tape even faster.

"Alex, please don't," I begged. "Terrell, what does my husband or I have to do with this?"

"Your man is the only one that I don't have beef with. He's Al's vendetta, not mine. Dawg was just in the wrong place at the wrong time as far as I'm concerned. You know I can't leave no witnesses. Shit, he's one of my favorite ball players. Now you on the other hand, you're payback."

"Payback? What do you mean payback? I've never done anything to you."

"Yeah, but your father did."

"You don't even know my father. You just met him for the first time today."

"Like hell I don't. I met your father for the first time at my daddy's funeral. Some gangsta niggas from back in the day who called themselves NGN, brutally killed my father. They carved some gang shit deep in his chest, left him with his nut sack slit open, and his fucking brains blown all over the dining room wall."

"Terrell, my daddy didn't kill him, so what does this have to do with me."

"My God father, Melvin Daniels stepped in after my daddy died to help my mama raise me. When your father got out of prison, his punk ass killed him. The day he did that dumb shit, he left me fatherless a second time."

I covered my mouth in shock because I knew he wasn't lying. What I thought about saying, I couldn't because it would have convicted my daddy and forced him to kill me for sure. My education in Social Work, and Clinical Counseling started kicking in, so I tried to talk him down. "Terrell, I'm sorry that happened to you, but Nikk, Kerwin, and I are not the ones that violated you. I'm sure my Dad didn't either, but maybe you should give him a chance to tell you what went down, if anything."

"Fuck that nigga."

"T, she's right. Maybe he can explain." Alex expressed, trying to help out.

At first T looked at Alex like he was hot with him for being on my side. Then he walked over shoving his finger in my face.

"What's his number!"

"What?"

"What's the number?"

I slowly rattled off Daddy's number, but for some reason he didn't answer. *Daddy, where are you? This is a time when I need you more than anything. How you not gonna answer?* I thought, watching him lower the phone as the voicemail picked up. "No answer, y'all better pray if you believe in God. I have wasted enough time with all this chit-chat. Al, I'm bout to do this."

"T, man, just think this through. You might be making a big mistake. Here you are about to avenge your God Father's death and you don't even have all the facts. Maybe you should try to call her daddy one more time," Alex suggested.

"Nigga, naw. If I didn't know any better, I'd think you were getting cold feet on me."

"What! Come on man, who am I?"

"I thought you were my nigga, but seems like you simpin' out."

"T, I've always looked out for you. Man, I'm just trying to get you to think about this first. You know if we get caught, it's life without for Murder 1."

"I don't care, let's get this done. Bring Nikk over here and lay her face down. I don't even want to look at that bitch when I blow her brains out," Alex demanded.

Alex had already expressed that I was the only one he was gon' protect, so as ordered, he grabbed up Nikk and drug her wiggling and screaming to the blanket. "Gag her. I don't want to hear her either."

"Terrell, Baby please don't do this," Nikk quickly begged. "Baby please, I love you. I'm pregnant with your child. How you…"

"Nikki, you think you can make me weak? I did have mad love for you, but you a rat ass tramp. For all I know that baby could be that Terryonto niggas seed. Hell any nigga with a dick for that matter."

"But it's not."

"Shut up talking to me!" he yelled, grabbing his face. Do you know I got an e-mail to my phone the other day from Melissa. It was a picture of you with some niggas dick in yo mouth and his nut all over yo face. That shit made me sick to my fuckin' stomach. I don't know how you got like this, but I'm numb to yo hoe ass. You can't hurt a nigga like me no more than you already have, Nikk."

"I'm sorry, lets just try, Terrell."

"I'm not fazed, and didn't I tell you not to say another damn word to me?" he paused, wiping tears from his face as he mean mugged Nikk. "That's what I meant," he expressed, opening fire on her. Terrell's first shot hit Nikk in the head and some of her brain tissue flew over on my lap. I freaked out and started screaming in her defense. Terrell had completely snapped and at that point he was on something else, totally tunning me out to put a second slug in her, which went in her chest. His chilling eyes silenced me as they told a story, a story about someone that had become bitter and merciless. "Bitch, you're next," he said, pointing his gun at me.

Once he said that, I looked into my husband eyes, and motioned the words, "I love you." I knew that it was the end of the road for me and I think he did too. My hands were about free when T started walking over to get me. Kerwin, feeling compelled to do something to defend me, struggled to his feet and flung his body forward in the direction of Terrell. Shots rang out like the Fourth of July, and Kerwin's body fell limp to the floor.

"OH MY GOD!!!!!!!! T, you dirty bastard. I hope you rot in hell for this," I screamed, freeing my hands. He pointed his gun at me with no remorse and opened fire on me while I was still in my chair. I stood to try to defend myself as bullets ripped through my body, quickly dropping me.

"T, stop," Alex yelled, making his way over to me. As he tried to stop T, he was hit in the arm. As my body fell over, I shook like I was having convulsions. "Damn, nigga you done killed her," Alex cried out in pain. "You promised you weren't going to hurt Asia. Nigga I can't …"

"Well nigga I lied."

"Man, I loved this girl," he stated as my eyes rolled up in my head.

"Fuck that, let's go before the cops come." T snapped. Alex held me for a second, crying. "Al, that bitch is dead, I said lets go." Suddenly, I felt him ease from up under me and the two of them ran out of the house. I laid there motionless for a little longer to ensure that they were gone, then drug my body over to Kerwin. The whites of his eyes were rolling and he was faintly breathing, "Baby," I cried, but heard nothing from him in return. Kerwin's head fell to the side and vomit oosed from his mouth. I felt myself becoming faint, so I dug my phone out of my pocket and dialed 911.

Chapter 35
Help Us

Seems like I couldn't get my fingers and hands to act right. They were not functioning as a team, but somehow God allowed me to push those buttons and finally the phone rung.

"911, what is your emergency?"

"Yes, I'm pregnant and I've been shot," I cried. "I think I'm going to loose my baby. Help us."

"Are you there alone?"

"No, my husband and friend are here. They've been shot too and I think their dead. Please send somebody quickly. I'm starting to feel weak."

"Sweety, do you know who shot you?"

"Terrell and Alex." I paused. "I need help, I can't feel my baby moving and I think I'm about to die."

"You're doing real good. What's your name?"

"Asia Phillips."

"Asia, stay with me honey, the police and paramedics are on the way."

"Kerwin," I screamed, pulling the phone away from my mouth. "How you gon' die on me before you get to hold our son? You said you wouldn't leave us," I cried, freaking out, as I observed his motionless body. "Please help us," I whined, putting the phone back to my mouth.

"Asia, baby calm down," the operator soothingly suggested.

"Please help us! My husband isn't responding. This is our first baby, and I want him to see our son."

"Asia, the paramedics and police have arrived. They're on their way into your house."

"Okay.

"What room are you in?"

"The den."

"Okay she's in the den," she repeated."

"They're here now," I stated, after one of them called my name.

"Sweetie, I'm gonna hang up."

"Okay."

The medics saw me lying on the floor and jumped right in. They started working on me and the baby because I'd lost a lot of blood. "Help us," I cried as the police tried to ask as many questions as possible. They didn't get in much, but I was able to at least tell them who shot us as well as the contact information for my dad. I didn't know all of what was going on with Kerwin and Nikk because they loaded me up and quickly zipped me to the hospital.

Once they rushed me inside the emergency room, the medical team started working on me. I heard the doctors talking and then suddenly I became distracted by this bright glow.

"She's in pretty bad shape," one doctor acknowledged, as medical professionals went scrambling everywhere, working to save me and my son's life. "We're losing her….. WE'RE LOSING HER!" A doctor yelled. I think I died because that was the last thing I remember hearing. Then my memory goes blank from there.

Chapter 36
Fight Butterfly

I was so heavily sedated my first few critical weeks in intensive care that I can't begin to tell you much of anything about them. I don't remember a whole bunch, but I do remember occasionally coming in and out from time to time, and whenever I did, I always recognized my parents sitting by my side. Most often when I came to, Dad was on duty. He was always tenderly kissing my left hand and fingers or crying. Dad knew Calvin Shaw ordered the hit on me, so the guilt from everything that went down was more overwhelming for him than anyone.

The bones in my right hand and arm were shattered from where I tried to block the bullets. That's why I could barely dial my cell that day. My large intestines had been destroyed by a bullet that grazed it and my liver, causing me to lose a portion of them both. An additional bullet lodged into the gristle of my nose, inches from my brain, so I had to have a minor operation on my face. I lost so much blood that I had to have several transfusions. My vitals were up and down and after I died and was resuscitated in the emergency room that first day, they observed me very closely because they didn't really think I was going to make.

Day in, day out, Dad was right there. "Fight Butterfly, fight," he'd insist, holding my hand to make me recognize his presence. "I love you so much. Baby, your Dad has made some major mistakes in life, but God, you bring my baby through this, and I'ma do better," he'd whisper in my ear, trying to make peace with God and keep me stimulated at the same time. Dad layed his face on the pillow right next to my ear, and cried as he sung an old gospel hymnal my Great Granny GG always sung…. *"Jesus paid it all, all to him I owe… Sin had left a crimson stain, but LORD you can wash me white as snow.* I knew from hearing my daddy compromise with the Lord that God had humbled him. Dad was at his lowest of low, his weakest of weak, his ultimate breaking point. Daddy Ruenae and GG always taught him when life was at what seemed like it's worst, to trust in the Lord. "God I'm trying to hold on." Dad teared. "I know this is not my baby girls' destiny.

Man, she has so much more to do. You done already took everybody else God, Bean, Ant, Daddy Ruenae, GG, Chew, J," Dad fussed, stroking my hair. "I'm trying not to question my faith and learn how to wait on you God. I know you have a way of making us know that it's not about us. No matter how much we have, God, you can always make the most prosperous.... humble. I'm begging you father, be with my baby, wrap my little girl up in your loving arms like you did for me so many times. Protect her and give her what she needs to pull through this. Amen." Dad uncontrollably wiped his tears, and intensely looked on at me.

"I love you Butterfly," Dad whispered one last time before showing me that I was still his little girl. He grabbed my hand, kissed my fingers, and sung the Barney song to me, "*I love you, you love me, ...*" *Boy, Dad has surely become soft in his old age.* I wanted to scream "Shut up, Dad," some days, but my body wouldn't let me do anything except lie there. It was as though I could hear the things happening around me, but my body was in a mild coma.

"P, you want some coffee," Uncle E, Mom or Teretta would ask, trying to occasionally pull him off for a break.

"I'm not leaving my baby's side 'til they tell me I have to. You can bring me something," he'd suggest, continuing to hold my hand the entire time. Dad would sit there and stare at me for hours. One day he just started rattling, "Asia, Daddy's sorry, baby. Had I known the outcome of my past actions would result in this, they would have been so different. I need you to fight. Daddy can't take another loss. The last time I hurt like this was when Bean left me. When my life was taken away from me the day I went to prison, you and my Ma became my everything. The day Bean died, she took a part of my soul with her. Butterfly you and me share a special bond that can't no man destroy. You've been to my life, what food is to the soul, *Umm Umm Good,*" Dad paused to plant several little kisses on my forehead. "I never got to tell Bean what she meant to me or how much I loved her before she died," he cried. "Sometimes I can't even sleep at night because I never had a chance to tell Ant or Daddy Reunae, either," Dad wiped his tears once again, and prayed. "God I know I'm not always right in my life as far as you're concerned, but please God, please, help my baby pull through this." With all Dad's prayers, it seemed as though he knew he lived foul, but he also knew enough to know the importance of calling on God for deliverance.

As the week slowly slipped by, I started to come to a little more, but due to the medication I was on, it was rare that I stayed coherent very long. I was waking up a little more frequently and engaging in brief conversations from time to time.

Finally, I'd come to my senses enough to form questions, which everyone dreaded.

"How's Kerwin and the baby?" I asked as blank expressions, dominated the room. "Did anyone hear me?" I paused, looking around the room. "I said how is Kerwin and the baby?" Dad stood to exit the room because he could relate so well to being in a coma only to come to some time later and find that his two best friends were dead and his whole world had changed.

"Asia, the baby died. He tried to fight after they took him, but his little body endured so much trauma that he just couldn't hang in there," Mom explained, crying.

"He died? Oh my God, how did all of this happen?" I cried, unable to hold back tears, screams, and moans.

"Baby, L'il Kerwin's mission was accomplished. He was conceived to ensure that his mommy lived. Had it not been for the baby, Asia, you would have died too. Those bullets did a lot of damage to your body, but the baby took one that surely saved you."

"How long did he live?"

"Not long."

"What about my husband?" I asked, crying even harder.

"Prince," Mama called.

"Yeah," Dad replied, wiping his face.

"Please come in here and help me," she begged, tearing.

Daddy walked over to me, kneeled on one knee in a chair, and bent over to talk to me. "Butterfly, you have to get it together. We've worked so hard to get you stable. Lets not over do it."

"Daddy, where's my husband? Please God," I cried out. "Please let somebody tell me something."

"Asia, calm down."

"Daddy, I need to know about Kerwin. Is he dead?" Daddy looked away, and then tears streamed from his face.

"Butterfly, Kerwin's fighting, Baby. They don't know if he's gonna make it. He's still in ICU. He took a bullet to the head, and one in the leg. He's been in a coma since June 3. The doctors said we'll just have to wait and see. Some of the swelling on his brain has gone down, but only time will tell. Dave, E, your mother, and Teretta rotate shifts to be with him. Steve was here last week for three days, but had to get back to his tour. He brought you some beautiful flowers, and sat talking to Kerwin for a few hours. He said he'd be flying in and out to check on you guys. Before he left, he said he was talking to Kerwin and was able to stimulate him some."

"What does that mean?"

"Kerwin was blinking a little, while Steve talked to him, so he thought he might have understood what he was saying. I've been here with you since day one, so I've only seen him a few times."

Immediately, I thought about my husband, and felt real pain for him. My heart literally throbbed at the thought of him fighting for his life without me. Here I'd been his only real source of family and support, and was unable to be near him during his time of distress. *I wish my baby's mother was here to comfort him in his time of need. God, there's nothing like a mother's love. Sometimes it's the only earthly thing that seems to be comforting enough when your aches and pains hurt so badly. I hope he knows I haven't abandonded him,* I cried allowing my tears to fall like a heavy rain.

All the news was so overwhelming that Dad didn't even bother to tell me of Nikk's fate, and I was so distraught that I neglected to ask. After all the bad news, my blood pressure went straight up. Dad called the nurse, who ordered everyone out.

"Everyone, she's been progressing so well. I think all the company today has been a little too much. I'm gonna have to ask you all to leave, and come back tomorrow."

"Ms. Neal I heard what you said, but I'm not going anywhere. I didn't leave my daughter when she was in critical condition and I'm not leaving today."

"I already knew you weren't going to leave, Mr. Prince. So I didn't expect you to."

"Teretta, take my bag home and bring me some clean clothes for tomorrow," Dad instructed. "Who's stayin' with Kerwin tonight?"

"Zena is," E replied.

"Okay. My gut is uneasy, would you stay at the house with little L'il Ant and Teretta?"

"No problem."

"I'll call you if something happens with Asia."

Chapter 37
Face Off

After everyone left, Dad made sure that I was comfortable and then crawled up in the recliner next to my bed to watched TV. The nurse came in right before shift change to give me some meds, and to see if Dad needed anything before she left. "No thanks I'm fine," Dad replied as she dimmed the lights. Before exiting, she slightly pulled the privacy curtains back and left the door cracked.

I quickly nodded back off after she left, but around three o'clock in the morning I opened my eyes to check on Dad, only to be startled by a man peering through my curtains like a real peeping tom. Looking right at me was this set of cold, dark, shaky eyes. This person dressed in dark clothing as he stared me down with this evil look on his face. Unable to speak from fear, I moaned a little, which awakened Dad.

"Butterfly, you okay?" He asked, turning pale as he observed the same thing I saw because at that point the man was completely in our view.

"Shhhhhhs," the gentleman whispered to us both, exposing a handgun, then backing away to completely close the three of us in.

"What the hell are you doing here?" Dad fussed, feeling for his gun.

"P, I told my beautiful little niece to tell you I said 4357. Why you seem so shocked to see me?"

"Calvin, I wouldn't holla at you or respond to yo message if we were the last two nigga's alive. The most I was gon' ever do for you, I already did."

"What's that?"

"Exhumed your corpse and buried you or who I thought was you with the Prince family."

"Yeah, I heard you did that. Thanks, that was mad love. Prince, you showed me you had some real compassion when you did that. That was something that you had to get from Daddy Ruenae or GG cuz Bean's ass was to cold for kindness."

"Yeah well that was then, and after you had your people do this to my daughter, I wish I would have left your grimey ass in the pet cemetery. And nigga for the record don't disrespect Bean in front of me."

"P, I didn't have this done. You think I'm that shallow?"

"Nigga you're a ruthless bastard. You ain't never cared about the Prince family, so why you gon' start now?"

"See that's where you're wrong. I got mad love for the Prince family, what happened was the Prince's stopped loving me."

"Yeah right that's why you took out your own twin, huh?"

"That's a very complex story. One of these days," Calvin paused, looking real disturbed. "Well fuck it. I'm gon' go on and lace you up, but you wouldn't understand because Bean always loved you the most anyway."

"This ain't got shit to do with Bean."

"Nigga, this got everything to do with Bean," Calvin snapped, gritting his teeth at Dad. "Her failures and poor decisions fucked up our family. Not mine. I didn't have a choice, she made my twin and I hate each other before we ever had a chance to meet."

"Man, she wasn't no better to Ant and me than she was to you. Bean didn't learn how to be a mother until I was convicted."

"P, and even then, she still only learned how to love you and Ke."

"Maybe so, but Ant Prince didn't care anyway," Dad boasted with pride. "Ant was the man, he was on his own shit. Shoot, he was the kind of nigga that didn't need nobody. He made things happen for himself. He didn't have feelings nor did he care about what a nigga thought. Bean and him hated each other. I just never really understood why."

"Nigga Calvin Shaw cared. That's why I started initially swaping in and out with Ant. I wanted a family to be a part of too. But when it came to Bean, being him wasn't no better than being me. Shit, she turned her back on us both."

"But that's where you and Ant were different. He wasn't moved by Bean, that nigga didn't have feelings."

"Ant had feelings, he just never showed 'em much. And you're wrong again, he didn't hate Bean. I know for a fact that he loved her more than anything. He just wanted her to love him back. Didn't you read his journals that were in the safe at Big Fellas?"

"Yeah, but wasn't nothin' in there about Bean."

"P, Bean hated Ant because you loved him more than you loved her. She was jealous of him and once her scandalous secret got out about us, she feared he'd tell you. That's why she hated the time y'all spent together. She hated her twin, because Ka'Nita spent a lot of time with me while I was growing up after my father and grandmother died."

"Why she go against Bean like that?"

"My father, Robert Shaw and Ka'Nita's husband Robin Porter we're brothers, fraternal twins to be exact. When my grandmother Minnie, had them, she took my daddy home and gave Robin to her sister Ethel because she was unable to have children. Aunt Pat raised Uncle Robin as her own. For the longest the boys were raised as cousins, but my Grandma's sister-in-law, Aunt Pat, told Robin everything. Robin understood my need to be embraced by family. P, there was nowhere for me to go, so that's why he and Ka'Nita spent time with me."

"I can't believe this. Our family is so fucked up."

"But that was my daddy and his brother's shit. Bean had a chance to love me and my twin and provide us with something different, her alcoholic ass just chose not to."

"Calvin, I'm not about to talk about my mother and my brother with you. Or maybe I should say our brother that you killed. As a matter a fact, you got some real big nuts coming here period. Don't you see my daughter's trying to recover?" Dad paused to look at me, but I pretended to be resting.

"I'm sorry about what happened to Asia, P. Man since she's been here, I've been by a few times to check on her. I just got the nerve to come in today. I usually stop by her husband's room from time to time because occasionally he's alone. Today I popped in here hoping to just catch a glimpse of Asia, and saw you. I was about to leave when she woke up. I'd already been standing here for about two minutes."

"What were you planning to do, catch me off guard and kill me like you killed Ant?"

"What happened with Ant was not my doing."

"You a fuckin liar."

"On some real shit, I didn't kill Ant or order no hit."

"I don't believe yo ass. Man, Ant meant more to me than I meant to myself. I would have taken a bullet for that nigga. He was my hero, and man when you killed him, you took one of the only three real niggas I ever loved. I hurt so bad the day they came and told me he was dead. All I could think about was how I never got to really tell him what he meant to me or thank him for being more than a brother, but also a father, and my best friend," Dad paused, looking around. "Man, I ain't trying to be in no gun war with you. I want to live my life and see my daughter recover in peace, so you gon' have to go or one of us gon' die tonight."

"P, I ain't come for no trouble."

"So why you here?"

"Man, if I wanted to get you, there were so many times I could have. My son CJ ran with Asia's ex boyfriend Alex. I've seen you at games. I've passed the stores from time to time when I'm in town, and since you just knew I was dead and no one tried to retaliate on you, you know you weren't watching your back like I always taught you to."

"Nigga, you ain't teach me shit. Ant was the one that told me 'Never trust anyone, not even family, always watch your back, and loose lips, sank ships.'"

"Well you failed two of the three lessons I taught you like I said."

"What!"

"P, you trusted some fucking hired hit-men that you didn't even know to take me out. Recardo and Barry worked for me. They'd been killing niggas for me since 86'. That's the only reason I'm alive and Melvin's not. And once you moved the body you thought was mine, tell me you didn't relax even more and stop watching your back all together."

"What you mean? Nigga, according to the news your body was recovered. Melvin is still listed as missin."

"Naw partna, Melvin's not missin'. That slimey muthafucka is very much so dead."

"How you know?"

"Because that's whose body you had exhumed. After Barry and Recardo drug me out of your store to the car, frontin like they were takin me out, they drove me and Mel to the lake. I did Melvin myself, so I know that nigga dead. And just like he violated me by stealing my journal and some of my property, I returned the favor."

"What?"

"I put my ID in Mel's pocket, took his, and like that Calvin Shaw was dead."

"You killed Melvin and stole his identity?"

"Hell yeah! Melvin was on some deceptive shit. He was working against the team. Settin niggas in the crew up left and right, narkin for the feds, and was very instrumental in the crashing of Silk's Empire. Sad part about it all was that he'd been doing grimey shit for so long that his punk ass got laxed. He was getting caught up, beating charges, and I couldn't figure out why, 'til my black ass got set up."

"So why you think he was the one settin' you up?"

"Melvin had T set up, and then tried to pretend like Ray Johnson and his boys did it. As time went on, the story on the streets that came out was that Mel did T over some drug territory, but it turned out that Melvin and T was sleeping with the same woman. T confronted Mel about the possibility of little T being his, and Mel didn't like that. Catherine had a blood test done after T died and it turned out that Little T was in fact Melvin's baby."

"How you know that?"

"Know what?"

"That Mel had T set up."

"That nigga was braggin to me about it."

"Nigga, you a lie. He wouldn't brag to Ant about killin T. Ant loved T as much as he loved me. T was like our brother. No way Mel was gon' bust himself out like that, he knew Ant would kill him."

"Yeah, but he would brag to Calvin Shaw."

"So when did he supposedly tell Calvin Shaw this?"

"After he killed him, thinking he'd killed me."

"Yeah Right. Man, why would he trust Calvin more than Ant?"

"You know the saying, 'Birds of a feather flock together."

"Yeah."

"Well, Cal was a snake like Mel, they grew up together, did dirt together, and that's why he told him about l'il T."

"So he told you about T, thinkin' you were Cal?"

"Straight up. Me and that nigga was eating at Fishbones. We were there drinkin' up some shit, and Mel and I were talking about some of the lames we'd taken out just on GP, and shit we regretted. That's when he confessed."

"What did he say?"

"He got this real serious look on his face."

"Cal, I got something to tell you."

"What?" I asked.

"Dawg, I've lived with a dark secret for a long ass time."

"Dark secret like what?"

"Man me and T were both fucking Catherine when she got pregnant with little T."

"Mel you dirty muthafucka. How you gon' fuck your niggas woman."

"It just happened. I was out checking traps one evening and ran into her at M&M's Shrimp Shack on Seven Mile. She was all up on a nigga's dick, talking about how fine I was and how she wanted me and I bit cuz I'd been wanting to fuck her."

"But she was T's main bitch."

"I know, but pussy was on my mind at the time. Nigga it was late, I was solo, didn't want to go home and sleep alone, so I told her we could hook-up if she promised not to tell T.... She agreed."

"And."

"Nigga, what you mean, And... And I fucked her, that shit was good, she let me go raw, and I bust one up in her."

"Forget that. How I know you ain't Calvin?"

"Cause I said so."

"That aint good enough for me, man do you know I ain't had no kick it for my Uncle Silk all these years because I thought he had something to do with settin' my brother up."

"Damn, fa' real."

"Yeah, and Silk was my boy, but after I came up off of my bid, I wasn't feelin' him. I didn't trust him and no one else for that matter."

"That's fucked up. Silk always cut hard for you."

"I didn't care, I wasn't feelin' him. I couldn't prove he'd set Ant up, but something wasn't right. But now that I think about it, I'm mad because what I'm hearing you say is Silk was innocent."

"Man, good thing you didn't try to kill him to avenge my death too."

"I thought about it a few times."

"P, Silk was the first nigga in the family that cut me off. He was so mad at me about what happened with you that he stopped supplying me because he said he didn't trust me."

"So everybody cut you off?"

"Yeah, pretty much, but when Daddy Ruenae did, I was fucked up."

"Damn."

"Let me finish, though."

"Go head."

"Melvin was always l'il T's Godfather and since Cat didn't want him to be confused, she allowed Melvin to be a more active part of his life. She never told him that Mel was his real daddy, but Melvin, started feeling guilty about what he'd done to T, he refused to call his son, L'il Terrance anymore."

"That's messed up."

"I know, so instead Mel told Cat he was going to call him Terrell after his brother who got killed on the block, and if she had a problem with that, then he'd tell L'il T the entire story about them. Cat didn't want any additional drama, so she agreed to the change of his nickname."

"So you mean to tell me that not only did that nigga sell out on Ant, he did T over a bitch?"

"Man, Mel was on some deceptive shit everyday. I swear he wasn't to be trusted. And the only reason I paid your pretty little daughter a visit a while ago is because I heard that Terrell was about to try to avenge Mel's death."

"Avenge it how?"

"Kill Asia, you, and the rest of your family."

"Who told you that?"

"P, I've been keeping up with you since the day you thought you killed me. Asia, was dating one of my little mellows. He's been good friends with CJ for a long time. When I found out Alex was dating Asia that was perfect. I immediately told CJ he was coming to Detroit to go to college to keep an eye on y'all for me. Alex told CJ about the hit in confidence. Al was so obsessed with Asia and wanted to know what CJ thought he should do. After CJ advised him, he told me. Once I found out, I flew in from New York on the first flight I could get to try to prevent anything from happening to you."

"Why would you do that for me after I tried to kill you?"

"Prince, I am the original keeper to the Prince."

"Naw, Ant was the original keeper to the Prince."

"So you still don't believe I'm Ant?"

"Nope."

"So how can I convince you?"

"You tell me."

"Okay, when you were young, I gave you a code to use when you were in distress. Remember 4357."

"Yeah, I do, but so did Calvin Shaw. That's how I knew you weren't Ant in the office that day."

"How?"

"You told me that code, but you didn't know the password Ant gave me."

"P, I know who gave you the code. When you were ten, I gave you the HELP code after dude in the projects tried to rob you." I slightly opened my eyes, squinting them just enough to still appear sleep, and did a double take at Calvin. Chills came over me as I listened to their conversation. "I'm Ant," at that point, I couldn't keep my eyes closed any longer. If I understood like Dad understood, Calvin Shaw was standing before me and my daddy, telling him that he was in fact his dead brother Ant.

"Damn man, so what are you saying?" Dad asked with watery eyes.

"P, I'm saying that you almost killed the wrong nigga. It's me. Ant. I told you that day, but you didn't believe me." Dad was stunned. He didn't know what to say as tears streamed down his face.

"I don't understand. Man, you had a chance in that office to tell me who you were that day, but you didn't."

"I tried to, but P you came at me so strong. And when I realized that your hit men were my men, I just said fuck it and played along."

"But why?"

"When I saw you at Big Fellas up in BBO that night, I was in disbelief. I didn't even know you were out. Man, I wanted to grab you, give you a hug, cry, and tell you just how much I'd missed you, but you gave me such a cold look. I walked up there and saw how much you'd matured and guilt immediately came over me. After I left you and Scooter at that table, I had flashbacks. I thought about Felica giving you your first blow job in the back of my Benz, the day I took you to that Playa's Ball, Silk had the night you begged me to gear you up, and the day we came to see you at the Michigan Reformatroy. When I saw all those bruises on you from where you were fighting, man I wanted to hang myself. Bean cried all the way home. I tried to tell her you'd be okay, but she cussed me out, blaming me for your outcome. And the fact that she was right on the money with her allegations didn't help." Ant paused to wipe tears from his eyes. "P, Bean hated my black ass. She always told me she wished it was me instead of you doing that life sentence and the fact that it actually should have been, ate at me daily. Dawg, to walk up in my club seventeen years later on top of my shit, and see you, my blood, who I loved more than anything, hurt. And to see you as a man and know that I robbed you of your youth for my own selfish reasons, hurt even more. I could barely look you in your eyes that day." Dad looked over at Ant and his head hung in shame. "Shit, P, I could barely look you in your eyes now."

"Fuck that, nigga we were brothers, if you felt all that you just said you felt, why didn't you say nothing to me then?"

"I remember when Melvin called me on my cell and told me to get to the club ASAP. When I asked him why, he said, *'Ant's little brother just walked up in the joint.'* I said Ant's brother who? *'The Prince himself.'* I couldn't believe it. I asked him how he knew it was you. And when he said, *'I came up in BBO to holla at Scooter and noticed him when he tried to conceal his identity.'* I felt like shit. I asked him did he make it obvious that he saw you, and he assured me that he didn't."

"I didn't think he noticed me either."

"Exactly! And that goes back to what I always said. You were never meant to be a player in this game. Mel asked me if I wanted him to kill you, I told him no, to just let you have your moment and try to avoid any altercations."

"Oh, so he was gon' try to kill me?"

"Naw, cuz I wouldn't allow it."

"Why not? Shit, you allowed me to do 17 years by myself?"

"Man, first of all, I wanted to see you. But once I did, I was reminded of all the love you had for your big brother, and the innocence I stole from you."

"You didn't think I was gon' strike?"

"Yeah I knew you were, I just didn't know how soon. When Mel called me the day after we saw you from the store, I knew what was going down from the way he was talking. That's why I came alone, with that envelope full of money. At first I thought I could give you a peace offering, tell you who I really was, kill Mel, cuz I was gon' do that anyway, and bring you in as a partner. But after talking to you and seeing all that pain in your eyes, I thought it would be easier to die as Calvin Shaw and move on. I knew it would make you feel good if you could do something like take me out for Ant, so I figured I'd vanished and let you live thinking you'd avenged my death."

"Man, I loved you. We could have worked through anything."

"But P, I hated me, and it was easier to disappear than to try to rebuild what we had as brothers."

"But we could have worked it out. We're family. You see I gave you a chance to fix it because I wanted it to be you more than anything."

"I knew I let you down. While I sat there lookin' at you, I remembered the day Daddy Ruenae told me I was a selfish ass coward. And he insisted that when I let you fall for me as far as he was concerned, I was no longer worthy of bearing the Prince name."

"He didn't mean that, he was just bitter and I was his favorite."

"Yeah, I know, but the fact of the matter is that he was right."

"So your guilt was so awful that you gave up everything? Your life, your son, your family, and all that could have been?"

"Yeah, and you loved me so much that you did the same for me without even realizing it 'til it was done. Didn't you?"

"I did, but I did it for the bond that we had."

"Well P, I died for me too, which confirms Daddy Ruenae's comment. To some extent it has always been about me. I lost a son and a portion of my life, but quickly gained another without any real sacrifice. See I still didn't have to really go without anything. I gave up a life, but I gained a new identity and started over somewhere else to continue to live my life as a free man. It wasn't that easy for you. Everyday, you woke up for seventeen years in confinement."

"Oh, I think you've gone without. Man, you lost real big on l'il Ant. I see him from time to time. He just graduated from college with a degree in

Agriculture, and got some big time job in DC last month. We don't see him much, but he calls occasionally."

"I know, CJ knows his Uncle Byron. B works at a party store on Seven Mile off Schoolcraft."

"Umm, I know him too. Your letter saved his life."

"Is that right?"

"Yeah, I almost killed him while we were in Standish together."

"Glad you didn't because he was another young buck that loved me as much as you did and I almost fucked his life up too."

"Yeah, but I made up for that and helped him clear his name," Dad paused to think. "Well tell me this."

"What?"

"Why did you steal Calvin's identity, he was our brother too."

"Melvin had Calvin killed thinking he was killing me. Since I'd just been caught up on some major drug charges due to him setting me up, and was looking at serving a life sentence with the Fed's, it was easy to die. I had more to look forward to as a dead Ant than I did when I was alive. I had a chance to start over. Daddy Ruenae didn't speak to me for months after I told him about your case. Bean hated me just because she thought you got caught up trying to follow behind me. Silk didn't fool with me as much because he didn't trust me. He always told me, 'Any man that would let his little brother who loved him like a father do his bid, was not worthy of the spit a nigga coughed up to clear his throat.' Whenever, I came around, Bean drank like a fish, cussed me out, and then put me out, but not before making it a point to tell me how much she hated me." Ant wiped fresh tears as he talked about Bean. "Man and need I tell you what it was like to see you at Bean's funeral. There I stood at the back of the church before the services started, looking at you shackled. When you were bent over in her casket, talking and kissing on her, I broke. I'd gotten there early so I could say my goodbyes, but you beat me there. I was gon' come in, tell her that I loved her, kiss her for the first time in over twenty-five years, and slip out before her funeral started. But after I saw you, I stayed."

"Why you didn't say something then?"

"Man, I wanted to. Instead, I watched you from the hall, wanting like a muthafucka to come in and hug you. But not for your comfort, my own."

"Ke said she saw you at the funeral."

"Yeah, I remember she ran out right after that video of Bean's life to that song by Boys to Men went off. At least she had you to comfort her, I had to do that service alone at the back of the church. *Mama...mama you know I love you...*" Ant briefly sung in a low dry tone. "P, there wasn't one day in my life after the age of three that I called Bean mama, nor was there one day after the age of ten that I told her I loved her before I sung it to her at her funeral." "Damn Bean, why me?" he sadly exhaled. "Man, Silk, Daddy Ruenae, Bean, they all hated me. I couldn't take the mental bullshit any longer. P all I ever wanted was to be loved, and once I became Calvin Shaw, I got it."

"Man I loved you"

"P, I know, but not once you were locked up."

"So instead of tellin'me what was up, you just die on me and not bother to say goodbye. Leave me in that fuckin' prison to rot from the inside out, stressing about the possibility of never seeing you or my freedom again."

"Prince, I wanted to do something I could feel good about. I started Big Fellas as Calvin Shaw with the money I'd stacked as Ant. And man, nigga's loved me like they loved Silk at one time. I had homies who would die for me. I made about thirty to fifty grand every two weeks with that spot. But what I discovered after getting my club just like I wanted it was, once all the loot was counted, the hoes were gon' and the lavishness of my lifestyle was removed for the day, I could never change the pain I felt or the disgust I saw when I looked at myself in the mirror. I made a bad decision when I let you fall for me. That's why I tried to make it up to you with all that money I put away. That safe in GG's basement, the bank account, and the money I buried in Bean's backyard was supposed to do exactly what it did. Move you to another status if or once you came home. I wanted to detour you from ever tryin' to be a balla or a repeat offender."

"Yeah, I guess. So what happened with Melvin?"

"I had that nigga's toes cut off and his lips slashed. I made Barry and Recardo do it right in my presence, so I could see that nigga scream and squirm like the rat he was. Then I walked up, gripped the hell out of his nuts, so he'd screamed, then I stuffed his toes in his mouth for steppin' to the wrong Prince."

"So did he know who you were before he died?"

"Oh yeah he knew."

"How you know?"

"Because just like I had a code of distress for you, I also had one for him. When I looked in his eyes and said 27277, he knew exactly who I was. His eyes bucked, as he frantically shook his head no. Then I spit in that nigga's face, for testin' a real G. I taped that bitches mouth, hands and feet, and then tossed his ass in the lake myself for killing my twin, and T."

"27277?"

"Yeah, ASAP-R *Alert...Sorry Ass Pig Run*. I always told him that whenever we had to move weight for a few dirty cops who kept our dope houses on protection."

"So Ant, what I need to do about them niggas that did this to my daughter?"

"We picked 'em up tonight. They're both strung up in the basement at my rent house."

"Where did y'all catch 'em?"

"Sittin' out in front of your house. They were waiting on you and your family to come home. E' pulled up in the driveway to drop off your son and wife. After he saw them in, he left. Once he was gone, they eased up on your street. I was sitting about a half a block down, watching your house when I noticed them. Barry and Recardo were already posted in your backyard just in case they tried to enter a different way."

"They were at my spot 'bout to kill my wife and Ant!" Dad asked.

"What you say?"

"I said they were at my house?"

"Naw, I'm talking about your son's name."

"Ant! You named your son after me."

"Yeah, Dawg, I was so proud to have a boy that I named him after both of us. I figured we could both live through him and DeMarques and Anthony Prince would have a second chance."

"What?"

"You know if he did something great in life then it would be a reflection of you and me. Doctor DeMarques Anthony Prince, or Honorable DeMarques Anthony Prince, and so on, you feel me."

"Damn, P. I did real bad by you man. I'm sorry."

"You made up for it today though. Man, you gave my family a second chance at life. I thank you for what you've done, but I don't want to be a part of anything that you decide to do to those boys. My life is so different now. Sitting here watching my daughter and son-in-law fight for their lives helped me know that there's more to life than trying to get revenge."

"I hear you."

"Do you really?" Dad paused, tenderly rubbing my hand. "See Ant, that's what all of this turmoil I'm going through is about anyway. You killed Ray to avenge T, The Caseys killed Chew, and J to avenge the ass whooping I put on Antonio Casey, Silk had those innocent girls and Antonio killed to avenge Chew and J's death. Calvin Shaw and Melvin was supposedly killed to avenged your death, but turns out that Melvin was the real serpent, so he was actually killed by you to avenge Calvin and T. I lost my grandson and almost my entire family because this Terrell nigga was gon' avenge Melvin's death and that nigga is the one that started this whole blood bath to begin with. This drama went full circle. Who are we to be trying to do acts of God? We're nobodies, that's why this foolishness got so out of hand, and when it's all said and done, Vengeance is really the Lords. From being *Hood Rich* to an out cold *Big Tymer*, we've made some bad choices that affected our entire family in a real detrimental way."

"I know man, GG always told me the decisions I made from day to day could and would affect me and all those connected to me for the rest of my life. To bad I didn't clearly understand what she meant then."

"Yeah, it's a damn shame that we don't understand or value experience and wisdom until it's too late."

"P, I guess it's my own fault that life had to come to this for me before I truly decided to change my ways. From talking with you today, I see that I lost far more than I realized."

"Ant, no matter what, I have always loved you."

"Thanks, bro, I needed to hear that."

"Man, I've lived such a carefree life since I killed you," Dad smiled. I ain't even on that Bad Boy shit no more. To be honest, once my children get through this, I want to go back to that lifestyle again. Dawg, this game ain't me or for me."

"So you want me to handle them nigga's that did this?"

"Ant you always have handled things. Hopefully, over the years you've grown and on some brand new shit, but whatever you do, I want no parts of it."

"P, it was good to see you. I love you, homie. And you know I've always been my brother's keeper."

"Naw Playa, you fell a little short on being your brother's keeper, but you have always been a keeper for the Prince."

"What's that mean?"

"Being brothers by far exceeds the biological connection. I learned that from E."

"He has been a real homie to you, huh."

"Naw, he's been a real brother and friend. Homies leave you hangin, and they tell you what you want to hear. Brothers and real friends cut hard for you and make mad sacrifices in spite of the situation," Dad paused, looking at Ant. "Like you." Ant was speechless as his eyes became glassy. "Stay up Big Bro. Daddy Ruenae would be real proud of you today."

"You think so?"

"I know it. Man, when I came home, he'd left this letter for me with GG that was written four days before he died. I've kept it in my wallet as a constant reminder of what he wanted the new Prince Family legacy to represent. Can I read it to you right quick?"

"Yeah."

"April 8, 1995

Prince,

The two Kings in your life left this gift for you. May you truly understand the meaning of the ultimate sacrifice you made to save your brother's life. You are my hero. I hope you learn from your past, and build yourself one heck of a future. Buy a few things you need with this money, and make sure you stay out of trouble. I'm counting on you to take our family to the next level. **Prince, Read, Reflect, and Realize that your life has a Real Purpose.** I can't tell you what it is, but trust in God, and He will direct your path.

Love,

Daddy Ruenae.

"Ant, I think you made some sacrifices that forced you to reflect over the years, too. After talking with you today, I see that you realize that your life has real purpose. I can't tell you what it is, but like Daddy Ruenae told me, 'Trust in God, and He will direct your path."

"P, *we fall down, but we get up....* Don't we."

"Yeah, you know why?"

"Why?"

"Cause a saint is just a sinner, who fell down, but got up."

"Look at you, P…"

"Man, I see that GG and Daddy Ruenae's raising us in the Lord, stuck with you as well."

"Yeah, some, but a nigga ain't gon' front, I'm far from a saint."

"Dawg, fa'sho… I'm already feelin' you."

"And you know what?"

"What?"

"I wonder do all Big Tymers feel the same as me. I wonder if after all the money is counted, the dope distributed, and the women are gone, do Ballas feel the same kind of void I feel. I wonder if they honestly find true satisfaction in being ruthless killers. I used to, but after loosing a child, a few homies, and a brother along the way, my mind stays in turmoil. My heart, damn, it's bitter. And my gangsta, though at one time it was on point, it doesn't seem to hold the same value it once did," Ant paused as if he were in deep thought. "P, somewhere along the way, I got soft. Somehow with the passing of each new day, I started to care about myself and those I was putting in harms way. "Aww hell naw, you ain't no real Thugizzo," my boys used to tease when I was fresh on the come up. And, I guess to some extent they were right. I say that because I believe what really happened was somewhere along the way, I realized that my life had real purpose, but ballin' wasn't it. Damn, I wish I would have discovered that long before all my losses. Then maybe I'd feel better about my current position and my life choices. It's a damn shame that life had to come to this for me before I truly decided to change my ways."

Suddenly, Ant dapped Dad down, then walked over to me, kissed my forehead, and apologized to me for my misfortune. "Asia, your daddy has always loved you," he whispered, setting an envelope next to my head. "I'm sorry about what happened, and I wish I could make things right," he turned. "P, I sure hope she pulls through. I've tried to make sure this little lady had all she needed since forever."

"How you figure that?"

"Everything Alex gave Asia over the years before he thought I died came from me, and afterwards I gave it to CJ who gave it to him for me. Alex knew Asia was my niece, but he was sworn to secrecy. When I found out what he did to her at that college, I had Raynard Hicks rally a few of my loyal little homeboys to kick his ass on a weekly basis for about two months straight. After a while, he started calling CJ, crying about how sorry he was and how much he really loved Asia. It was then that I called the dogs off because they were about to kill him."

"Well thanks cause she never told me or I would have killed him myself."

"Yeah, sure you would have," he teased.

"Ant, thanks for the HELP."

"4357 for life, L'il nuts."

"No more L'il Nuts up in these boxers. That was 1984, this is 2010."

"Yeah my bad, shrivled nuts."

"Ant, a nigga like me well hung in his old age."

"I don't doubt it. It's in the genes. You a Prince, right?"

After Ant's little remark, he laughed and peacefully exited the room. I peeped over at Dad, watching him wipe tears from his eyes. For some strange reason, I felt the kind of pain for him I used to feel when I visited him in prison. I really hurt for him, but to respect his privacy, I never bothered to let Dad know that I heard most of his discussion. Sometimes it's best to let a person have their privacy and let family secrets stay a secret, so I did just that.

Chapter 38
Recovery

After one month in ICU, they moved me to a private room. After being in the hospital for two months, I was finally able to go see my husband for the first time. I had Dad wheel me over to Kerwin's Room. I didn't know what condition my loving husband would be in, so I tried to prepare myself. I ain't gon' lie, we'd all been leaning on GG and Daddy Ruenae's spiritual teachings, so sung Yolanda Adams song, all the way there. *"There's no pain... Je..sus can't feel. There is no hurt....that he cannot heal..... All things work... according to, the master's purpose, and his holy will.. Asia, Phillips, No Matter What, You're Going Through........, The Battle is not mine, it's the Lords......."*

Woooo, after thinking about the storm God delivered me from, I was totally broke down. At that point, I knew once God let me live, he was going to use me as a living witness. I dried up my tears right before we entered the room. Suddenly, I saw Kerwin and fresh tears dominated my eyes as I fought like hell to keep them from falling. Dad, finally seeing us together was able to envision first hand the reality of what we'd gone through as a family, and he teared up as well.

"Hey Baby," I greeted my husband as Dad pushed me by his bed. Kerwin kind of laid there paralyzed. He was unable to move and couldn't say much of anything because of his trachea. I grabbed his hands and tenderly caressed his fingers as tears streamed down both of our faces.

"You look so handsome," I expressed, reaching up to gently touch his bald head and wipe away his tears. "I missed singing with you so much?" I expressed, forcing a smile. "Hey guess what? I got a song for you." Kerwin lay motionless as his eyes did all the talking for him. They lit up as I started to sing, *Musiq, I'll love you when you're hair turns gray,yeah, and I'll love you when you gain a*....Oh hold on, I got another on," *Let me cater to you because today is your day...* "Kerby, *my life would be purposeless without you,*" He just looked on as I kept talking. "Do you remember that song by Destiny's Child? I know you probably don't. It's a throw-back, but anyway that was the first song that came to mind when I saw you.... I love you so much, Mr. Philips. I don't care if you ever walk again; I love you and will provide for you forever if necessary. I'm in this for the long haul. It's you and me baby 'til dirt do us part." After I caught a glimpse of the small scar on his head from where he'd undergone surgery, I leaned over and cried on his arm like a baby. Dave, Steve, and Dad looked on with glazed eyes. I peeped back and caught Dave wiping his face a few times.

"Do y'all think he understands me?" I asked.

"Yeah, he does," Steve answered, optimistically.

"How you know?"

"He'll communicate with you by blinking."

"Blinking?"

"Um'hum, watch," Steve suggested, getting up from his seat to engage Kerwin in conversation. "Sup, homie, can you hear me?" he asked with the brightest smile. Kerwin, immediately blinked once for yes. "Do you know who this is?" he asked, pointing at me. Again, he blinked once before tears streamed out of his eyes. I could only take so much and that broke me down.

"Okay, can everybody give me like five minutes alone with my husband, please? I haven't seen him in over two months. I'd like to talk to him by myself."

Everyone got up and made their way to the hall. I scooted in as close as I could to him. He intensely looked on at me with tears still streaming down his face.

"Baby, I hope you're feeling okay today. I've missed you more than anything in the world. Do you know how much I love you?" I asked in a soothing tone, without waiting for blinks. "My GG and great granddaddy always told me to pray for what I wanted because there was power in prayer. I can't tell you how many days I have thought about you since this happened and whispered small prayers of healing for you. Baby, my faith in God is rejuvenated. Obviously God heard my cry. I'm thankful for that cuz you know me and you are some serious sinners, but that just goes to show how forgiving he is. You know we were about to bust up in hell with gasoline draws on," I teased, smiling. That comment must have tickled him, because it brought a mild smirk to his face. "Did I just see a smile, Mr. Phillips?" One blink immediately followed. "I'm so sorry about this. Had I only known something was gon' go down, I would have never put you in jeopardy. You're my best friend, and whatever I got to do to help you get through this, I'm here for you. I promise, *My loves gon' be right here*," I stated resting my head on Kerwin's arm. Suddenly, I noticed his index finger slightly moving. Maybe that was his way of showing compassion for my tears, or maybe he was telling me it was gon' be okay. I don't know, but

I linked our fingers together, tenderly kissing his. "Baby, when you married me, we married for better or for worse, for sickness or for health, 'til death do us part. We got this unconditional thang that can't nobody take away. I'm gon' show you what Agape love is all about for the rest of our lives. As soon as these doctor's tell me you can come home, I'm gon' show you that I married you for you, not who you became or what you had."

Dad eased back into the room. "Butterfly, are you okay?"

"Yeah, I'm fine."

"Your nurse told me not to keep you out to long, so we better get back to the room."

"Okay," I paused, taking one last long look at my husband. "Remember when you picked me up that one night from the airport in that Bentley? You treated me like such a queen. No one has ever made me feel that special in my entire life. You know what else? That very day, I realized just how much I loved you. Actually, it was then that I knew I'd never love another and I'd only love you for a lifetime. Kerwin Phillips, all this time you've given me mad love and *I Can't Get Enuff*. See, even after you were mad at God for so long, he still found it in his good graces to pull you through."

Kerwin moved his lips, but his words were faint.

"Say that one more time, Baby," I suggested, focusing on his mouth.

"Don't give up on me," he motioned.

I grabbed Kerwin's hand, then placed it on my mouth for a kiss.

"Get well soon, Baby, I'm ready for you to be at home with your wife."

"Come on Butterfly, I better get you back. Son-in-law, keep fighting. We need you, man."

"You know what, Daddy?"

"What?"

"I remember when I was about fifteen or sixteen you told me that once I understood that there was more to life than material things, I'd select a man that treated me like a lady, and loved me unconditionally. You were right. After I think about Nikk, I realize that she was looking for love in all the wrong places. She came up with knuckleheads that didn't give a shit about her and she paid the ultimate price for her neediness in the end. I thank you for your fatherly advice because I could have easily been her."

"So you see parents sometimes do know what's best."

"Yeah, yeah, yeah, I didn't tell you all that for a lecture."

"But you know I'm gon' give you one, right?"

Chapter 39
The Conclusion

Kerwin went through rehab and came home almost eleven months after our incident. When he first got to the house, he struggled to do simple things, but his determined spirit wouldn't allow him to succumb to his injuries. Everyday he'd work out to strengthen his motor skills. Though the doctors told him he might not ever walk again, my baby was encouraged. He was a fighter and was gon' show the world that he believed in God's healing power and himself more than anything, which to him was most important for his recovery.

Kerwin's first six months home, I pushed, and pushed, and pushed him. We started going to Fifth Street Baptist Chuch on Fifth and Woodward, and God really started working on my soul. The first sermon I heard Pastor Coleman preach was called, ***"Don't get caught up in a Power Failure."*** He said, *"Life will go through flip flops and trouble will come double, but focus on God at all times, not just during the storm, and he will keep your mind, spirit, body, and soul right. Be careful of the witness you bare your delicate issues to, especially if they are non belivers. Learn to trust in yourself and your own judgement. People were not meant to be your source of Power, and as long as you live a life without God, you'll never have power."* GG always told me that the blood of Jesus would never lose its power. Pastor Coleman re-instilled that point for me when he said, *"Your friends, family, and homies don't give you power. However, it can be obtained by God through your own deeds."* I immediately thought about how Nikk tried to encourage me to leave my husband and take his money. Then I thought about how far he and I had come together. Considering our victory, I was so glad I trusted in my own judgement. I was blessed with enough wisdom to know better than to let the serpant get into my business to much.

I guess that's exactly why Kerby and I were granted favor. Agape Love is something that God does so well. In spite of me and Kerwin's shortcomings, God smiled upon us, and I knew it. Oh yeah, Pastor Coleman inspired me that day. Once he finished preaching, I couldn't sit in my seat. No one knew my story better than God, and he'd sent me a Word on how to get a real spiritual break through in my life. With my arms lifted on high, I walked to the front of the church, bawling. "I surrender, Lord," I shouted to the top of my lungs as tears poured from my eyes. "Thank you, Jesus, Thank you," I continued to cry, standing before the pastor. Suddenly, I felt a hand clutch mine. It was Kerwin's. He'd walked up without his cane to stand before the church with me. As the choir sang, *"I need you to survive,"* My heart felt overwhelmed with joy as I reflected on my childhood and spending time with my Grandma Bean. The song *"Be Grateful,"* quickly invaded my mind. That was the song she blasted every Sunday to get her church on, but mostly to endure Daddy's incarceration. I finally, understood the comfort and peace my grandma found in a good gospel song after weathering a storm.

My baby walking to the alter without his cane for the first time confirmed the sermon, ***"Power comes through deeds."*** I thought about how his body ached daily after working so hard in rehab. When he made it home, I'd strip him naked, give him a hot bath, and then rub his body down in warm baby oil to soothe his pain. Once I tucked him in, I'd snuggle up under him and read a few verses from the Bible. "Weeping may endure through the night, but Joy is coming in the morning." The strength he gained in God from us reading The Word every night was truly revealed that day.

Yeah, yeah, yeah, I know I said we were sinners, but just because we were lost, didn't mean we had to stay that way. Once we saw Gods miraculous blessings, we had to keep finding refuge in him. Well, I know I did because I realized He'd spared my life for a reason. What my purpose was or is I've yet to figure out. I guess if I just keep on living, He's gonna expose it to me one day. But for the time being, I'm thankful that He gave me a second chance. I got a real life testimony, and I'll tell our story everywhere I go.

...◆◆◆...

Well, it seems like all the years that went along with my uncles gangsta ways finally paid off for the good. Instead of killing Terrell and Alex, he had CJ turn them in. Both went through the court proceedings and got 35 to 50 years for attempted murder, breaking and entering, kidnapping, and conspiracy to commit murder. They also received two additional natural life sentences for the murder of Nikk and my son. After court, Kelly approached me to extend her condolences and cried on my shoulder. When I hugged her, she cried even harder about how things had turned out between us. Yeah guilt will eat at a nigga for years when they know they have done you dirty. Nonetheless, I consoled her, expressing that she and her babies were victims just like me. I was robbed of my best friend and my child, they were robbed of a father, provider, and so much more. I knew about loving a Daddy from the confines of a correctional facility. I could relate to it so well. Not to mention the many voids they were about to encounter; therefore I knew what was to come, and my heart ached for all of them.

When I walked out of the courthouse that day, I caught a glimpse of Alex sitting in the county van. I noticed him zooming in on Kell and his daughters as they crossed the street. He grabbed and shook his head in pain. I'm sure he was probably thinking of all he'd sacrificed based on having foolish loyalty like my dad had back in his day. I walked down the stairs holding my daddy's hand. When I reached the sidewalk, I finally made eye contact with Alex. He looked over at me and waved with this soft smile. I dug up a frown from Hell, mugged him with squinted eyes, and flipped him off. Don't get it twisted, I said I was working on my spiritual walk. I ain't say I'd totally arrived.

Kerwin and I decided to stay in our home. We agreed that in time we might look at moving somewhere else, but since our house had so many special memories that truly outweighed the bad, I wanted to be there to remember life as it was before the tragedy. It took me a year before I ever went into my son's room, but that is because thoughts of his life and the dreams I had for him hurt so badly when I thought about the fact that I never got to see him, touch him, nor bring him home.

I also thought about Nikk and all the good times we used to have. I cried quite a bit that first year because what I lost in her was more like a sister than a friend. Every week like Grandma Bean did after Ant Daddy Reunae died, I'd truned on my gospel music to endure my losses, and think about the past. Grandma played Amazing Grace, I played STAND by Donnie or Hezakiah. "I love you, you love me" *"What do you do...when you've done all you can. Seems like you can't make it through....You just STAND,"* I'd sing, tearing like crazy. Shoot, I spent so much time reminiscing on the good times me and my girl had in college that I would literally laugh out loud when I thought of how open she was about being a gold digger. For emotional comfort, sometimes I'd wrap my arms around myself and hug me, pretending like it was a hug from Nikk. *Darn, I miss her*, I'd sometimes think, skimming through photos of us. In memory of her and little Kerwin, Mom suggested that I plant a tree or a rose bush. Nikk was more rugged like a tree, but in my heart, she was truly a beautiful rose. So to honor her, I went with both. To honor my son, I donated countless hours of community service to the Children's Crisis Center. Those sick, abandoned, and abused babies truly helped me identify with my maternal side. After Kerwin got better, there were days when I'd drag him along just for the experience.

With time, Kerwin recovered pretty well from his injuries. Of course he could not go back and play professional ball, but we'd spent wisely, saved wisely, and invested wisely, so we were okay financially. He opened a few businesses around the city, and had a community center built on the Eastside, right up the street from his high school. Him, Dave, and Steve organized a basketball camp for some of the underprivileged shorties in the hood. They got some additional corporate investors, found the most troubled kids on the block, and took their teams on a summer tour to keep them legit over the break. As much as I missed my husband when he played in the NBA, giving back was always in him, so instead of fussing about his little summer get aways with a bunch of hardheads, I'd fly to a few cities on their calendar and serve as Coach Mom.

What's a Coach Mom? You know the one that brings extra shoestrings, socks, band-aids, rubber bands, snacks, tape, towels, soap, deodorant, and lots of love, hugs, and kisses. Coach Moms scan the gym one last time for things that might have unnoticeably fallen out of gym bags or been left behind. We give words of encouragement, wipe away tears when the loss hurts more than it should, and so on. Actually, my community service and becoming the mom of the team helped me heal emotionally regarding the loss of my son. I lost one child, but over the years that passed, I gained hundreds. And Kerwin and I loved each and every one of them like they were our very own. We established a grant for kids who desired to play organized sports, but, their parents could not afford the fees. I know we blessed so many kids over the years, but it has been a two way street because they've blessed us in return.

Dad and Teretta, well they still live in their fancy house, drive their fancy cars, and run their fancy businesses. Uncle E, he's still himself. Single, good looking, and a hoochie to the tenth power. Dad doesn't get out with him as much as he used to. He said our little family encounter was enough for him to know that home is where the heart is and if he can't find adventure at 1113 Valley Woo Circle, then he didn't need it.

He did call and apologize to Uncle Silk for his behavior without ever mentioning that Ant was alive. The two of them try to get together monthly to watch a game or talk about old times. Dad realized that he was wrong and is trying to re-establish their relationship. When I asked Dad what had actually gone on with him and Uncle Silk, he told me that he was real bitter with Silk because he never visited him in prison. And the fact that he didn't come until Grandma Bean's death made it even worse. Dad said he always despised him for that because he worshiped Silk as a kid, and for someone he viewed as a hero to forget about him the way Silk did, it hurt and broke Dad down emotionally.

"Asia, to be let down by someone that you think is all that, really eats at you like a parasite. I think what hurt more than anything is discovering that I didn't mean near as much to Silk as he meant to me."

"Dad that's why you don't store all your hopes, dreams, treasures, and loyalty in someone else. Nobody should be a greater hero to you than yourself."

"I didn't share that with you for no lecture."

"But you knew I was gon' give you one, right?"

"You're starting to sound like your pops."

"Hey, I'm a Prince, it's in my genes."

That's how that conversation ended, and to this day Dad always teases me about how am I gon' enlighten him as his child. Shoot, kids teach their parents something about life everyday. If more parents took the time to listen maybe we'd have less black men falling victim to gangs, death, and prison. But then again, that's a whole different story on an entirely different day.

As for CJ, well, he moved back to New York to be closer to Ant. Ant was so caught up in all the lies and family deception that had come from him being so *Hood Rich* that he had to continue to allow CJ to think he was really his daddy. In all actuality, Calvin Shaw was, but Ant had grown to love CJ like he was truly his own. I guess in sacrificing a relationship with Ant Jr., he grew closer to his twin's child to make up for the loss.

Detroit's too risky, so Ant doesn't visit us here that often. From time to time, Dad and Ant talk on the phone and occasionally when him and Uncle E are in New York, they stop in and spend a day with him. I thought that was a blessing in disguise. Here Dad had gone years thinking he'd lost a significant person in his life, and out of nowhere God blessed him with a second chance to cross his brother's path. Distance and growth is a wonderful thing, isn't it? I am grateful that my dad learned the real definition of being *Hood Rich* during his incarceration, but I am even happier that my Uncle Ant, finally got a clear understanding of what being a real ***Big Tymer*** is really all about.

When this story first started, Ant gave us his definition of a Big Tymer in the opening. Though I can never replace my best friend or my son, I couldn't hold grudges. Forgiveness is so important when it comes to finding inner peace. There are so many people I could be angry with, but I'm just as responsible for some of the misfortune I experienced. Wisdom and experience is a wonderful thing. I can't dwell on what I should have done. Like Mom and Dad had to go through their own trials and tribulations to have a testimony, so did I. One thing for sure is that God's gon' do what He says He's gon' do. He'll stand by his word, and He most certainly comes through. GG always told me, '*No Weapons Formed Against Me Shall Prosper*. She was right. Once I stopped pointing the finger at everyone else and came to grips with my own mistakes, I learned that Real Big Tymers also shine like priceless diamonds when they can admit their own faults, learn from them, and progress.

Real Big Tymers also make a difference in the lives of others when they share what they've overcome to get where they are. My stuff may not make the next person's life any better, but I promise I'm gon' witness whereever I go. Just like the Prince family, each person's gon' have to go through their own mess to recognize that every life has a purpose. It sometimes requires mistakes, heartache, and losses to discover who you truly are, but that's what living is all about, RIGHT?

Read, Reflect, and Realize that life has Real Purpose.

Dedicated to
LaTonya Bell.
My life long friend.
Also....
The real victim and blessed survivor
of a senseless shooting similar to the one in this story.

I love you Sis.... God truly has something great in store for you.

Ant

"A real stupid **Hood Rich** nigga gon' always fuck himself with his shallow mentality, but a **Big Tymer** on the other hand, goes through his hard knocks, endures his sacrifices, has his regrets, learns from his heartaches, and shines in the end like a freshly polished set of chrome rims."

Silk

"Young Playa, most **Big Tymers** got to beware all who cross their path. Trust is always a factor with everyone. **Loose lips, STILL sink ships.** Most improtantly, when you're on top of your grind, understand that no matter what the profession, any Big Tymer can end up on the bottom."

About the Author

Crystal Perkins-Stell was born April 5 in Newark, New Jersey, and raised in Detroit, Michigan. She is a loving mother, educator, counselor, and motivational speaker, who pulls no punches when writing her reality based novels. She is a proud member of Delta Sigma Theta Sorority, Inc., and a six-time Who's Who inductee. Days before BT's went to print, (March 14 2006,) Crystal was inducted into Who's Who Amongst America's Educators. She's an advocate for HIV and AIDS awareness, a member of Oklahoma City's Urban League Young Professionals Club, TRiO, Tau Beta Sigma National Band Sorority, and several professional, literary and educational organizations.

Crystal double majored while completing her undergraduate studies at Langston University. She later went on to the University of Oklahoma where she graduated Summa Cum Laude with her Master's degree in Human Relations/Counseling.

Crystal is not only a gifted writer, but also committed to African American college students. A percentage of the proceeds earned from all book sells go towards scholarships for first-generation and low-income college students.

Crystal's novel Hood Rich is an Essence Bestseller that was written after she wept over the number of young black men serving life sentences in our penal system. In April of 2005, she expanded her literary mission to incorporate an outreach program for African American youth that are, have been, or are on the verge of being incarcerated. Realizing that our youth saturate their minds with urban lit., Crystal felt compelled to spark intellectual thought about the consequences of making poor choices. She created a literary slogan and has made it a major factor for completing all her novels. "Will the reader be able to, Read, Reflect, and Realize that Life has Real Purpos?" If she can answer yes, this blissful dreamer calls it a story, puts it out, and allows her literary skillz to take readers there.

D. Brown
Thanks for Everything

Quick Order Form

Fax number for P.O.'s (405) 216-0221

Telephone orders: Call (405) 414-3991.

E-mail orders: www.crystalstell.com click on Order link. All Credit Card purchases are handled through Paypal

Postal orders: Crystell Publication, Attn: Crystal Stell, PO Box 8044 Edmond, Oklahoma 73083-8044

Please send the following book(s):

___*Soiled Pillowcases: A Married Woman's Story*

___ *Hood Rich, Sex, Status, and a Baller's Confession*

____ Big Tymers, Can't Get enuff

____ I'm in Luv With a Stripper

___*Never Knew a Father's Love*

Name:_____

Address:_____

City:_____State:_____Zip:_____

Telephone:_____

Email Address:_____

Sales tax: Please add 8.75% sales tax to all purchases.

Shipping by air
U.S.: $4.00 for the first book and $2.00 for each additional book.
International: $9.00 for the first book and $5.00 for each additional book.

Thanks for your support

CRYSTELL PUBLICATIONS

Presents
The M. Alexis Stell

COURSE BOOK SCHOLARSHIP FUND

Eligibility Requirements: This scholarship is designed to assist first-generation and low-income, minority college students with the purchase of course books. The applicant must meet the following requirements in order to qualify for this scholarship.

The applicant must:

1.) Must be a first generation or low-income continuing student.
2.) Be a U.S. Citizen
3.) Have a grade point average of 2.9 or higher (on a 4.0 grading

scale at an accredited 2 or 4 year College or University.)
4.) All applicants must provide a current official transcript with a

College or University seal and 2 letters of recommendation from a faculty or staff on institution letterhead.
5.) Include a 500 word type-written, double-spaced essay best describing the applicant concluding with his/her long term career goals. Essay should include full name, current address and contact number
6.) Include a photo and submit all material no later than May 30, for consideration of fall awards.

Scholarships will be awarded the 2nd week of the semester. Submit applications to:
CRYSTELL PUBLICATIONS,
Attn: Karolyn Lewis, Scholarship Coordinator
PO BOX 8044
EDMOND, OK 73083-8044
Any questions, please e-mail comments to **cleva@crystalstell.com**